P9-ASE-909

HOUSE
OF A
THOUSAND LIES

HOUSE OF A THOUSAND LIES

A NOVEL

CODY LUKE DAVIS

CROOKED
LANE

NEW YORK

This is a work of fiction. All of the names, characters, organizations, places and events portrayed in this novel are either products of the author's imagination or are used fictitiously. Any resemblance to real or actual events, locales, or persons, living or dead, is entirely coincidental.

Copyright © 2022 by Cody Luke Davis

All rights reserved.

Published in the United States by Crooked Lane Books, an imprint of The Quick Brown Fox & Company LLC.

Crooked Lane Books and its logo are trademarks of The Quick Brown Fox & Company LLC.

Library of Congress Catalog-in-Publication data available upon request.

ISBN (hardcover): 978-1-63910-005-7
ISBN (ebook): 978-1-63910-006-4

Cover design by Meghan Deist

Printed in the United States.

www.crookedlanebooks.com

Crooked Lane Books
34 West 27th St., 10th Floor
New York, NY 10001

First Edition: August 2022

10 9 8 7 6 5 4 3 2 1

For Louise Hames. I love you more.

America does a poor job tracking and accounting for its unsolved murders. More than 256,000 victims have died in unsolved homicides committed in the United States since 1980. No one knows all the names of these victims because no law enforcement agency in America is assigned to monitor failed homicide investigations by local police departments. Even the official national statistics on murder are actually estimates and projections based upon incomplete reports by police departments that voluntarily choose (or refuse) to participate in federal crime reporting programs.

Coroners and medical examiners reported nearly 2,200 more homicides to state and federal health authorities in 2015 than police departments reported to the U.S. Justice Department, a long-standing discrepancy that has gotten worse in recent years. The reasons for these reporting failures are not well understood. Local police tend to blame clerical errors.

—The Murder Accountability Project
For more info, see www.murderdata.org

PART I

She-Wolf

There's nothing you can ever do to lose my love. I will protect you until you die, and after your death I will still protect you. I am stronger than depression and I am braver than loneliness and nothing will ever exhaust me.
—Elizabeth Gilbert, from *Eat Pray Love*

The unexamined life is not worth living.

—Socrates

CHAPTER

1

Diana

October 8, 2019. 3:12 AM

Diana Wolf clicks *"Confirm"* on the thirteen-grand purchase saved in her cart.

As her browser goes white loading the next page, it hits her that she has no clue what it is she just bought and no memory of having gone online to shop. Nor of demolishing a fancy cheese platter and two sleeves of water crackers, nor of buying *Princess Bride* on Apple TV, but the forensics are damning.

Westley's getting tortured in the Pit of Despair, so she'd guess her last hour is gone. At least.

Shit. Blackout Santa strikes again. It's been a while.

"How do you feel?" asks the six-fingered man.

Westley whimpers in pain.

"Interesting."

Diana snorts. Droplets of red wine fleck her iPad. She wipes it on her pants.

She opened only two bottles tonight too . . . one more reminder she's turning fifty-four in a month. It may be time to accept her tolerance isn't what it was and adjust her nightly intake.

Or not.

It's only a little money. Diana wouldn't have put it in a shopping cart if Diana didn't want it. It's not like she bought a car again . . . is it?

What would thirteen get her, a Kia? No. There's not enough alcohol in the state of Tennessee to get her that drunk.

She stares at her browser, waiting for it to change, but the next page stays white and blank. Still loading. Stuck.

She swipes over to her inbox, hoping to find a confirmation email. To her delight, there are two.

The first one is the drapes Thad asked her to buy for his man cave so he won't see cars pulling into the driveway. Good. Thad would've thrown a fit if she forgot his drapes, and it looks like she sprung for two-day shipping. So that's good.

The second email is . . . less good.

It's okay. It's not a car. It just isn't something she needed, wanted, or ever thought she might want in the future, which is a bit of a letdown. Blackout Santa usually gives better gifts.

"It's like you don't even know me anymore," she says to her wineglass.

She hired a cartographer?

A quick Google search reveals that cartographers survey parcels of land in order to draw maps of said land. So, it's a map. She spent a Kia's worth of dollars on a map of Wolf Hollow, including the thousand acres of poplar woods they own behind the main house. But why? Talk about an impulse purchase. Minus an impulse. Do maps usually cost five figures?

Diana googles it. No. They do not.

The cartographer's website clears up the price after a little digging: her map is *period accurate*. He makes it how the Pilgrims did it or some shit—there's a whole spiel.

She keeps clicking.

Mr. Cartographer's name is Kerry Perkins. She peruses his blog and is pleased to find photos. He's a handsome Asian guy, looks like in his late twenties . . . athletic, tall . . . often shirtless . . . and he's got a jaw-line that reminds her of Christopher Reeve. Oh. Oh yeah. She suspects these photos played a role in her map purchase. That, plus she loves to throw money at these hipster artisans.

This one takes his Pilgrim shtick seriously. His *"About Me"* page says he walks every inch of every property he maps.

Walks.

Wolf Hollow is over a thousand acres. How long will he be out there? And then Diana remembers. "Oh, fuck me."

She puts her wineglass down to type with both hands, but she misses the coffee table and it shatters on the floor.

Well. Thad will be unhappy if he finds out she broke another one, but she's got bigger issues than cleanup. It's late as hell and he played with Otto today, so it's safe to assume he's sleeping it off somewhere. Diana golfed with them once. By the thirteenth hole, the two men were so drunk they bet a thousand dollars on whether Thad could hit a squirrel. He could not. Since her husband won't be back until morning—noon-ish—and America, their maid, will show up for work in just four hours, the broken glass really isn't Diana's problem.

Diana's problem is Kerry Perkins.

She rereads the cartographer's confirmation email.

There it is. Shit.

The survey portion alone is going to take a week.

Seven days of a stranger walking around in their backyard from sunrise to sunset. As if that won't piss off Thad enough by itself, it gets worse. In just three days, the day *she chose*, Kerry plans on driving over from Nashville to Leiper's Fork to get started on it. He expects to stay with them at Wolf Hollow, eat meals with them, and sleep in the main house.

For a week.

Nope. None of that's happening.

At best, she might be able to put Kerry in the barn. Thad would sooner burn the house and start over than let an employee sleep in the guest bedroom. "It's for *guests*," she can hear him snarling.

Three days. She's got seventy-two hours to whip up a good lie. Kerry Perkins doesn't offer refunds.

She decides to sleep on it.

* * *

Three days later, Diana waits for the cartographer in the kitchen with a glass of Malbec.

The glass itself is identical to the one America cleaned up the other day. Not her first replacement. There were eight wine glasses in the custom set when she commissioned it (another *artisanal* purchase) two years back. Three left intact now. Thad thinks six but, as evidenced by the fact he hasn't shut down the cartographer thing yet, alcoholics are easy to gaslight.

She told Thad it's going to take a single day. Next week.

Not her best lie, but the idea of a map grew on her once she sobered up. She doesn't know any women in town who have one of these. All she has to do is hide a stranger living on the property for six days.

What could go wrong?

She got the drapes installed in the man cave yesterday, so Thad won't be able to see any lights on in the barn, and she told Kerry Perkins via email he'll be eating meals alone, which he okayed. On the off-chance Thad discovers Kerry in the barn, her plan B is simple. She'll throw the cartographer under the bus, act like he's a stranger, and tell him to get the fuck out—then, once Thad's back inside, tip the guy *very well* and move him into the Songwriter's Cottage.

Deny, deny, deny. That's her motto.

If Thad finds Kerry in the Songwriter's Cottage . . . well, he's shit out of luck. The chances of her husband entering both buildings in a week are minuscule, but even so, her mind wanders to the pistol Thad wears on his belt. Going from L.A. to Leiper's Fork was a rough transition, so she can forgive the initial purchase, but ten years later he still wears it. Thad claims it's for shooting rattlesnakes. It's an ugly thought, but she wouldn't be surprised if he bought the gun to shoot people.

Old people do that.

Thad turned seventy-one in January. Seventeen years older than she is. Ever since they moved, the age difference feels more and more like thirty years, or forty. She can't decide if it's a psychological thing or if he had a mild stroke on the plane or what, but her husband got *old* in Tennessee.

Thad Wolf is an old person now. And it shows. Hence, the drapes. Hence, a lot of things: he watches Fox News eight hours a day; he's made a sport of yelling at the maid; America has become well-acquainted with the word *eyesore*.

Tires crunch to a stop in the gravel driveway outside.

Diana gets up and opens the front door. She leans on the frame, swirling her wine.

An old black sedan sits behind three other cars in the gravel parking circle: her dark green Jag, Thad's neglected red Mercedes, and the ancient blue family minivan (*eyesore*) in front.

Kerry Perkins steps out of the black sedan, closes his door. "Hello there. Are you D?"

He is as advertised: six foot four, flannel shirt, biceps, *jawline*.

Diana bites her lip. She waves from her perch in the doorway. "You found me. Diana Wolf." She signs off with just the first letter for correspondence. Minimalist.

"Nice to meet you in person, Mrs. Wolf," he says as he climbs the three steps up to the porch and reaches out a hand. "I'm Kerry. The cartographer. We emailed. Kerry Perkins."

Diana looks down at his hand. Shakes it. "I know. Come inside. Welcome to Wolf Hollow."

"Gorgeous," he says, following her into the entry hall.

"The house? Or is that just what you say to all the girls?" She glances back over one shoulder and arches her spine, the way that makes her ass look good.

Kerry gulps. "The house," he clarifies.

Diana smirks. She leads him into the kitchen and pours him a glass of wine. "Sorry for missing your texts. Cell service is spotty down here."

He eyes his wine with suspicion. "Oh. Thanks. I shouldn't. Maybe tonight?"

"I insist. One glass. You'll walk it off." She thrusts it into his hand, smiles, and sits at the island. "So, how does this work exactly? Now that you're here."

"Well, Mrs. Wolf," he says, taking a stool across from her, "for about a week, given the acreage we discussed, I'll be surveying your property. Then I'm going to draw you up a map."

Diana's blue eyes sparkle. "Oh great!" The conversation is going to be one-sided, she imagines.

She flirts with him for a while.

Kerry can't keep his eyes off her breasts once he has a glass of Malbec in him, which is flattering. Other women her age might get offended, but not Diana. She loves it. It reminds her she still *has it.*

That said, she's a huge tease. She'd never cheat on Thad in a million years. She owes him too much.

How many teenage girls grow up to marry their celebrity crush? Not a lot. But she did. Diana used to sing *"A Thousand Lies"* walking to school back in Ohio. The trip was six blocks from her last foster home, just long enough to get through the whole song twice if she didn't rush. Never in her wildest dreams did she imagine that just a couple years later, she'd ride a bus to L.A. to visit her sister, Kristen, and they'd go to a big party, and she'd run into the rich, famous, blue-eyed Texan hunk who wrote that song, and he would swoop into her life to *rescue her.*

But it happened. He did.

It's been thirty-two years since then, though.

These days, it's nice to be reminded now and again that what she sees in the mirror over the sink at night isn't what men see. All she sees is decay. Wrinkles. Dark blue veins pulsing in her forehead like worms. But this young specimen, Kerry Perkins, God bless him, he just sees a code-red rack on a bombshell blonde whose husband isn't home, and he's going to think of her tits tonight while he jerks off in the barn, fifty yards from her bedroom.

Because Diana Wolf still *has it*.

The knowledge puts her in a good mood. She decides to jump her husband's bones when he gets home tonight, and makes a mental note to text him so he can take his pill.

Nothing stupid happens with Kerry.

She gets a good laugh out of how nervous the poor kid is when she shows him to his bedroom on the second floor of the barn. But that's it.

Once he's all set up, she takes his arm in hers and walks him down a gravel path behind the house so he can get his workday started.

"Trust me, you want to survey the woods first," she tells him as the path ends at a cobblestone bridge over a deep ravine. Nothing but tall, thin poplar trees on the other side, a thousand acres of it. Her hope is Kerry won't meet Thad until the seventh day if he saves the main clearing for last.

Diana stops halfway across. "Well, this is it for me."

She goes up on her tiptoes and pecks Kerry's cheek goodbye, then shoos him off.

The big lunk gets fifty feet or so before he turns back and waves her down. "I forgot to ask, is there anything I should know about in there?" he shouts from just inside the tree line, where a shadow falls so dark she can't make out his eyes. "You know, like a landmark or two you want me to mark on the map?"

Diana shrugs. "I don't—"

Know.

That's what she means to say. But she stops.

It's true. She doesn't know any landmarks. How could she? She never sets foot in the woods out back.

Now that she thinks about it, it seems strange. She never makes it past this exact spot on the cobblestone bridge. Halfway. Every time she walks the gravel path in the yard to its end, this is where she gets chills, stops, and hurries back to the main house.

The poplar woods scare her.

Why?

She stiffens at the appearance of a little voice in her head, not her own. It's been silent for years. Therapy was supposed to help. It did. For a while. Now it's back.

But her answer to its question is what gives her pause. She has no idea *why*.

The poplar woods were a big selling point when they bought Wolf Hollow. She was the one who begged Thad to let her build a path out back, and then a bridge to reach the tree line, because she thought she'd take walks to watch the leaves change. She picked out these cobblestones. They're from Spain.

"I . . . my two sons built a treehouse when we first moved," she says. "But it's probably just sticks now. It was eight or nine years ago, the last time I saw them go out to it."

Maybe a decade, since Jonah and Cy look like teens in her memory—as they crossed the bridge into the woods that last time, both of her sons were smiling. Joking like they did back then, when the two boys still looked alike, before Cy got so muscular and Jonah so thin and gaunt. Almost twins. Platinum-blond hair like their mother, tall like their father, as good-looking as you'd expect.

Best friends. Happy.

Or she used to think they were.

"Don't go looking for it," she trails off, eyes stuck on a quivering dead leaf wedged between two cobblestones.

"What was that?" he shouts.

"Nothing!" she shouts back, wondering the same thing. "I'm sorry. You go on."

The little voice is gone, but a stung feeling lingers. It's like waking up in bed after a spider bite. She knows a tiny pain woke her up, but not what it was or where the wound is. Not yet. You never do until it starts to itch, so you just close your eyes and go back to sleep.

She glances up, smiles.

Kerry nods, waves.

Diana watches the cartographer disappear in the trees.

She walks back up the hill to the main house and sees it. *Oh*. Oh no.

Not even a day in, and there's already a gaping hole in her plan. It's going to be hard for Thad to miss the black sedan parked in the driveway.

CHAPTER

2

Kerry

October 11, 2019. 3:21 PM

H AVING FAILED TO "walk off" four generous pours of Malbec, Kerry Perkins stumbles out of the poplar trees into a huge, sundrenched clearing. He felt sick, and the grass looked inviting.

Huh. The clearing isn't empty.

He shades his eyes, hoping to get a better sense of what he's looking at. He's not tripping; it's a house.

Kerry rifles through his fanny pack and pulls out what he's looking for: a handheld GPS, his dirty little secret. All those old brass sextants and quill pens he brought? Stage props. Truth is, only a moron would use paper and ink to survey an estate like this: a thousand acres, ninety percent of it dense forest. Forget a week. It'd take a year.

Work smart, not hard. That's his motto.

Less than two miles as the crow flies from the main house. Still in Wolf Hollow. This must be that "treehouse" her kids built, then.

In her emails, Diana specifically said there are only three structures on the estate: a main house, a barn, and a cottage. He saw those. This makes four. She must have never seen it. There's no tree. It's got an L-shaped foundation, painted white walls, a black tile roof, glass windows . . . and most of them aren't even broken.

It is a *house.*

This right here is some serious rich kid shit. It'd cost a fortune just to haul materials out here. Then again, these are celebrity scions he's talking about—who knows how much unearned capital they had access to?

Kerry googled Diana Wolf the second he got her full name, same as he googles all his new clients. When he started the artisanal maps racket in Nashville, he used to think he'd get hired by a lot of country singers. Nope. Not one in three years. His real clientele is mostly stay-at-home wives who found him on Pinterest, and their husbands all work in biotech or finance or semiconductors . . . nothing cool. He was starting to think the singers weren't real. So, imagine his surprise when Google revealed who the mysterious "D" is.

Holy shit.

This estate belongs to *the* Thad Wolf. That was his house. She's his wife.

Thad Wolf's wife hit on him!

Dad would be proud. A con man doesn't get to think that often.

Back in the seventies, Perkins was a fresh-off-the-boat Chinese immigrant in Austin, Texas, with nothing but a made-up name, a dishwashing job, an apartment with thin walls, a racist neighbor, and an understandable eagerness to broadcast his deep patriotic love of all things American and capitalist. Anyone can do that math—of course he listened to The Pack. What's more American than crossover country music?

Sixteen years later, his new wife died giving birth to a baby boy. Art, ever the patriot, named his son after a senator.

Kerry remembers riding in cars a lot as a kid, always traveling to new cities so Art could interview for a new job or meet some new woman he'd been pen-palling with (neither ever worked out). In the Perkins family, it was a rule: driver picks the tunes—meaning Art, and he picked The Pack. Kerry knew the lyrics to *"A Thousand Lies"* before he could speak. It was Dad's favorite song. When Kerry was nine, they played it at his funeral.

Today, Art can brag in heaven about how his only son is working for the man who wrote and sang that song. Kinda cool.

And . . . *yup.* The fucking chorus is stuck in his head now. But he's alone in the woods, and it just so happens that's the best place you can be when you've got a song stuck in your head. Out here, he can belt it out if he wants to, and nobody'll hear a damn thing.

Moments like this make him wish he'd studied to be a real cartographer. Three years into it, selling maps is the only scam he ever ran that makes him *happy*. Lots of exercise, sun, nature, and the cherry on top is his marks never even realize they got screwed. The end product they receive—he gets his maps made in China for three hundred bucks and change—is indistinguishable from what he promised, so his reviews are stellar. No one gets hurt, for once. No one comes after him. It's nice.

Hands in his pockets and a smile on his face, he doesn't feel so sick all of a sudden.

Kerry sings as he walks into the clearing, flat as hell.

I can cast aside a thousand lies
I can close my eyes to keep you close to me
I can let you in, forget your sins
All you need to promise is you'll never leave . . .

When he gets to the treehouse-cum-starter-home, he tries the front door. Locked. Door is solid teak, so he meanders over to the east-facing side and peers in through a broken window.

The interior is dirty. Dark.

But the dirt and mess all looks recent, like a bad storm came through a few weeks, not years, ago. Leaves on the floor, dust on the moldings, spiderwebs—but that's it. No real damage. It's nicer than his house in Nashville, that's for sure. *Christ.* They got an onyx countertop installed in the kitchenette: a single massive slab of polished black stone with big splashes of white.

Little fuckers. That alone must've cost twenty grand.

Kerry decides to explore a little.

He wraps up a fist in his flannel's sleeve, clears a few glass shards from the frame, and vaults in.

Inside, the sounds of the forest die.

He meanders into the kitchenette, intending to check if the onyx slab is real, and if so, if it's light enough to carry out.

But then something else catches his eye. Around the corner of the ell, where he couldn't see before, a clear plastic tarp covers most of the floor. Four open cans of slick black paint hold it down, one in each corner, and there's an easel in the center with a six-by-six-foot stretched canvas propped up on it. A painting.

Near-finished, all in black and white oils. *Grayscale,* he half remembers from an art class he flunked in high school. Whoever painted it was no amateur—it looks *realistic.* And *wet.*

Kerry shivers, suddenly aware of how much colder it is in here than outside. Like an air conditioner is on.

He rounds the corner and stares at the painting.

It's of two devils. He's not sure what else to call the two life-sized figures writhing on the canvas. Both have big, curved goat horns growing out of their shoulders. One is male, bigger, and the smaller one is female, which he can tell because the two devils' anatomy is human where it counts, and boy are they *fucking*. It doesn't look fun. Not for the female. He walks up to it for a closer look. Where the male's claws dig into her breasts, little black trails leak out and run. *Blood*.

Kerry backs away.

The big male's eyes follow his. It's a cheap illusion created by the paint's texture, but the eyes look alive: vertical white slits, hungry and smiling.

Kerry's heel catches on the edge of a pile rug against the wall. The corner flips back, just for a second. A black flash. "What the fuck?" he whispers, glancing down at the rug.

He kicks it again. It slides an inch.

He isn't crazy. There's a metal hatch in the floor. He can see a corner of it.

He gets on his knees and rolls up the rug, and there it is—a hatch. Black iron, just big enough for a man to fit. The kind you'd expect to open and find a ladder inside, like the ones they put on top of submarines. But where does it go? A basement? He tries the rusted handle. Pulls once. Twice. It won't budge. Not locked, he realizes. *Sealed*. Fused shut at the edges, like someone took a blowtorch to it.

Kerry hears a sound like loose clothes behind him.

The hairs on his neck stand up, and he glances over his shoulder. But there's no one. It was just a cross-breeze blowing dead leaves in from the far window.

For the first time, he notices a leather notebook lying on the tarp. Pocket-sized.

He crawls over to it.

He picks it up, flips the notebook open. Tiny black droplets dot the lined white pages here and there. Other than that, it looks empty. But a page is marked. He flips ahead to it. A single note is scratched into the margin in pencil: *39.3851 N, 119.7064 W.*

Kerry knows coordinates when he sees them. On a whim, he takes out his iPhone and snaps a photo of the marked page. Then he closes the notebook and puts it back where he found it.

A twig snaps somewhere in the woods. Close by.

Kerry crab-crawls to a wall and flattens his back to it. Holds his breath.

But there's nothing. No one.

When he realizes it was just the wind again, or a rat or a bird, his face gets hot. This is stupid. He is thirty-one years old, and there's no good reason for him to be this scared. But still . . . he should leave. If only to get on with the survey.

From the ground, he looks up at the unfinished painting.

The big male looks back.

Kerry scrambles to his feet, finds the broken window he used to get inside, vaults out into the clearing, and makes his way back to the tree line. He jogs this time. He doesn't sing.

*　*　*

Hours pass.

The sun goes down.

Right as it's getting truly dark and he's fighting through a patch of brambles and choke vines in the thickest woods yet, right when he's nearly forgotten all about the two Wolf brothers, the air-conditioned house no one knows about in the clearing, the two devils, the iron hatch, and the coordinates jotted in the paint-smeared notebook—or, at least, right when he's finally convinced himself he only got so freaked out because he watched the first *Blair Witch* movie alone last week, and it's not worth worrying about, and obviously there's no mad painter running around out here with a blowtorch, he just scared himself stupid in the woods like a jackass, Kerry Perkins kicks something lying half buried in the dirt. Hard.

He trips and staggers forward, cursing.

The something rolls a few yards, lopsided.

Kerry toggles his phone's flashlight on and aims the beam down past his feet at it. "Whoa. *Whoa.*"

An earthworm wriggles and falls out of an eye socket. Lands in the black dirt.

No more jogging: he runs.

*　*　*

Kerry bursts out of the trees and sprints over the cobblestone bridge, then up the gravel path into the main clearing, past the firepit, the parking circle, and all the way to the barn. He takes the stairs three at a time up to his room, where he grabs his MacBook Pro and a day bag packed full of clothes—only what he can carry—then he's down the stairs and in the parking circle again, power-walking past a big red pickup truck that wasn't there earlier. He pops his trunk with the key remote and dumps his stuff. Slams it shut.

Then he takes a much-needed breath.

Kerry slips his iPhone out of his pocket to check if he has a signal yet. Twenty minutes, he's been trying to get through to the cops. Anyone.

But no. Still nothing.

"Jesus fuck." He rubs his temples as he trots to the driver's side of his car.

Ch-Chck!

Right next to his ear. It's a metal sound you only hear in movies: the slide cocking back on an automatic pistol. He stops in his tracks. Drops his car keys to the gravel. Raises both empty hands, slowly, to the back of his head.

"Where'd you get those keys, *boy?*" says a drawling voice, so close he can smell whiskey on it. "This car belongs to America."

3

Diana

October 11, 2019. 7:08 PM

L EIPER'S FORK IS a one-street town.
"Ooh! Thad, look at that!" she said when she first saw the street sign forty-five minutes outside Nashville, tugging on her husband's sleeve in the backseat of the town car, like Jonah and Cy used to tug at her dress when they were little. "Isn't it adorable? If we move here, we'll be able to relate when politicians talk about Main Street!"

Thad rolled his eyes. Sighed. "Yep."

Diana still loves it. But a decade later, the Leiper's Fork she loves is dying a slow death. Every year, it feels a little less like an authentic small town and a little more like a movie set.

Puckett's is the epicenter of activity on Main Street. It's been in Leiper's Fork over fifty years, owned by the same family that whole time. Never closes. It's a general store in back, a butcher up front, a restaurant on one side where the folding chairs and card tables are set up, and a liquor store on the other.

There are two restaurants, one on the north end and one on the south. Country Boy is better.

There's a coffee shop called The Cuppa; a renovated Civil War–era building called The Store of Northern Aggression, where they sell jackets and gardening tools; and a real estate office. All with long histories. Locally owned.

Then, there are six antique shops and an art gallery. Not authentic. Other than Old Shit, none existed when they moved in to Wolf Hollow. All new, all high end, all built to cater to a new class of residents in town—hers.

Diana cringes, shaking her head as she drives past a line of identical storefronts.

It's only been ten years since they got here, but Leiper's Fork has transformed. It's nothing like how it was. Then, it was a rural southern hamlet. Now, it's a full-blown, rich, white, liberal boomtown. The secret got out. All of a sudden, Johnny Depp lives a few minutes down the road in one direction, Justin Timberlake and Chris Stapleton in the other—*live* is a stretch, but all three do own land, and every once in a while Diana spots Justin or Chris in line at Puckett's. Mostly, the big celebrities use their sprawling, ostentatious swaths of land out here as vacation homes or to raise horses. Or bison. Or alpaca.

Diana and Thad came in with the first wave of the rich. When they arrived, locals still dominated the spiderwebbed dirt roads and private lanes off Main Street. Dilapidated farmhouses. Broken-down, rusted cars on lawns. Basketball hoops with frayed nets and bent rims lying on their sides next to shacks that looked abandoned but weren't. That's all been cleaned up. The rich own it all. The hillsides are green and empty. Horses graze in distant meadows.

You never see houses anymore. Just gates. Or, if you're lucky, a long, winding driveway you can't see an end to.

A few farming families still eke out an existence on the edges of town by renting unused fields from the new owners. Most of the poor locals weren't so lucky, or savvy, or healthy enough to work. They lost their land outright. Old debts got called in. Landlords found any excuse to evict their local tenants, eager to combine and trade and sell the lots to out-of-state buyers. No one wanted to miss the gold rush. But a few stubborn undesirables stayed in Leiper's Fork anyway, fleeing their old homes to camp in the woods. Every once in a while, deep inside a tree line or between two gates, Diana will see a shack, a trailer, a rotting barn, or a shadowed garage with a shotgun leaned up against it, and she'll wonder if a family of six is asleep inside on the floor.

Diana knows what it's like to sleep that way. To be poor.

She pulls her Jaguar into a parking spot outside Old Shit. The owner, Robyn Clarke, was the second woman she met in Leiper's Fork.

Diana had complimented her on the name of her shop. "Classy," she'd said, giggling at the sign.

"You know what? You just passed the friend test, stranger," Robyn replied. "You like Old Shit, we can probably get along."

And they could.

Now, the two women gossip and chat about wine and the latest glitzy arrivals in town a few times a week, usually in Old Shit or on the creaky swing on its balcony out back, facing the trees. Robyn can't leave the shop much. She works full-time, so any time she comes to visit, Diana buys something small to support her—it's what best friends do, isn't it?

Diana walks into the shop. Above her, a string of twine pulls and a bell rings.

Robyn Clarke comes around the corner, smiling wide, hands clenched in front of her chest. "Look what the cat dragged in. To what, pray, do I owe the pleasure?" She grabs Diana's hands in hers. The two of them stand there like an old portrait of chaste lovers, eyes locked and glittering like they can't believe how lucky they are to have each other.

"Oh, you're too sweet," says Diana, holding out a cheek. Robyn pretend-kisses it. "I was in the area. You know how it is. I just thought I'd stop in and say hi."

"Well, I didn't hear a 'hi,' missy."

"Oh. Sorry. Hi."

"All right. You did what you came to do, so . . ."

"Har-har." She's all set up to brag to her about the map, and Kerry Perkins, the six foot four cartographer in her barn with a jawline that makes him look like an Asian Christopher Reeve—but then she sees a black-bobbed head through the cracked door to a back room where dried antlers are sold out of big metal buckets. Just a flash. A blur in her peripheral vision, like a body moving past the crack on the other side.

Five foot nine. Cashmere shawl. Red stiletto heels.

"Is that Sally Davis?" she asks after a pause.

Robyn's face turns grim. "Diana . . ."

"I know."

"I don't want trouble," says Robyn.

"No trouble."

If Robyn was second, Sally Davis was her first best friend in Leiper's Fork. The first friend she ever made in all of Tennessee, if she doesn't count people she paid.

Sally and she had a lot in common. Both grew up poor then married rich in their twenties; both are drop-dead gorgeous blondes (or Sally used to be, before she dyed her hair black); both got boob jobs in their thirties to go from a B cup to a tasteful single D; both raised two boys, all grown up now; and severe mental illness ran in both their immediate families. They used to joke that Sally's father and Diana's mother, both paranoid schizophrenics who died young, had been lost soul mates . . . which made the two of them sisters in a roundabout way. If not for Sally being taller by four inches, it'd be hard to guess they *weren't* sisters. The two women had held hands when they walked in town. Despite all that, it only took three years for their friendship to sour.

Rumors started to fly. About Sally and Thad.

No truth to them, of course. Thad would never do that to her. Never. Diana knows that. Not after thirty-two years, three houses, two kids, Cy's schizophrenic meltdown, and everything else they've been through together. But even though it wasn't true, Sally never did anything to stop people talking. Never.

It bothered Diana. A lot.

"No such thing as bad publicity," Sally had joked when Diana finally prodded her over brunch one day.

Diana's blue eyes had flashed above a white smile, and she'd stabbed her fork into a cold Belgian waffle, staring at a former best friend as she ate the rest of her meal in silence.

"Do you want me to text you when she leaves?" says Robyn now.

"No, thanks," says Diana, backing out of the shop. "Really. It's okay. I've got to get steaks and run home. Dinner won't make itself."

She leaves. The bell above the door rings again as it closes.

* * *

Robyn Clarke watches her go, frowning.

Robyn doubts that last part is true. Diana Wolf can afford to hire a cook if she feels like it, judging by how much money she spends in Old Shit on a weekly basis. And oh, how the magnanimous old cunt just *glows* every time she walks out with a new knickknack.

Sally Davis exits the back room, stiletto heels clicking on the old wood floors. "Well? Is she gone?"

Robyn sighs. "I got rid of her."

* * *

Back in her Jaguar, Diana's phone buzzes.

She digs it out of her Prada bag and looks at the screen. One notification.

It's a text from Thad:

Get yr ass back here NOW

That is not good.

Still, she stops at Puckett's and picks up the steaks.

CHAPTER

4

Diana

October 11, 2019. 8:21 PM

WHEN DIANA GETS back to Wolf Hollow, steaks in hand, a stale, earthy scent hangs in the entry hall: cigar smoke. Cohiba.

To her left, the white double doors to Thad's man cave are shut. Fox News blares inside, too loud for healthy eardrums, but perfect for an aging musician. She knows it's Fox by the crusty male voice ranting about a *"war on men,"* which is just . . . not a thing.

She drops off the steaks on the kitchen island, then backtracks to the man cave and takes a deep breath to prepare herself.

As she slides the doors apart, hateful bullshit fills the air:

"Remember Andrea Dworkin? Still influential! Still taken seriously! And now Lena Dunham, an admitted child molester . . ."

Inside, Thad Wolf sits bolt upright in his big leather chair, asleep. The angle gives her a nice view of all the stiff black hairs in his nostrils, thick as foxtails. He's been neglecting to use the trimmer she got him as a stocking stuffer last Christmas.

She plucks the remote off his armrest and presses a red button. The sound cuts out.

Somehow, the lack of noise wakes him up. His head jerks forward, neck stiff, and he looks up to find Diana standing in front of the TV.

"What?" He's drunker than usual.

"You texted me," she says, holding her ground.

Thad blinks. "Mm. Yeah. Found a homeless Chinaman set up in the garage."

"You found a *what*?"

Thad digs in his pocket and pulls out a black key fob. "How'd he get the keys to America's new car? Huh? I asked him. He said to ask you." He presses it.

Out in the parking circle, a cheerful *beep-beep*.

Diana's caught in a lie.

When Thad had gotten home earlier, after a quickie in the master bedroom, she'd told him the black sedan was America's. The lie was simple: she gave America permission to park in the driveway for just this week because the maid has a sprained ankle. Thad usually makes the maid park at the top of the hill, so her crappy real car (*eyesore*) doesn't sit all afternoon in the gravel parking circle, where, until his drapes got installed the other day, he would *have to look at it*.

Now that her simple lie is blown, she's only got one option: go bigger.

"Honey. You misunderstood. That's my cartographer's car. Kerry Perkins. Remember? I told you. He came by early today because he happened to be in the area." She pauses. "Why do you have his keys?"

Thad frowns. "Wait a minute, you said . . . why'd you tell me it was America's?"

She shakes her head. "I never said that."

His brow furrows. "Yes, you did!" There's a hint of uncertainty.

"How many drinks did you have on the course?" she asks, striking a careful balance between judgmental, concerned, and exasperated.

Thad sulks. "I drove back, didn't I?"

"You sure did," she says with a cruel laugh. "Forget it. What happened?"

He scratches his scalp, like he doesn't remember. At seventy-one, Thad still has a full head of wispy brown hair. The man is a born outlier. "Well. I mighta overreacted. But I thought we were gettin' robbed. I mean he came runnin' outta the woods like a bat outta hell, straight into the barn, started loadin' up all in a hurry, and I crept up with my pistol an' . . . . shit. You know, I think I locked him in the pantry."

Her eyes get big. "You did *what*? Jesus Christ. Thad!"

She sprints out of the man cave, grabs her keys out of her bag, and flies down the kitchen stairs, two at a time, to the pantry. Unlocks it.

Sure enough, Kerry Perkins is sitting on the cold concrete floor in the far corner, head propped on a bag of flour like it's a pillow. His eyes flutter open.

She stops. "Kerry, I am so sorry," she whispers, real fear in her voice.

The cartographer's body language says "*relief*" more than "*pressing charges*," which is great because this definitely counts as kidnapping. "Mrs. Wolf, I'd like to use your phone, please."

"Okay. Sure. Who do you need to call?"

Kerry stands and dusts his jeans off. "I'm calling the police."

She drops the calm facade. "*Please.* Wait. Before you do that, please, just tell me what happened."

He stares at her for a long time, and she knows something's wrong. Something *else*. "Diana. How well do you know those woods? You said there was a treehouse, but have you seen it?"

"I don't," she says, lost. "And no. That's why I hired you, isn't it?"

Kerry nods. "It's not a treehouse."

"I don't understand."

"Your sons built a *house* back there."

"Oh. Okay." She's not listening. Tears form in her eyes as she imagines the legal fees.

It hits her: this could ruin her family.

What family? says a little voice, not her own. *How many years since you hosted a real Thanksgiving? Your sons haven't spoken to each other in five. One's a paranoid schizo just like grandma, and the other never calls. Your husband's an old drunk. Your brother and sister despise you. You never stopped treating them like little kids, and now they've spent the last four Thanksgivings in Santa Barbara, and your entire relationship is conducted in a group chat full of dusty happy birthday texts. Your friends lie to . . .*

She shoves the little voice aside and tries to focus.

Kerry breathes like he could make use of a paper bag. "Your two sons. Which one is the painter?"

She snorts. "Jonah. My eldest. Wait. Is *that* what scared you?"

"Depends what you think I—"

"A painting." The look on his face tells her she's dead-on, and her confidence rises from the grave. "One that would make Hieronymus Bosch and Francis Bacon throw up in their mouths a little. Black and white. Demons. Blood. Nasty sex. Stop me if I'm close."

Kerry blushes. He nods. "There was a big painting inside. It was . . . disturbing."

"I can guess. I bet I'd agree." She dares to smile. "But what do you and I know about art?"

"Sorry?"

She sighs. "Jonah works at Christie's auction house. In Manhattan. He's got a degree in it."

His eyes look like they could burst from thinking so hard. "So your older son, Jonah . . . he's always painted like that?"

"Since he was a teenager in Los Angeles. I think it started on a trip to the Los Angeles County Museum of Art, but he got a crush on Francisco Goya, and it spiraled from there. It's his thing. I've come to terms with it." That's a lie. Secretly, she thinks her son's art is shit. Misogynistic. Crude. Repetitive. And her opinion isn't without heft. Diana knows art theory and history, if not practice. She has her mother to thank for that (it's one of the very few things she has Bonnie to thank for). On both sides, art runs deep in the Wolf family's genes. Thad composes music and lyrics, Bonnie painted butterflies and fruit, Kristen paints vases filled with wilting flowers, and her eldest son paints demons murdering and raping each other in caves. To each their own.

Kerry frowns. "Who's Francisco Goya?"

"Dead Spanish painter. He got sick and painted a lot of witches on the walls of his house."

"Ah." He puts a hand on his chin. If he had a pencil, he'd chew on it.

Silence.

"I'm not going to press charges over this," he says suddenly. "I think I had a little part in it. I got scared, like . . . it was like the first *Blair Witch* movie. You know?"

No, she does not. "Sure."

"It's fine. I get what happened, man." He looks up into her eyes, earnest. "You lied to your husband about me being here, right?"

"Yes."

He nods. "It's happened before. I get it." A coy smile materializes.

She clutches her shoulders. "I'm not sure what you're implying."

"It's okay. I get it. Plus, my dad was a big fan. If I sued Thad Wolf, it would be, like . . . dishonoring his memory." He sighs. "I just want to go home. Okay?"

Diana knows not to look a gift horse in the mouth. "Okay."

"But," he says, lifting a finger to silence her, "I need to show you something first. I found it in the woods, and it's the reason I still need to call the police." He measures his next words, deadly serious. "You let me call. I lead you to it. And that's it. I leave *right after*, forever, and you don't get a refund. I think that's a fair deal. Right?"

It's more than fair, she thinks. Thad put a gun to his head and locked him under the house; he could sue for millions if he felt like it. "Yeah. Okay."

Kerry pushes past her and walks upstairs.

She follows him.

They find Thad pacing at the top of the staircase, wringing his hands. He jolts at the sight of them. "Mister, I-I owe you an apology. Is there anything I can . . .?"

"Autograph," says Kerry, monotone. "On something good."

"No problemo, partner." Thad holds out a bear paw.

Kerry shakes it anemically with two fingers loose, the exact way her husband claims means a man is spineless and untrustworthy. She's not sure if it's all Texans or just him, but the man treats handshakes like horoscopes.

Thad grimaces down at the limp hand in his.

"Thad," she hisses, "Mr. Perkins needs to use our phone. Then he needs to show us something serious. In the woods. After that, if all goes well, he's going to *leave us alone.* Got it?"

Thad nods, shoulders scrunched up to his ears like a kicked dog. "Okay. Sure. You two go ahead. I'll just . . . wait here."

*   *   *

Halfway across the cobblestone bridge, Diana stops.

At the edge of the woods, Kerry looks briefly over one shoulder to nod at the path he took earlier, beckoning her to follow. She doesn't. Just watches him fade into the trees as he walks deeper. The forest is so thick, it's only a few seconds before he disappears.

Even his flashlight beam is gone.

Diana breathes in. Out. In.

She takes a step off the cobblestone bridge, and her foot lands on the other side of the ravine. In. Out. Another step, another, and so on as she closes her eyes and prays: *O Lord . . .*

When her eyes open again, she's in the trees.

She drifts along the path she saw Kerry take, keeping her eyes down on the soil. Catches up to him after a minute or two. They walk in silence. The only noises other than their rustling movements are insects and bare branches creaking in the canopy fifty feet up, but the night is loud with those two sounds. It's slow going in the dark. Kerry keeps losing the trail as he tries to retrace his steps.

Half an hour or so later, poplar trees are all she can see in every direction.

"Kerry?"

He's gone. She must've fallen behind without noticing.

When no one answers, panic sets in.

Everywhere she looks, it looks the same: trees. "Kerry!" She keeps moving, but she doesn't know where she is, and soon she's getting dizzy, disoriented. That fluid in her ear canal, whatever it is that controls balance . . . it feels like someone's stirring it with a spoon.

She steadies herself against a tree and vomits. A mixture of bile and half-digested red wine spills onto the brown leaves, sticks, and shriveled weeds. *Look. It's a Jackson Pollock.* She wipes her lips, smiling weakly. Jonah would like that joke.

"Here," says a loud voice in the distance. Kerry's. "It's here. Now do you see, Mrs. Wolf?"

She can't see him yet, but her ears tell her where he is.

There's a small clearing up ahead and to her left, a spot where moonlight bathes a circle of grass in cool blues and grays. Beautiful. But that's not where he is. No, his voice came from off to her right, where there's nothing but suffocating overgrowth: fallen trees, black tangles of moss, weeds, dead bark, and damp soil.

Somehow, she resists the urge to run into the clearing and goes right.

She sees his face first. Pale white. Even when she shines a light on the rest of Kerry, his body is nearly invisible. The green-and-brown plaid flannel he's wearing might as well be camouflage out here.

"How'd you ever find this place?" she asks.

"Bad luck. I fucking tripped over it." He points.

And that's when her flashlight beam locks onto the something on the ground: a human skull.

It's tiny is her first thought. A woman, or a child. Off-white. Covered in webbed roots. Clumps of black dirt and shadows cling to the deep bony holes where teeth should be, but aren't. But that's not the part Diana figures must've scared Kerry so bad. It scares her too.

There are two wolves carved in its forehead.

5

Kerry

October 12, 2019. 1:24 AM

IT'S EARLY THE next morning by the time the local cops come to let Kerry Perkins out of the barn.

"Wake up. He's ready to talk to you," says the big corn-fed deputy who's been standing guard outside his door all these hours. "Hey. Don't look so bummed. After this, you get to go home."

Kerry rolls his eyes.

He sits up in bed. Still at Wolf Hollow, waiting in the tiny spartan bedroom Diana set up for him. What a joke. "Oh, I get to go home? Eventually?"

"Yep." The deputy gives him a thumbs-up. Smiles.

Kerry stares in awe as the big idiot whistles on his way back out and down the stairs. When he's alone, he stands up and stretches his shoulders. He's six foot four, so he gets tight, and it gets worse when he's stressed out. Like right-the-fuck now. Cops are treating him like a suspect, not a witness. Yeah. It's that kind of stress that gets him *real* tight.

Lenny from *Of Mice and Men* leads him out of the barn and past six inert police cruisers parked in the gravel circle, then up the three steps to the Wolfs' front porch. The big front door is open. Warm light spills out of the entry hall. But the deputy blocks it with his back and points a meaty finger at a pair of wicker chairs set at the far end of the porch.

Kerry walks half the length of the house and sits down in one.

This is nothing like how he expected it to go with the police. Warning bells are ringing in his head. Loud. It's weird. All of it is. Unless every single cop show, movie, and true crime documentary he's ever seen is full of shit. And he's seen a lot.

Not letting him leave the property this whole time while most of the cops went off with Diana into the woods to see the skull with no teeth. *Ding-ding!* Weird. Why wouldn't they take Kerry? He's the one who found it.

Oh, and the cops searched his car. And his room. And his bags. They asked for his permission first, and he said it was fine . . . but still. *Ding-ding!*

And now, this. The lead detective is holding official interviews at Wolf Hollow. Why here? Don't they normally take you to a police station? *Ding-ding-ding!*

Ten minutes into waiting for the detective to emerge, he pipes up: "Do you know why he's doing this here, and so late? Is this normal?"

Lenny shakes his head. Shrugs.

Kerry nods, shuts up.

No. This is cool. This is fine.

The detective backs out of the open front door, waving bye to someone inside with the hand that isn't firm on his belt buckle—presumably Diana Wolf, which would explain the dumb grin. He imagines her at the end of the entry hall, with a big honking glass of red wine, arching her back to show off her ass.

Kerry laughs as quietly as he can. *Dang. Wasn't just me.* Does she just do this to every man she meets? It has to be on purpose.

After a last tip of his hat, the lead detective turns his attention to Kerry, and his demeanor changes instantly. Not for the nicer.

The detective walks down the porch like a killer in an old western: long, slow strides, stepping heavy in his cowboy boots, head silhouetted by the overhead porch lights so Kerry can't make out much of his face. "Well, well," he drawls. "Mr. Cartographer."

Kerry smiles, all lips.

The detective stares down at him for a second, measuring. Then he nods once. Slow. Sits down in the open wicker chair so they're facing each other across a squat glass table. "My name's Ellison. I'm in charge. Just have a few questions about this statement you gave us earlier, that's all."

Ellison pulls a folded document out of his shirt pocket and whaps the air with it. Places it on the table, still folded.

Kerry blinks. "I told your guy everything. It's all in there."

"Sure it is."

Ellison takes a notepad and a pen from Lenny, who leaves them alone and backtracks into the yard. As soon as the big deputy steps off the porch, darkness swallows him.

Ellison taps his pen to regain Kerry's attention. "I'll ask you, kindly, to start at the end and work your way backward in time. Helps to remember details."

He tells Ellison everything. Again. Starting with the moment the cops arrived and he gave his statement the first time, then working back to the beginning. Taking Diana out to the skull. Diana letting him out of the pantry. Thad throwing him down there, pistol to his head, and locking it.

Et cetera.

Ellison just writes and writes. Silent. His pen makes more noise than he does, scratching away at the pad. It's not until Kerry gets to what he saw in the Wolf brothers' "treehouse" that he stops him.

"Hold up. This painting you saw," says the detective. "Let's talk about it a minute, now that I've had a chance to go see for myself. Nasty shit. But you heard from Mrs. Wolf it was her son's artwork, did you not?"

"Yes. She told me."

Ellison scratches down a big check mark in his notes, never glancing up. "I'm curious then. In your statement, you insisted a few times that you think that painting is connected to our girl. Old Toothless. You even made sure to mention you think we should check up on these two kids. Cyrus. Jonah. But it was hours later when you found her. I don't see it."

"I mean . . ."

"Jonah Wolf is in Manhattan and has not left in six months," Ellison says, sighing. "And Cy was in California last anyone in the family heard, broke as hell, so he ain't flying back on a whim. Time lines all add up unless the maid's lying too. Neither son is a person of interest at this time. Ain't sure those two boys'd love to hear you put both their full names in a police report like this. To be clear, I don't love it neither."

"There's a maid?" asks Kerry. "Oh. *America.* I just got that."

Ellison ignores him, unfolds the statement on the table and reads it silently. "You made a big fuss about this wet paint."

Kerry nods. "It was wet."

"That's the thing," says Ellison, looking back up at him. "It was not."

Kerry leans back in his chair, tries to gauge the tone of this interview so far. "You're wrong."

Ellison sighs. "You touch it?"

"No," he admits.

"I did. You think to ask Mrs. Wolf why that paint might look wet?"

"No."

"S'not commercial paint he uses. Mixes it himself. Just keeps its sheen when it dries, is all. Momma says he likes it that way. Something 'bout the skin looking more alive when it shines. More *realistic*." Ellison rolls his eyes. "Now, I ain't sure about all that." The detective smiles, shaking his head like it's all a big laugh the two of them can share.

Kerry manufactures a chuckle.

"I met him once. Jonah."

"Oh."

"Very intense guy," says Ellison, looking hard into his eyes. "But he's no killer."

"I never said he was."

Ellison shrugs. "I read between lines for a living, kiddo. Come on."

Kerry leans forward, full of nervous energy and not sure what to do with his hands. "No. No, you're misunderstanding me. I am not accusing *anyone*. I have no dog in this fight. I told you what I saw and what I thought of it. That's it."

Ellison nods reassuringly. "I believe you. Loosen up. Both of us are just doing what we're s'posed to do."

Kerry crosses his arms, not reassured in the slightest. It still feels wrong. None of it adds up, not as clean as this detective is insisting it does. "Why was it so cold? And that notebook—did you find it? It was on the tarp."

Ellison's smile disappears in an instant. "How many drinks did you imbibe this afternoon, Mr. Perkins?"

"Four. But I wasn't drunk. Not really." Not a lie—more of a fudge. It's not like he was blackout. "What does that have to do with—"

"No notebook."

Kerry can feel the blood draining from his face. "It wasn't there?"

Ellison nods, slow and serious. "I'm not saying you're an unreliable guy. Just today."

Kerry's leg is hot. His iPhone feels like it's burning a hole in his pocket. "I understand."

"You said before there was a set of numbers inside. In this notebook."

"Coordinates," Kerry corrects him. "A location on a map."

Ellison nods. He looks down at his pen and notepad again. "Did you recognize this location?"

"No."

"Did you get a chance to look it up, then?"

"No. I haven't had service since I got down that driveway."

Ellison looks up. "Lemme guess . . . Sprint?"

Kerry glares at him. "It's a good deal."

"No doubt. So, I guess you don't actually remember these coordinates. Is that accurate?"

Kerry feels sweat droplets sprouting on his forehead, even though it's dropped about thirty degrees since night fell. He wipes at it with his sleeve. Hopes Ellison didn't notice. The detective's body is all casual. Friendly. His eyes are different. Harder to read. Intense. And there's something else . . . Fear?

"Yes," he lies. "That's accurate."

Ellison stares. "No memory at all?"

"None."

The detective's face stays blank. "Too bad. You didn't take a picture on your phone, did you?"

Kerry shakes his head. "No service."

Ellison makes a face like he's talking to a moron. "Huh. You wouldn't mind if I took a peek at that camera roll, just to check? Maybe you forgot. You know. Given your state."

Kerry musters up all the anger and irrational confidence in his being. The end result feels a lot like courage. "Yes. I would mind. My photos are private. You already searched my other shit."

Ellison's face melts into a death glare. "Your call."

Kerry shrugs. Courage is working out for once. "Let me know if you get a warrant, but there's nothing illegal on it. I just don't want your guys looking at my naked exes."

All of a sudden, the detective snaps his notepad closed. Stands up. Cracks his neck. "All right then. Thank you for your time, Mr. Perkins. If I need anything else, we'll be in touch. But I think we're done here."

Kerry stays rooted in his seat. "That's it . . ."

Ellison holds out a hand to shake. "Yeah. That's it."

Nervous, Kerry takes the hand. Shakes it. The detective pulls him up like a football player helping up a downed opponent after a play.

"Jumpy as hell, boy," says Ellison as they walk down the porch to Kerry's black sedan in the parking circle. "Do everyone else out there a favor, and stop to get a bite before you get on the highway. You good?"

Kerry nods. "Yeah. I just thought you might . . ."

"Arrest you?"

Kerry nods again.

Ellison claps a hand on his neck and brings him in close. "For what? Never doubted you. I doubt those four or six drinks she fed you in there." He makes a motion with his thumb and pinky to imply what he really thinks of Diana: a drunk. The town lush. "Shit, kid. Catch on. Why ya think I kept you here so late?"

Kerry feels stupid as it hits him. "You didn't want me driving."

Ellison smiles, nods.

Kerry laughs half-heartedly. "Oops."

"Oops," the detective agrees. "Go home. If you need me, call the sheriff's department. Not Franklin. But you ask any cop in a hundred miles for Big Rod and they'll probably point you in my direction."

Big Rod. For real. "You don't have a card?"

"Nah."

They get to Kerry's car.

"Keys are in the ignition," says Ellison, slapping the roof of the black sedan. "Rest of your gear should be in the back. Let me know if you end up missing anything."

Kerry stops. Remembers something. "Wait. You didn't tell her about my bag . . . I mean, when you talked to . . ."

"No. Your little secret's safe."

Kerry feels a swell of relief. "Thank you. I just wanna say it's not like these people are *ever* unhappy with the end result, you know? It's just way harder to do it the way my website—"

"It's fraud."

Kerry's face goes white again. "Oh."

"Listen." Ellison opens the driver's side door and ushers Kerry inside like a kid late to soccer practice. "One last piece of advice. You ever find yourself in a situation like this again, shut up. Hear me?"

Kerry gulps, nods as he climbs into the driver's seat, and buckles up. Closes his door.

Ellison leans in close to the window, a hand on his belt buckle again. With his free hand, he makes a gun and points it at Kerry. Drops his thumb like a hammer on a revolver. *Bang.*

The detective smiles, turns, and walks back to the golden light shining out of the house.

Kerry exhales. Flicks the ignition.

His tires climb the steep driveway all the way back up to the gate at the top that leads out of Wolf Hollow. It's open. He puts on a turn signal, checks both ways, and weaves out onto the road.

Finally. Off Thad Wolf's fucking property. As it fades in his rear-view mirror, he hopes he never sees that gate again.

At the first stop sign he hits, he reaches into his pocket and pulls out his iPhone. Unlocks it. Opens his camera roll. *There it is*. A page in a notebook, stained with black oil paint. A set of coordinates scrawled in pencil: *39.3851 N, 119.7064 W.*

Kerry deletes it.

He slams his foot on the gas pedal and tries to ignore the tremors coursing through him. He has every number of those coordinates memorized, photo or no. Can't help it. That's his job—memorizing coordinates.

A few miles down the road, GPS finally picks up his location. A female voice politely requests that he turn left in one hundred feet. He obliges.

The black sedan's engine clanks, makes that noise again. Half the time now, it sounds like there's a ten-pound kettlebell tied to his under-carriage. Kerry silently promises the cheap car gods that he'll take it to the dealership as soon as he's home. As he turns onto a bigger road with four lanes, he watches his speedometer and brakes sporadically to keep his speed at thirty miles per hour, fifteen below the limit. Just in case.

When he gets to the edge of Leiper's Fork proper and turns onto Main Street, he decides to take Ellison's advice since he really could use a hot coffee and some food. Calories. Sugars, fats, glutens, something bad for him to eat and digest on the forty-five–minute drive back to Nashville so he doesn't start to lose it.

Near the southern end of town, he pulls up at the lone coffee shop, The Cuppa. What drew him in was a green-and-red neon sign in its window, a stark contrast to the old wooden storefronts on either side: *"Open 24 Hours—Free Wi-Fi!"* An oasis. A well in the desert. If it's true. Not even Thad Wolf can get reliable Wi-Fi down in this hole, judging by the nonexistent download speeds he clocked in the barn.

Still worth a shot. A coffee will do him good either way.

Lo and behold, Kerry feels like the worst is over as he puts his park-ing brake on. When he walks in and sees four busy young people on laptops, working late, he feels even better. Calm, even. These laptop folk are his people: mustaches, MacBooks, and flannel.

By the time he sets down a coconut-milk latte and a gluten-free doughnut on the cafe's big common table, he feels right at home. He uses a paper slip with the password he got from the barista to connect to the Wi-Fi, then opens the *New York Times* app on his phone. To his shock, it loads in a blink: high-def pictures, video previews, everything. Forget *reliable*. The Cuppa has better Wi-Fi than he does at home. As he digests the bland, same-old headlines—stories about an oil spill in the ocean, deaths in the Middle East, and skyrocketing Manhattan housing prices—his worries fall away like autumn leaves. *What skull? What cops?*

Ten minutes later, he notices the thin man staring at him.

It's not your average, non-creepy stare. Seated in a secluded booth, the thin man hasn't blinked in minutes. A laptop is open on the table in front of him. He's not looking at it. The man's face is pale and soft, but his hazel eyes are like sharpened spikes in a pit. His clothes are stained and worn; he's got on a fleece pullover, baggy slacks, a beanie, and an ancient pair of cross-trainers held together by duct tape.

Other than the laptop, it all screams homeless.

Kerry frowns and gets back to his phone. He's a city boy at heart. You get used to homeless people staring in coffee shops.

But ten minutes after *that*, the thin man is still staring at him. The laptop, open before, is now closed. The thin man has no drink. No food. As far as Kerry can tell, he still hasn't blinked. So, now it's scary. Then right as Kerry works up the courage to confront him, the thin man rises out of his seat, with his laptop in an armpit, and hobbles to the exit.

The thin man never stops staring as he puts his back to the door, dirty-nailed fingers fumbling blindly for its handle. He gets it, kicks the door open with a heel. A little bell on a string tinkles, and he shuffles out onto Main Street, like a crab, as the door creaks shut.

Kerry sighs, thinking the thin man is gone, but then he jumps and spills his latte when he notices a pair of yellow eyes pressed up against the front window.

Kerry stares back.

Finally, the thin man retreats into the dark.

Okay. That's it. Fuck this town.

Kerry's seen enough. He abandons his unfinished latte on the common table as his feet carry him out of the coffee shop like it was their decision to leave.

Once outside, he checks for the thin man.

But there's no one. The sides of the road are empty in both directions, so either the thin man ducked into another shop, got in a car, or . . . Kerry glances back at the dense woods looming behind The Cuppa: grayish trees with no leaves, fifty feet tall, packed tight as rows of corn for miles.

In the dark, he doesn't see it until he's a foot away from his door, reaching for the handle.

When he notices it, his hand recoils. There's a white piece of paper folded and stuck under the black sedan's windshield wipers. A note. It says *Kerry Perkins* on it—in painstakingly perfect, tiny cursive.

Kerry flips it over. It has his home address written on the back. His house in Nashville. No one here except the cops should know that . . . his website doesn't have an address listed.

He opens the note:

leaving so soon? the map was supposed to take a week.
judging by her bank accounts, you took the money. please email me.

pink@jkjkxo.com

The fuck?

When he's read it twice, he drops it and grinds it in the dirt with his heel, jumps in his car, reverses onto Main Street, and guns it.

6

Diana

October 17, 2019. 1:08 PM

DIANA WOLF WAKES up alone.

Thad must be at the golf course already. His pillow is empty and his sheets are tossed aside.

She rolls onto her side, rubs her eyes.

The alarm clock with green numbers on her side table says . . . *fuck.* Again.

She sighs as her head flops back down onto her pillow. It's wet. Cold.

She has nowhere to be today, no appointments to make, but it still makes her feel like a piece of shit when she wakes up past noon. There's none of that light, hello-world-how-are-you? feeling, no endorphin rush at the thought of a cup of coffee. The sunlight even looks less vibrant, filtering in through her shades.

The bed smells like a gym bag, and it's all coming from her side, so she wipes her forehead. Yeah. No surprise when the back of her hand comes away slick, dripping sweat.

Again. The last six nights haven't been pleasant. On Monday, a cartographer showed her a mutilated skull in the woods out back of her house and called the police, and the police came, four cruisers' worth, because it was fucking real. Every night since she saw it, she's had the same nightmare. Six in a row. It's like she's a kid again. "Night terrors," doctors said whenever Bonnie was lucid enough to arrange a free visit for her insomniac eldest daughter—mostly through her disability benefits or one of the charities that irregularly checked in on her three kids. It took a lot of years and a lot of therapy to get to where she was at last Monday: dreamless sleep. Eight hours a night, seven nights a week. No night terrors. No voices. But she's moving backward now, and it's all because she can't forget the fucking carving on its forehead. The two wolves.

Diana *knows* that design. She knew what it was, and who carved it, the second she saw it.

The two wolves have names: Jonah, Cyrus. Her two sons.

The boys used to sign their paintings with it.

Cy gave up on painting with his big brother at the tail end of elementary school, which is when his attention swiveled to drugs, computers, and rare sneakers, in that order. But Jonah didn't. He painted and painted, then painted some more—and he kept using the two wolves to sign it all. He didn't switch to his initials until college. That design is scattered all over old photos of his work, and today you can see it on the backs of half the paintings he's got stored in Wolf Hollow's basement. Hundreds of canvasses. Hundreds of wolves. Thousands of demons. The old paintings are wrapped in plastic and leaned up in orderly rows, asleep in a locked crawlspace ten feet below where she sleeps—or where she doesn't.

She closes her eyes, wishing it'd all go away.

She knows Jonah carved it.

But for six days, she hasn't been able to marshal the nerve to call her eldest son. To ask him: *Why?*

He must have done it one of these years he visited Tennessee for the holidays, which would explain why it was so close to the boys' treehouse. Jonah probably got bored, went for a nostalgic walk in the woods, and found the toothless skull the same way Kerry Perkins did. But instead of calling the police, he saw an artistic opportunity. He carved on it. Carved a sentimental image from his childhood into a dead girl's forehead, trying to make some sick, vague, immoral, shocking, provocative, misguided—and *harmless*—statement piece. But alas, the cops won't buy that story.

They shouldn't. It sounds crazy.

So, she lied.

She told Rod Ellison and the rest of the cops she has no idea what the carving means.

To a stranger, the real explanation might seem far-fetched, but it sounds exactly like Jonah if you know what his art is all about: *"Domination and penetration . . . the nonconsensual violation of female flesh and bone by a dominant male."* Jonah's words, not hers. She can practically hear her eldest son's high, reedy voice as he explained the intent of his oeuvre to a small crowd of friends, family, and curious hipsters at his first (*only*, to date) gallery show in Manhattan: sixteen life-sized, colorless paintings of demons hate-fucking each other to death in torchlit caves. The show flopped. No mystery as to why. It was a good turnout, as openings go, but the sixteen paintings Jonah chose to showcase were repulsive. Hateful. So much so that she felt a guilty tinge of schadenfreude when not a single painting sold. Not one. Her long-held, silent beliefs about her son's "art" had been vindicated at last.

"Art." Like this.

Digging up a murdered girl's skull—and instead of calling the police or even trying to do the right thing, desecrating it. Where's the empathy? Or the intelligence, even? He signed it. It's like he wanted to taunt the cops, to position himself as the prime suspect in a murder investigation. To waste their time. Why? "Art" again?

What is he, fucking differently abled?

It's not even a question whether Jonah killed her.

No. No way. She didn't raise her boys like that. Whatever Cy does or Jonah paints, they're both sensitive people, just artists—like their dad, their aunt, their uncle, and their grandmother.

Bonnie.

Diana's mother was a painter too. Butterflies and fruit. And she was twenty-eight when she first hallucinated. Diagnosis came a year later when they committed her the first time, gave her all those pills she refused to take.

Jonah's twenty-eight.

On mornings like this, she thinks about that.

Unsurprisingly, her new night terror is about the dead girl. Jane Doe.

She never realized homicide police actually call unidentified corpses that name. Thought it was something Hollywood invented, that in real life they'd use numbers or letters of the alphabet or a code, maybe even Dewey decimals. But no. Jane Doe is real. Jane was in her early twenties, white, petite, five foot one, wide hips, a hundred pounds. *Either a supermodel or poor then,* Diana muses, still lying on her back in bed and staring up at a huge ceiling fan with old mahogany oars for blades (*artisanal*).

It's a weird thing, to know her weight. But she does. The police can guess all those details now, ever since they found the rest of Jane's skeleton, minus hands or feet, a few yards away from her skull. A couple days ago, detective Ellison had revealed the worst details yet. Jane Doe had been buried a few hours after she died, apparently around seven years ago. Diana keeps hoping the cops will revise those numbers, because she and Thad have lived at Wolf Hollow for ten. If they're right, she was living in this house when someone murdered a girl in their woods. Took out her teeth. Cut off her hands and feet. Buried her in a shallow grave. In all likelihood, Diana Wolf was home when it all happened.

Which explains her nightmare.

*   *   *

It starts in her kitchen.

It's silent. She's in the middle of cooking a big turkey as the sun sets over the cold woods outside, taking it out of the oven the way she used to on Thanksgiving when she still held the catch-all family dinner. But she's alone. No guests in the house, none out in the yard. She muscles the twenty-pound roasted bird up onto the kitchen island. Cooked to perfection as usual. As she removes her oven mitts, she hears a high-pitched scream outside: piercing, blood-curdling.

She looks up, out the trio of bay windows over the sink. At the woods.

The scream ends abruptly—with a wet *gurgle*.

Silence again.

She sees nothing except the firepit, where all the stump seats are unoccupied, and the cobblestone bridge over the ravine. Beyond that, there's nothing but tall, bare poplar trees and an empty gray sky.

She shrugs. Shakes her head. *Hearing things,* she tells herself as she grabs a chef's knife out of her block, sharpens it a few times on a whetstone, and carves the bird on the kitchen island. Thin slices. Quick, confident cuts. *Sic. Sic. Sic.* Breast meat falls off its body. Brown, greasy liquid pools and eddies in the tiny reservoirs around the edges of her cutting board. When it's down to exposed bone, Diana discards the chef's knife and grabs a leg with one slick hand, the bird's ribcage with the other, and pulls.

The drumstick snaps off. *Crrk!*

*   *   *

And that's it. That's when she wakes up.

It may sound like a pretty benign dream, as night terrors go. It doesn't feel that way.

But maybe she'll still forget. Maybe it'll go away. If she just gets out of bed. If she just makes herself coffee.

Even as she does it—gets up, puts on slippers—she knows she's telling herself bullshit. After six nights, it's safe to say the nightmare about Jane Doe has joined a small pantheon of her very worst dreams:

1. Bonnie, naked but for heavy makeup on just one half of her face, chasing her with a knife through their rat-infested apartment in Los Angeles and screaming nonsense as she desperately tries to make it into Kristen and Luke's room in time to lock the door.
2. Cy, as a small baby, crying in their old dark house in Brentwood, California, while she tries to find him in every room, but she can't. He's nowhere to be found, she's alone, and his little wails keep getting littler and sadder and farther away.
3. A dead coyote lying in the road at night, lit by headlights as its corpse returns to life, stands, and stares at her while dark blood and intestines fall out of it.

All connected by a feeling of dread. All the kind of nightmares you carry through life like stones tied to your neck.

The nightmare about Jane Doe is a stone kind. She's not going to forget.

Diana throws on a robe and walks into the main room. America sees her and waves from the kitchen, a hundred feet or so away on the other side of the cavernous open-floor-plan space. Diana waves back as she navigates through the living "room," then the dining "room," and finally into the small nook where Wolf Hollow's espresso machines live. There are three machines now: Thad's black Nespresso, her silver Breville, and a brand-new gray Mr. Coffee she bought for the seven cops, give-or-take, who show up to dig at the crime scene every morning.

She crafts herself a dainty two-shot latte, topping it off with a perfect inch of foam, courtesy of the Breville's steam arm. Then she hits a button and the Mr. Coffee spits out a gallon of black, caffeinated sludge. Italian and American engineering in a nutshell.

She pours the sludge into a thermos and grabs a stack of Styrofoam cups. She ditches the slippers for green rubber boots at the back door, because it looks wet outside, but she doesn't bother switching out her robe for a jacket. Ellison likes her in a robe—it's obvious. He's always a little less guarded when she wears it, always willing to slip her a few more details about Jane Doe, the investigation, even his personal life—she knows the names, ages, and attitudes of all three of Big Rod's teen daughters. Zelda, his eldest at sixteen, is going through a bit of an *awakening* and seeing if she can fuck every senior boy at school . . . but who isn't at that age?

Diana steps out into the backyard. Her boots sink into the damp grass as she walks past the firepit with all its empty stump seats, down the gravel path, over the cobblestone bridge above the ravine, and finally arrives at the middle of it. Halfway across.

She stops. Takes a deep breath and thinks a prayer—not for Jane Doe, who doesn't need it, but for her sons, the two wolves, because they do.

O Lord, let this pass . . .

She exhales. Closes her eyes.

She takes a step, then another and another. It's not so bad until the bridge ends, and the ground changes into something soft and wet. Sticks and leaves crunch under each step.

When she finally opens her eyes, she's in the woods.

* * *

She knows the way now.

When she gets close, blue ghosts flit between distant trees like will-o'-the-wisps: cops in their ponchos.

A line of taut yellow-and-black tape rises out of the overgrowth, blocking her path. "*CRIME SCENE DO NOT CROSS*," it reads.

Diana ducks underneath. The wet tape slides down her back as she straightens up and walks into the thicket where Jane's corpse still rests in the soil, one part here and one part there, each bone highlighted by white plastic markers that stick up out of the earth like headstones.

The coroner was supposed to come get what's left of her yesterday, but his van broke down. Bad engine.

And so, Jane Doe remains.

One of the young rookie cops notices her first. He waves, eyes tracking the big steel thermos tucked in her elbow. The rookie jogs over to a blue ghost facing the other direction, taps his shoulder, and nods at her.

Rodney Ellison has a big smile on his face as he swivels and finds her gliding up to the crime scene in a white robe. "Mrs. Wolf," he drawls, both hands resting on his belt buckle. "Our patron saint of caffeine. I must ask: What in God's name is a jewel like you doin' in a mineshaft like this?"

Diana snorts as she passes him the thermos and cups.

Ellison pours a cup, then hands it to the rookie. His eyes never leave hers.

She places a hand on his wrist, goes up on her toes to kiss his cheek, and lingers a second longer than *polite greeting* calls for. It has the intended effect. When she pulls away, his pupils are glazed over as if she'd drugged him.

Diana smirks, unable to contain a sense of pride at still being able to work a married cop like this.

"Please, Rod," she says as she surveys the other cops, purple plastic gloves stretched across their hands, excavating and brushing dirt off bones, bagging evidence in Ziplocs, one guy snapping photos on a big, outdated camera. "God's got nothing to do with it."

"Sure he does," he says with the nervous energy of a southerner who fears the Lord.

Diana nudges him. "So. Where were we? Any suspects yet, compelling leads?"

Ellison shifts weight from one leg to the other. Clears his throat. "Been meaning to have a word with you, actually. You know, it's frowned upon to talk shop about an ongoing . . ." He stammers when he notices her idly fingering the cinch of her robe.

"Oh?" A red-painted fingernail grazes his hand.

Ellison looks at it, breathing heavily. "Sorry. We can't keep talking about an ongoing investigation," he clarifies. "If one of my guys ever heard us, he could get me thrown off this case. Or I could lose my job."

She shrugs. "Oh. That's okay. I get it."

She wanders off, pretends to be interested in a cheap box of doughnuts left open on a fold-out card table set up in the trees. Two remain out of a baker's dozen. She picks up the one that isn't custard and studies it, mouth pursed. As if she fucking eats doughnuts. *Please.* She's got assets to maintain if she wants to keep a rich husband interested, and the wine makes it hard enough.

"We ain't found shit," says Ellison, a little too loud.

His eyes dart back and forth to all his younger officers, but if they heard, none of them care.

Diana drops the stale doughnut and sidles up to him again. "Knew you'd come around."

He nods, sips his coffee.

She decides to push her luck. "Well, what's your theory, then?"

Ellison gives her a look. "What, about her?"

"Yeah. What would you guess her story is, if you had to?"

Ellison scratches his chin. Smiles.

"Humor me, Rod." She bites her lip. "Please?"

"Hoo-boy. Fine." The detective's head shakes while he says it, as if it isn't on the same page as his brain and mouth. "I'd guess she was a drifter. A local. One of them off-the-grid types we used to get around here back in the day. Baby doll's bones don't match a single missing person's report in the whole national database. Means nobody's looking for her. So that says hooker, druggie, runaway, a girl who fell through the proverbial cracks." He stops. Sighs as he stares off at a dense cluster of trees. "The girls do tend to come out the other side like this. Breaks my heart."

Involuntarily, she thinks of Cy. "What about the boys?"

Ellison frowns. "I suppose boys don't fare much better." He sips his coffee.

She nods. Stares into the forest at nothing. Trees. Dead leaves.

Is Cy still in there? In the cracks? It's tough to say. She hasn't spoken to her baby boy in over six months. That was the last time Cy called her or anyone else. Nobody knows where he is or what he's doing. Thad doesn't give a shit, says it's for the best. His mom is the only one who still cares about him.

And do you, really? says a little voice, not her own.

Maybe not, if she's being honest. It's not like she's been trying to track him down or call. She has a number. But ever since he threatened to kill Jonah with a skeet shotgun one morning and Thad had to physically throw him out of the house, everyone's been afraid to speak to Cy, even Luke and Kristen (to be fair, she can't remember the last time either of her siblings spoke to *her*). And for good reason—she can't imagine Cy's gotten better these last five years, all alone. She wonders, how does her baby boy support himself? Does he get enough to eat? Is he warm? Does he have a job? Decent socks, underwear, shoes? Is he happy?

No, says a little voice.

Her heart breaks.

You failed your sons, worse than your mother failed you. At least Bonnie was insane. Sick. But you're a liar. You tell yourself this isn't your voice.

Diana closes her eyes. Prays.

After a few seconds of it, the voice is gone, and she gets her head right. "So you'd guess she's a drifter. But I meant it like who do you think murdered her? A john?"

Ellison raises an eyebrow. "Where'd you go and get that idea?"

"What, that it could've been a john?"

"No, no. It's not a *murder*. Who told you it was—one of mine? Shit." He glances around the dig site, searching for likely suspects.

Diana bristles. "No one. Rod. Our girl seems to be missing her teeth, hands, and feet. Jesus Christ, how do you think she died?"

His eyes narrow at her use of the "*J*" word. "Look. Some asshole killed her. Don't misunderstand me."

She waits expectantly.

"Murder is a legal term," he says, as if he regrets correcting her. "This is just a dead body, a Jane. Why do you think we were checking the missing person's database?"

Her eyes turn to slits as she puts two and two together. "It's not a murder if there's no victim," she says, staring at the white markers scattered among the pits of dirt and dead leaves.

He nods gravely. "*No humans involved*, we call these."

She sees her opening and goes for it. "What about the carving on the forehead, the two wolves? Your guys still need to look into it. Don't they?"

This is it. The moment of truth.

He waves it away. "It's nothing. We did. I know you were worried it was a threat on your family, but I'm happy to report the timing don't work out. Looks more like some dickhead dug it up and carved on it a few years after she got buried. I'd guess last winter, if that. It's a sick prank, is all. Teenagers or some such. I seen it before. Mighta been that boy, Christian, and his friends, the ones you let hunt up here . . . or it mighta been anyone. So it's not a concern of ours no more, and it shouldn't be yours neither." He winks at her. Proud.

A great weight lifts off her shoulders as she digests what he said. The carving doesn't matter. So that's the end of that.

Cops aren't wrong about it having been a "sick prank," but that's all it was, and now that's all it ever will be. Good. Nobody else needs to know what Jonah did. It was just a mistake. Her baby is safe. Her family is safe. It'll all be over soon.

"So? What's next?" she asks, settling into real curiosity now. "How do you identify her if her bones don't match a missing person in the database?"

"There is no next," he whispers.

Ellison doesn't elaborate, nor does he look at her when he says it, or after . . . like he's ashamed.

"What do you mean?" An inexplicable fear wells up in her chest. *This is good news,* says a little voice. *Remember?*

"We might be able to pull DNA from the marrow," he says, doubt-ful. "I wouldn't hold my breath if I were you."

"You're still going to try?" she says, accusatory, and notes of anger are creeping into her voice now. "Your little dig here is just the start of a big investigation, right?" It's funny: now that she's not worried about the carving coming back to haunt Jonah, her momma-bear instincts have shifted and she's worried about the dead girl instead. Jane. Who-ever she was, Jane deserves better than this. Even seven years after she died, she deserves someone who'll *try* to solve her murder, who'll *try* to make her a person again, not a Jane. It would certainly make Diana feel better about lying to the police.

Ellison looks up at the sky, pleading with his eyes for a reprieve. "Why'd you think I'd ever talk with you about this stuff? We got no leads. It's been a week."

"It has been six days."

"Even that is a long, long time for this kind of thing," he says softly, like he's explaining a dead pet to a toddler. "A long time. And then you pair that with a seven-year-old body, no vic, no witnesses, no cause of death, no murder weapon . . ." He stops to weigh his phrasing. "There wouldn't be a point to it."

Diana's face gets hot. "*No point?* You can figure out her fucking name!"

She yelled that. Oops. A few cops stop what they're doing in the dirt pits, pop their heads out, and stare like groundhogs.

Ellison, eyes on fire, gives an all-around glare that puts everyone back to work in seconds. Then he turns his wrath on Diana. "Frankly, I'm insulted by your tone. Didn't you say you worked as an ER nurse?"

She had. In another life.

After her foster parents kicked her out, she worked the graveyard shift at a hospital in Cleveland for a year before she met Thad on a trip to visit Kristen in Los Angeles . . . at the Playboy Mansion, a detail she hates remembering and avoids thinking about when possible. A "talent scout" invited the two sisters off the street— just another pair of naive young blondes from the Midwest, oohing and aahing as they walked the Sunset Strip.

She nods.

"Right," says Ellison. "So in the ER, you ever have fewer than three patients goin' at once? Ever?"

"No," she admits.

"I supposed not. So do you want to venture a guess as to how many cases I'm on right this second? All corpses. All suspicious deaths, since

I work in *homicide* and the sheriff does not send for me otherwise. Do you?"

No. But Diana refuses to answer rhetorical questions as a rule, so she waits for him to finish.

"Fourteen," he says, sniffing. "This is not a *Law & Order* episode. We're not all hands on deck on a single case until it gets resolved, start to finish. We work 'em all at once, which means we solve the ones we can solve. And yeah, sure, we spend more time on those. That's reality. Okay? And far as I can tell, all thirteen o' my other bodies have got a better chance at clearing than your Jane Doe, here, because those cases have got names and witnesses, or a family who knew the vic, or evidence. This girl? We got nothing. It is a dead body. That's it." He stops, cools off. Sighs. "I'm sorry I raised my voice at you. Are we clear?"

She lets it all wash over her. "You're never going to solve it, and you're not going to try. Right?"

It's Ellison's turn to ignore a rhetorical question. He just sips his coffee like she's not there.

Diana cinches her robe tight, waves goodbye to the other officers, and stomps back into the woods.

*   *   *

Rodney Ellison watches her go out of the side of his eye.

Her skimpy white robe only goes down to mid-thigh, so there's more than enough smooth, pale skin to keep the detective's attention as she walks off in a huff. Ellison loves an angry woman. It's no fun when they like you.

He wolf-whistles as she arches her back and ducks under the crime scene tape in the distance, out of earshot.

"Yo, Rod!" says a voice behind him. Ignacio, the rookie.

Ellison doesn't look. "What?"

"I found a thing down here. Could be hers."

His smile disappears as he turns around and glares down at Ignacio in his hole, kneeling in a two-foot-deep pit with dirty toothbrushes and used purple gloves scattered around his legs.

"Bullshit. What is it?" says Ellison, feet planted at the pit's edge. "Give it here."

The wide-eyed rookie rises to his feet and steps out of the pit, holding a cloth the size of a napkin, like a baby bird, in both hands.

"Iggy. You think it's evidence, you wrap that shit up."

Ignacio puts it in a plastic bag. Zips it. Hands it over.

Ellison holds the clear bag up to the sky, examining what's inside: a brass button.

It looks like it's from a pair of jeans, maybe. Top button on a fly. In good shape for how deep it was in that pit, which means it's not old enough to have gotten there naturally. Someone buried it. And where you'd expect to find Levi's or whatever brand name embossed on it is a slogan he's never seen: *"LOOK AT ME LOOK AT YOU!"* The tiny letters spiral around the button's edge, so he has to rotate the plastic bag as he reads it.

"Well?" says Ignacio. "Was it hers?"

A chill skitters down the detective's back. He shakes his head. "Nope. I'd say it's been in the ground two or three years, if that. No dice. Hop back in your pit, rook."

Ignacio looks disappointed. "You got it."

Ellison waits until the rookie is in a hole again, eyes down.

After a final scan to make sure nobody else is looking, he slips the evidence bag with Jane Doe's brass button deep into his back pocket. Sips his coffee. Tries to act casual. But the tremor in his hands is *bad*, and he spills on his chest.

He wipes it up with a sleeve.

If any of his men saw, they're doing a good job pretending otherwise. Good boys. If they know what's good for them, they'll keep those fucking heads down.

Ellison certainly wishes he'd done the same three years ago, when that first encrypted message appeared on his cell phone. Like a virus. It just popped up on his home screen. He wishes he'd 'fessed up to it when that first deposit landed in his account—told someone higher up. They might've protected him and his family. But he didn't. No one can protect him now. No one but God. He took it. Spent it.

He regrets it every day. No amount of money is worth this fear.

CHAPTER

7

Cy

September 2, 2004. 6:32 PM

CYRUS AND JONAH Wolf hiked up a steep hill at the top of Tigertail
Road, with light camping chairs slung on their backs.

Halfway up, sweating and out of breath, Cy stopped to look over
his shoulder.

Los Angeles dominated the southern horizon, dotted with the first
lights turning on at dusk. Even in the half dark, the view was breath-
taking. The hill's vantage point offered a hundred and eighty plus
degrees of unobstructed sight lines, so almost every landmark in the
city was visible at once: Santa Monica Pier and the sun sinking into the
Pacific Ocean to his right; downtown's skyscrapers in the south; and if
he squinted real hard to his left, he could even make out two and a half
letters of the Hollywood sign in the far east.

Beautiful.

"You were right," he said.

"I'm always right," said Jonah, way ahead of him and not slowing
down. "Come on. It gets better."

"Fine," he said, starting back up the hill. "Hey. Chill out up there."

"You need a break, big boy?"

Cy's face got red. "No. But if you fall up here, your arm's coming
out again, and I threw up last time."

"Shoulder," Jonah corrected him. "It's my shoulders that dislocate."

"Whatever. It's gross."

"Maybe I like them loose." Jonah popped a shoulder out, then right back in without missing a stride.

Cy shivered. "Stop it."

When they got to the peak, valleys fell off on both sides, and a mountain ridge dipped to meander north along the coast toward the Palisades.

Jonah unzipped his camping chair and set it up behind a fallen tree, where he sat and propped up his feet on a dead branch. Cy chose a spot beside him, then dug in his pockets for rolling materials: sandwich bag half full of weed, grinder, loose tobacco, king-size papers, filter tips, fold-out tray, *Yu-Gi-Oh!* card. Not a rare one. Mystic Clown. He used it to cut the ground-up pot and tobacco together.

He took his time on the spliffed joint, taking pains to do it just like he'd been taught. He was still a newbie to all this. Last summer, he barely knew what weed *was*. A lot of things had changed since he started hanging around with his older brother.

Jonah watched over his shoulder. "Not bad. You don't need to worry so much about losing some. It's okay."

"Says you," said Cy, who got half the allowance, being two years younger. "I skipped out on lunch for three weeks to buy this, butthole."

"Bullshit," said Jonah. "You just packed one every day out of the fridge."

"Same thing."

"No. You didn't go hungry. You didn't hunt."

"Fine. I guess you're right."

Jonah smiled. "Always." He stared at the rolling tray. "I like that card."

Cy held it up. The art on its face was dark, even for *Yu-Gi-Oh!*: a clown demon crouching in an eerie green light, with eyes all over its skin and two fanged mouths. "It's just a common. But it's cool." His brother was making fun of him—he was sure of it: Jonah always said trading cards were for babies. He'd never even played Pokemon.

"Give it to me."

Cy handed it to him.

Jonah examined it seriously before pocketing it.

*   *   *

They smoked for half an hour, looking out over Los Angeles as the sun disappeared.

The freeways morphed into great red and yellow snakes. The two snakes slithered over a drunken grid of black-shadowed streets and boulevards lined with tall palms.

"I feel like we live in *Blade Runner* sometimes," said Cy, as if it was a deep thought.

"How so?" said Jonah, as if it wasn't.

"Just like all the millions of lights. I know every one of those is a house or a car. And for every one of those things, there's a person. But to me, instead they're all just like . . . *people*." He stopped, embarrassed. "Sorry. Is that stupid?"

Jonah stared off at a big house in the distance. "No. That's true."

"I mean, it's like in the movie. Los Angeles. I don't . . . people here don't care about each other."

"I agree."

Cy blinked. His big brother never *agreed*, not when something wasn't his idea. "Cool."

"It's not just here. No one cares about anyone."

"Yeah. I bet you're right." Cy waited for a variation on *"I always am."* But none came.

A rare silence hung over the two brothers.

Jonah broke it. "I get it."

"What?"

"I get why you said you were going to hang yourself."

Cy shrunk into his chair. He felt tears in his eyes and hid his face. "Who told you?"

Jonah blew a smoke ring. It gained height as it deformed into nothingness. "Dad. The counselor called at home. Mom took it in front of him."

Cy sunk deeper. "Mr. Warren swore he wouldn't tell anyone. Not Dad. He swore."

Jonah shook his head. "He has to call. Dumbass. It's the law. You knew better."

Cy put two and two together. "That's why we've been hanging out so much this summer, huh? Mom and Dad made you."

"Just Mom."

Cy gave up on holding back tears. "I knew it." Two silent streams ran down his cheeks. "Just don't tell anyone at school. They'll make fun of me."

"Let me finish," said Jonah, holding up a palm. "Yes. I hung out with you at first because she made me. And yes, the deal ends when school starts next week. She also made me promise to never ever mention how you threatened to commit suicide." A beat. "But I just broke that promise. Didn't I?"

Cy nodded, silent.

"Fuck the deal. I don't want this to end when school starts," said Jonah, a big smile appearing on his lips and in his eyes. "I always thought you were just . . . Cy, I'm sorry for all this. But I can't say I regret Mom making me do it. I want us to stay best friends. That's what we are."

Cy's tears ran dry. "Really?"

Jonah stood up. "Really." He walked a few steps closer and motioned for a hug.

Cy hesitated. "I love you." He stood up and wrapped his arms around his older brother, cried into his chest.

"I love you too. It's okay." Jonah ran his fingers through Cy's short-cropped hair as he spoke quietly in his ear. "I never thought I'd know someone so much . . . *like me.*"

When Cy had calmed down, he spoke into his older brother's damp shirt. "I've wanted a best friend for so long." He could hardly believe it. It was a dream. Jonah was thirteen, a middle-schooler. Popular. And he was choosing *him* for a best friend? Cy? Cy was eleven. A fifth-grader. Quiet. Not popular. A big, hairless soprano who sounded like a girl. A fat one. "Baby fat," Mom called it, but he knew it was a lie. Google said *baby fat* was bullshit, and so was *big-boned*, and *husky*, and *slow metabolisms*, and he was just fat.

Jonah hugged tighter. "Win–win. I want a partner."

After laughing at each other for getting so sentimental, the brothers sat down in their camping chairs again.

Jonah relit the joint and sucked a hit into his lungs. Passed it. It glowed red in the dark.

Cy took it. Puffed on it, hands cupped around its tip to block a breeze that wasn't there. "What'd you mean, a partner?"

"Oh. Nothing."

Cy frowned. "Don't be a jerk."

A floating set of teeth appeared in the dark like a Cheshire cat. "We're going to start painting together. I can teach you."

Cy flinched—his big brother used to *teach* him to fight. It was just a cover story to use on Mom and Dad when Jonah wanted to practice a new Krav Maga move . . . on a real person. The ones they only let you do on dummies in class. He knew his little brother would never tell anyone how he got hurt. Mom would always make up a reason to tell the school if a teacher asked, then she'd get home and yell at Dad. And Dad would drink. And drink. And no one would mention it again. Ever.

"No tricks," said Jonah. "I just want us to make art together. As a team. I've got a few ideas I want to share with you as far as styles go, but I do want your input. This is going to be our work. *Our* art."

"Okay," said Cy. "Yeah. Let's do it. Our signature can be, like, two wolves. Or is that dumb?"

Jonah made a face like he was surprised: *not bad*. "No. It's perfect. Romulus and Remus were raised by a she-wolf."

"Who?"

Jonah ignored the question, lost in his own excitement. "Yeah. Okay. I'll draw something up tonight. See what you think."

Cy smiled. "Cool."

But then something changed in his big brother's face—a shift, dark and heavy.

Cy took notice. There was a storm coming. A bad one.

Jonah stood up, walked a few paces, and inspected the city spread out beneath him. A black cloud rolled in front of the moon, and its shadow seeped down his back like sweat. "One thing."

"What's up?" Cy said it agreeably, but the shift in tone was scaring him now.

"It's about how you threatened to kill yourself. I'll only say it once, then we never bring this up again after tonight. Do you hear me?"

"It's okay. Go."

Jonah turned and loomed over him, thin and tall, blue eyes cold as meat hooks in a slaughterhouse. "Never do it again."

Cy looked at the dirt. "Okay." Tears flowed down his cheeks again, but it wasn't sadness this time. It was *fear*.

Jonah sat, and it was clear the storm had passed. "That's it."

Cy coughed and his hands shook as he passed the roach. It was tiny by now.

"Thanks." Jonah took it and waved its red tip over Los Angeles like a paintbrush. "Look at all these *people*." The last word oozed out.

A sprawling city twinkled beneath the two boys. Millions of lights.

Jonah took a long drag and held it in. "Cy. Have you noticed yet how much smarter we are than them?"

"Who?"

"All of them." Tendrils of smoke drifted out of a white smile hanging in the dark.

Cy pawed at his face with a sleeve. "Yeah." It was a lie, but he suspected it was what his best friend wanted to hear.

8

Diana

October 17, 2019. 2:12 PM

Diana storms out of the woods.

As she crosses the cobblestone bridge, she notices Thad's red pickup parked out front. She digs her phone out. It's early. Thad doesn't get home before dark, normally, once he's had time to get good and drunk at the clubhouse bar.

She closes the front door softly and sneaks past the man cave, but then her ears perk up at an unexpected sound, so she doubles back.

In disbelief, she puts her ear against the white double doors: laughter. Thad is laughing. Hard. This is abnormal. Thad must be on the phone, seeing as how he's the only person talking, but her husband doesn't answer the landline as a rule—he leaves that to her or America. And he certainly doesn't laugh on the phone. *Unless it's Jonah.* The two of them have special in-jokes.

She backs away.

She's been putting off talking to her firstborn son for six days. Jonah never calls *them.* She has to talk now, but what if Thad told him about the skull or about the carving? What does she even want to say to him? Briefly, she considers just denying she ever connected Jonah to the carving at all.

To her horror, the sound of Thad's voice moves on the other side of the white double doors. She can't see him, but he's standing up from his leather chair. Now, he's swerving around the oak barrel he uses as a side table. "I think that was your momma," says Thad, getting closer. "I'll see if I can grab her for ya."

Diana stands in the hall, frozen.

Why are you so afraid? asks a little voice, not her own. *He's just your big boy. Your son.*

Thad throws open the white double doors and almost runs her over. "Fuck, Dee!" Their feet tangle and they trip, but at the last second, he drops the phone and catches her in one wiry arm. He smiles, inches from her face. "I mean, what's goin' on, beautiful?" He mimes slicking his hair back.

Diana giggles. What do you know? He can still be romantic, when she least expects it. "Hey. Sorry."

He waves it off. He helps her up, then picks up the phone. "You wanna talk to Jonah? He asked for ya."

She nods.

Thad narrows his eyes at her like she's acting weird. He puts his ear to the phone and listens. "Son. I'm gonna stop you there. My game is comin' on TV, and your mother wants to say hi. Okay? Mm-hmm. Okay. Love you, bud." He smiles. "Yeah, yeah."

He hands the phone to her, pecks her cheek with a kiss, then withdraws back into his man cave.

The white double doors slide shut. She's alone.

The other end of the line crackles in her hand. "Hi, Mom."

Diana closes her eyes and breathes. "Hello, gorgeous."

Jonah laughs. It's a great laugh he's got. Just like his father's but more contagious, disarming. "So when were you going to tell me?"

She shivers. Walks into the kitchen just to keep her feet moving, pulse pumping. "What, you mean our unexpected guest at Wolf Hollow? She's not much trouble. Quiet. Sleeps in the woods."

"Nice," says Jonah, with a dry fake laugh. "How long's that bullet been in the chamber?"

"Six days," she says. "I haven't told anyone yet, so you're the first victim I had a shot at. Seriously. Not even Robyn."

She hears Jonah smile, a wet sound, spit sticking to opening lips. "I'm honored."

Diana finds herself circling the kitchen island, doing laps like a meth head, so she reaches down to the wine cooler on her third pass. Grabs a bottle of Malbec and a custom glass. "Well, where do I start? How much did your dad tell you?"

"Oh, he told me. Skeleton in the woods with no hands, no feet or teeth? Fuck that. My friends and I used to walk out there all the time. It feels weird, and I don't even live there, so I can't imagine how you . . . you okay?"

She puts her glass down. Feels her eyes getting watery. *It's time.* "No, honestly. Did you carve your old signature into that girl's skull, Jonah? Tell me the truth."

Silence. Crackling and white noise.

"Yes," he whispers.

She waits for an explanation, but none comes. "Why?"

Jonah sighs. "I was drunk. It was after Thanksgiving last year. I took a walk in the woods, bottle in hand, and went to the old treehouse, and it got dark. I tripped over it." He sounds appropriately ashamed. She imagines him looking down at the floor, wherever he's calling from. "I know that doesn't excuse what I did. Not in the slightest."

She takes a seat at the kitchen island and pours herself a glass of wine. Swirls it. Takes a long drink. "No. It doesn't. How *could* you? What were you thinking?"

"I wasn't. It was a spur-of-the-moment thing and it . . . if there is a silver lining, it was a big moment for me. My rock bottom. And since, I haven't swallowed a drop in over nine months. I'm sorry for what I did. But I learned something important about myself. I'm an alcoholic."

Diana spits out her wine, mid-sip. "Hold on, what? You have a drinking problem?"

Just like that, all is forgiven. The carving on the skull is peanuts compared to her eldest son admitting weakness for the first time in his life. Even as a baby, Jonah almost never cried. People always commented on how quiet he was. Cy was like a broken smoke alarm at that age, always going off for no reason, but not Jonah. When they had him baptized at Brentwood Presbyterian, the reverend slipped on a wet stair and broke his hip in the middle of the ceremony. Little Jonah slid into the basin of holy water. To the horror of everyone in the pews, he sunk like a stone.

Diana was the first one up to the basin, stepping over the injured reverend.

But when she looked down at the bottom, her baby smiled up at her with open eyes through a surface like glass. Calm. Still.

She lends a sympathetic ear as he pours his heart out: story after story of how he hid his battle with alcoholism all these years.

It started his freshman year at NYU.

He says by sophomore year, he couldn't go two hours without it.

By junior year, he couldn't paint at all unless he was blind drunk. Explains a lot.

Diana pours two more glasses of red wine by the time he's finished, vaguely aware of how fucked up it is to get drunk to these stories. "Have you told your dad any of this?"

"No," he says, pain in his voice. "I was afraid you'd feel awkward drinking a glass of wine at dinner with me. It was my problem. It is."

"Don't worry about us," she coos, touched by his small display of empathy. "I won't tell him until you do. Do you need me to fly up? I've got no plans."

"I'm fine with you and Dad right where you are."

"Okay. But let me know."

The rest of their conversation is pleasant.

Diana can hardly remember why she was so apprehensive about speaking to him, even as the topic veers back to Jane Doe, the skeleton in the woods, and the police investigating it. "They're not going to solve it," she blurts out.

"Really? How do you know?"

"The fucker told me. Ellison." She explains how after recognizing the signature on the skull's forehead, she decided to work on the detective a bit to see if she could sniff out whether he was in trouble.

When she's done, Jonah sighs. "I can't believe you lied." He pauses. "*Fuck.* You know? I thought it was like an old Indian skull or something, not a girl who got murdered seven years ago."

"I still can't believe you *did* that . . . even if you thought it was *an old Indian skull.* Not cool, mister, you know better. Native American."

He snorts. "What was your favorite baseball team growing up, again?"

"Cleveland." She realizes her mistake and freezes. "Oh, shut up. Asshole."

Then Jonah says something troubling. "Mom. Did you call Cy? Does he know?"

Her inexplicable fear returns. It comes on slow, like sitting in a bath as it fills up with ice-cold water.

Jonah hasn't asked about Cy or spoken his name in five years. Not to her. Not since the day his little brother tried to kill him. The day Thad disowned Cy, threw him out of the house and said to never come back, and her baby boy drove off in the car she had bought him for his sixteenth birthday, into the sunset and out of her life.

"No," she says, thoughts moving at a mile-a-minute clip. "Why do you ask that? Why now?"

A second passes in silence.

Jonah chuckles. "Honestly? I only asked because Haley made me promise I would. She's got this weird thing about wanting me to reconnect with Cy, says he's my brother and always will be, it's probably killing our parents how we don't speak . . . on and on like that. You know how she gets."

No, but Diana can imagine. Haley is a nag if she's anything like her mother, whom Diana and Thad have been forced to spend an inordinate amount of time with this past year now that their offspring are engaged. A few holidays, even. Easter was a shit show. "Oh. Well, tell Haley I agree. I think it's a great idea. I don't know about your dad, but you know how much I'd love to see you and Cy on speaking terms again."

Jonah makes a noise like he's unsure. "I'll tell her. And we'll see. If you hear from him, let me know if he's sane enough to carry on a conversation." A pause. Crackling. "You don't know where he is . . . do you?"

She feels her throat closing again. "No."

"Well. I hope he's safe."

"Me too."

"I love you, Mom."

"I love you too."

They say goodbye. Diana hangs up.

9

Pink

October 17, 2019

Diary #4167

Last modified: today, 9:21 AM

I must stop this. Now.
I do not want to hurt anyone.
But ever since I moved here to be with them, it keeps getting worse. How could it not? I can't avoid thinking about them. They are here. She is here. I live in the same forest that at some invisible line melds into Wolf Hollow. The lands we own, like our lives, are joined. This is what I bought. This is what bankrupted me. Fifty yards from this shack where I sleep and wake up, there is a road where Diana Wolf sometimes drives past in her Jaguar. The coffee shop where I write this has a big window, and through it, some days, I catch a glimpse of her walking.
Only glass between us. I lose my breath.
Then, I feel ashamed.
But how can I avoid the Wolfs? How can I, since I bought this place in a fit of lunacy?
God help my soul, if he or it exists.

* * *

Diary #4168

Last modified: today, 11:36 AM

I cried again in the shop. They were unhappy with me.

I wish so many things.

I wish I never heard the voices in his songs. Or if I had to hear them, to be sick, I wish I had ignored them and never followed them east.

I wish I had just run away when my father hit me for the last time. Is it a sign of just how low I am that if he were here, I would ask him what to do next?

I wish the nightmares would stop. The guilt.

I wish I could just be stupid. Numb. I wish I could just go to sleep.

Most of all though, I wish I had never learned to use this computer. This device that tortures me, that has become my only lens through which I see reality, my portal into it but also my prison, which keeps me removed from a world that shuns me and burns when I look upon it truly after hours spent in a daze, huddled in my corner sipping hot caffeine, staring at a backlit screen. Thousands of hours spent rearranging letters and numbers, like a toddler hammers pegs into holes.

This is life? Then I am tired of this life.

And some healthy corner of my mind always knows, knows it for a certainty even in the bad times. The longer I remain here, convincing myself of awful things that cannot be true, the more danger she is in, and her family. If I truly were their protector and savior, as the man in blue tells me I am, my path forward would be clear. But it is not.

I am lost.

It is a conundrum. I am too much a coward to kill myself.

* * *

Diary #4169

Last modified: today, 12:18 PM

I can feel the man in blue coming. Only hours now. Lights hurt to look at. They are bright like the sun. When I finish this entry, I will go home to weather him, and the bad time. I must. I must remind myself that the last time I strayed in the shop too long, mistakes were made. A man got scared.

And I know too well that scared people are capable of scary things.

I get scared. Too often.

Today, I must be brave. Fear only brings him faster. Anger only makes him worse. But denial is worst of all. Denial will get people hurt.

I wonder if Diana's mother could feel the bad times coming. I can. These are things I wish we could speak about. Illness. Even now, I care for her and believe in my heart we have a real connection, a common history that binds us.

Even now. That is frightening.

Dr. Winters would turn me in to the police if he knew I followed them to this place. For years now, he is afraid of our missed appointments. He tries to contact me at my old email address, pleading with me to recommit to treatment.

He is right to be afraid.

When I look back at things I have done, lists and forum posts and code I have written, thoughts I have typed down in the bad times . . . I am scared of myself, this me who appears when I am seeing the man in blue. I know he will hurt the Wolf family. I know. It is only a matter of time. How can I possibly justify it to myself, that it only happens sometimes? That the other eighty percent of the time I am a good man?

There is no justifying it. I am here. I came to this place. I doomed myself.

To anyone reading this, if I have done something horrible, I am sorry.

Some pathetic part of me knows I can stop it. I can get help again. So why do I not?

Do I want this?

Is he me?

* * *

Diary #4166

Last modified: today, 3:14 PM

top ten d outfits

0. red chanel train nightgown + red mb stiletto heels, last worn 1.21.18 for t birthday
1. red d&g maxi dress + thigh black leather boots, last worn 1.20.19
2. black silk blouse w/white floral print + white jeans + black mb heels, last worn 10.13.19
3. gold chanel backless + ?heels, last worn 7.01.19
4. red hermes maxi dress w/black straps + black mb heels, last worn 1.21.19 for t birthday
5. sky blue? sundress w/sunflower print + yellow flats, last worn 8.11.09
6. forest green givenchy maxi cutout back + woven sun hat, last worn 1.20.16

7. black cashmere sweater w/white heart graphic + black jeans + white heels, last worn 2.18.10
8. white+green mcqueen jumpsuit + black mb pumps, last worn 3.21.08
9. red latex halloween costume "satan," last worn 10.31.14

top ten t songs

0. a thousand lies
1. trust in texas
2. gunslinger
3. she-devil
4. i'm the goddamned best
5. all my little girls
6. blackout tuesday
7. kiss my ass (if you insist)
8. red cars for rock stars
9. i'm so tired, babe

* * *

Diary #4170

Last modified: today, 6:21 PM

!!!WOLF BROTHER WATCH!!!

IS JONAH A MONEY LAUNDERER?
theory

EVIDENCE FOR:
—slip of paper he discarded at tigertail, mar 2009
  —partial registration app for corporation in wyoming, dated jan 2008
    —"r&r holdings"
—single transaction traced to r&r holdings
  —purchase of one lot from christie's auction house fall sale, 2008
    —j.m.w. turner painting: fishing boats in a stiff breeze
      —$4.2 million
—r&r holdings dissolved, jan 2009
—jonah drills holes in his hard drives before trashing them, ?—present
  —only wolf family member with this habit
  —forgot twice, jun 2007 + may 2009
    —recovered files almost entirely composed of coded messages(!)

—what is the buffalo hunt?
    —referenced repeatedly
    —bh initials show up in almost every email
—jonah starts @ christie's auction house as fine arts intern, sep 2012
    —hired full time immediately after graduation from nyu, jun 2013
        —fine arts specialist
        —never promoted
        —has never connected to christie's intranet. how?
—no 18-yo has $4.2m to spend on a painting
    —if it was him, had to be using someone else's money
        — t?

EVIDENCE AGAINST:
—no non-circumstantial evidence found in 10+ years of monitoring
    —circumstantial evidence extremely weak
        —you also drill holes in your old hard drives
            —"coded messages" possibly just partial data corruption
        —painter working for auction house is not surprising
—not his name on shell corp registration doc
    —being in his trash does not mean he put it there
        —if he did, still does not make it his
—jonah bank accounts consistently normal
    —why launder money if not being paid for it?
    —spending normal
        —never more than what he earns ($60k yearly)+ what t gives
        him
        —biggest vice is art supplies
        —frugal?
            —two exceptions: treehouse + nyc penthouse rent
                —but t paid/pays for both
—lives in a penthouse, free access to t's money if needed, beautiful
fiancée
    —no plausible motive whatsoever
—you are sick

CONCLUSION:
keep watching accounts

WHERE IS CY?
no sign since blip outside reno last november
completely off grid
or dead

worried about him
not on drugs again, you hope. but nothing you can do
imagine this is how diana feels

CONCLUSION:
:(

*   *   *

Diary #4171

Last modified: today, 10:18 PM

no more talk of help. no going back to doctors.
no one can know what you are. murderer.

you are here for a purpose.

remember always always what t said:

CAST ASIDE A THOUSAND LIES
NEVER LEAVE
ONLY YOU CAN SAVE HER

10

Diana

October 17, 2019. 5:01 PM

FOUR GLASSES OF wine pass.

As the sun gets dim outside, Diana Wolf sniffs and tilts her head up.

On cue, Thad exits the man cave in a puff of cigar smoke and dust.

Well. It's now or never. She catches her husband's eye and pats a stool, beckoning him to join her at the kitchen island.

Thad stumbles over. Sits down. "What's up beautiful?" Surprisingly gentle, he takes her hand in his bigger one and kisses her ring finger.

Diana smiles at the light touch of his lips. Even now, he can be charming when he wants to. "I wanted to ask you something."

"What about?"

"Jonah."

Thad looks up. "What about him?"

She takes a deep breath. "Have you ever worried he drinks too much?"

He shrugs. "Nope."

She nods. "You ever seen him get drunk?"

Thad thinks about it. "Seen him drink wine at dinner, but he's always good about it. I guess no." He makes a face, but it's hard to read.

"Me neither."

He squints. "What are you askin' for, then?"

Diana stares out the bay window above the sink, at the woods. She doesn't answer.

"Total space cadet." Thad gets up off his stool, shaking his head at her. "Jesus, Dee, gonna take you to a doctor if you keep doin' this shit."

"Maybe you should," she whispers.

"What?"

"Nothing. Sorry."

Thad glowers at her as he stumbles out of the kitchen, then doubles back to visit the liquor cabinet. He pulls out a bottle of George Dickel rye and a tumbler. Grabs a full tray of ice.

Finally loaded up, he heads back to his man cave.

She listens. The white double doors slide shut. Leather crinkles. Fox News pundits whisper in the walls. A lighter snaps, and the smell of cigar smoke intensifies.

Diana sits at the kitchen island, sensing Thad and all his self-loathing.

She chugs the rest of her glass and reaches for her black Prada bag, pulls it over, rummages inside for her phone. No new notifications. On a whim, she opens up her texts and composes one to Haley Jackson:

Just spoke to J. He told me you encouraged him to reconnect with Cy. You have no idea how that touches my heart. Thank you honey!

Diana hits *"Send."*

Oof. Now that she's looking at their texting history, she's even more glad she reached out. She should know Haley better. Jonah's been dating this girl for three years and engaged to her for one, but somehow Diana and her soon-to-be-daughter-in-law have exchanged just four texts in total.

Ting!

A reply comes in, startling her. She always forgets how fast young people text back and forth. The world keeps speeding up.

Diana checks the message, smiling.

Her smile fades.

?

A single question mark. Does that mean something new, now . . .? Or maybe Haley deleted her contact info.

Diana types a second text in hopes of clarifying:

Jonah told me it was your idea for him to reconnect with Cy. He asked me about him earlier today when we spoke on the phone. It's D. Jonah's mom. btw

She stares at her phone, anticipating another immediate buzz.

Each passing second is agony. Easy to understand why millennials are so impatient, growing up with these things. Diana misses the simple, slow tech she grew up with. It's why she still keeps a fax machine on her desk, even though she only gets penny stock tips on it nowadays. Cy used to make fun of her for it all the time.

Ting!

There. Finally.

In her rush to read Haley's reply, she swipes it off her locked screen by accident. She curses as she types the password to unlock her stupid phone.

Finally, she sees it:

I know, hi D! just confused, who is Cy?

Her fingers type out a desperate response:

Cy. Jonah's younger brother. They haven't spoken in five years.

She hits "*Send.*"

Her head spins. How could Haley not know who Cy is after three years of dating his older brother? Does she know him by a nickname?

Diana waits.

As the wait goes on, at some unnoticeable point her inner monologue dies out, and everything is quiet. No little voices chime in. Time passes like fog drifting over a lake.

She sits there, staring at her phone.

Hours pass. Darkness falls outside.

No notifications.

A few more hours sees Thad stumble drunkenly out of his man cave. He teeters down the hall to the master bedroom.

Diana notices his emergence vaguely from her stool at the kitchen island. And she's sure her husband noticed her too, still sitting in the same spot after so long. But neither partner acknowledges it. No good nights are exchanged. Like always, they pretend to miss each other.

It does remind her to check the time: her phone says it's 2:00 AM.

* * *

At 3:36 AM, Diana gives up.

She pads down the hall and curls up next to Thad in bed.

Wide awake, she stares up at the ceiling fan with its mahogany blades. Worried. Praying she doesn't dream:

O Lord . . .

It works. She doesn't even sleep.

* * *

Pale sunlight stabs through the curtains.

He lied, says a little voice in her head, not her own.

And for once, she listens.

Diana snatches her phone off the nightstand, unlocks it, and looks up a number deep in her contacts. As her thumb hovers over it, she hesitates . . . but she needs to know where her baby boy is.

She presses her thumb down on the number.

It rings once. Twice. Three times. Four.

Click.

Under the crackling white noise, she hears faint highway sounds. A siren blares in the distance.

A breath catches in her throat. "Cyrus?"

PART II

Remus

There is a luxury in self-reproach. When we blame ourselves, we feel that no one else has a right to blame us. It is the confession, not the priest, that gives us absolution.

—Oscar Wilde, from *The Picture of Dorian Gray*

11

Cy

October 18, 2019. 4:43 AM

CYRUS WOLF DREAMS of the dead.

Hundreds of rotting corpses stand in his way, blocking the path down to the sea. As he paces in the wind-blown grass on the cliffside, their rictus faces swivel to follow his movements like an army waiting for a speech from their king.

Cy wishes he could give them what they want, but he has no words to say. They're dead. They hear nothing. Nothing he does will ever help.

He sighs and turns his back on them. Hikes up the steep path.

Near the top, the ridge plateaus and a horizon appears in the sky. A sliver of sun sinks into a gray ocean, painting the nearest clouds dangerous shades of pink and crimson. *Beautiful.* As always. The path ends in more tall grass. He wades through it.

At the edge of a white cliff, a man in black stands and looks out at the sea. Tendrils of smoke drift around his head.

Cy gets ten yards away and stops. "Jonah."

His older brother turns to face him, smiling. Long white teeth flash in the half-light. "Isn't it beautiful?"

Cy nods. "The sunset?"

Jonah shakes his head. "All of them." A shadow passes over his face and drains all the blue from his . . . *its* eyes.

Cy backs up.

The Jonah-Thing cackles as its skin turns black as ink, starting at its hands. Its body jerks. Both its shoulders dislocate with a *pop* and its arms stretch grotesquely until they coil up in piles at its feet. Black blood sprays its face as antlers erupt violently from the base of its neck.

Cy glances back to see if there's any escape to be made. But no. The corpse army has formed a wall across the path, penning him in. Staring.

So . . . fuck it.

He calmly joins the Thing that was his brother at the cliff's edge and hangs a sneaker over the two-hundred-foot drop to the sea. Sighs. He tries not to look at It to his right, but It looms in the periphery of his vision. Black but for Its teeth. Ten feet tall.

"It gets easier." A black claw comes to a rest on his shoulder, squeezing gently. "I promise."

Bzzz!

Cy nods wearily. He looks down past his shoes at a thin beach nestled against the bottom of the cliff. Black sand. Huge dark waves slam the tips of white rocks, forty feet high.

Bzzz!

There's someone standing on the beach, staring back up at him. A woman. Blonde. Familiar. "Mom?"

No way to be sure at such a long distance, but it looks to him like the woman nods.

As he bends his knees, she screams. He hears her voice clear as day: "No! Baby, no don't do it!"

Cy dives off.

The Thing reaches out to catch him, but only gets a clawful of shirt and bloody skin.

He drops fast, and a foul wind whips at his open eyes: salt, foam, fish stink. The black beach gets bigger, closer, and so does the screaming woman. It is her. Mom. She steps out of harm's way as his neck breaks on the cold sand.

*   *   *

Cy's eyes shoot open. He coughs. A mouthful of air floods his lungs.

A weak but practiced hand clenches the loaded sawed-off shotgun on his lap and raises it to his shoulder.

Twin barrels point at the motel room door. Finger on the trigger.

Cold sweat drips down his nose.

He breathes. In. Out.

Nothing's there. The door is closed.

He checks the web of fishing line rigged across the locked door and all the room's little depressing windows, also locked. It looks like a giant spider is renting the room. His lines all end in silver bells, all situated at ear level next to the armchair where he sleeps.

All his lines are taut. Bells aren't tinkling. No noise. So what woke him up?

As if to answer him, his phone jitters across a side table. *Bzzz!*

A pile of black fur stirs in the shadows by his feet. Poot yawns, stretching out his muscular back legs like an oversized bird. The pit bull stands and ambles over to the face-height table, and his head turns sideways as he studies the buzzing phone. Then he licks it. Over and over.

Cy frowns, but it's a half smile. He shoves Poot's soggy face away from the burner.

The big puppy looks up at his dad, tongue hanging out like he did good.

Cy can't help but laugh at his bad luck. Here's a guard dog who can't bark, ever since his asshole first owner cut his vocal cords, and chooses not to bite. Perfect. Just what he thought he'd get when he rescued a pit bull: a giant lapdog who eats four cans of meat a day. But Poot needs him . . . and maybe that's love, and that's the only thing that keeps him going these days. If he weren't so torn up about what it would do to his dog, he might shoot himself in the head tonight. End it.

This isn't life.

A hunger spasm twists his abs into knots, but the shotgun stays steady.

Bzzz!

It'll stop soon if he lets it. That would be the smart thing to do.

But he can't help it. He's curious. Nobody ever calls. No one has the number except his Mom and Luke, and he hasn't spoken to either in months. He hasn't heard a friendly voice in a long time. The one he gives Poot in his head doesn't count.

So forget playing it smart.

Playing it smart is what got him here: to a Super 8 twenty miles outside Reno, Nevada, sleeping in an old armchair with a loaded shotgun on his lap. Half starved. Ribs showing. Waiting to die.

Cy lifts the burner up and checks its caller ID: "*MOM.*"

There are two options: green to answer, red to decline.

He props the shotgun against his chair, uses his sleeve to wipe off his phone. Puts it to his ear as he stares at the web of fishing line and bells. All still. All silent.

Cy clicks the green button.

On the other end, he hears a woman breathing. "Cyrus?"

"Do you have any idea what time it is here?" Exhaustion creeps into his voice despite his efforts to hide it.

Diana sighs. "No. We don't know where you are."

We. It's always *we* when she talks to him. "I can't believe you still won't use Signal."

"I remember you told me to use an app, but it's been so long . . . I just . . ."

"I know. I'm sorry." It's the truth, but he's not paying attention. He watches the door and the windows.

A long silence falls.

"It's okay," says Diana.

"It's after four o' clock," says Cy, as if it excuses how mean he's acting. He's just tired. That was his first hour of good sleep in a week she ruined.

"Oh, honey," says Diana, "did I wake you up? Do you want me to call back later?"

"No."

"Okay."

A pause.

"Are you okay, baby?" says Diana, in a more panicked tone than usual. *Something's happened.* "Just tell me you're okay. I just need to hear it. That's all."

Cy considers his response. "Then I'm okay."

"Okay."

Another long silence.

Cy just watches the fishing line. Listens. Fingers the loaded shotgun propped against his chair, caressing the tips of its two barrels in a figure eight along the edges.

"Did anyone tell you what happened?" she blurts out. "We have had quite a week down here at Wolf Hollow. Quite a week."

What a stupid question. "No," he says, humoring her. "No one's told me anything."

"Well. I hired this cartographer, right? We thought it would be nice to have a map made of Wolf Hollow, your Dad and I. Just for fun."

Cy closes his eyes. "Uh-huh." He pinches the bridge of his nose, massages his sinuses.

Mom has a bad habit of babbling to him about all the lavish purchases she's made recently. It pisses him off. He's hungry. Work's been real thin lately, the work Cy can get: cash work, under the table. Untraceable. Safe. He spends most of what he earns on dog food.

"So, he shows up. *Cy.* I'm not kidding." She laughs. "On his first day in the woods, guess what he trips over?"

Cy sits in silence and counts his protruding ribs. Not listening.

"A *human skull.* Can you believe it? Real."

He stops counting ribs and looks up, eyes wide.

She drones on. "I was so scared, Cy—like, we could see it had no teeth, so I'm thinking murder. And guess who was right? It turned out it was a young woman's head and the sheriff's department came back with shovels and dug up her whole skeleton the next day, so all week we had six cops . . ."

It's her.

It's the girl who was going to Asheville.

So, they found her. She's the only one buried in the woods. Only took seven years.

His fingers go numb, and the burner drops to the floor. *Cl-clack!*

Poot jumps up, startled, and pads over to the corner of the room with his ears down and tail between his legs.

Cy sinks back into the chair and holds its armrests to steady himself. He stares at the dirty bed in the center of the room, still made, its sheets pulled tight. His arms and legs shake. He starts to cry.

With a trembling hand, he picks up the burner again. Listens.

Diana rambles on: ". . . and your dad hates it when they park their cruisers out front—he says it's an eyesore—so I told them to . . ."

Cy interrupts her. "What are they saying to you about it? The police?"

"What? I don't un—"

"Shut up, Mom," he whispers. "What do they know?"

She doesn't respond at first. He sweats.

"Nothing," she says. "I talked to the detective from the sheriff's department, and he doesn't think they'll solve it. He said it's a waste of—"

They're in control already.

Cy ends the call.

He rises to his feet and stuffs the shotgun into his coat—olive green, heavy, lots of pockets. Then he sets himself to the task of ripping down lines and bells: all the windows, every vent. He throws it all into an army surplus duffel bag. Zips it tight. Hefts it over his shoulder, opens the door, and holds it as Poot squeezes past his legs into the Super 8 parking lot, trembling.

12

Kerry

October 18, 2019. 7:12 AM

KERRY PERKINS DRIVES back into Leiper's Fork a week after he vowed never to return.

Sick vow, bro, he thinks as the poplar woods get thicker on both sides of the road and a green sign lets him know he's on Main Street now, not the highway. After a final curve, the town itself comes into view. *Shithole. Fuck this place.* He aims a middle finger out his windshield. It makes him feel better.

It's not like he wants to be here. He has to stop this shit before it gets worse. Or at least find something out, if he can't stop it.

It was a miserable week.

First, it was the note on his car.

The next morning, he woke up and his front door was ajar. He spent that whole day tiptoeing around his house with a baseball bat. By that night, he had found nobody, nothing out of place to indicate anyone had ever been there, and he had broken a lamp and two small glass picture frames with his bat.

The next day, he finally worked up the courage to google the coordinates he found, and it was a random Super 8 motel in middle-of-nowhere Nevada. Creepy as fuck.

Two days later, he ran an antivirus program on his laptop, and it told him he had malware in his webcam. The kind where whoever wrote the malware had access to it and was downloading footage from a laptop he keeps open most nights on his desk, facing his bed.

There's a square of duct tape over it now.

There's no questioning it anymore. Someone is *watching* him.

He has a hunch as to who it is.

The thin man.

Kerry parks his black sedan outside The Cuppa, since he doesn't know where else to start searching.

He locks his car and walks inside.

A string pulls, and a bell above the door rings.

Standing in the doorway, he suddenly feels ridiculous. Why did he come here? It's not like the thin man is just going to be in the exact place he last saw him.

He heads to the register as he scans the café, full again with busy flannel-people on laptops. He intends to ask the barista manning the café if he knows who the thin man is or, if not, where to start asking after him—but then he stops. Does a double take.

Oh.

There he is.

The thin man is sitting in the same corner booth, wearing the same fleece sweater and beanie. He must hang out here a lot? Local weirdo. The way he looks in the daylight doesn't exactly scream "criminal mastermind." But it could be an act.

Kerry walks to the corner booth. "Hey."

The thin man stares up at him, mute and terrified.

Kerry slams the man's laptop shut. People at nearby tables jump, flashing him disgusted looks. "You left that fucking note on my car last week, right?"

The thin man nods pathetically, like a dog caught eating furniture.

Kerry nods back. "Yeah. Come outside and let's talk, then."

Every patron in the café is whispering now, sneaking looks at the tense conversation taking place in the back corner.

The thin man cringes as he notices all the eyes on him. He nods and pulls at his collar, holding his breath like the air just turned poison.

Kerry leaves first and waits out front.

The bell above the door rings and the thin man joins him, rubbing both hands together and blowing. "Thank you for that," he says in a soft, precise accent. Not a local. But what is he?

Kerry squints. "For what?"

"I hate when people stare. I know this makes me a hypocrite." He talks like a kid reading aloud in class, all stilted, like he wants to get every syllable right. Definitely learned English from an immigrant, but he could just as easily pass for Eastern European, part Japanese, or Hawaiian. *And he's just pathetic enough that you already want to forgive him and forget him.*

Kerry finds himself thinking the thin man would make a good con artist. He frowns. "What do you want from me?"

The thin man blinks. "Nothing."

Kerry hardens his stare. "No. Fuck you. What did it mean? Why are you downloading shit off my webcam?"

The thin man shakes his head, bewildered. "What webcam? No. Not me. I left your note, but it was a misunderstanding. My fault. Okay? No? Look." He digs in his pocket for a ratty wallet, flips it open and rifles through it. "I don't have much, but if I can pay for your gas—"

Kerry slaps the wallet out of his hands and eight or so crumpled dollars flutter into the street. He shoves the thin man with one hand, forcing him a step back. "Why are you watching me at home, and what does it have to do with Diana Wolf!?"

People a half mile up the street turn to look.

The thin man tucks his chin, withering under their stares. "Not here. *Please.* Only the note is me. But I can help you."

Kerry shakes his head. "*Here.* How?"

"You said shit is being downloaded. I assume from a laptop? And you have it with you?"

Kerry nods suspiciously.

"If someone is watching you, I can find them."

"Yeah. Sure. How do either of us know you can do that?"

The thin man shrugs, exasperated. "I know where you live, even though you don't list it on your website. I knew about her map, and that you took her money. Thirteen thousand? How do you think I know all this?"

Kerry makes a face. That is why he suspected the thin man in the first place. "Touché."

"Please. It was my misunderstanding, that note. I am sorry. Truly. I thought you had . . . wronged her." He makes sure no one else is close by, then whispers, "Diana Wolf."

Ding-ding!

Kerry starts to get it. "What are you, a stalker?"

The thin man winces, clearly fighting an urge to take off. "Please. Not here." A tear runs down from his eye.

Kerry groans. Stalker or not, he can't stand to see a grown man cry. "Well, where the fuck do we go?"

*　*　*

They don't go far.

Laptop case under his arm, Kerry follows the thin man around back of The Cuppa to what looks like an old outhouse . . . as in, a rotting shack people used to go shit in when this town didn't have plumbing. He watches in horror as the thin man opens the door, sits down on a wooden bench—its hole, thank God, is filled in with sand—and opens his laptop.

Kerry stands in the threshold, nose scrunched up. "Dude. No. Why here?"

The thin man taps the cramped bench next to him. "Two reasons: fast internet, privacy. I have a deal with the owner. He gives me a discount and lets me sit at the back booth since I set up a modified modem for him last year to mask his MAC address." He smiles up at Kerry, but he's met by a blank stare. "I . . . uh . . . I help him steal free internet. Now he sets his own speeds, and it also hides user activity. Win–win. You see? The smells are not what you think. This outhouse hasn't been used for years." He taps the bench again. "Come. Sit."

Kerry reluctantly walks in. The door creaks shut behind him.

He picks up the thin man's empty laptop bag and throws it down to use as a cushion. "I'm regretting this. This is fucking weird, man."

The thin man sighs. "Please. Just sit. I promise you after this, you will see there is no reason to fear me."

Kerry doesn't sit. "Uh-huh. I don't even know your name."

The thin man smiles and digs out his wallet again. Slips out a New York State ID, hands it to Kerry.

He reads it. *Panaggiotis Gopsikopolis.* It's either the worst fake name of all time, or it's genuine. And the card feels real. "Okay, but what do I call you?"

The thin man thinks about it. "Pink."

"Big *Reservoir Dogs* guy?"

Pink shakes his head. "No."

"So what are you, Greek?" He doesn't sound it.

Pink sighs, ignoring the question. "You want me to fix your computer, or no?"

Kerry nods.

"And then we're even, and you forget the note?"

Kerry thinks a second. If the note was a mix-up, fine. If this guy is a stalker, fine. That's Diana Wolf's problem. This is his. He nods.

"Then sit."

Kerry sits as far away from him as possible. It's still cramped, so their knees bump whenever Pink taps his right foot up and down . . . which is *constantly*. "Please stop that."

He doesn't stop. "Hand me your laptop?"

"This better be good." Kerry slips it out of its case and hands it over.

Pink flips it open on the bench beside him. "MacBook Pros are shit. You can get this same performance for much cheaper."

Kerry rolls his eyes. Computer people are all the same: evangelists, every last one. A Linux recommendation is coming, he bets. "I'm a Mac guy. I like the way it works out of the box. I like the look. I'm used to it."

Pink shrugs. "Fair enough. Password?"

"Can't you just hack into it?"

"Yes. *Password?*"

Kerry looks away, embarrassed. "*v-e-g-e-t-a*-sixty-nine."

"A man of culture. No caps?"

"No caps."

Pink enters it in. The desktop appears. "Congratulations. You are hacked." He starts to type.

Kerry leans in. "Whoa. Dude. What the fuck." He shifts his weight on the laptop bag to get a better look at his screen. Windows open and close faster than he can keep track. A single shortcut, and all but one closes. Text starts flowing. "You went to GitHub and . . . are you just casually writing your own software right now?"

Pink shakes his head. "I wrote this years ago. Most of it I downloaded, and this is only optimizing for your system."

"What is it?"

"Magic. Shush."

"Fine." Kerry watches the code take shape, mesmerized. "This is so sick."

Pink smiles.

* * *

"There." Pink hits "*Enter.*"

"So?" says Kerry. "What happens now?"

"We wait. And when it's finished, I will know what malware, if any, is truly in your system."

"But I already ran an antivirus scan on it. I told you. Someone is in my webcam, downloading footage."

Pink shakes his head. "You ran Mac Helper Professional. Yeah?"

Kerry nods. "How'd you know?"

"Because Mac Helper Professional is shit software and always returns this false result when a user doesn't quit out of Photo Booth first. I noticed it open on your task bar."

"You didn't look at any pictures on it, did you?" asks Kerry, concerned.

Pink raises an eyebrow. "No. Why would I do that?"

Phew. Got lucky. Lot of bad ones on that camera roll. "So . . . you think I'm fine? No one's watching me after all?"

Pink nods. "You're fine. No one wants to watch through strangers' webcams. Or the sickos who want to are seldom capable of doing it, and those capable see no profit in it. But I understand why you came back here. I scared you."

Kerry frowns. "How'd you get my home address?"

Pink sighs. "Trust me when I say you won't understand even if I tell you."

Kerry bristles at that. "Try."

Pink looks at him like he's explaining a dead hamster to a child. "When you renewed your website registration last year, you put it in as your billing address."

"Oh. I get that. See? Why would I not understand that?"

Pink laughs. "You don't."

"Fuck off. I do."

Pink shakes his head. "If you did, you would ask me how I got private billing info from your web registrar. And now you will keep yourself up at night googling to try to understand. I tried to spare you. But *no.*"

Kerry feels the sting of an accurate assessment. "How'd you learn all this stuff?"

"I googled at night. I do not recommend it. I had a lot of time alone and good reasons to learn. It's how I survive."

"You have a job?"

"I fix code others have written, for a fee, from my laptop. I'm good at it. I told you."

Kerry never taught himself anything except how to lie and steal. But that's all he ever needed to survive. "What's your deal? You're too smart to be like . . . this. Why are you wearing taped-up Nikes and hanging out at a coffee shop in Leiper's Fork, not making bank at some tech company in San Francisco? I promise if it's a style thing, you'd fit right in."

Pink fidgets and looks at the ground. "I'm sick. It's like you said."

Kerry realizes, suddenly, he's not the only one feeling like a stranger saw right through him. "So you left the note, thinking you were protecting Diana Wolf, because what, you saw me leaving after a day, and thought I stole her money?"

Pink nods. "Yes. I need to save her."

Kerry laughs, then realizes it's a shitty thing to laugh at and stops. "From what?"

"I don't know. Probably nothing, but I can't stop. So I hide from her, and I protect her from a distance. Sometimes . . . I go too far."

Kerry frowns. If there's a good stalker to have, it sounds like this guy is it. But he can't help feeling like there is no such thing. *He monitors her bank account.* "Like how?"

"I steal her garbage. Things like that."

Kerry sighs. "Do you live here because she does?"

"Yes. I followed her. And I know this means I'm sick, but my choices keep bringing me back to her. It's my fault, in the end."

"I don't know if it is, man," says Kerry, who means it. "Have you ever seen a psychiatrist?"

"Yes," says Pink, embarrassed.

Kerry puts a hand on his shoulder. "Did you ever get a diagnosis? Medicine?"

Pink stares at the hand touching him, taken aback. "Yes. Why do you care?"

Kerry looks him in the eyes, serious. "Because I know a sick person is different from a bad one. And my dad was scared of going to hospitals too."

Pink gets the stung look again. "What makes you think I'm scared of hospitals?"

Kerry shrugs. "Call it a hunch."

Pink blinks, nods. "You're not like I thought you would be, after seeing your website and maps."

Kerry feels a tinge of shame again, same as when he realized he never closed Photo Booth earlier. "How so?"

"I thought someone who cheats rich ladies out of thousands of dollars in exchange for Photoshop maps would be, you know . . . a bad guy."

"You caught me too, huh?"

Pink nods. "But you're not a bad guy, Kerry Perkins. I won't tell."

Kerry looks up, surprised. He nods. "You seem like not a bad guy too. Hey, Pink. Sorry I was a dick to you earlier."

"It's okay. Sorry I scared you."

"No, tell you what. We should get a beer after this. On me. You can have beer, right?"

Pink looks up, glowing. "Really?"

"Yeah. I'll try to sell you on hospitals."

Pink starts to say something, but just then, the laptop makes a sound, and his eyes are drawn back to it. "Oh. We're done." He scans the results. As he reads, his expression changes.

"What's wrong?" Kerry leans in. "Your search thing found some shit, didn't it?"

"Yeah."

"I told you there was shit in there!"

Pink shakes his head. "Why would they . . .? What did you do? You didn't tell me something."

Kerry looks at the screen to see what he means, but it's just as indecipherable as before. "Hell are you talking about? What did it find?"

"No one is controlling your webcam," says Pink gravely. "This is a keylogger."

"A what?"

"Someone is monitoring your activity on this laptop. Keystrokes is what they're downloading."

So . . . everything he does on it? That sounds worse than just webcam footage. "Fuck. You said you could find who it is, right?"

"No need," says Pink. "I know this keylogger. Only police use it."

13

Cy

October 18, 2019. 7:23 AM

C Y DRIVES NORTH in the fast lane. I-580 falls away beneath him. The old camper van he lives in is a piece of shit in the wind. Its tall shell lurches and sways, and his steering wheel pulls to the right every time he passes an eighteen-wheeler.

Poot sits in the passenger seat, panting. Spit dribbles into a cup holder. *Christ.* It's almost full.

Cy gives him a sideways glance. "What are you, dying? I wish you'd sit in back, where the sun doesn't hit you right in the face."

Poot stands up and licks his cheek. Just stays there panting, blissfully unaware of how his big head blocks all but one mirror.

Cy reaches inside his glove compartment and takes out a little collapsible bowl, then, one-handed, twists open a water bottle and fills it. Most of the water makes it, but a few droplets end up on the floor, turning dust into mud. Which is fine; he doesn't mind cleaning. It feels cathartic to try to make a thing as good as it used to be or better. For once.

Poot buries his face in the water, splashing more on the seat than into his mouth.

Cy smiles. Briefly.

The yellow gas light flicks to life on the dash display. It's that time again. He shudders as he prepares to deal with a real person.

Cy throws on his right-hand turn signal and gets off at the next exit. He pulls into a 76 station and stabs a fuel hose into his tank, then walks into the little shop to prepay and buy food with the last of his emergency cash: canned beans, venison jerky, and an elk antler for Poot. Gas station inventories are wildly different in towns where people hunt, he's noticed.

As he walks up to the register, he freezes.

He stares past the cashier at a girl with a cardboard sign across the street. She's in her mid-twenties. White. Brunette. Pretty. Not the type to normally end up homeless. An addict, most likely. She's too skinny. Like him, he realizes as he looks down at his nigh concave torso.

Cy reads her sign. She's hitchhiking to Reno. He doesn't bother with the rest of her sob story because he's looking at her outfit: traveling clothes, an olive-green jacket with holes in it, and hiking boots. Paralyzing guilt ripples through him. Worse than hunger.

The resemblance is uncanny. The hitchhiker across the street looks just like she did. The girl who was going to Asheville. If they stood next to each other, they'd look like sisters.

"Sir?"

Cy snaps back to reality. The guy behind the register is looking at him funny.

"Bag?"

Cy shakes his head and collects his meager change: three quarters and a dime. Gathers his food purchases. Walks back to his camper van and fills it up with forty dollars' worth of gas.

*   *   *

Cy pulls up next to the hitchhiking girl and rolls down his window.

She's hesitant. Very.

He's learned not to take this sort of thing personally. She's not worried about him; it's the big black dog in the passenger seat. "Don't worry. This is Poot. He's an idiot." His timing is perfect. A fly lands on Poot's nose, and his eyes cross to stare at it.

The performance seems to calm her down. "Thanks." The girl laughs and gets in. She shoves Poot into the back. Begrudgingly, he obliges her.

The two human occupants of the van are quiet. Cy doesn't mind; he likes to keep his attention on the road. Keep moving. Keep occupied. Bad thoughts run rampant if he lets his brain wander. Thoughts like how this girl's face is different up close. Sadder. *Her* face was happy right up until the end. The only expression he ever saw her make was a smile.

Eleven minutes pass in silence.

The hitchhiker girl speaks up in a tiny voice. "So, what's your name?" Too high-pitched. Nothing like *her* voice.

Cy looks at his passenger. The girl's head and shoulders are pressed against the window, knees tucked to her chest. This time, he can't say it's the dog. She's frightened of him, the big drifter with bags under his eyes who picked her up and then didn't speak a word to her for fifteen miles.

Idiot. He's been alone too long.

Poot walks up between the front seats and puts his chin on Cy's lap.

Cy shoos him off, but not before the dog's mouth leaves a spit stain on his jeans. Bits of elk antler in it. "Sorry." He brushes away the meat parts and blends the spit into a patina. "I'm Corey," he lies.

The girl relaxes. "Abby."

"Nice to meet you, Abby," he says, trying to affect warmth. "Why are you headed to Reno?"

She scowls. "Didn't you read the sign?"

Rude. "I confess, I did not . . . except the Reno part. I'm headed there."

"Cool." She digs under her fingernails for dirt, grooming idly. "I'm meeting a friend. Car died on the way up from Gardnerville."

Cy forces a smile. "Gardnerville! I know that town. I've spent a lot of time there."

The girl laughs. Also forced. "Oh. Cool. I haven't. I was just there a few days working."

"Oh." Her makeup is caked on and she smells like sex, so he has an idea what *working* could mean. "You shouldn't hitchhike."

She looks up, eyes narrow. "Why not?"

"Dangerous."

Abby doesn't respond at all.

"I didn't want to make you feel . . . or . . ."

"No. I get it," she says icily.

"I would never . . . I'm not . . ." He stumbles through an indecipherable apology.

"It's okay," she says once he's done, colder than ever.

"It's just you could have got someone else. Not me."

Abby laughs—*at* him, not with. "Yeah. I sure am glad I got you." She goes back to picking at her nails, but she keeps a wary eye on him.

It makes him feel like a predator, unworthy of trust. A starving lion staring at a little bird.

"Sorry."

They keep to themselves after that, to his extreme relief.

Abby never asks why he's going to Reno. Or about the iron bars reinforcing his camper's doors. The custom bulletproof windows. The machete in the center console. The green trash bag full of fake IDs stuffed under her seat. The gun locker in back.

Good. He doesn't like to lie.

CHAPTER

14

Kerry

October 18, 2019. 2:54 PM

K ERRY PERKINS SITS in his black sedan, engine idling like it's full of
rocks. Staring.

He's parked a ways down the road from it: a huge metal gate with a
flower design worked into it, flanked by tall privacy hedges. Gorgeous.
The street is called Nimes Place, a quiet stretch of asphalt in an afflu-
ent neighborhood hidden just outside Nashville city limits, halfway
between his own house and Leiper's Fork. This particular home he's
staring at—or this big-ass gate, since that's all he can see of it—belongs
to Rodney Ellison.

Pink told him where it was.

True to his word, he took the little weirdo to Country Boy for
brunch and drinks after Pink discovered it was the cops watching on
his laptop, and the two men nursed craft beers while Kerry gave him
an elevator pitch for going back to a doctor:

"Did I mention my dad yet? Art?"

Pink shrugged.

Kerry smiled, reminiscing. "He was pretty cool. Big fan of The
Pack, like you. Know how he died?"

Pink waited.

"Skin cancer. The treatable kind."

Pink made a face. "Treatable?"

"It was stage one. Ninety-five percent survival rate . . . but he didn't tell anyone he got diagnosed, he was so scared. Horror stories in his head about dying on chemo machines with no hair. He went to a traditional Eastern medicine place instead, and the man there gave him water pills." Kerry shook his head, quietly furious. "Dad didn't tell me for months, because he knew what I would say, and he didn't want to hear it . . . and he didn't want me to worry. Eventually, he couldn't hide the cancer in person, so he just hid from *me*, and I didn't see him again until the week he died. You know what they call Eastern medicine that works?"

"What?"

"Medicine," said Kerry, sighing. "You know what happens at the end of stage-four skin cancer if you don't treat it?"

Pink just waited again.

Kerry nodded. "Black sores break out all over your skin like there's bugs eating you from inside out." He paused. Breathed. "Go to a doctor, Pink. Get treated. It may not work, but at least you're fucking trying."

Pink nodded seriously. "Okay."

"Say you promise."

"I promise."

"Okay." Kerry clapped a hand on his shoulder.

After his duty as a decent human being was done, he steered the conversation back to more pressing issues—his—and the two of them brainstormed possible reasons Ellison might have to illegally surveil Kerry, and then a plan for what he should do about it. Clearly the cops installed it when they searched his car, but what did it mean? That he's still a suspect in that girl's murder? Okay. Then why install *an NSA keylogger* on his MacBook? Pink said they'd need authorization through the Patriot Act to use it, so any evidence they got off it would be inadmissible at best.

Neither one of them could make any sense of it, so the plan was slow-going. But after the biscuits and grits had come and gone, and all that was left was drinks—wham. Pink let it slip he knew where Ellison lived. *Nimes Place.* He had looked up the guy's home address, like, a week ago, soon as he knew there were cops at Wolf Hollow. He refused to say the exact house number at first, but eventually he gave it up on one condition: that Kerry not go to it.

"Trust me. You want to wait," said Pink, four beers in. "See what this detective does when he realizes we disabled it. Okay? Now you promise."

Kerry huffed. "Fine."

An hour later, the two men exchanged contact info and agreed to keep in touch. Then Kerry hopped in his car and google-mapped the address at the first stoplight.

Google said it was on his way home. He plugged it in.

Fuck Pink, he remembers thinking at the time. This isn't computers. It's real life, and what Ellison is doing to him is super illegal. Since the house was on his way, he decided he'd just stop in, say hi, meet the detective in person at his home, maybe vaguely threaten him, see if the two of them couldn't work something out. End this.

Now he's here. This is Ellison's house—or, his gate. Which is pretty fucked up and terrifying.

Pink was right. He never should have come.

Thick yellow tape is drawn tight across the big metal gate with flowers on it. Even from this distance, he knows what it says: *"CRIME SCENE DO NOT CROSS."*

Four black-and-white cruisers are parked on the curb out front. Nashville cops, city boys, not from the Williamson County Sheriff's office like the ones at Wolf Hollow. He keeps his distance. Bad idea to draw any attention to himself until he can wrap his head around what's going on here . . . *here.* In this ultra-bougie neighborhood Ellison can somehow afford to live in. No sidewalks on Nimes, probably so the riffraff don't wander in. No noise. Tall, manicured hedges line both sides of the street. This stretch alone is long enough for twenty houses, but there are only four gates. One at the far end has a little security hut next to it where a private guard has his feet up watching TV.

A sentence rattles in his head: *Cops don't make this much money.*

Kerry slips his phone out of his pocket, keeping one eye on the four black-and-whites. Too far away to tell if they're occupied.

He types into Google: *"rodney ellison detective sheriff big rod."* Hits *"Enter."*

A local news article pops up at the top of the results: *"Local Homicide Detective Missing, Says Sheriff."*

Jesus Christ. It's dated two days ago.

Surely, there's a good explanation in the article . . . but no. There's not. He feels himself starting to hyperventilate, so he stops reading, but the implications of what he's already read are enough to keep his pulse thumping. Nobody knows where Ellison is. Not his wife. Not his three kids. They're all worried sick.

It's been two days. Kerry's binged *The First 48* enough to know what that means. He's totally dead.

Down the street, the doors open on one of the police cruisers—both sides, driver and passenger. Two cops get out, and to his horror they start walking in his direction. The bald one whispers into a radio while the other rests a hand on his gun.

Kerry gulps. *Shit.* He should've listened to Pink—the guy is smart. Why didn't they google Ellison's name earlier? Why does he keep trying to drive places after four drinks?

He steps on the gas pedal, but nothing happens: no rev, no engine.

"No fucking way," he whispers, fumbling at his keys to restart it. "No. Not now." He tries again. Again. Again.

The engine roars to life.

Kerry clasps his hands in front of his face, closes his eyes and thanks the cheap car gods for their mercy, shifts into drive, and pulls away so fast his tires screech.

In his rearview mirror, both cops stand in the road and watch him go.

Once he's safely back on the highway, Kerry emails Pink a link to the article, typing on his phone with one hand:

Ellison is fucking missing. Scared. Can you meet to talk? What do I do?

He sends it, puts his phone down, and waits for a reply. And waits.

He keeps waiting all the way home, driving silently. No radio.

All night long, sitting at his desk alone, he waits.
No reply comes.

15

Cy

October 18, 2019. 9:08 AM

CY DROPS ABBY off in the parking lot of a Harrah's casino with an Original Mel's attached in one corner.

As she walks around a corner, he loses sight of her.

Picking the girl up was a mistake. He shared his food with her, the last of it, just because she looked as hungry as he is, and he thought it might be good karma, but it was just stupid. He feels nothing. The guilt remains. Still there. The girl who was going to Asheville? Still dead. Nothing's changed. He isn't sure what he expected. It'll always be there, no matter what he does, who he helps, what they're wearing, or how much they look like her. Guilt like his doesn't wash off. Not ever. Lady Macbeth tried, and look how far it got her; it drove her insane.

Cy parks the camper van in the same lot he left Abby in. Puts Poot in the back and leaves a fan running, then gets out to stretch his legs.

Then, a miracle: a piece of green paper wriggles in a light breeze, pinned under the front tire of a white sedan parked three spaces over. *Money.*

He jogs, then runs to it as a number in one corner becomes legible: *20.*

Cy kneels and pulls it out from under the tire, careful not to tear it. Pulls it tight between dirty fingers, holds it up to the sky, and makes sure it's real. It is. A twenty-dollar bill. Right when he most needs it. Karma. One last good meal. Or maybe it's more.

He looks across the parking lot, up at the casino. Harrah's.

Why not? One meal won't make much of a difference. It'll just prolong things. *Fuck it.*

He locks his doors and walks to the entrance. Goes in.

The casino interior is twilit and depressing. There are mirrors on every available surface: ceilings, walls, gaudy Corinthian columns. A few old women sit at slot machines nearby, eyes glued to spinning wheels, clawed hands buried in cups of quarters. A man wearing a trucker hat with a Marine Corps insignia is either asleep or passed out at a bar, arms folded under his face. A waitress collects an empty glass next to his hand, walks back behind the bar, and disappears into a hidden door.

Cy stands with his hands flat on his lower back. Stretches. Scans. Casino layouts are purposely disorienting, and he gets the reason for it, but he's always wondered why they can't just put up an arrow that points you to the restaurant. He's been drifting on the outskirts of Reno for a year and a half now. Too long. Enough time to develop opinions about this sort of thing.

As he weaves through slot machines and craps tables, he spots what he's looking for and changes course.

A sports bar. Basketball is on all the televisions inside. One of the teams playing is the Lakers, unless there's another gold-and-purple squad in the NBA he forgot about. He seats himself at a booth where he can play the Wheel of Fortune game at his table. It used to be one of his favorites when he still had money to burn.

He bets his twenty dollars. Orders a Corona and a plate of sliders, then plans his escape route in case the bet goes south.

Cy sips, eats. The Lakers are losing to the Bucks. Bad. Down by twenty-five, which seems out of character. Last time he paid attention to the Lakers, Shaq and Kobe were still on the team, they were coming off a string of championships, the Wolf family homestead was still in Brentwood, on Tigertail Road in California, and Jonah was his best friend, his idol, and his closest confidante . . . and the Bucks were fucking terrible. Times change.

Lights start flashing at his table.

He looks up at the Wheel of Fortune board in disbelief.

He won. It's real. Karma is real.

What's the payout—a thousand dollars?

He laughs loud, in the middle of the casino. He has to. Today, he's lucky. Something he hasn't felt in a long, long time. Certainly not in the last seven years.

He feels like he's walking through a dream when he turns in the ticket, cashes out, and watches a floor manager slide a crisp, heavy set of fifty-dollar bills under the bulletproof glass.

*   *   *

In the parking lot, his luck runs out.

The first sign of trouble is when he hears Poot banging against the door of the camper van, twenty feet away.

Then he hears another noise: feet running up on him.

Before he can look, Cy feels a cold metal edge dig into his throat, and an arm shove into his spine. A man's hand holds a rusty blade to his neck. A butterfly knife. There's a star tattooed between thumb and index finger. Uneven linework. *Meth head.*

The tweaker's hand trembles, and his knife slices a layer of skin deep.

Cy winces and scans the parking lot nearby. Abby, the hitch-hiker girl, is leaning against his van. Looking out for cops. Passersby. Witnesses.

"We just want the money. Just what you won," a raspy voice breathes into his ear. "Now, tie that fucking dog up and let's go inside, or I'll make sure he doesn't bother me some other way you won't like."

A shiver ripples down the muscles in Cy's back. "Don't threaten my dog."

The pressure of the knife on his neck lets up just the tiniest bit. "I'll do whatever I damn well pl—*urk!*" Cy shoots an elbow back into his attacker's temple, and the pressure is gone just like that.

He listens. The knife drops to the hot asphalt and lands on its handle. *Plink.*

He spins, legs bent.

The tweaker staggers back, cursing, eyes spinning in his head. They focus just in time to catch sight of a steel-toed boot flying at his chest. *Thud.* His neck whiplashes forward as he leaves his feet, and when he falls, the back of his head hits the ground. *Crack.*

Cy knows not to take chances. He walks over to where the tweaker is moaning on the asphalt.

Seeing him coming, the tweaker reaches into his waistband. *Mistake.* It doesn't look like he has a gun, but you never know.

Cy stomps on his stomach, pinning him. "Take it out." He lets up, and the tweaker removes his hand from his waistband, coughing and crying. It's empty.

Cy grips his shirt collar and pulls him up so their eyes meet.

"No more. Please . . ."

Cy laughs.

His first punch busts the tweaker's nose open. Dots of blood flick all over his chest and face.

His fist snaps back and cuts through the air a second time. There's a sickening wet and crunchy sound as the tweaker's right brow crumples.

"Ben!" Abby screams. Close by.

A third fist hits, and the tweaker's upper lip splits into two red mangled halves. Pain shoots deep into Cy's knuckles. Blood drips from his left hand where half a front tooth sticks out of the webbing between his index and middle finger.

He smiles at the gruesomeness of it, letting it fuel his adrenaline, then he slams his fist into the tweaker's face again.

Again.

Again, harder.

He hears footsteps. *Wait for it.*

Cy spins and catches Abby with a back fist. Her feet fly out from under her, and she grips the rusty butterfly knife tight as she falls. She lands awkwardly on the blade, cries out, and when she sits up, her arm is bleeding.

Not an artery. She'll live.

As if to prove him right, she goes for the knife again.

A steel-toed boot crushes her fingers, trapping the blade. He shifts all his weight to his toe and grinds back and forth. Another pathetic scream.

He lifts his foot and her broken fingers curl into a claw. He kicks the butterfly knife away. It skitters across the asphalt, twirls to a stop under a pale blue van.

Abby sobs in the fetal position.

Cyrus Wolf stands over her, blue eyes wild. He reaches down to his ankle and slips it out: a long matte-black hunting knife. A relic of his youth. He presses it into the muscle of Abby's throat, hard enough that she has difficulty breathing.

The dark, clean blade stays utterly still. No shakes. No tremors.

He laughs. The city noise comes back—a white, shapeless drone. Tires. Engines. Slot machines.

Satisfied Abby isn't a threat, he looks over his shoulder. Her boyfriend lies still and silent a few yards away.

Cy turns his attention back to Abby. She's crying now, quiet, pathetic tears that stream down her cheeks, ruining her makeup. "Oh no. Ben. No god, please . . ."

He grabs her by both cheeks and squeezes, forcing her to look at him as he glances around at the wasteland of cars. "You'd think a parking lot at a casino would have more security cameras. But that's why you felt comfortable jumping me here, right? Nobody coming to help, even with all the noise you're making. No security. No cops. No sirens." He pauses. Sighs. "A thousand dollars. Your life is worth more than that." It's true, and he knows *exactly* how much more. The number haunts him.

She wriggles out of his grip, cries out to her tweaker boyfriend again: "Ben!"

Cy slaps her face. "You need to appreciate this," he warns her.

Abby nods.

"I could have killed you, easily," he says, softer than before. "I still could. No one would ever know—or care. You have no idea. I envy you."

After that, he lets her go and walks away.

He climbs into his camper van, pushes an anxious Poot into the passenger seat, and starts it. Throws it in gear. Drives.

In his rearview mirror, Abby crawls to her boyfriend and cradles his head in her lap. Cries.

When he's far enough to be sure she won't see, Cy bursts into tears of his own.

Poot licks his elbow, trying to help, big eyes staring up at him sadly.

He puts all his weight on the gas pedal and accelerates. It's time to disappear. For good.

*　　*　　*

Eight hours pass.

Cy drives. No destination but nowhere.

Disappearing isn't complicated. Never was. Ask D. B. Cooper. It just requires a plan, a clear head, and the will to do so. People disappear all the time.

The hard work is already done. He has a list of potential problems and contingency plans, strict rules to follow. Rules like don't stop in big cities, never draw attention to yourself, ditch any cell phones.

But he's not following the rules he set.

The black burner phone sits on the camper van's dash, laughing at him. He should chuck it out the window, but he can't. It was too good to hear Mom's voice, and after what he did to Abby, it's good to feel like he has someone nearby. Family. He keeps seeing her in his rearview mirror as he drove off. Bleeding, sobbing in a heap.

Why did you hurt them so bad? You could've just taken the blade. Easily. How did you lose control so fast?

The true answer scares him: because it felt good.

It's been a rough day, but that's no excuse for what he did.

I-80's dotted yellow lines zip under the camper van as he accelerates. At a hundred miles per hour, the camper shell starts to shake in the wind.

Poot gives him a nervous lick, so he throws the cruise control on at ninety-five and leaves it. No cops in sight. It's possible some highway patrolman makes his way onto this stretch of I-80 once a month or so, but the next big city is Salt Lake, eight hours away. There's a lot of highway to cover out here. Getting pulled over for speeding now would be a statistical anomaly, a stroke of bad luck on par with a getting bit by a great white in three feet of water.

It's been forty minutes since he even saw another car.

Cy flips down his sun visor to look at his reflection in the tiny mirror. Not pretty. His face and eyes are stark shades of red, and a bruised line bisects his Adam's apple. The bruise has gone through half the rainbow these last few hours: red, purple, yellow.

As he stares at the face of a stranger, he forgets where he is.

Behind him in the mirror is a girl in traveling clothes. A ghost. Black-and-white, dripping oil paint. It's the girl who was going to Asheville. The only girl he's dreamed about for seven years, the one who waits to torture him in hell.

Brrrrrraaapppppp!

The rough tread at the edge of the highway catapults Cy back to reality. The steering wheel jerks his thumb nearly out of its socket as the camper jumps off the road into a ditch. Not deep, which is lucky. These campers flip.

He veers back out of the dirt. *Brrrrraaappppp!*

Poot hides under the dash, ears flat to his big head.

He reaches down and rubs Poot's head. "Sorry, boy," he says, feeling guilty. "I'm so, so sorry . . . I don't know what I'm doing."

The dog licks his hand.

Need to calm down.

No mistaking it—a second attack is coming. He's hyperventilating. A sharp pain stabs rhythmically in his chest.

He pulls over to the side of the highway and passes over the tread again. Slow, this time.

He parks in the emergency lane.

The sun is going down. It's twilight in nowhere.

On both sides of the highway, nothing, not even proper desert. *Chaparral.* An empty dirtscape stretches to the horizon, flat and gray and cold. A patch of gangly bushes ten miles to the south is the highlight of the view. Mountains rise in the far distance, shadowed and unknowable.

No cars in sight.

No one is following him. Yet.

Cy undoes his seat belt and climbs into the back.

The living space is cramped; storage, bed, and sink are all crushed together like Tetris blocks.

He climbs onto the bed, pushes loose a false section of hard-plastic wall, and pulls out a wrinkled ball of Ziploc bags held together by rubber bands.

He sorts through what he's got left. In each bag, he keeps a different coping mechanism: pills, grass, acid, molly, mushrooms. The mushrooms are what he's after. Shrooms have always worked better for him than therapists. Therapy is dangerous for liars. When you can get someone else to tell you the lies you want to hear, they're a lot easier to believe.

He measures out an eighth ounce of brown, wilted caps, then puts his drugs back in their hiding spot and climbs down from the bed.

He makes a sandwich out of the shrooms because they taste like shit. Literally—they grow on cow shit. Peanut butter, on the other hand, does not, so it almost evens out.

He winces through his "meal."

When the last bite is gone, he climbs back into the driver's seat, feeling better. The anticipation of a high makes everything else move to the back of his brain, frees him from the prison of memory. If only briefly.

It'll be an hour or so until the drugs kick in.

Cy looks at his travel guide and finds an isolated place on the map called Vernon. A ghost town. A real one. He might be able to make it and set up camp before his fine motor skills start to go. Description says it's not worth visiting, which sounds promising.

How many rules is he breaking now? No driving on drugs. Check.

Tomorrow, he'll worry about rules. No point tonight. He doesn't feel like making himself vomit.

Cy exits the highway at Lovelock.

* * *

On a deserted road near Vernon, the shrooms kick in. It starts with his skin crawling. The yellow white lines in the road slow. He sees the asphalt gaps between them now: one, two, three, four. The lines grow hairs. Gray fuzz. Giant fuzzy caterpillars inching under his camper one after the other.

Poot sits up in the passenger seat and frowns at him, disapproving of his driving. *Do dogs frown?*

In a moment of lucidity, Cy realizes he needs to stop and make camp.

He pulls off the road. Asphalt gives way to dirt as the camper van clanks and lurches into a black abyss. The view out his windshield reminds him of one of those nature documentaries about exploring the ocean floor. He drives a football field's length, slow, crushing bushes under his tires. Then he parks.

He climbs out. Lets Poot do his business while he assembles the shade overhang. As he unpacks the cooler, he makes a checklist of his remaining supplies: three bottles of water, a pound of jerky, three cans of beans, and two cans of dog food. That's it. In his rush to get away from Reno, he forgot to buy anything with his winnings. No big deal. He'll run to a store tomorrow and re-up, maybe even splurge on some Gatorade powder.

Cy opens one of the dog food cans and sets it out for Poot, with a dish of water.

Last, he breaks out his fishing line and bells. Runs a few lazy trip lines across all the doors, the windshield.

Cy stumbles back inside. Locks himself in. Drinks a full bottle of water in a single gulp. Poot is on the floor under the dash again, trembling. Ears back, teeth bared, yellow eyes staring past him into the back of the camper.

Cy spins and looks.

Two black-skinned demons writhe on his bed. Naked. Fucking. Their mouths open and close in pleasure and pain as they silently rock back and forth. Shoulder horns scrape. The big male thrusts in and out of the struggling female, both wrists pinned above her head by a single hand twice as large as her own. His free hand rakes a long, sharp claw across her back, and the skin splits open, exposing raw muscle.

Cy turns his face away, disgusted.

Then he notices a third apparition in the back of his camper. In a cramped space below the storage closets, a teenaged boy sits cross-legged, head hanging to avoid the low ceiling. Blond. Face obscured in shadows. Its arms bleed out onto the floor, growing and coiling.

Cy climbs in back and sits across from It.

The Jonah-Thing looks up. It has no face. That's new.

Cy gulps. "I'm not afraid of you anymore," he lies.

The Jonah-Thing smiles, or something like it. "Confess . . ."

"I don't get it," says Cy as tears pool in his eyes. "What do you want?"

The Jonah-Thing shakes its head, giggling. "It gets easier. And easier."

Cy breathes. "Not for me. I'm not like you."

It laughs at him, cruel and mirthless. "And that's why no one will remember you when you die. The runt. The Wolf who didn't. Wasn't."

He rolls his eyes. He's heard it all before. "I don't care. I'll be dead."

It trains its black hole of a face on his and studies him. Nods. "You are dead, little brother. You just don't know it yet."

"Sure I do."

"Stop it," It says in a low voice, pitched like a record spun backward with a dirty fingernail. "Cy. Come home. To me." Its pitch drops and drops until it's a bass tone, two octaves lower than any human being can speak. "I love you. You're my best friend. You are me. I am you. It is only us."

"No. It's not."

It grins, revealing a shark's mouth in the center of its face full of row after row of white teeth. "I vouched for you." It glances up at the bed, at the two demons fucking. "Protected you from them all these years. You owe me. And you know it."

"*Jonah.* Enough. I won't come back. I can't. How does it end?"

It laughs, but the laugh is his mother's laugh. "Cyrus?" it says in her voice. "Just tell me you're okay."

Tell me.

An epiphany strikes, and his head pops up. He leaps to his feet.

He knows exactly what he has to do: *confess.* To someone they'd never expect this time.

He glances at the burner phone on his dash, then walks in what feels like slow motion, leans over the headrest, and reaches for it.

It's got a single bar of service.

C H A P T E R

16

Haley

October 18, 2019. 6:54 PM

H ALEY JACKSON WAITS until dinner the next night to ask Jonah about his brother, Cy. The one he's never told her about. She can't imagine why he wouldn't. After three years . . .?

There must be a good reason. He's her fiancé, the man she decided to spend her life with. Why couldn't he trust her? She trusts him.

Haley sets the table meticulously: two forks, two spoons, two poured glasses of cabernet sauvignon, spare bottle on ice, three candles, the old china plates with delicate blue designs on the edges.

Once the table is set, she checks on the food. It's ready to go.

Then it's a matter of waiting.

The grandfather clock in the entry hall, the one Diana and Thad sent them as an engagement gift, rings seven times. *Bong!*

Jonah should be home from work any minute. He gets back late sometimes. Getting to be more often in recent weeks, sure, but nothing alarming, and not a big enough deal to bring up with him in anger or out of insecurity. She trusts him.

Haley takes a seat on the couch in the living room. Swirls the red wine in her glass. Sighs.

The apartment they share is on the west edge of Chelsea in lower Manhattan, ritzy modern digs that belie the fact she's an underemployed fashion model and Jonah makes sixty thousand dollars a year with his oh-so-lucrative art history degree. Luckily, they were both born into ungodly wealth. The two of them are the only young couple they know in Manhattan who live in a penthouse apartment. There's a greenhouse on the roof. Glass. Dark green steel. Haley uses it to grow tomatoes.

The front door opens.

Jonah is home.

Tall. That was the first thing she ever noticed about him. That and his eyes. They're a cold blue she'd only seen before in sapphires. In sleek pin-striped suits like this one, he looks thin at first glance, but up close you can't help but notice his posture: shoulders back, neck straight, head high. Relaxed.

Her first guess, off the bat, was an athlete. A rock climber.

Nope. An artist. A talented painter. So, so very hot.

Haley knew he was husband material the first night they met, at a little cafe near her childhood home in Chicago, where a writer friend of hers was reading a short story. It was shit. No one liked it, not even her own friends. But Jonah clapped.

Hot. Talented. *Kind?* She practically dragged him back to her apartment. When his business trip ended a few days later, she bought a ticket to visit him for a weekend in New York. And she never left. There are more modeling jobs in Manhattan anyway.

Jonah waves to her from the door, wordless. His phone remains stuck to his ear.

Hayley returns the wave, then glides to the kitchenette to put final touches on her dinner prep.

They don't speak until a few minutes after he sits down at the table.

"You have a little brother." She tries to keep any lingering resentment out of her voice—and fails. The accusation lands on the table the same instant as his plate of grilled salmon. "Cy. Right? Your mom said so."

Jonah sighs. Then he looks up and smiles.

It's absurd how he always knows *exactly* how to look at her—that smile has gotten him out of plenty of arguments in the past. But not this time. She sits down across from him and presses on. "Why did you never tell me?"

He drops the fake smile, and a scowl replaces it. "Mom had no business mentioning Cy to you."

"But she did, and that doesn't answer my question, and it's not the point. Why? That's the point, baby."

"I hate it when you call me that."

"*Why?*"

Jonah folds his hands and stares at his plate. "I'm afraid of him." He says it soft, quiet. "And *for* him. It's the most painful thing in the world, so I don't talk about it."

Haley looks down at her lap, ashamed for making him feel that— the most painful thing in the world. *Hold on.* She frowns. "Are you quoting Sylvia Plath now? That was a line from *The Bell Jar.*" It's her favorite book, and he knows it. That line was originally about an electric chair and what it might feel like to die in one. It's in the opening paragraph or two.

"Not intentionally." He shrugs.

She's not so sure. "Fine. Sorry. I don't . . . want you to feel that way." The way Sylvia Plath did, an author famous for killing herself.

"Well? What were you expecting?"

"I don't know. Why are you so afraid of him?"

Jonah reaches up and pops one of his shoulders out, then pops it back in. He does it when he's nervous, like a tic. "He tried to kill me."

Haley spits out a bite of salmon. *"What?"*

Jonah nods. He picks up a fork, plays with his food. "Yeah. I woke up, and Cy was at the foot of my bed pointing a skeet shotgun at my head. My parents kept one at Wolf Hollow. We used to shoot clay pigeons up on the hill, other side of the driveway."

Haley shakes her head, dumbstruck. "Why would he do that? How did you talk him down? What the hell, Jonah?"

"It's a long story."

"Clearly. Fuck. I'm sorry." Haley decides she needs more wine, so she pours herself a fresh glass and downs it. Pours another.

Jonah drops his fork. He clears his throat. "We were best friends growing up. I'm a year and a half older, so I think Cy idolized me a little bit."

She makes a sad face, cooing.

"It's okay," he says softly. "He threatened suicide the first time in elementary school. I thought he only wanted attention, but now it feels like a red flag we just . . . missed. In high school, Cy got into drugs, and something changed in his head. He started lashing out. He came at me with a pocket knife once when he was high, and hurt me pretty bad. He felt awful once he was sober. Claimed he didn't remember doing it. Mom and Dad started sending him to a psychiatrist three nights a week after that. We started talking less. When Cy was at NYU with me, we never hung out. A year after I graduated, when we both visited Leiper's Fork for Thanksgiving, it was really hard to see how bad he'd gotten. He would cry and scream in the middle of the night. I'd hear him across the hall. It'd wake me up."

"Oh God." Haley takes another sip of wine, riveted.

"Night terrors. It runs in my family, on my mom's side. Anyway, we found Cy outside one morning. Naked. Cutting himself with a razor blade."

"Was he high?"

Jonah blows air out through his nose, shaking his head.

"Did your parents commit him?"

He laughs sarcastically. "That next morning, I woke up and there my brother was, holding a shotgun on me. I still remember how I could see so far down the barrel, could see the rifling. It's all spirals."

Haley pours both of them another glass of wine. Her fourth. Jonah's first. He's never been much of a drinker.

He sips it, mouths a *thanks*.

"How did you calm him down?"

"I didn't. I just kept him talking. Dad came upstairs to check on us, and tackled Cy from behind. The gun fell, and I picked it up. It was loaded."

"Fuck," says Haley. "I can't imagine Thad tackling someone."

Jonah frowns. "Old fucker hits hard."

Haley giggles, but he doesn't smile like it was a joke, so she stops. "Was that the last time you spoke to him? Cy?"

He nods. "I hadn't even talked about him since, until today."

"What was he like before all that?"

Jonah looks caught off guard by the question. A rare thing. His eyes get moist, and right away he wipes at the tears like he's embarrassed she saw it. "Like me," he says in a trembling voice.

Haley reaches across the table and cups his hand gently in hers, almost satisfied. "Thank you for being honest with me. I love you."

"Love you too." He pulls his hand away and lifts his fork.

"There is one other thing . . ."

"What?" says Jonah, chewing a mouthful of salmon. It's his first bite since he sat down, so it must be cold by now.

Haley braces for a bad reaction. "You told your mom that I was bugging you to reconnect with him. Why?"

Jonah blinks. "I never said that." He tucks back into his plate.

"Baby." That'll get his attention. "Be honest."

He shrugs. "Why would I lie?"

Haley frowns. "Then why did she think that—"

"No idea." He stuffs a bite of fish in his mouth. Chews. Grins. Picks a thin bone out of his teeth and puts it in his napkin. "This salmon is delicious, Hay. What did you glaze it with?"

*   *   *

Three hours later, Jonah shoves her back onto their bed. He claws at her blouse, too hard.

"Don't rip it," she says in between forceful kisses. He bites her lip. Pulls on it again, ignoring her.

She likes it. Haley holds her arms up over her head to help him get it off. The sheer white fabric twists as it rolls off her fingertips.

Jonah uncoils next to the bed, holding her blouse in one fist like a rag. Shirtless.

He gets up every morning at five to train at the gym, and it shows. Six foot three. A hundred and ninety pounds and *wiry*, not an ounce of fat. A torso like smooth river rocks.

Haley does a sit-up. She pulls him closer by his belt. "Any girl ever tell you that you look like the statue of David, but with a way bigger dick?"

Jonah wraps the blouse tighter around his knuckles, not smiling.

When she pulls his pants off, they take his boxers to the floor with them. She follows, sliding off the bed onto her knees. She looks up at him, doe-eyed. Jonah pulls the twisted white blouse tight around her throat, enough to make breathing painful.

She uses her hand first, staring up at him with his flaccid dick held next to her face. Choking. Tearing up. He likes that, usually. Not working right now, though, so she switches to her mouth. He eases up on the blouse, lets her get a gasp of air in. Then she closes her eyes and shoves it in all the way. Gags on it. But that's not working either.

It's a new experience: a guy completely limp after five minutes of all his favorite tricks in her arsenal. In college, boys came when she took off her bra half the time. Because that's who the fuck Haley Jackson is. She models jeans for Dior. This doesn't happen to her.

Not fun. She can literally feel her confidence deflating in her mouth. He's not even bothering to choke her now. Loose white fabric dangles off her shoulder.

It doesn't take a doctor to call it: the mood is dead.

Haley lets him fall out. *Plop.* "Sooo . . ."

Jonah's cheeks go red. "Yeah."

"Yeah."

"Sorry. It's work."

"No, baby, don't be—"

"Don't call me that."

"Okay."

Jonah falls down on the bed, staring up at the ceiling.

Haley curls up next to him. There's a first time for everything. Tomorrow, the two of them will laugh about it over breakfast. She grabs his arm and wraps it around her. Calloused fingers grip her shoulder, tight. She smiles. Closes her eyes.

* * *

Haley wakes up. There's no arm around her. It's early morning. The room is blue-dark. Sun hasn't come up, but wan light is starting to leak in. She rolls over in bed, notices the bare pillow beside her and almost sits up. But then she hears him.

She pretends she's still asleep, but she opens one eye and points it past her feet.

Jonah stands in the darkest part of the room. He's naked. Moving, his blue silhouette quivers. A taut canvas sits on an easel against the wall. Black and white oils in open jars on a stool nearby. Two tall mirrors are angled to face him, one on each side, and his twin reflections flutter in the dark like wings.

A sound like ruffled skin: *fip-fip-fip-fip*.

Haley shuts her eyes, grinning. It's a kink. He always does this when he finishes a new painting.

Artists.

She only caught a glimpse of what's on the canvas: a flayed woman on a rack, arms pinned down by nails. Gruesome. Stark. Familiar subject matter for him.

She drifts back to sleep.

* * *

Haley wakes up to the same bare pillow puffed up just like last night.

Jonah never came back to bed.

Warm golden light streams in the windows. An empty easel and canvases in various states of completion are stacked against the wall. The oil paints and stool are gone, put away.

No sign of him in the living room.

When she gets to the kitchen, still naked, there's a note stuck to the refrigerator. She reads it.

Got a call last night. Office needs me to fly out to visit buyer pulling out of a big sale. Up to me to save it. Got a flight to LA out of JFK at ten, so might be in the air by the time you read this. Only gone two days. I'll bring a present back for you.

Love,
Jonah

Tears form in her eyes.
Business trip. Again.

A despised memory bangs on the door of her consciousness, but she drowns it out by assuring herself that there's no reason to suspect anything like that. Yet. Nothing but a bad feeling.

She snatches her cell phone out of her bag on the counter and dials the number she has saved for his department at Christie's, pacing into the living room.

The office assistant picks up. "Fine arts."

"Hi, Lena. It's Haley, Jonah Wolf's fiancée."

"Hey, girl! How's he feeling?"

Her stomach twists into a knot. "Why do you ask?"

"He called in sick the next two days. Are you not with him?"

"No."

"Oh. Did you leave town for a shoot? He told us you're taking care of him."

"No. You're right. Sorry," Haley says, tone suddenly light and airy. "I just got out of the gym, and I guess I had a brain fart from being so exhausted."

Lena laughs. "It happens."

Haley keeps babbling. "Yeah. He's here. At home, lying on the couch. Ha. I'm such an idiot."

Lena clears her throat. "Oh. Um. No worries!"

"I'm gonna go check on him."

"Happy to help. Tell him I say hi!"

Haley ends the call and her knees buckle. She collapses onto the wool rug and pulls her bare knees up to her breasts. Dips her head until her spine curls up like a question mark. Sobs.

Grips the soft pile with her toes. Lets go. Grips again.

He's cheating on her again.

Who is it this time? she wonders? One of her friends? A colleague he met on one of his *actual* business trips? No. It's not like him to make the same mistake twice.

He promised. Never again. That's what he said. And she believed him.

This time, she's going to stand up for herself. This time. She repeats the words over and over to herself like a mantra: *this time.*

She's said it before. It's always bullshit.

What can she do? Leave him in the middle of planning a wedding? Her parents would be heartbroken, and she can't just go back to square one and hop on Raya and Bumble—or, god forbid, *Tinder.* Gross. Fuck that. She can't.

And she loves him.

Honestly, does she have proof of anything? Actual *proof?*

Now that she thinks about it . . . no. Can't prove shit. She's just acting crazy again, he'll say. Lena could have been confused. Or the higher-ups at Christies just wanted to keep hush-hush news of this big buyer withdrawing from the sale, so he had to tell the office assistant he was sick rather than the truth. Which is . . . he's headed to a save meeting in Los Angeles, on a ten AM flight out of JFK.

JF-fucking-K. That's it.

Haley picks up her cell phone and googles a number. Dials it.

A woman at his preferred terminal picks up. "Alaska Airlines. How may I help you?"

"My name is Haley Wolf," she lies. "Would you mind looking up my husband's flight number for me, and tell me if he checked in this morning? I lost the info. His name is Jonah Wolf, and he should be on your ten o'clock flight to LAX."

A pause. "I'm sorry, ma'am. I'm not authorized to give out that information."

Shit. "But . . . even to his wife?"

"No. It's the law."

"Oh."

"I understand that's frustrating, ma'am, but there's nothing we can do. Passenger privacy is something the TSA takes seriously. Your husband is the only one who could tell you whether he checked in or boarded a flight."

She opens her mouth and then closes it.

Garbled noise from the terminal hums in the background. "Can I help with anything else, Mrs. Wolf?"

"No, no."

"Okay. Bye now." *Click.*

No way to check, then. She feels stupid for even trying; that woman probably put her phone number on a watchlist as a *possible stalker*, or something like that.

Just as she's about to spiral again, she notices it on her phone's screen: the red bubble that reads *1* hovering over her texts. She must have missed the notification in her scramble to call his office.

When she opens the app, she sees a text from Jonah. No words. Just a picture he sent. It's of him, sitting in a cramped leather seat on the plane and blowing her a kiss. The time stamp says 10:04 AM.

Haley leans her head against a cabinet, relieved. He told her the truth.

She gets up, goes to the kitchenette and brews a pot of coffee, and thanks her lucky stars she didn't confront him about all this. She shakes her head, laughing.

But then all of a sudden, tears are in her eyes again and the laughs turn into sobs; the bad feeling never went away. Her period must be coming, she decides. Jonah always tells her how crazy it makes her.

C H A P T E R

17

Diana

October 20, 2019. 2:38 AM

DIANA IS SITTING at her desk, on her eighth glass of Malbec and surfing the internet, when her phone buzzes inside her Prada bag.

She unzips it, pulls the phone out, checks the notification. It's an email from Cy. He's never sent emails before. On her home screen, the message body is truncated to a short preview:

Mom. I need to tell you something. It's about the girl in . . .

She recoils. Her finger trembles as she swipes into her inbox.

It's about the girl in the woods.

Read this whole email. There are attachments at the bottom, links to files. Don't open any of them yet. I'll explain everything.

I'm sorry. I wish you could've seen what was happening in our family. The rot. I tried to tell you, but you didn't want to hear what I had to say. You didn't want to see it. Smell it. You couldn't. You don't see it in Dad. I wish he was a good person, Mom, but he's not. He doesn't love you. He needs you is all. You don't see it in Jonah. No one does. And you never saw it in me.

I killed her, Mom. It was me. I murdered the girl in the woods.

It was seven years ago. I never knew her name. I still don't. She said she was going to Asheville. I used a needle filled with suc—"

Diana deletes the email.

Then she calmly deletes her Gmail account, her iCloud account and everything in it, both her other email addresses, and her Facebook, and she cancels her cellular plan. Any method Cy could conceivably use to get in touch again, she needs to destroy. She grabs her iPad and powers it down, then she pulls her desk out from the wall, unplugs her desktop power supply, and picks up the tower.

The fax machine beeps and whirs.

Fuck. Cy used to make fun of her for still having a fax machine.

She stares at it, frozen.

A page drops out into the tray. Black text in a huge font, so big she can't help but read it:

Re: Jonah. See for yourself.

Diana curses and struggles to put down the tower, then realizes she can just drop it. She drops it. Its insides clatter as it hits the floor.

By the time she gets to the fax machine and unplugs it, two more pages have printed out. Not text this time. A photo and some sort of map.

She doesn't look at either. Just crumples both up in her fist, then picks up the wrecked desktop tower and carries it through the living "room" into the kitchen, where she dumps it next to the patio door. From the pantry, she gathers lighter fluid, a box of fireplace matches, and a metal bin she used one Thanksgiving to show Avner Bindley how to bob for apples. The patio's screen door *clacks* against its frame as she drags it all outside, and then down to the firepit: bin, computer, phone, iPad, fax machine, papers.

She stacks it all up in the bin, tucks in kindling, douses the heap in lighter fluid, and strikes a match. Tosses it in.

The heap burns. Plastic melts into conjoined, unrecognizable blobs. Screens crack and shatter in the heat. Papers shrivel and dissolve into floating bits of ash.

Soon, a horrid black smoke rises from the firepit. It climbs up above the trees, past the bare branches in the canopy, where it lingers in a swollen cloud.

Diana says nothing and thinks nothing. She only watches as the black cloud over Wolf Hollow grows and grows.

* * *

Two hours later, while it's still dark out, Diana drags the last of three wet, steaming, heavy-duty trash bags to the top of the long driveway, leaving a glistening trail like a slug. She heaves it into a black garbage bin, then closes the lid and starts sobbing as she goes back the way she came. She makes it halfway down the hill before she keels over and vomits. She kicks dirt over her puke to hide it, and then she stumbles the rest of the way to the house and finally into the master bedroom, where she lies down on her back on top of the duvet, next to a snoring Thad.

She knows she won't fall asleep. She closes her eyes anyway.

*   *   *

When a trash truck pulls up at Wolf Hollow in the morning, a man hops off its back and opens the black garbage bin.

It's empty.

He shrugs and hops back on. Signals the driver. As the truck moves on to the next gate, he air-drums with his one free hand and sings along off-key to a song in his earbuds:

> *I can cast aside a thousand lies*
> *I can close my eyes to keep you close to me*
> *I can let you in, forget your sins*
> *All you need to promise is you'll never leave . . .*

18

Jonah

October 19, 2019. 11:54 PM

THE NIGHT IS dark and cold in Nevada. The highway is deserted. Jonah Wolf is furious.

To a stranger, he might appear calm, even bored. The expression he wears is one you'd see on a junior accountant typing up a spreadsheet after hours, the last at his cubicle. A man who wants nothing but to finish his work and go home. He is close now. Driving north on I-80 in a gray rental Hyundai at sixty-four miles per hour, he uses his turn signals and listens to pop on the radio. Two hands on the steering wheel. Eyes on the road. Seat belt on.

In his head, a clock ticks.

Cans of gasoline and recapped water bottles filled with piss line the floor in the backseat. He hasn't stopped driving since fifteen minutes after his plane landed at LAX. He can't afford to. The trip has to seem impossible. Jonah Wolf is *in Los Angeles,* on a fake business trip he made up so he could cheat on his fiancée. He is *not* on I-80, halfway between Reno and Salt Lake City. How could he be *here*? Why would he be?

In truth, he should have made this trip years ago. He is only furious at *himself.* The Hunt gave him every chance to prove them all wrong, to bring Cy back into the fold, and he failed . . . all because he thought his little brother was as smart as him. But he was wrong.

He is close now.

His mouth twitches as he checks his GPS. It's the next exit, Lovelock. Then it's a half hour to Vernon and the spot two hundred yards off-road where he picked up Cy's signal.

A red dot blinks on his map. Lovelock exit is in half a mile.

He checks all three of his mirrors. No cars in sight, but he flips on his turn indicator just in case. Even alone in the dark, it never hurts to act like a good person.

*   *   *

Thirty-one minutes pass.

Jonah pulls off the road at the spot where the red dot blinks on his GPS. He turns his radio off.

Almost right away, he sees it: the twenty-four-year-old camper van that Cy had bought three summers ago, in cash, off a Craigslist ad. An anonymous seller. He knows all about it. He never stopped watching Cy. There is no going back, not after what he's seen and created. Their art.

Jonah knows the camper's doors are reinforced with iron bars, and the cab windows and windshield are custom—bulletproof, shatterproof, impossible to jimmy.

He knows there's a dog inside. A pit bull.

He knows the dimensions of all the camper shell's windows. He knows his little brother ran out of money before he could replace these, but Cy probably figured the openings were thin enough to keep a man out—and they are, if the man has healthy shoulders.

He knows there are little bells on strings.

But he hoped he'd never be forced to use knowledge like this. He had convinced himself his little brother was just going through a phase and that one day he would come around and get in touch and come home, and everything would go back to the way it was. When they were just boys. Two wolves. Cy would be his assistant again, his protégé. A new him.

It wasn't meant to be.

He turns off his headlights and drives two hundred yards.

He parks.

He kills the engine and waits for both eyes to adjust to total darkness. They do.

He takes off his shoes, then his socks, and retrieves his Gigli saw—a thin flexible wire, like a garrote but sharp as a scalpel—and a syringe full of succinylcholine from the center console. He carefully tucks his tools in his pockets. Then he slips out of the car.

It feels strange being out in a cold night like this without his teeth on. Naked. But dogs hate masks, and there's no point worrying about a witness in a literal ghost town.

The dust and rocks and dried-out weeds feel good on his bare toes. He has more control barefoot. And he enjoys it, so why not? His feet leave a clear print, but no identifying marks, same as his hands: unique, but *useless*. There is no him. He is a nonentity, free to do as he pleases. Sixty-two people on Earth would be able to pick the real Jonah Wolf out of a lineup, and he watches them all closely.

He can see the camper van even with just the stars for light, so he makes his way to it. He can see better in the dark than most people, he thinks. It comes naturally to him. But then, most everything does.

He steps over and through the strings and bells with ease and approaches the small half window on the left side of the camper shell. This model year had a bad problem with it swinging open on windy nights, even when it was locked. The latches are useless.

He reaches up with his right hand and tugs on his left shoulder, jerking it out of its socket. He swings his neck and his right dislocates as well. It still hurts, as intense as it did the first time. It always does. But you get used to it.

He yanks the latch open, pulls himself up and slithers inside.

19

Cy

October 20, 2019. 12:42 AM

CYRUS WOLF DREAMS of a painted girl in traveling clothes. Her skin drips black-and-white oils as she dances on a decrepit stage. A one-woman cabaret, she spins like a ballerina, but her eyes stay trained on where he sits alone in the cavernous theater's front row.

He stares back at her in awe. Mouth agape, crying.

An outstretched hand beckons him to come up onto the stage. To dance with her.

The painted girl retreats behind the dusty curtains, curling her dripping finger over and over until it, too, disappears backstage.

Cy stands. He climbs onstage, lifts the dusty curtains aside and follows a trail of paint spatters. He lets go and the curtains fall behind him.

Everything goes black.

PART III

Romulus

He wasn't raised that way.

—Louise Bundy, at her son's execution

20

Thad

January 22, 1998. 5:39 PM

THE LOCKED DOOR to Jonah's bedroom creaked and shook, its doorknob rattling. Diana's screams blew in through the keyhole like an icy wind. "Stop it! Thad, he's six! He's our little boy! No! Please God, no! *Thad!*"

Thad sipped from a bottle of George Dickel rye. Wiped his lips. Smiled.

On the bed, Jonah sat with his legs dangling halfway to the ground. It was a Cal king, too big and too high end for a kid his age. Diana was the one who'd picked it out, did it when she was pregnant and said he'd *grow into it*. So far, she was wrong.

The thin boy stared at the quaking door, petrified. Crying like a girl.

Thad placed the fifth of rye on a side table, uncapped. "She ain't gettin' through without no crowbar, so you had better look at me. *Boy.*"

On cue, Jonah looked up. Ice-blue eyes, empty and sunken, the boy looked like a gut-shot buck staring at a hunter walking out of the trees. *That color.* Too gray, too cold and pretty—they were his mother's eyes. Not Thad Wolf's eyes. A girl's.

And it wasn't just that; all of him was the same way. Small. Delicate. Prissy.

Thad curled his lip in disgust. "We got to have us a talk. Man to man."

Jonah said nothing.

Thad shook his head, slow. "Momma tells me you the one broke my red Fender to shit. Says you confessed."

"Yes, sir. I just wanted—"

"You just wanted to be like me—Daddy."

Jonah nodded and a dim light appeared in his face. Hope. "I watched your old tapes, sir. You did it on the Johnny Carson show, smashed it on your drums at the end. It was cool. They all clapped."

"Heard you said all that too. Your momma might care, but she ain't here."

"I said sorry. It was just, I wanted to practice for when I grow up. I didn't know."

"Don't lie. You knew what you was doin' was wrong."

Jonah looked down at the floor. Swung his shoes. "I just thought you had so many guitars it wouldn't mean nothing . . . you never, ever play the red one. Ever."

Thad stared at him, too furious to speak or move.

"I was pretending to be a rock star. Like you. Dad. I said sorry."

"Boy. I ever tell you about your granddad? My poppa?" As Thad talked, he gripped his big gold belt buckle in one hand and calmly unclasped it. A Texas state flag with a diamond-encrusted star flashed in the warm overhead light. He pulled on it and a thirty-six-inch leather strip slithered into his hands, coiled up in a ball around his fist. Stiff. Heavy.

Jonah stared at the belt. Its big shiny buckle.

Thad started to pace. "Granddad was a carpenter. You know that. But you know why?"

Jonah shook his head, eyes still on the belt.

Thad nodded. "Because Jesus was a carpenter. And he did love Jesus. We all loved Jesus, your aunt Linda and me and your grandma. Had to. Else we got"—he held up his fist with the belt—"a life lesson."

Diana shrieked and cried on the other side of the door, louder than ever. *You fucking bastard!*

Thad ignored her.

He raised his voice and spoke over the din like she wasn't even there. "My daddy taught me everything I know. He was a great man. You know I love you boys. Don't ya?"

"Yes, sir."

Thad let the belt uncurl, its buckle end dangling to his feet. "Good." He wound up to swing it—

—and was surprised to find that his son didn't flinch, or cry. Not even a blink. The little boy just stared up at him, and suddenly an old memory surfaced: an intense emotion, one he had felt many years ago but never named. *Hate.* It was what he felt whenever his own father hit him with a belt, way back when Thad Wolf was just another bored preteen hellion in West Texas getting rides home in the back of a cop car every weekend. *How many of those life lessons did you learn, really?*

It made him feel strange, acknowledging that this truly was his son. Diana was the one who'd always wanted kids; he'd been more of a passenger on that train, and after the boys were born, he remained a passenger—albeit one who complained and lashed out whenever the ride got bumpy. He thought of Jonah and Cyrus as *her kids*. If they weren't the boys he wanted . . . that was his fault.

Thad relaxed his arm until the gold buckle came to rest on the floor with a soft *clink*.

"*Let him go!*"

He had finally had enough of those screams. Thad roared back at her without turning around: "Baby! You go to Cyrus right now, or I will take you to him! *Git!*"

Just like that, the door stopped shaking. The screams died out.

Footsteps outside, walking away from the door and down the hall. Silence. *Easy.*

"Thass better." Thad walked to the side table next to the bed and took a deep swig of rye. He coiled up his belt and put it down next to the half-empty bottle.

Jonah stared at him.

Thad stared back, unsure what to say. "I ain't your granddad. And you ain't me." *No kidding,* he thought, his guilty epiphany already fading in an alcoholic haze. He sneered at the little boy's thin ribs, arms, and legs. *Like a bird's bones.* "You couldn't live through one beating like I took. Momma raised you too soft to start now."

Jonah's lip wobbled, and he started to cry.

It annoyed Thad how he could never predict what would set the boys off. Far as he was concerned, neither of them had a single god-damn thing to cry about. Ever. "Stop it. Now."

Jonah didn't stop. He just cried harder, and harder, and his dad's blood started to boil.

Ungrateful little shit. Thad slapped him. He held back, but it still sent his son sprawling on the bed.

A nasty red welt appeared on Jonah's cheek. He sobbed.

"Sit. Up."

His son stopped crying and sat up, shaking.

Thad lifted his chin up gently. "You know I didn't do that to hurt you, don't ya?" he said, meaning it and aiming for a fatherly tone as he kneeled to look his son in the eye. "I just need you to learn this lesson, boy, about me and trying to be like me." He hesitated. "*Don't.* You think I'm some sort of superhero or a god. But I'm not. I was a goddamn *product.* I had the look, and I was marketed at the right time to the right demo, and they used me until I was old and used up. It's a big lie. All of it."

Jonah sniffled and shook his head. "Is not," he whispered as if he only half believed it.

"*Is.* I ain't special, kid. Never was. I got lucky, and that's it. That's the big secret to being a great artist. Art ain't nothin' but an industry, and some man in a suit chose me is all, and there are a million singers, guitarists, and songwriters who coulda done what I did—better. *But I got lucky.* And you won't. It was a one-in-a-million chance I got rich, and it will not happen for you. It wouldn't make you happy if it did anyway." He laughed. "Trust your old man. If it takes fifty years or a hundred, it don't change nada . . . no one is gonna remember my name. It is a lie. Rip that Band-Aid off. You are never gonna be like me no matter what, so listen to your daddy, and *do not ever try again.*"

Jonah's eyes flitted up to meet his, and this time they were cold blue fires. Full of hate. "Mom said you're just afraid of me."

Thad felt a blood vessel pumping damn near out of his forehead. "Hell did you just say . . .?"

Jonah smiled, and his gums were streaked with bright-red blood. "She said you only get so mad because you know if I try to do the same as you, I'll get more famous than you ever did. She said you're a jealous old drunk and a has-been!"

Thad punched his son in the ear.

The little boy fell off the bed and to the floor in a heap, landing awkwardly with one shoulder blade bent under his little chest. *Shoulders don't bend.* The more Thad looked at it, the more it didn't look right.

He breathed. Panic started to set in.

For what felt like an hour, he waited for his son to writhe or moan. But his son didn't move.

Thad unlocked the door, marched down the hall, and got Diana to call the hospital.

He told her she had to lie about what had happened, what he did. "I didn't mean to hit him," he told her, and in his mind it wasn't a lie.

She agreed to lie on one condition: he would never hit Cy. Ever.

Thad promised. No sweat off his back. As if parenting one kid wasn't hard work enough.

Huh. *No sweat off my back.* There was a song in there, a catchy one. So, while the bird named Inspiration was still perched on his shoulder, he started writing the bones of a chorus in his head. Kept humming it to himself in the passenger seat as Diana drove one car-length behind a blaring ambulance to the nearest trauma ward, speeding in the wake of its blue sirens. Traffic parted ahead of it, and they got to blow through all the red lights. It was fun. He had never got to do that before, not even back in his prime, back when everyone in the world knew his face and name.

"No wood on the stack. No girl in the sack," he whispered at his own transparent blue grin reflected in the passenger window. "No wolves in my pack. Hell. No sweat off my back." Oh. That was it. A melody. Change a few words and that right there? Hit chorus.

He done did it again. Easy money.

As the hospital at UCLA came into sight, he crossed his arms and leaned against the door, satisfied at a job well done.

He closed his eyes.

*   *   *

Thad Wolf woke up at home with a pounding headache.

When he walked into the den and sat down, he noticed a guitar conspicuously missing from its stand: the red Fender.

When he asked Diana where it got put, she started to cry. Wouldn't tell him what had set her off. It was like she'd gone crazy. She locked herself in the master bathroom soon as he pressed her on it, then refused to come out or speak to him at all.

He could hear her in there. She just put her back to the door and cried and cried.

After a few minutes, he sighed and let it go. Not worth it. *Women.* It was just her time of the month was all.

A vein in his head throbbed painfully while he got dressed, walked out to his truck. On the drive to the golf course, a bird he used to know well alighted on his shoulder, and he hummed an unfamiliar tune, like it had just come to him in the night:

"Hell. No sweat off my back . . ."

Hot damn. He done wrote a hit song in his sleep.

21

Haley

October 21, 2019. 4:59 PM

*D*ING.

Haley Jackson steps out of the elevator at the top floor, exhausted from a long shoot for Chanel with one of her least favorite photographers. The guy named something pretentious like *"Benoit,"* who likes to point out all her body's flaws every time he works with her, riling her up on purpose just before he snaps a shot; he says she has a sexy mad face. She'd love to show him how sexy her fist looks up close, but assault is so much easier to prove than a gay man sexually harassing a female model—or so her agent says. Usually followed by *"That's just fashion."*

No shit. Benoit is one of the worst, not *the.* Far from it. It's not the job she dreamed it'd be.

Jonah keeps telling her she doesn't need to work, but she worries. Haley never says it aloud, but if they ever broke up, she'd want a career to fall back on.

He's been distant. He spends less and less time at home lately.

It's always business, but still . . . it makes her wonder if he's looking for a way out. *Maybe Benoit is right.*

She pinches the last bit of stubborn fat on her waist as she walks. She sighs.

Halfway down the small, carpeted hallway that connects the elevator to the penthouse, she hears something strange and stops, frowning.

She looks over her shoulder, but the elevator is already descending. She's alone. The sound came from behind the penthouse door.

Skkrit. Skkkrit. The door rattles a little in its frame.

She takes a wary step forward.

Could a bird have flown in? All the windows were shut when she left.

Skkrit. Skkkrit.

"Hello?" she whispers.

Skk-skkk-skkriiit-skrriit! The door jumps as something big pounds against the other side. Haley screams and leaps back.

Then it stops, and she hears a voice. "Hey! Stop it! No!"

Jonah?

For a second, there's silence, and then the door opens a crack. Jonah's head pops out, smiling. "Sorry." He looks her up and down, still wearing all her makeup and body glitter. He whistles. It's cute. "You look sparkly. I missed you."

Haley walks to him. "What *was* that? Why are you holding the door closed?" She gives him a kiss.

He gets a coy grin on his face. "I got you a surprise. To say sorry."

"For what?" It was a business trip.

"For being such a ghost recently. Close your eyes. I'll show you."

She does as he says, confused. "What did you do?"

He leads her inside by the hand, shutting the door behind them. There's the sound again, but softer, scratching at the floor this time. Something heavy *thuds* against a cabinet in the kitchenette, then it *thuds* again and again, in a slow rhythm.

Thud. Thud. Thud. Thud.

"All right. Open them."

She opens her eyes, and they go wide as saucers. Her mouth stretches into a toothy grin as she sucks in air. "Oh! You didn't!"

Thud. Thud. If the big black dog can feel its tail slamming the cabinet every time it wags, it doesn't act like it.

Haley drops her bag on the counter and runs to it with open arms, squealing. "Ooh, little baby bear!" She squats down to its level.

The dog shies away from her at first, nervous, but then it tiptoes up and puts its massive blocky head on her knee. She scratches its ears, and it kicks its back leg.

"You adopted?" She looks back at Jonah, tears in her eyes. She always wanted to adopt, but he said he'd only go for a purebred. Too many mutts at the pound, too many pit mixes. If he was going to own a dog, he wanted to know exactly what he was getting. And plus, he said, they had plenty of money to pay for it. Why settle for someone else's cast-off?

He nods. "Thought you'd like that."

She looks back at the dog. "But . . . you got a pit. I thought you hated pit mixes." Her smile fades for a second. She blinks and stops scratching its ears.

It looks up at her. Its eyes are huge, and they look sad; its whole face does. She knows dogs can't frown or cry, but it certainly looks like this one is trying to. All that tail-wagging isn't the happy kind. *Thud. Thud. Thud.*

"Poor baby," she coos, pulling its torso sideways so it stops hurting itself on the cabinets—a feat that drains all of her remaining strength because the dog fights her every inch of the way and it's strong as fuck. "Jesus, babe. You got a *big* pit. Like what . . .?"

"People change their minds." He shrugs. "I love you."

She looks over her shoulder at him, giggling. "What's its name? Is it a he or a she?"

"It's a he. And he doesn't have one yet."

Haley blinks again. Shelter dogs always get names. "Which rescue did you go to?"

Jonah scratches the back of his neck, embarrassed. "I didn't."

"Then where—"

"Long story. He was running in traffic near LAX, and my flight was delayed, so I caught him, drove him to a vet to see if he was sick or chipped, and he wasn't, and the vet said the local shelter was a kill place, so I just . . . felt like I had to take him home."

She laughs. "*You?* And then you brought him on the plane? How?"

Jonah shrugs. "Easy. Just said he's an emotional support animal and paid extra."

A stray. Must've been living on the streets a long time, then; he's no puppy. That would explain the trembling, all the anxiety. "Poor big baby. What have those eyes seen?" she whispers. "Bad shit, I bet."

The dog licks her face, but then he sees Jonah approaching over her shoulder and his body stiffens, tail tucking under his back legs.

Jonah rests a hand on her clavicle. She takes it in hers.

The dog stares at the floor, hackles raised, as Jonah reaches down to pet his head. He stiffens again at the touch and twists away from it.

"Doesn't seem to like men very much," says Haley, frowning.

Jonah sighs and withdraws his hand, clearly hurt but trying not to show it. "Maybe this was stupid." He looks at her, concerned. "Listen. If you don't like him, we can go—"

"No!" She plants a big smooch on the dog's face against his will. "No, I love him. I love him. I do." It's just hard for her to imagine what her fiancé was thinking when he decided *this dog* was the one to bring home, and on a three-thousand-mile flight to boot. There are a ton of pits at rescue places. Surely he could've found one in a local shelter that wasn't deathly afraid of him.

But maybe that was the point of this stunt—to show off his soft side by going to heroic lengths to rescue the neediest dog possible.

Haley looks up and squeezes his hand.

He squeezes back, but his eyes are on the dog. It almost looks like there are tears welling up.

Whoa. Maybe it isn't a stunt.

"Thank you, babe," she says. "I mean it. Best surprise ever. It's actually really sweet you just felt like you had to."

Jonah nods.

"I bet he'll warm up to you. You saved his life. Dogs don't forget that stuff."

He wrinkles his nose. "Yeah."

She turns back to the dog and stares into his deep brown eyes, almost black. "You're so quiet, big bear." She smiles, worried, as her finger traces a thin raised scar on his neck. Like from a surgery.

He stares back, sad and mute.

"There's food for him in the cabinets, and a bowl. I already put out water." Jonah walks past and sits on the couch. "So, we're calling him Bear?"

Haley thinks about it. "Yeah. I like Bear. Big ol' Mr. Black Bear, with his big ol' head." She scratches his chin and squeals again. He may be scared and he may be a stray pit, but he's pretty dang cute. Plus, isn't it normal for dogs to act weird their first night in a new home?

The dog's powerful tail wags and wags. He leans his head into her chest, and she hugs his neck, laughing, but then he leans in harder and knocks her off balance, and she topples over onto the cold vinyl floor in a heap. Bear stands over her in a power stance, licking her face repeatedly. It's like wet sandpaper dragging across her chin and lips.

"Big baby! Oof, you're so gross and clumsy and dumb, but I don't *care!*" She pinches his lips like a grandma might pinch a kid's cheeks, then shoves him away and stands. Dusts herself off. "Let's get you fed."

She goes to the cabinet and opens it, and Bear follows so close he almost trips her.

The whole time she's making his dinner, he never looks up at her or the food. The dog keeps watching Jonah instead, even though her fiancé is just sitting on the couch ten feet away, reading something on his phone quietly. The TV isn't even on.

Thud. Thud. Thud. Thud. Thud.

She frowns, following the dog's stare.

Jonah looks up and meets her eyes, expressionless.

She shakes her head, forcing a smile. "How was the rest of your trip?"

He sighs, face buried in his phone again. "Boring."

22

Cy

May 25, 2008. 5:50 PM

HALFWAY TO JOSHUA Tree, Cy turned the stereo off.

"Yo, that's a fucking cop," he said, pointing out the windshield of Jonah's old Prius at a cruiser hidden on the side of the highway. "Slow down."

Jonah laughed. "I'm only going seventy. Calm yourself."

"The speed limit's sixty-five. Why give them an excuse? Slow down."

Jonah rolled his eyes, but he slowed down to sixty-four. "Happy now?"

"Super." Cy turned the music back on—they were halfway through *The Chronic* at the start of a lengthy Dr. Dre playlist—once they were safely past the idling black-and-white. He watched it get smaller out the back window as they left it in their dust. "Are you getting excited yet?"

"About what?" said Jonah, eyes on the road. "Doing shrooms?"

"Yeah, man. I tried these with Alistair last weekend and they are *bonkers*. I'm hype."

Jonah made a grossed-out face. "I knew it. I knew you bought from Alistair. Ugh. Why do you hang out with him? That kid is fucking weird."

"Sure, but he's got good drugs."

"Yeah, but that's—"

"Bonkers," said Cy. "He's not that bad. Don't be a dick."

Jonah frowned at him. "You shouldn't hang out with people just because they have good drugs."

"I think that's extremely arguable," said Cy, laughing.

* * *

Four hours later, Jonah vomited into a crevice between two rocks. "You were so fucking right," he said, laughing up bits of peanut butter and mushroom caps and staring wide-eyed at his fingers. "This is *crazy*."

Cy was sitting cross-legged on a boulder above him, trying to meditate. "Uh-huh."

To the west, the sun was going down over distant mountain peaks, already bisected into a jagged half circle. As he stared out from his vantage point, the whole landscape pulsed and quivered. The colors were all wrong. When they'd arrived, sober, the park was all tans and browns and grays, with the exception of the Joshua Trees themselves. Then, they looked to him like something out of a Dr. Seuss book. Now, they looked like part of a desolate alien landscape.

"These trees are freaking me out, man," he yelled down to Jonah. "Are you coming back?"

No answer. No sign of his brother near the rocks he'd vomited on.

Cy stood up, panicked. "Jonah?" He crawled down from his rock and found a trail of vomit leading down to the dusty flatland around the formation they'd climbed. "Jonah, where the fuck did you go?"

"Here," said a soft voice.

Cy stopped at the bottom of the rocks. It came from the other side. "Why are you wandering off?"

No answer.

"Dude. Are you okay?" He walked around the whole rock formation, leaning his head into every crevice he passed to check if Jonah was hiding from him. "Dude!"

Then he turned a corner and saw it. In the side of a nearby formation, there was a cave. A deep one.

He walked to its mouth.

Inside, Jonah stood deep in the shadows, back toward him and looking up at the low ceiling. Something was off. It was his posture. Tense. Elbow glued to his side.

Cy walked in to join him. "You're such a dick, dude . . ."

Jonah turned his head, slow, as he brandished a long black hunting knife. Its blade glinted in the dark. "Why did you follow me here, Mr. Tani?"

Cy froze. It was a knife Dad had given Jonah two Christmases ago, but Cy had no idea he carried it. "Jonah. It's me. Cyrus."

Jonah gave him a suspicious look, shaking. "Is he dead?" Tears started to stream down both cheeks.

"You're safe. No one's dead." Cy took a cautious step forward, hands held flat in front of his chest. "Put down the knife."

Jonah shook his head. Then he retreated into the cave, backing into the darkness until he vanished in it.

"Dude!" Cy followed him in, eyes adjusting slow to the pitch-blackness in the rear of the cave. "You just ate too much drugs. Stop . . ."

Jonah had reached the back wall by the time Cy caught sight of him again. He was standing in a sort of natural crevice, and he had his arms flat against the rock on both sides, chest heaving like he was having a panic attack.

Cy stopped when he saw what he was doing. There was a slit in the rock, a thin tunnel or passage, that looked like it might lead deeper underground. It was hard to tell. Nothing but more shadows on the other side. "Are you trying to squeeze in there? Stop it. You're gonna get stuck, man!"

And then something impossible happened. Jonah's body jerked like that of a dying insect. Both his arms grew a foot in length, he squirmed, and a second later his entire body had disappeared into the rock slit—an opening that looked eight or nine inches wide.

Cy stood there, speechless. Terrified. *Was that real?*

No sound or movement came from the dark on the other side. "Jonah?" He waited a minute, but it was the same as before: nothing. He shivered from the cold. *Fuck it.*

Cy walked out of the cave and made a beeline for the parking lot, ignoring the tent they'd set up. The Prius was the only car in the lot. He climbed in back, wrapped himself up in blankets, and locked the doors. Outside all the car's windows, nothing but blackness.

Twenty minutes passed in silence.

Then, as he stared out the window on his side and saw nothing but his own dark reflection, a pale face appeared inches away, swallowing it, and he jumped half out of his skin.

Jonah rapped a knuckle on the window. "Let me in—it's cold."

Cy hesitated, then he unlocked the door, and Jonah jumped in back to join him, taking a share of blankets and nestling in for the night.

"I agree," said Jonah. "Fuck that tent."

Cy looked him up and down. His arms were the usual length. "Did you just pull a knife on me in a cave?"

Jonah stared at his fingers again, twirling them in front of his face, and Cy realized it was the most fucked up he'd ever seen him. "It was a mistake. I thought you were someone else."

So that was real. "Who is Mr. Tani?"

Jonah smiled big. "An imaginary friend. We hunt buffalo together." He holds a finger to his lips. *Shh.*

"Did you pop out your shoulders and wriggle into that gap in the rock?"

Jonah's smile disappeared. "No."

"Okay."

They said nothing for a while.

"We ate way too much shrooms, didn't we?" said Jonah, who seemed to be more lucid again, at least for the moment.

"Yup."

"Shit. Sorry about the . . . I forgot I had it." Jonah took the black hunting knife out again, but left it safely in its leather scabbard this time. He tossed it at the front seat and missed, and it thudded on the floorboard. "You wanna talk about space and shit?"

*   *   *

As the sun peeked over the eastern horizon and the sky transitioned from black to lavender, the two brothers were still wide awake in the backseat, discussing life, semantics, religion, ethics, drugs, music, consciousness—all the big, important thoughts Cy never usually had time or headspace to devote energy to, what with school and football practice and chasing girls. The more abstract, the better.

"Do you think you're happy?"

"You sure you wanna go there?" said Jonah, frowning.

"It's just . . . I'm not." Cy leaned his head against a window. "I don't even know what it's like."

Jonah took his hand and squeezed it hard. "I know." Hand in hand, they sat in silence for a minute. "No. I don't think I'm happy. Not yet."

Cy nodded as his mouth turned down at the edges, and his eyes started to water. "I wonder if anyone is, man. What if people all just lie to themselves about it? Look at Mom and Dad."

"Not everyone's got personality disorders. There are people who die happy. Just not a lot."

Cy wiped away a tear on his blankets. "How do you know?"

"Well, let's define the word *happy*. I think you meant to ask if I'm satisfied with my life. Right?"

Cy thought about it. "I guess. I thought being happy was a little stronger than just satisfied, though."

Jonah raised an eyebrow. "What, like constant euphoria? That's what you think happiness is?"

Cy shrugged. "Yeah, I guess."

"No. Think about it. What's the point of good feelings? All those chemicals in our brains that trigger something like the opposite of pain. Serotonin, dopamine."

"I guess they're to reward us for doing things that help us survive?"

"Close," said Jonah, in his element with a captive audience. "Things that help *our genes* survive. Why do you think sex feels so . . . well, you wouldn't know yet, but it feels good. And it has nothing to do with our own *personal* survival. Euphoria is a trick. That's what most good feelings are—biological tricks to keep us making babies."

"I guess," said Cy. "But, man, that's depressing if we're just meat robots."

"No, it's not."

"How is it not?"

"I was just making a point. The happiness you just described, like it's a goal that you just *achieve* one day? It's a myth. Nobody's happy all the time. That would defeat the purpose of happiness. It's a moving goalpost. A carrot on a stick. A lie. If you spend all your time trying to catch it, prepare to be disappointed, because you never will."

Cy shifted uncomfortably in his blankets. "I guess."

Jonah slapped the back of his head, just hard enough for it to hurt. "Stop saying that. It makes you sound stupid. Tell me what you *think*."

"I did, asshole . . . you're right, okay?" he said, glowering. "Life is meaningless. Free will doesn't exist. I get it. You don't have to beat nihilism into me. I just think it's depressing to talk about."

"If you think I'm preaching nihilism, you're not listening."

Cy rolled his eyes. "Okay. Explain, then."

Jonah's eyes gleamed. "I don't want to feel good. I want to *know* satisfaction. That's true happiness."

"I still don't get the difference."

Jonah shook his head, smiling. "One lasts. It can't be taken away. You control it."

"Cool. So, what's your grand plan to achieve satisfaction?"

Jonah lit up again, like he'd been eager to share it with someone for a long time. "I want to build a legacy that will last forever. Not a family or a business or a useful invention with my name on it, but a legend. I want to leave behind a story so powerful, it won't just be my name that lives on. It'll be *me*. My art. My thoughts. I want my ideas to haunt the minds of all men, forever, at all times. I want to be remembered as they try to sleep, when they're alone at home, in their cars, while they eat and fuck, and the only thing that dominates a mind like that is what it fears. Death. So, my legend is going to be a ghost story. I tell people my art explores death, but the truth is, my art *is* death. The paintings are only studies. The surest way to defeat an enemy is to know him so well, you become him."

A pit was forming in Cy's stomach. "You want to scare people? What do you mean, your art is death?"

Jonah flashed him a strange look, like a doctor evaluating his patient's response to a medication. "What would you do differently if you knew for certain that good and evil don't exist?"

"You lost me again."

Jonah plowed ahead. "I read an article in *Nature* about a physics experiment they did at Harvard. It was super dense, but the takeaway was that they observed an object existing in two quantum states simultaneously."

This meant nothing to Cy. "Okay."

"They found proof of a multiverse, Cy," said Jonah, like he'd witnessed a miracle. "Not definitive, but if someone else can replicate it, do you know what it means?"

Cy tried to remember. They had talked about this "multiverse theory" stuff before, a bit more sober, which at least gave him some confidence that the concept wasn't total hooey. "It just means every possible outcome in history gets its own, slightly different universe, and there's infinite universes all layered on top of one another. Infinite versions of me, you, everyone. Right?"

"Correct," said Jonah, beaming. "And they keep finding more evidence for it. But what does it *mean* if they prove it? If every time *you* choose to do good, *another you* chooses the opposite?"

Cy thought about it. Then it hit him. "If I pick up a piece of trash, it still doesn't get picked up."

"Exactly. Every event has happened, is happening, and will happen again, again, and again. Good or bad. You can never prevent an atrocity, even one of your own. So, you and I, knowing this, no longer have any use for things like guilt or ethics, do we? You and I are free to do as we please. We can rise above our programming to help others, our short-sighted desire to *feel good*, and focus entirely on what matters."

Cy stared out the car window at the black sky and his own faint reflection over it. "Like what? Art?"

Jonah put a hand on the back of his head, massaging his hair. "Yes. That's how you and I write our legend. Together. Imagine all the possibilities at our fingertips once you accept that there's no logical reason to be or do good unless it benefits *us*." His blue eyes flashed, studying his little brother's reaction.

"What are you saying, though?" Cy didn't like where this was headed. "We can hurt people? Or like, you want to?"

Jonah could sense his discomfort. "Never mind," he said, sinking into his blankets. "We can stop. How're the ladies treating you at school? Any cute girls you've got your eye on?"

Cy eagerly bought into the pivot. "The girls in my grade are the worst, dude. Amanda hardly talks to me anymore, and Stacy, she likes that asshole Ben Watterson . . ."

The sun rose. It flooded the car with light. And still the brothers talked and talked.

Neither of them slept the whole weekend.

Instead, they had ten or twenty arguments in the same vein: good and evil, right and wrong, over and over. It was all Jonah wanted to talk about. It was an obsession.

After the second night, Cy was already running out of reasons to disagree.

By the time they packed up the car on the last day, Jonah's victory was total. He'd convinced his little brother he was right again, like always. Cy didn't think good and evil existed either. Morality. Ethics. In fact, he was *sure* it didn't. The two wolves were free to do anything they wanted, even hurt people, and nothing would change as long as they didn't get caught.

CHAPTER

23

Diana

April 4, 1989. 5:48 PM

THEY MADE LOVE on the private beach, on a white towel under a
sand bank where no neighbors could see.

When things were building to a climax, she whispered in Thad's
ear, "Wait. Take it off."

Thad stopped, and they made eye contact. Held it. "You sure . . .?"

She nodded.

He rolled the condom off and pushed back inside her hungrily, and
she moaned. Closed her eyes and basked in the moment. It was the hap-
piest she had ever been, so she wanted to remember exactly how it felt.

Thad grunted and shivered. Then he relaxed.

They lay in the sand together, breathing heavily in each other's
arms.

Thad stroked her back, tracing shapes with his fingertips. It always
gave her chills.

Diana was twenty-two years old, a newlywed, and hopelessly in
love. She sighed, gripping his strong arms tight. "Thad Wolf. I think
you may be my best friend."

Thad kissed her neck. "You are the best thing to ever happen to
me."

She smiled. *Liar.* "I'll never leave." As it left her lips, she knew it
sounded corny. *A play on his lyrics? Really?*

But Thad liked it. It got him hard again. He flipped her over, and she screamed . . . in a good way.

*   *   *

An hour later, they were still naked on the beach. Alone, wrapped in their towel, watching the Malibu sunset. It was a good one. Rippling clouds glowed pink and orange above the horizon, where the sun was sinking into the Pacific Ocean like a scuttled ship.

Seabirds flapped their wings in the distance. Gentle waves lapped at the pale sand. Thad's heart beat slow and steady against her ear, pressed tight to his chest. Otherwise, it was silent.

After their first honeymoon in Bora Bora, Thad surprised her by renting a beach house in Malibu for a three-day weekend—he knew it was always her dream to live in one of these. So, now they were enjoying their second honeymoon.

Thad rubbed her shoulder. "I think we go for Tuesday too."

Diana laughed. "Can we just extend it like that?"

Thad looked at her like it was a stupid question. "Wallace at the office, he set all this up. He'll make it work."

She stared at him in awe. "So. When does this honeymoon end?" It had to end. Right?

Thad shrugged. "Whenever we want." He said it like it was a given, like it was just what he was *used to*. He ruffled her hair, sat up, and started making a neat double scotch with the contents of a little cooler they'd brought outside.

Diana shook her head. It was hard to believe, the things she'd gotten used to. Thad's life was intoxicating. His freedom. His spontaneousness. The casual luxury of it all.

Thad Wolf was thirty-nine. Seventeen years older than her—practically middle aged!—but no one who watched them together would ever guess there was such a big gap. Thad always said that when someone gets famous, they stop growing up, like their personality gets stuck and preserved in amber until they die . . . and he had gotten famous in his early twenties, so she supposed that explained it.

Neither of them spoke again for a long time.

They just held each other and watched the sun sink.

When night fell, they made love again. Slower, this time. It was even better in the dark.

*   *   *

Diana woke up from a nightmare, naked in the cold sand and shivering. For a horrid moment, her mother's stale perfume lingered in her nostrils, but then she smelled salt and seaweed, and it was gone.

Thad had stolen most of the white towel. It was rolled up around his legs.

She shoved him awake.

His eyes fluttered open. "Shit. What time is it?" A scotch glass and an empty bottle stuck out of the sand near his head.

Diana hugged his neck, tight.

Thad hugged her back, confused. "What's wrong?"

Tears welled in her eyes. She hid from him, pressing her face harder into his skin. "What if we're bad parents?"

Thad scoffed. "Oh, come on."

"We didn't have good parents," she whispered. It was the understatement of the century. "What if we don't even know what it looks like?"

Thad brooded. "My daddy is a great man. He did his best."

Diana didn't push it. Thad's father was borderline senile, and he spoke in tongues on the phone with her sometimes if he felt she needed a demon or two exorcised. His nickname for her was *"that harlot."* Lovely man. Very devout. "I lied about my dad being dead. He isn't."

If her husband was shocked by the revelation, he didn't show it. Thad ran his fingers through her hair. Listening.

"I think he lives in Ventura with his family." She paused. "He and his new wife could've taken us in after my mom died. Or before. He had the money. Any time he wanted, my dad could've saved us. But Tara didn't want to raise some other woman's three kids. So my dad just abandoned us to social services . . . and made new kids."

Thad whistled, shaking his head. "I see why you lied. I woulda found his ass by now."

"Do not. He's not worth it." Diana sighed. "I only brought him up so you'd understand why I'm so . . . *scared.*" She couldn't protect Luke and Kristen. She was the one who had called 911 that day after Bonnie died, and then all the social workers had come and split them up into three foster homes.

She'd practically invited them in.

Then she couldn't save Luke when he ended up in a hellhole with an abusive foster father. Her little brother had it worst, by far.

But you found them, she reminded herself.

It was true.

Kristen she found in the phonebook when they were both still teens. They had managed to keep in touch ever since. But when Luke had run away from his last home, and both sisters lost track of him for eight years. They had all but given up, and then, three weeks ago, Diana finally convinced Thad to let her hire a private investigator, and it took him just under four days to find Luke in Michigan. She'd spoken to him on the phone, and after some negotiating, he'd let her book him a travel itinerary to visit her at her new home in Brentwood. Kristen agreed to drive down from Santa Barbara too, so now—for the first time in a decade—the three of them were going to be together. Reunited. They'd probably see each other at holidays for the rest of their lives.

All because she'd met Thad. It wasn't just freedom that she'd gained being with him; it was the power to make bad things right for the people she cared most about. Things were so good, and only getting better. Lois Lane had never had it half as good. She and Thad were in love. Rich. Good-looking. Healthy. Why should she be worried?

And yet, you are, said a little voice in her head. Her own.

Thad nudged her and stood. "Come on. You're freezing. Let's get in bed." He pulled her up by her elbow. She didn't fight it.

He left to gather their clothes.

Diana stood on the beach alone, naked, staring out at a black ocean. A swelling tide splashed her feet, ice cold, and the sand felt coarse and filthy between her toes.

CHAPTER

24

Cy

December 1, 2008. 3:13 AM

FRESHMAN YEAR AT Harpers-Exeter was halfway over.
Cy was in his bedroom, surfing the internet on a laptop he
wasn't supposed to have. Part of his big punishment: no video games, no
internet, no phone. He was allowed to read. The rest was contraband.

"He's suspended is why!" Mom had screamed when Thad complained about her hiding all the confiscated shit in his man cave, both
of them oblivious to how well conversations in the house traveled up
the A/C vents. "I thought I'd hide it somewhere he never goes. Oh
look, Dad's room!"

It was a two-day suspension for selling drugs on campus.

Not good, but it could've been worse. The administration had
agreed not to put it on his permanent record. Other kids would've been
expelled, but Thad was a big donor.

It had only taken a minute to locate his computer, once his parents
were asleep. The man cave was the biggest room in the house, but it
didn't matter. He'd found it hidden in the barrel side table next to
Thad's armchair, the same one where he hid his empty rye bottles. No
bottles today. Mom must have thrown them out when she hid the contraband, which was almost certainly what had gotten Thad so upset.
She'd already known the bottles were in there—they all did—but the
old man liked to pretend it was a secret. If there was one thing Cy

knew about his parents, it was that they hated nothing more than a punctured bubble.

Thad didn't have a drinking problem—he was doing better.

Mom wasn't depressed—look at her.

The boys were *amazing*—thanks for asking.

Mom was already telling her friends the suspension was *"all a big misunderstanding."* It was not. Cy had been averaging ten grand a month in profits selling stepped-on coke to senior girls.

He checked his Facebook again, wishing he could sleep.

It was stupid, but part of him was sad Mom hadn't made a bigger deal of it. Every year, she became a little more like Thad. She was even drinking a glass of red wine at night now. Every night. Sometimes a glass turned into a bottle.

The only person actually pissed at him was Jonah, but only because he'd gotten caught.

Cy powered off his laptop. He left his room and crept down the hallway to his brother's.

He rapped on the door four times, in the rhythm they'd practiced.

No answer. Not a sound.

Jonah never slept through a knock, which meant he had slipped out for the night again.

Cy returned to his room, disappointed, and shut the door. As he lay down on the covers, a ringtone shattered the quiet he'd been living in since his parents went to sleep. It was his phone. *Contraband.* He reached over to silence it, cursing under his breath. Then he saw who it was.

He frowned as he answered. "Jonah?"

Nothing but a sound like rasping breaths on the other end.

"Did you butt-dial me?"

"Cy," said a distant voice, like it was on speaker.

He groaned. "Dude. No. Put it to your ear, I can't hear you." This was a habit with Jonah.

Nothing. More rasping.

"Hello?"

Suddenly, a noise so loud it hurt came out of the phone: a car horn. *Bwaaaaaahhhh!*

Cy dropped it, scared shitless. As he went to pick his phone up, rubbing his ear, he noticed something: the car horn. He could still hear it. It sounded like it was coming from somewhere down the street.

A cold, damp fear settled over him like mist. He checked his phone. His brother hadn't ended the call. "Shit."

Cy peeked out through his curtains at the world outside. Dogs were starting to bark. A light turned on upstairs in the house across the street.

He kept hoping the sound would end. It didn't.

Did Jonah get in a fucking car accident?

He put on a pair of sneakers, and then he was running down the stairs and out the front door.

Cy ran down Tigertail. The street was unlit and empty. But he could hear it, louder and louder as he ran: a car horn.

Half a mile from the house, he turned a corner and saw the source of it. A gray Prius. Jonah's car. But it didn't look like it had been in an accident. The car was parked on the shoulder, lights off, windows tinted just dark enough to stay legal. To a deaf person, nothing would seem wrong.

"Shut that fucking thing off!" a cranky old man shouted from a distant window.

Cy sprinted to the Prius. When he saw his brother through the windshield, he gasped.

Jonah was slumped over the steering wheel, cheek pressed against the topside leather grip. There was blood all over his hands and face, glistening. His eyes were open.

Cy tried to open the driver-side door, but it was locked. "Jonah!" he yelled, pounding on the tinted window with a fist. "Can you hear me?"

Inside, a specter of movement. The door locks disengaged.

Cy flung the door open.

Jonah's limp torso would have fallen right onto the asphalt if not for his seat belt. But he was still breathing. Cy peeled his brother's face off the steering wheel, and the horn stopped blaring.

"Cy . . ." Almost a moan. Jonah's clothes were soaked in blood, so much it was impossible to tell what part of his body it was coming from, or if it was one wound or a hundred.

Cy felt tears in his eyes. *Is this what it looks like when a person bleeds out?*

"I need . . . you to drive . . . now."

"It's okay," he lied. "You're not gonna die."

Jonah's lips formed something like a frown. "*No.* You. Drive. Me. Out of here. *Now.*" Blood spilled out his mouth and down his chin. He choked on it, hacking.

Cy noticed the black hunting knife held tight in his brother's hand. The same one he'd threatened him with in Joshua Tree. It was dripping wet.

He retreated a step, wary. "Is this all your blood?"

Jonah shook his head and pointed at something on the floorboard: his iPhone, right where he'd dropped it after calling for help.

Cy reached down and got it. "What do you want me to . . .?"

Jonah gestured at the phone, eyes furious, each breath shallower and raspier. "*Read.* Drive me to that fucking address . . . or I'll kill you."

"It's locked."

"*Eight-nine-nine-two,*" said Jonah. His eyes closed.

Frantically, Cy entered the PIN. His hand was shaking so badly, it took three tries.

A notepad was onscreen, with an address written in it. "Venice? What . . .?" The big hospitals he knew were all in the opposite direction: UCLA, Cedars Sinai, USC.

Jonah gurgled.

There was a note under the address: *money in spare tire.*

Cy undid his brother's seat belt and struggled to shove his wet, limp body out of the driver's seat.

*   *   *

The whole trip, he looked out for cops.

Twenty minutes, and the car's GPS told him his destination was on his right. He was in Venice, just a few blocks from the shops on Abbot Kinney. "Fucking kidding me . . ."

It was a bungalow, the kind that look shitty on the outside, but only rich dudes can afford. Rich dudes who surf or dive for lobsters off their kayak. And there was no parking.

Cy threw on his hazard lights. He climbed out, ran up to the gate, and pressed a button on the intercom.

There was no ring or dial tone. "It's late," a thin voice finally said.

Cy realized he had no clue what to say to this man. "My brother's hurt. He gave me your address."

The thin voice laughed, which was not the response he had expected.

Cy blinked. "My brother is Jonah Wolf."

An intake of breath.

"Hello? Can you help? Please!" He started to cry and meandered down the sidewalk, yelling, "Help! Someone! He's dying!"

"*Quiet,*" the thin voice hissed behind him. It wasn't coming from an intercom. It was real. "C'mere."

He turned around, pawing at his eyes. The bungalow gate was open. A man leaned out. "You know him," said Cy. "Are you gonna help him?"

The man looked like a rich surfer. He wore a vintage "*Big Lebowski*" T-shirt and sweatpants. "Sure. Then I'm gonna fucking kill him."

Cy frowned. "Who are you?"

The man didn't answer, just stared at the blinking Prius double-parked in the street. He shook his head angrily. "Turn the lights off and pull it into my garage. I'll open it." He stomped back inside.

Cy did as he was told: slid into the driver's seat, turned off his lights, and waited for the bungalow's single-car garage to open. A second later, it did. Empty. He pulled in. The man flipped a switch on the wall, and the garage door lowered again as Cy got out.

"First. Where is my money?" the man asked.

Cy remembered the note. "In the spare tire."

"Show me."

He opened the Prius's hatch and lifted up the plastic board over the spare tire well, not knowing what he'd find there. What he saw didn't make any sense. The well was packed to the brim with twenty-dollar bills, each rubber-banded stack labeled "*$10,000.*" There had to be two hundred grand in it.

The man grunted. "Okay. Give me your cell phone."

Cy did.

The man pocketed it. "Now help."

They lifted Jonah out of the car and carried him inside, Cy carrying his legs, and the man his torso.

The inside of the bungalow was cold and modern, and there was nothing about it that screamed *surfer*. The walls and surfaces were white, and the floor was stone. "There. Gurney." The man nodded at a corner, where there was an actual steel gurney against the wall.

They got Jonah's body up onto it. When they dropped him, he moaned.

"What are you gonna do?"

The man got behind the gurney and pushed it, rolling it to a door on the far side of the room. "Fix him. You wait here. I only talk to your brother."

"What if he doesn't wake up?"

The man stopped, and the gurney creaked to a halt. He hung his head, laughed, then he pushed the gurney at and through the door, and Jonah's body disappeared into what looked like a DIY operating room beyond. The door slammed shut.

* * *

Cy sat on a white leather sofa and stewed.

After an hour or so, the door opened, and the man stepped out. "He's stable. You need to sleep here. You can have this couch."

"I can't. Our parents will freak out."

The man gave him a stone look.

Cy stayed right where he was, seated.

The man snorted and got him a thin blanket out of a closet. Tossed it at him. "You can go once I talk to him."

* * *

Cy woke up in the night to shouting in the next room. It was the man: "*. . . little fucking brother! You know what Tani said to do with him!*"

A second voice was less audible, its tone measured and serious. Jonah's. "Be quiet."

That was all he caught.

Cy closed his eyes tight and tried to go back to sleep.

* * *

At ten AM, true to his word, the man gave their phones back and let them both go.

Jonah had a black eye, bruises and stitches on both arms, and bandages wrapped tight around his ribs, but he was still the better choice to drive home. A rattled Cy climbed into the passenger seat.

As they pulled out of the single-car garage, he finally had a chance to ask, "What just happened?"

Jonah put a finger to his lips. "I'm sorry, but you need to trust me. I *will* tell you what this all means. But not today. It has to be like this."

Cy shivered the whole drive. He didn't bother asking again.

He was starting to wonder if all of it had been a nightmare, and he'd wake up soon.

He wondered it again, more intensely, when Jonah parked on Tigertail, unwrapped his bandages, and ripped out all his stitches.

"What the fuck are you doing?" Cy yelled, horrified.

Jonah was bleeding all over the car again as he stuffed the evidence in a trash bag and dumped it in a neighbor's bin. He got back in, drove the rest of the way home in silence, parked again, and ran into the house.

When Cy got inside, he found Jonah in Mom's arms, crying like he was terrified, telling her that his little brother was high on drugs and had attacked him with a knife.

Diana looked up at her youngest son, fear in her eyes.

CHAPTER

25

Kerry

November 14, 2019. 4:39 AM

Kerry wakes up, and it's still dark out his window. And there's someone inside his house.

The front door closes downstairs. *Shunk.* The sound of it opening must've been what woke him up.

Kerry flicks a light switch, rubbing his eyes. He throws his covers off and listens. Hears footsteps climbing upstairs—slow, heavy steps, a man being careful not to make noise. His brain short-circuits as he realizes, *This is the killer.* The one who did Ellison. Kerry's not a fighter; he only lifts weights to make his biceps look good; he skips every leg day; he's got back problems. He's about to die.

The killer's footsteps climb, almost to the landing now, where the door to his room is. There's no lock.

Kerry jumps out of bed and grabs the nearest object he can use as a weapon: the lamp on his side table. He rips its cord out of the wall, and the room goes black as he sets his feet, ready to bring it down on whoever walks in.

The footsteps stop on the landing. A pair of heels shuffles at the door to his room.

Its brass knob turns slowly. The door creaks open.

"Yahhhhhrg!" Kerry's voice cracks as he rushes forward, eyes shut, swinging blindly.

"I'm sorry!" yelps a puny male voice, in retreat. A swing makes solid contact, and the lamp breaks into pieces as the intruder howls, "My fucking face! Oh fuck you, Kerry Perkins, you asshole. *Why?"*

Wait a minute. Kerry opens his eyes, breathing heavy. "Pink?"

Pink leans against a wall on the landing, shaking, holding a red hand up to his bleeding forehead. "Was that a lamp?" He slides down the wall until he's sitting, and a ratty backpack slips off his arm.

Kerry drops what remains of his improvised weapon. "What the fuck are you doing in here?" he hisses. "Did you break into my house?"

Pink shrugs. "Yes."

"Why?"

Pink's voice gets serious. "I rang the doorbell, but you slept through it. And we need to talk. In person."

Kerry scoffs. *"Now* you want to talk! At four in the morning! No, no, I'm not an asshole. *You* are an asshole. Where the shit have you been?"

"Hiding," says Pink, softly. "Searching for answers. I was scared after what you sent me about Ellison. I'm much more scared now."

Kerry's heart drops into his stomach, like on one of those tower rides where they strap you in with your feet dangling, and the carney counts down from five, but he blasts you off at three. "What?"

"I know who killed your girl in the woods, but I fear knowing will be the death of us both." Pink stands, a little unsteady on his feet. "You need to read this email I found. Now." He reaches into the backpack, takes out his laptop, pushes past Kerry, and flips it open on the bed.

Kerry stands frozen in the doorway. "What do you mean, 'the death of us'?"

Pink says nothing. Types.

"Dude, does someone want to kill me?"

Pink looks up at him, and even though it's still dark in the room, he can see a glint in his eyes. *Tears.* "I don't know. Read it. Then you tell me if I'm overreacting."

Kerry shuts the door, numb. He closes his eyes and pinches his own thigh, hard, trying to wake up. It doesn't work.

At the foot of his bed, keystrokes echo in the dark. *Tick-tick-tick-tick-tick . . .*

26

Diana

November 25, 2011. 7:18 PM

THANKSGIVING AT WOLF Hollow was in full swing.

Diana's arms were crossed. She was in the kitchen, looking out the trio of big bay windows over the sink, gauging the mood of her guests. *Going well.*

Everyone had assembled on tree stumps around the smoldering firepit to listen to Thad play his guitar and sing the hits. It was a good turnout. From her vantage point, she could see her sister, Kristen, and her husband, as well as the Bindleys, Otto, Cy, both of her brother Luke's daughters, and a few people whose names she couldn't remember.

At first they were mingling, drinking, and eating hors d'oeuvres, but soon everyone was silent and listening.

Thad was in his element, telling a folksy story in between songs like he always used to do onstage. Diana couldn't hear him from inside, but she could tell just by watching the rapt faces of his audience that he was halfway through the one about how he wrote *"A Thousand Lies."* It was still an amazingly sexy thing to watch, even after all these years. He transformed when he was entertaining people. You couldn't look away. And it made him smile in a way nothing else really did anymore.

She sighed happily.

Cy was looking like a real adult for the first time since his diagnosis. He was taking his pills. Stable. She always knew he'd do better once he got to NYU with Jonah.

Her boys were all grown up. She'd broken the cycle. She was a good mom.

Luke knocked into her elbow on his way back outside. "Oops. You good?" He held two over-filled wineglasses, one in each hand.

Diana nodded. "Are *you* . . .?"

Luke's cheeks were red already. Dinner wasn't for another hour or two. "I'm, uh, fine." He dangled one of the wine glasses at her like an olive branch. "Eh? Come on—quit working so hard."

Diana shook her head. "I'm okay. Thanks."

Luke frowned, but he kissed her on the cheek. "Hey. Thanks for inviting me and the girls. The house looks amazing." He pushed through the screen door and walked back outside, where he handed his extra wineglass to a waiting Robyn Clarke.

Diana watched out the window as her friend giggled at one of Luke's jokes, grazing his arm with a fingertip.

"Careful," she said to herself, grinning. Luke and Robyn. Oof. Talk about a match made in financial hell. Her baby brother was broke with a capital "B," to a degree even Robyn couldn't understand. Luke owed Thad how much money, now? Even that sum wouldn't include any of the ludicrous favors . . . like the two-month period when they let him stay with them at Wolf Hollow, sleeping in the barn while he wrote a novel.

Diana slipped on her mitts and checked on the big turkey in the oven. Immaculate. One hour away, max.

"Sophie," she called out.

The cook she'd hired came running from the other side of the kitchen.

"It's an hour out. Is everything else good?"

Sophie nodded, standing at attention. "All under control, Mrs. Wolf. I've got it. Go enjoy yourself."

Diana gave her a look. "I would '*enjoy myself*' a lot more if I felt you could handle things in here. Don't let my brother drink any more wine until dinner. Tell him *I* said so, if he asks."

Sophie nodded. "Of course, ma'am."

Diana turned back to the window. Pretty much everyone was accounted for, it seemed, except for the one person she wanted to talk to. "Did you see where Sally went?"

"Which one is Sally?" asked Sophie.

"My friend. The one who looks like me. Blonde. White dress."

"Oh! I saw her on the path out to the Songwriter's Cottage," said Sophie. "About a half hour ago."

"Thanks." Diana walked out the front door, down the porch's three steps, and followed the gravel path away from the overflowing parking circle.

After thirty paces or so, the hum of conversations in the backyard faded. The only sounds were the little creek, tiny birds chirping, and poplar trees swaying in the breeze. The gravel path turned a corner and angled down into the ravine, and the Songwriter's Cottage came into view: a tiny log cabin, a place she built for Thad to have sessions with all the songwriters in Nashville he always wanted to collaborate with. After two years, he had yet to use it. The boys watched TV and smoked pot in there sometimes, but that was it.

Diana could see lights on inside. She was just about to call out to Sally—*"Hey bitch, where'd you slink off to?"*—when she heard noises coming from inside.

She stopped in her tracks. Frowned. Listened.

These were fairly easy noises to interpret.

"Fuck me like that . . . oh, fuck . . . you're so fucking bad . . . *oh, fuck!* . . . yes, yes, *yes!"*

Diana broke out in a wicked grin. *Who're you fucking in there, Sally?*

Not her husband, that was for sure. Diana hadn't invited Gerald, and anyway, Mr. Davis was in Europe on business. In her head, she tried to catalog who else had been missing around the firepit. Was it a server? A few of the boys Sophie brought would do in a pinch, if memory served.

Diana tiptoed to one of the windows, giggling, intending to surprise Sally mid-coitus as a prank.

But when she ducked under the window, she heard something else: a *thud*. A cry. *Pain.*

Diana peeked through the glass, confused.

Inside, Jonah pumped in and out of Sally Davis, flat on her back on Thad's great big wood desk.

"Yes!" screamed Sally, eyes rolling back. "The men in your family have such good fucking cocks. But your dad's was better."

He slapped her, hard.

Sally cried out in pain, then it morphed seamlessly into laughter. "You love when I talk about fucking your dad, don't you?"

He punched her in the gut this time, knocking the wind out of her.

"Oof." Sally looked dazed, head lolling back. "Hit me again."

Jonah grunted, but he didn't hit her.

He reached down, coiled his fingers around her throat and squeezed, silencing her. His muscular forearm flexed as his hips pumped.

Sally's face turned bright red. Her eyes bulged.

Jonah held on, but his head swiveled. He made eye contact with his mother at the window.

He didn't stop, just stared at her.

Diana dropped to her knees in the dirt and sat there with her head resting on the logs for thirty seconds.

Hoping against all reason that she hadn't actually been seen—that it was just her *imagination*—she climbed up the side of the ravine, staying off the path, away from the sightlines out the cottage's windows.

A minute later, she appeared at the firepit in the backyard, disheveled, eyes red from crying. She marched up behind Luke, who was telling a story to Robyn Clarke—he held yet another wineglass, fresh, full of red, and thus Sophie was *so fired*—and stole his drink without announcing her presence. Kept walking.

"Whoa, hey . . ." said Luke.

Diana didn't look at him. She downed the glass of wine, then she chucked it into the fire and it smashed into a thousand bits, silencing the rest of her guests' conversations. "Anyone seen Sally?" she said aloud, to no one in particular.

No one said anything.

"Funny. Me neither." She shrugged, then walked back to the house to check on her turkey as everyone stared at her, help included.

* * *

That night, she had the dead coyote nightmare. First time in years.

Diana was driving her old Mercedes station wagon, the one they had in Los Angeles when the boys were just toddlers. It was a foggy night, and visibility on Tigertail was so bad that she had to slow the car down to a crawl. This wasn't normal fog—she couldn't see her own hood ornament. There was a smell like rotting meat in the air, and when she rolled down her window to try and see the road, the fog flooded in like a thousand pounds of water, filling the car so fast she had to pull over and purge it through the A/C vents.

She navigated the station wagon to her house, five miles per hour.

When she finally got to Tina Bollenbach's house next door, she figured that was good enough and parked.

Right then, her headlights caught movement.

Diana looked closer. There was a dying coyote in the road ten feet from her driveway, twitching in the mist. Her first thought was that someone hadn't seen it in the fog and had hit it, but it didn't look like roadkill. On its torso, a mess of big, ugly cuts had been made with a heavy edge. Black blood poured from its chest cavity and ran into a gutter.

It howled pathetically.

As she watched, its body stopped rising and falling. Dead.

"I just wanted to try the butcher knife," said a high, tiny voice in the backseat.

She didn't look back, just stared straight ahead at the dead coyote. She heard a low, angry noise like a swarm of bees—quiet at first, but swelling. Getting closer.

The dead coyote stood. Its spindly legs moved like a stop-motion puppet, out of sync with its body and too fast. Its stomach fell out and splashed on the asphalt.

It took a step toward her.

The insects buzzed louder. Closer.

"If you don't tell," whispered the tiny voice, so close she could feel it on her neck, "I won't."

Diana looked in her rearview mirror, crying. In the car seat behind her, there was a mutilated coyote with its eyes burnt out. Cruel black zip ties kept it in the seat, posed like a human child. Its head moved suddenly and its no-eyes met hers in the mirror.

"You would clean it," it said in Jonah's old voice—a little boy's.

He was nine when he said it in real life.

"You would clean it," it repeated, lower.

The noise of insects was so loud now, it was painful.

Suddenly a swarm of locusts streamed in through the A/C vents until they filled the car, every inch of air occupied. She swatted and screamed, but the more she opened her mouth, the more flew in. As she choked and twitched, she felt a thousand tiny, barbed legs digging in her throat and ears.

* * *

Diana woke up clawing at her neck.

27

Kerry

November 14, 2019. 5:04 AM

PINK TURNS HIS screen around. "Look."
　　Kerry looks at the desktop, and there's a folder open: "*dwolfHDrecover.*"
　　"Pink," he says, frowning.
　　Pink drops his eyes, ashamed. "I know. But it does not matter how I got this."
　　"How did you get it?"
　　Pink glares at him. "I took what was left of it out of her trash."
　　At least he's honest. Kerry yawns, shaking his head. "Goddammit, what is all this? Why is half of it corrupted?"
　　"Because she tried to destroy her computer in a fire. I was lucky to recover what I did, and only because she didn't do a good job of it. Most of what melted was casing."
　　Kerry looks up. "She tried to *burn* it?"
　　Pink nods. "Yeah, and also her phone, fax machine, and tablet. One week ago in the middle of the night, she made a huge bonfire of it all. And that same night, she deleted all her social media, changed her email address, and opted out of online banking. None of her passwords are the same." He lists the old passwords as if he's bitter about it, particularly the online banking one.
　　"Why would she do that?"

"To hide something," says Pink, talking too fast. "Something that scared her. I believe it was an email she opened earlier that night about the skull you found. But now that I've read it . . ." He leans over Kerry's shoulder and checks his progress onscreen, tutting impatiently. "You scrolled too long. Go up."

"I don't get it," Kerry says, redundantly, as he scrolls back up through her email history and gets closer to the present day. "She was the one who hired me to go out and map the place."

Pink sits on the edge of the bed. "Yeah. I wonder if she even knows what she did."

Kerry looks up again. "Sorry? What?"

Pink sighs. "Did I ever tell you how long I've watched Diana Wolf?"

Kerry shakes his head, *no*.

"I didn't think so. Twelve years, I've spent following the Wolf family. Her. Thad. Their sons, Jonah and Cyrus." Pink digs out his wallet and pulls a faded Polaroid from it. It's an old family photo of the Wolfs—all four of them—posing on a lawn in front of a painting the two boys made. "Ever since I started hearing the messages in his songs telling me to save her."

Ding-ding!

Twelve years. Messages in songs. Holy shit. No question now: Pink is not the good kind of stalker; he's the untreated psychotic kind. "Okay."

"I know this means I'm sick."

"What's your point?"

Pink twiddles his thumbs, nervous. "She's done this before. Twice."

Kerry's head spins. "Why?"

"Once, it was because of me. I tried to show her . . . what Thad was doing to her with a so-called best friend. Then the very next day, her accounts were all gone just like this, and . . ."

Kerry waits, but the sentence hangs in the air unfinished. "And?"

Pink bites a dirty fingernail, deep in thought. "It was like she didn't remember any of what I sent to her after that. Like she just forgot."

"What? How?"

Pink shrugs. "I don't know. Read the email."

Kerry looks back at the laptop screen. He's not scrolling anymore. His cursor sits at the top of the folder, back at the present day, so he opens what must be her most recent email and starts reading. "Is this it?" he asks, not wanting to waste any more time. "The one from her son? Cyrus?"

Pink nods.

Kerry reads. It starts out pretty normal, but then he sees it and his stomach drops.

I murdered the girl in the woods.

"Fuck."

"Yeah. Tell me when you finish."

"Can you just tell me what it says?" Kerry asks, voice quivering.

"Read."

He reads it, and the message body appears to be fully intact.

I murdered the girl in the woods.

It was seven years ago. I never knew her name. I still don't. She said she was going to Asheville. I used a needle filled with succinylcholine, that muscle relaxant you told us about. Remember? It gave you nightmares when you used to work in the ER. It really is perfect. I got it from a nurse, and it wasn't even hard. You were right. They don't get paid enough.

I hate what I did. But as awful as it is, it's nothing compared to Jonah. What he's done and is still doing.

The problem is, you won't listen to anything I say or write about my brother. You'll come up with a reason not to believe it. I know you—you need to see it for yourself. Luckily, you can. He is careful and smart, but he is not a god, and he never needed to hide things from our family. We hid it all for him. Mom, this part is IMPORTANT: go to the location in the photo I sent. It's the first attachment at the end of this email. I'm faxing it too, so you can't accidentally delete all this.

Find the iron door. Look inside. That's it.

There are directions in the second attachment, the spreadsheet, that can tell you exactly how to find it. It won't be on any map. I don't think I can say much more, not accurately. Already forgetting things. I'm not sober. You just need to trust me and find it. Please.

Do not go to the police or the press. I tried. It only got more people hurt.

When you see it, open the other attachments, because what's behind that door is just the start of it. Then you'll understand what I'm asking you to do. You are one of the only people he still relaxes around. You need to finish the job I couldn't that last morning.

I'm sorry for all this and for being so stupid all this time. I wish I knew ten years ago what I do now. I wish I had just pulled that trigger instead of letting him talk. I wish I could give the girl who was going to Asheville her life back, or trade it for mine. But I can't. I wish you and I could see each other one more time or talk again, and maybe we will someday. But I doubt it.

It meant the world to me when you called. I love you. Bye, Mom.

—Cy

Kerry closes the email and buries his head in his hands. "I *knew* she recognized that skull. You should've seen her face. And see here? She told him what drugs to use to kill this girl. She's been lying this whole time, man, covering up for her kids. She probably knows whatever it is Jonah did too, and that's why she burned her shit."

Pink's mouth gets thin and a skeptical noise escapes. "Eh . . ."

Kerry whirls on him, unhinged. "I am in no mood. No noises. Use your words."

"If Diana knew he murdered the girl, why send this email? What need is there to tell her what he did, how, or when?"

Kerry stares at the wall. "Hmm."

Pink stands and starts to pace. "This is a confession. A cry for help. But what's interesting is how concerned he is she will *choose* not to believe him, *come up with a reason*. I wonder if this has to do with her bouts of convenient amnesia."

"You mean she's just faking it?"

"What I mean is," says Pink, "Diana is in denial. She has learned that when a bad thing happens to her, it hurts less to pretend it never did. Or if that's impossible, that it wasn't bad. So, she pretends to not remember the truth, until maybe one day . . . she truly forgets." He pauses as he makes a connection. "Maybe the very worst memories, she dismisses as nightmares."

Kerry nods, staring at the email again. "What did he mean here, about finishing the job he couldn't?"

Pink makes a face like it's obvious. "He wants her to kill him. Jonah."

"Shit. You're sure?"

"Yes. He's talking about the day Thad disowned him five years ago, after he pointed a shotgun at his brother."

"Hold on," says Kerry, overwhelmed by it all. "Back up. Cy got disowned? Who pointed what gun at who?"

Pink sighs.

* * *

An hour later, he's caught up on most of the relevant Wolf family history. The sky outside is starting to get lighter.

Kerry yawns, exhausted. "Did you recover any attachments?"

"No. She downloaded none. I can only see that he sent six. Big files. And that the first one was a photo." Pink pulls a mangled, burnt piece of paper out of his backpack. "But I also found this crumpled inside what I can only guess was a melted fax machine. Diana must have exotic taste in photo paper or ink, or both, or it would've burned to ash. Remember he mentioned a fax? I believe this is what came out before she could unplug it. The first attachment." He flips it around.

Kerry looks at it, and what he sees makes him shiver.

A photograph.

It's wrinkled to shit, all four corners are torn and jagged, and there are two large holes in it, but the image is clear enough. It's of a black iron door set into a cliff. The door—and the rock on all sides of it—is charred black, like someone started a fire on the other side. Above the cliff, there's a strip of blue sky bisected by a jet trail.

Looking at the photograph reminds Kerry of how cold he felt when he first leapt into the brothers' so-called treehouse. "What do we do? Who do we take this to?"

Pink frowns. "No one. Especially not police."

Kerry laughs. "So what? We just sit on it? Pretend we never saw it?"

"It would be the smartest thing," says Pink, but something's bothering him. "But what if Cy is right?"

"Right how?"

Pink gets a dark, sad look on his face. "What if his brother has done worse than kill a girl and bury her in the woods? Is still doing it? Diana has already chosen to pretend. Whatever it is Cy was trying to stop . . . what if we are the last two people who can stop it?"

Kerry shivers again. "It's not our problem."

Pink nods. "Maybe you're right. But if I'm going to pretend this doesn't exist, I would rather know what *this* is. Or I'll spend the rest of my life imagining . . . won't you?"

Got a point. "Cy said to find this door," says Kerry, "so, say we want to . . . how are we supposed to do that if he left the directions in the second attachment?"

Pink shakes his head. "I don't know."

Kerry breathes in and out, hyperventilating again. He needs to start carrying paper bags. "You know you smell, right?"

Pink laughs. "My Lyft driver down here said the same."

Kerry nods. "Go take a shower. Leave your nasty clothes outside the door, and I'll throw them in the wash. If we're gonna be working on this all day, I want you sterilized before you sit on anything else."

28

Cy

February 12, 2009. 2:19 AM

IT'S A FUCKED-UP thing, knowing you're not crazy when you're surrounded by people saying you are. You start to not know.

Therapy wasn't going well.

"Tell me about the man following you," said the salt-and-pepper-haired psychiatrist, who was sixty but looked forty because he lifted weights and got up at six AM to jog.

Cy blew out a breath of air. "I don't want to talk about that." He'd regretted it the second he let it out the first time. Of course it sounded crazy. It *was* crazy. Everything that had happened since that night with Jonah, it was like the world had gone insane.

But it was true.

A man had been following him.

The first time he'd seen him was at school. The man had been standing across the street, leaned up against an old blue van. He was white, around five foot ten, with a bald head and a short black beard, and wore a white T-shirt with oil stains on the chest. And he was watching Cy. Intently.

The next time Cy had noticed him was at Alistair's house, across the street again. Same van. Same outfit. Same stare.

Then Cy had caught the man strolling behind him as he walked the seven blocks from school to therapy. He broke into a sprint. Lost him.

But of course, then he'd been forced to explain to the salt-and-pepper psychiatrist why he was sweating and out of breath. And now the psychiatrist thought he was crazy too, even though it wasn't even a stretch to imagine; Mom had gotten a restraining order against a stalker a few years back, some dude who was going through her trash and sending her love letters. Maybe this was him again, but coming after her kid this time.

"All right," said the psychiatrist. "What *do* you want to talk about?"

Cy thought about it. "Jonah won't speak to me."

The psychiatrist nodded. Scratched a sentence onto his notepad.

Forty-five minutes later, Cy walked out of the medical building and to Mom's waiting car with a prescription for lithium. Antipsychotics for his budding schizophrenia.

They drove to Brent-Air Pharmacy on the way home and picked the drugs up.

*   *   *

That night, Cy passed Jonah's room on his way to bed and stared at the door.

It had been over three months since he and his older brother had had anything resembling a conversation.

Jonah shouldered past him. "Watch it," he said.

Cy moved aside so he could get to his room.

Jonah leaned in and whispered in his ear, "Don't take the pills."

Cy was stunned. He blinked.

Jonah slammed his bedroom door.

*   *   *

The next morning, Cy was eating Honey Nut Cheerios in the kitchen when a local news story came on.

"Mysterious Killing Thought to Be Gang-Related," read the ticker along the bottom of the screen.

"Los Angeles police are asking the public to help identify a man brutally murdered in the street last night," said the pretty blond anchor. "The slaying, which occurred at one AM in Studio City, was captured on CCTV camera. Take a look."

The news couldn't show the full footage—it was too graphic. But they could show everything leading up to it: a white man walking out of a convenience store, eating something, a burrito maybe, then walking across the street to a dark-colored van. Another man, in black, rushed out of the darkness behind him and put a blade to the man's neck.

Then the footage froze.

Cy dropped his spoon. Milk splashed onto his shirt.

He recognized the van. The man's stained white shirt. The way he walked.

It was him.

It was the man who'd been following him.

And now he was dead.

"Police say the suspect is likely a black male in his thirties, six foot two to six foot four, under two hundred pounds . . ."

Cy shivered, grabbed his backpack, and ran out the door. He didn't want to think about it. Didn't know if it was even real.

After all . . . he hadn't taken his pills.

He drove to school and tried to forget.

* * *

He almost did.

Until that night.

Cy was dreaming when suddenly he was yanked back into reality by a voice at his bedside. "It's time to wake up, little brother."

Cy blinked the sleep away, then turned his head and shrieked.

A black-gloved hand shot out and clamped down on his mouth.

The figure standing at his bedside didn't look like Jonah. It was dressed all in black: black sneakers, black sweatpants, oversized black hoodie with the hood up, black gloves, and . . . a mask. With realistic latex dark-brown skin.

"What the fuck?" Cy mumbled, voice muffled by the glove.

Jonah laughed.

He took his hand off Cy's mouth, then held an index finger up to the mask's lifeless lips.

"Why are you in blackface?"

Jonah didn't say anything.

Cy sat up. "Halloween's not for like, eight months. Racist."

"I know."

Cy stared at him, not knowing what to make of it all. Finally, the question that had been burning in him forced its way through his teeth, and tears bubbled up in his eyes: "It was all real, wasn't it?"

Jonah nodded.

Cy put his head in his hands, not wanting to look at the mask. "Why? Why did you do this to me?"

"To protect you."

Cy shook his head. "From what? Who?"

"More danger than you know."

"Like the man on the news? The one who was following me?"

Jonah stared through the eye slits of the mask, unblinking.

"Did you kill him?"

Jonah shrugged.

"What does that mean? Did you or not?"

"You decide what it means."

"No, Jonah," said Cy. "What is this? The money you had in the spare tire well. Where did it come from?"

"My work," said Jonah simply, as if that explained it all.

"What are you, a hitman?"

Jonah shook his head. "An artist."

Cy groaned. "What the hell do you need more money for?"

"Why were you selling drugs?"

Cy thought about it. "Because I wanted to buy things without Mom and Dad knowing."

Jonah nodded. "The art I make is expensive." He produced a draw-string bag from behind his back and tossed it onto the bed.

Cy opened it nervously while his brother watched.

It was a rubber mask. Like Jonah's, it was a black man's face. But where his was expensive and realistic, Cy's was not. "Fat Albert. Are you fucking kidding me?"

"Put it on."

Cy bristled. "Why do I have to be Fat Albert?"

"Shut up, and do what I tell you." Nothing joking in his tone.

Cy shut up. He put on the mask. It was hot, and it smelled inside. "I can barely see."

"We can fix that later," said Jonah, satisfied that his orders were being followed now. "Get dressed. We're going out."

Cy stood up and went to his closet. "All black?"

Jonah walked up from behind, close enough to make him nervous. "What do you think?"

Cy selected a black hoodie and black jeans. Jonah handed him a pair of leather gloves—black.

"Where are we going?"

"Out." Jonah opened the bedroom door and checked the hallway. Empty.

*   *   *

The drive took half an hour.

It was 3:23 AM when the gray Prius pulled up and parked on the corner of Fifth and Towne streets in downtown. Skid Row.

"Dude. Don't slow down," said Cy, mystified. "What the fuck are you parking here for?"

There were blue tarps strung between poles, cardboard box forts, and camping tents crowding the opposite sidewalk: a full-blown shanty town in the middle of one of the biggest, most well-heeled cities in the developed world. A couple of addicts were openly shooting heroin in the entrance to one of the tents, backlit by a lantern swinging from a rope inside.

Cy could feel hundreds of eyes on them. The clean car that just parked across the road. A Prius.

It always felt strange, seeing this place, being reminded of its existence. You tend to forget it's there, living in L.A. Sandwiched right between the Diamond District and the Arts District: hell on Earth.

Cy pawed at his neck where it met the rubber mask.

"Stop it," Jonah whispered. "We're meeting someone. He's coming."

Cy ignored him, kept itching.

Jonah grabbed his hand and squeezed. "I said, stop it."

Cy twisted out of his grip. "Why?"

"Because I can see your skin when you mess with it."

"Anyone who gets close is gonna be able to tell our eyes are blue."

"Up close, all these are for is to scare people. But to a CCTV camera or a cop down the block, we don't look out of place." Jonah shifted in his seat. "Shut up. Sit still. Let me talk."

A shadowy figure was approaching, jogging down the middle of the street, silhouette lit by a distant trashcan fire.

Jonah rolled his window down a few inches but didn't turn to face it.

A thin black man came into view, hunched over and skittish. "What do you need, bruh?"

Jonah reached under his seat, and his hand came back holding a brick of cash: twenties and hundreds only, stacked and tied into two bundles. Judging by the size of it all, it had to be tens of thousands of dollars in total.

He handed the bundles off through the window, still facing ahead.

The man stuffed them into his coat, looking around again to make sure no one saw.

"One of those is for you," said Jonah, monotone. "The rest is for the traffic cop writing tickets on Fourth Street, around the block from here, number five-fourteen on the hood. But before you give it to him, you're going to give him this card." He reached into his own pocket and produced a Hallmark card, the type you buy at a pharmacy when you forgot your nephew's birthday.

The man at the window took that as well, even more carefully than he had taken the cash.

"Good boy," said Jonah.

Cy flinched at the remark, but the man didn't act angry or even surprised by it.

The man just nodded and left. He slunk back into the street and disappeared in the smoky, sweat-drenched night.

Cy hit his brother on the shoulder, incredulous. "What are you, friends with that guy?"

"No."

"Then what are you doing? He's just gonna take it and you'll never see him again."

Jonah shook his head, rolled up his window.

"How do you know?"

He started the car and pulled away. "It's the same reason you won't ever tell anyone what we did tonight."

Cy paused, wary. "Which is?"

"These people know me."

The next twenty minutes, they drove in silence.

When they got to Sunset, Jonah finally removed his rubber mask. Taking it as a signal, Cy did the same.

He couldn't hold it in any longer. "What was that? I still don't get it." He was questioning his sanity again. None of it made any sense. It was all dream-logic bullshit. *Did we really just drive to Skid Row and give a homeless man, like, forty thousand dollars, or is this what being sick is?*

Jonah smiled, teeth shining in the dark. "You will in the morning. Tonight was a demo. If we're going to make art together, first you need to understand something about money and the things you can buy with it."

"Things like what?"

"Anything."

That was all the explanation he got until they pulled into the driveway outside their house on Tigertail, right next to Thad's red Ford GT.

Jonah turned the engine off, then turned to face him. "Starting now, there are going to be lessons three nights a week."

"Lessons?"

"The first one is in two days. You're going to learn how to use an onion router."

Cy's head was spinning. "An onion router?"

Jonah nodded. "A couple years ago, you'd need a computer science degree to do it, but there's a version now called Tor you can pick up in an hour."

Cy had heard the word but never in a good context. "Isn't that what pedophiles use to share stuff over the internet and not get caught?"

Jonah opened his door, got out. "They're not the only ones."

The boys crept inside.

Jonah took both masks, and they parted ways in the hallway outside both their rooms without another word.

Cy got undressed, folded the black outfit back up, stuffing the pieces in three different drawers, and slipped into bed.

As he lay there, he couldn't stop thinking he should take his meds tomorrow.

It was time to admit it. He was insane.

*   *   *

Cy woke up to a familiar sound: Thad barking at someone on the phone downstairs. "What the *fuck* do you mean, don't know who did it?"

He stretched. Got up. Brushed his teeth.

He took his pills.

He walked downstairs in his underwear. The sound of Thad yelling was now muffled, as he had clearly taken the conversation outside. In the kitchen, he found Jonah eating the remainder of an omelet at the island. As he entered, his brother promptly stood up, took his plate with him, and exited the room without a word. *So it was a dream.*

He sighed.

He was pouring himself a bowl of cereal when he realized whom Thad was yelling at on the phone outside. It was the cops. "I *will* take this up to the commissioner, ya sorry dispatch minimum-wage piece o' shit!"

He walked outside to see what the fuss was.

What he saw in the driveway was funny at first: Thad throwing a tantrum in his full golf outfit—plaid pants, spikes, one white leather glove on his hand like Michael Jackson. Then Cy realized what he was so mad about, and his blood ran cold. Standing in the doorway, Jonah smirked as he held a finger to his lips.

There was a yellow metal boot on the wheel of Thad's Ford GT. A parking cop had locked it.

29

Kerry

November 14, 2019. 6:28 AM

WHILE PINK IS in the shower, Kerry grabs some old clothes from deep in his closet—middle school era—and folds them neatly on the bed. Then he walks down the hall in his socks, as stealthily as he can.

He told Pink to leave them out, and sure enough there's a pile of dirty clothes next to the bathroom door. He gathers it all up and brings it downstairs, plops the pile on top of his laundry machine, and then systematically turns out all the pockets.

The ratty wallet falls out of his pants.

Kerry starts the laundry, then thumbs through its contents while monitoring the sounds of running water upstairs. Inside is about what he expected: four single dollar bills, crumpled; two neatly folded napkins covered with notes in blue ink, illegible; the NY State ID card he saw earlier; the faded old Polaroid of the Wolf family, still creepy; a twenty-dollar Visa gift card, long expired. That's it.

Kerry frowns. He's about to put the wallet down and forget he was ever suspicious in the first place . . . then he notices the weight.

There's something else in it.

He feels around the tattered old leather, and right between two duct-taped seams, something hard pokes through. *There it is.* A gap. A slit in the duct tape behind the billfold.

Kerry teases it open and pulls out the three cards inside.

Driver's licenses: California, Montana, and Georgia. All three have Pink's face on them, but it's three different pictures of him, and none say his name is *Gopsikopolis*. The names are all different. All three cards feel like the real deal. Fakes this good are expensive. *Who is this guy?*

The water shuts off upstairs.

He slides the fake IDs back into place and puts the ratty wallet on top of the machine, like he never opened it.

*   *   *

Kerry is sitting at a desk in his bedroom, freaking out, trying to distract himself by scouring the internet for discreet methods to locate the iron door in the photo, when Pink appears dressed in a vintage black "*Metallica*" T-shirt and a pair of baggy Levi's. There weren't any shoes close to his size, so his taped-up Nikes complete the look.

He admires himself in a mirror next to the bed. "I can't remember the last time I felt so clean. Thank you, again."

Kerry looks up and winces. Now that Pink isn't wearing a beanie, the top half of his head is exposed for the first time, revealing a nasty scar on his left ear. Pity stirs deep in Kerry's chest. It's not a scar you can miss—or ignore.

Pink notices him staring and holds a hand up to hide it. "Is there a hat I can . . .?"

He nods, feeling like a jerk. "Sure." He rises to help, then he remembers. "I wanted to ask you a question first, though."

Pink sits on the bed and hangs his head, not listening. "I have a confession to make."

"What's your *real*—" Kerry sputters to a halt, mid-accusation. "Wait, what?"

Pink glances up at him sadly, then his eyes return to the hands clasped tight in his lap. "You've been to me, I think, kinder and more trusting than anyone I ever met. And I was wrong to chastise you for it, because kindness like yours is something very rare. Rare and precious." He sighs, shakes his head. "I was lost, and you reminded me: *I must try to get better.* I need help. But so did you when you trusted a stranger with your laptop." He fidgets and chews on his lip, like he's struggling to articulate an important point. "I think I . . . need you to have been right to trust me. And this is a problem because all I have done so far to repay your trust is steal your passwords."

Kerry narrows his eyes. "Go on."

Pink takes a big breath, and his hunched shoulders drop from his ears. "I lied to you. My name is not *Panaggiotis*. I've never been to Greece—or to any country outside this one. The ID I showed to you is a fake. Just one of several I use."

Kerry waits. "I know."

Pink nods, unsurprised. "You went through my wallet."

Kerry smirks. "Not as trusting as you thought."

Pink laughs. "Maybe not."

"What do you mean, *maybe*?"

Pink ignores him. "If you want, I'll undo all of it, change all your passwords to two-factor, answer any questions you have, and teach you how to lock me out in the future. I'll also understand if you ask me to leave now, or call the police. You can. Maybe that's the best thing for me, if it leads me back to treatment. Just please, for your sake, if all this with the Wolfs is not in my sick head and is as real as I fear it is . . . do not mention that email to them. Forget it."

Kerry thinks about it. "All right. Lots to unpack here." He rubs his eyes, too exhausted to say with any confidence if he's making the right call or if there even is one. "First thing: What accounts did you get access to, and what did you do with it?"

"All of them." Pink sighs. "And uh . . . nothing."

"Bullshit." On both counts; he can't know it's *all*. And who would even want to hack an XVideos account?

Pink blushes. "No. You see, I watched you for longer than I said."

Kerry's stomach sinks, full of dread. "What does that mean? How much longer?"

"The day after Diana Wolf contacted you, I logged into your bank accounts. Both of them."

He knows about the stash. "Fuck you. How?"

Pink scratches the back of his head, not sure how to say it tactfully. "Your passwords suck. Numbers on the end do nothing if they are always *sixty-nine*." He gets a guilty look on his face. "And you need to stop clicking links in strange emails."

Fair. "Yeah. Cool. Blame me for it."

"Sorry," says Pink.

Kerry shakes his head, trying to get his thoughts in order again. "Jesus, man . . ."

Pink nods.

Kerry rolls his eyes. "You know as well as I do, I'm not calling the cops on you. Dick."

Pink looks up, shocked. "I do?"

Kerry nods. "I was freaking the fuck out *well* before you showed me that email. And *I'm* not crazy." He's pretty sure, at least. "I can't trust cops, and I don't want to be alone. This is real."

Pink nods. "Shit."

Kerry smiles in agreement. "That said, why should I believe anything you tell me now? How can I?"

Pink shrugs, alarmed. "I had no reason to tell you other than shame."

Kerry isn't so sure he agrees, but that doesn't mean it's a lie. "What's your real name, Pink?"

"Please. Don't make me say it aloud." Pink trembles, on the verge of tears.

Kerry frowns. "What? Why?"

"I will answer any other question you have. *Please.*"

Kerry digs his heels in. "No. This one."

Pink starts to cry. He sobs.

Kerry lets him this time. He waits. And waits.

The sobs peter out.

When Pink finally speaks, he does so slowly and seriously, as if giving voice for the first time to a painful thought he's heard thousands of times in his head. "My *real* name is my father's name. I won't say it. His memory dies with me."

Kerry looks into his eyes . . . and believes him. "Fine." He pauses, thinking of a suitable replacement question. "What happened to your ear?"

Pink laughs. "Funny. The answer to that is also my father's name."

Kerry says nothing, waiting.

"He was sick too. I don't know if it was sick like me, but . . . . sick. It doesn't matter. Everything bad humans do, we could say, is due to sickness, and no one sane is ever responsible for the bad things. No one can ever be blamed." He sneers. "*Fuck that.* I blame him. For this ear, and every other evil choice. It's like you reminded me: we are not to blame for who we are, but for the world to be a decent place . . . we must be to blame for who we try to be."

Kerry waits patiently, but the story never arrives. "Pink?"

Pink stares at him, glassy-eyed.

Kerry stares back. "What did he do to your ear . . .?"

Pink closes his eyes and nods, resigned. "We were living in a tent we shared with his dealer. I woke up to a stranger holding my arms down, while my father broke a bottle and took it to my ear. I kicked and screamed. They told me there was a chip in me, and it needed to come out. They were laughing." He grimaces, reliving it. "It was two years after that, I ran away for the last time."

Kerry frowns. *Two years after that.* "Man. I'm so sorry."

Pink smiles. "I know you are. That's why I told you."

"Why did you stay . . .?"

Pink takes a second, as if asking himself the same. "He was all I had."

Kerry says nothing. Nothing *to* say. So, he just walks to the bed, sits down right next to Pink, and bear-hugs him.

Pink is taken by surprise by this and doesn't hug back. In fact, he actively squirms. "What are you doing? Stop."

Kerry hugs harder. "Shh. It's just a hug."

A moment passes in silence.

Pink eventually stops struggling and lets it happen, more or less.

Another moment passes.

Pink hugs back.

Kerry smiles, then pats his back as they part. He stands up. "When this is all over, I'll drive you to a psychiatrist myself. Promise." He walks to his desk and sits again, motioning for Pink to come look. "And you *will* be changing all my passwords and teaching me how to lock you out. But today, we've got work to do."

Pink stands up and wanders to the desk, looking over Kerry's shoulder at his computer screen. "Why on Earth are you on *4chan*?"

Kerry looks back at him, grinning. "You know it?" Anyone who browses the internet long enough eventually hears a story about *4chan*. Home of alt-right incel trolls, Bronies, the best and worst memes anywhere, and if you know where to look, a smattering of terrifyingly capable hackers, anarchists, and wannabe domestic terrorists.

Pink reads what he sees onscreen. "Tell me this post isn't you. My god."

Kerry's grin disappears. "What?"

"*Kerry,*" says Pink, panicking. "You posted the photo? On *4chan*? And you *asked* for their help?"

Kerry gets defensive. "What's wrong with that? I made up a fake story." Not a stellar one, but still; he'd said the photo had been left to him by a distant aunt, and the iron door supposedly hid a stash of his great-grandfather's ill-begotten Krugerrands. He just needed help locating it, that's all.

Pink frets. "Yes. I can see that." His eyes linger on one line, and he pauses. "Nice touch with the racist coins."

Kerry beams. "Right?" He hangs a hand in the air, but he doesn't get the high-five he was after. "Look. I checked online, and I don't think there's anyone we can pay to just, like, pinpoint the location in an old photo. We can't go to cops. So where else is there for us to start?"

Pink's eyes get big. "So many places!"

Kerry swats away the criticism. "So what? It's just a dart throw. No one will even see it."

Pink seethes. "But why take the risk at all?"

Kerry pulls up a new tab. Googles *shia labeouf flag 4chan* and opens the first result, a *Vice* article. "Read it. I always thought it'd be cool to try something like this. Crowdsource detective work. It works! You won't believe how easily they found this art project Shia was doing."

Pink looks at the page, and his face scrunches up in recognition. "I know about the stupid flag. Idiot. These degenerates are not just going to do the same for our door."

"Why not?"

"You're not famous, and they don't despise you. And if you know this site, you must know they don't take kindly to outsiders who want to use them as a personal army. Idiot."

Kerry opens his mouth, but a rebuttal doesn't materialize. "Hey, man," he manages, "I don't see you bursting with ideas."

Pink laughs, but it's not a happy laugh. "You posted here because you have seen these trolls do impossible things. No?"

Kerry thinks about it. "I guess so."

"Yes. I know. I have seen things too. Awful things." Pink shivers. "They're not genies who grant wishes. This is more like . . . wishing to a monkey's paw."

"The fuck is a monkey's paw?"

Pink makes a frustrated noise, and a big vein throbs on his forehead. "It's bad. Trust me. Let me sit."

Kerry leans back and crosses his arms. "Trust me, he says . . ."

"Shush. Damage is done. I may as well try to salvage what you gave me."

"How?"

"*Shush.*" Pink shoves him out of his office chair and takes over at the computer. He starts typing furiously.

Kerry pouts as he tries to keep up with what's happening onscreen. It's not easy until Pink starts writing in full sentences. "You're just doing the same thing!"

Pink shakes his head gravely. "Oh goodness, no. What you did was a terrible idea. Awful." He types another line, capping off his post. "But it's done. What I'm doing now is mocking you and inviting others to do the same."

"Hey!"

Pink ignores him. "Now. You will post as a new identity on your phone. You will then also mock yourself. Then I'll use a third identity to go against this new trend of us mocking you, and announce how I've played along and concluded *exactly* where our photo was taken because I'm so good at this, it was child's play. This post will be very detailed and *very wrong*. So wrong, hopefully, that a real troll will swallow the bait and take it upon himself to prove how wrong we are to us, out of spite. And then, if enough of them start to despise us, like what happened to Shia LaBeouf's stupid flag... your stupid plan may just work . . . or more likely, it still doesn't." He pauses, a dark look on his face. "Or this mob of lowlifes turns on us, doxxes us, and ruins our lives. But if I supervise, I doubt it."

Kerry grins. "You really hate these people, huh?" It's a side of Pink he's never seen before—pissed off. *Been this way since his dad came up.*

Pink snorts. "I think this is kind, to say *people*."

"But you think this, uh, modified plan has a chance."

"Tiny."

Kerry slips out his phone, ready to help. "I'm sold. Lead on."

Pink nods. "Good. You now." He hits "*Enter*" and posts his first message, a four-paragraph rant on how offensive and utterly entitled he found Kerry's original post, and a call to arms for other users to dox him based on a long, flawed investigation into his supposed posting history on /poll/, the site's politics board.

"Cool. So. *Doxxing*," says Kerry, reading. "That's when they find out where I live and post it online, right?" His nerves are flaring up. The part of the plan where *they* suggest someone should dox him went unmentioned just now. "What if they actually do it?"

"They will not," says Pink, confident. "I asked them to."

"Ah."

They type in silence for a good twenty minutes, both of them getting into faux arguments with each other and themselves. Playing both sides, teasing new blood to join the fray.

Eventually, there are real users posting in the threads. Arguing.

Then one of them tells Pink (or one of his fake users) he's a *fucking moron*.

How else does someone think that photo is in Tennessee? the thread says. *The plants SCREAM cali.*

Pink gets excited, tapping his foot. "Do we see . . . a lead? I may have spoken too soon about this plan."

Kerry grabs his shoulder encouragingly, then gets back to work.

Ten minutes pass, then suddenly there's a breakthrough. An anonymous user posts a version of their photo with a filter applied—some algorithm that sharpens details. There's no text in the post. The altered photo speaks for itself. It now shows two—not one—jet trails in the sky above the iron door. One of them was too faint to notice in the original. The white lines cross thousands of feet above the cliff, like swords slicing through blue air.

Pink recoils in surprise. "My god. It's like the stupid flag."

Kerry punches the air. "Shia LaBeouf!"

* * *

An hour later, several more users have concluded, by analyzing the angle of the two jet trails and cross-referencing all the flight paths of major airlines operating in America, that the photograph was taken somewhere in Malibu, California. Judging by a streak of seagull shit on a rock nearby, says one user, the cliff face—and the iron door—is near the coast, maybe a mile inland from the Pacific Ocean.

Git gud cuckie, a user replies to Pink's original identity.

Pink starts to reply, but before he has half a post written, someone else beats him to it: *Wheres it in Malibu smh u guys didnt find shit.*

New users swarm in this new set of replies.

Pink sits back, hands off the keyboard. "I guess . . . we just supervise now." He frowns.

Kerry slips his phone back into his pocket. "That was fast." He leans over Pink's shoulder and watches as the chain of posts grows and grows. "This is good, right?"

Pink takes a long time to answer, staring at all the new posts like he's staring at a wildfire.

30

Cy

May 16, 2009. 8:34 PM

THE LESSONS WERE boring until they got to Krav Maga. Jonah presented his little brother with a black hunting knife, identical to his own. "Do you want to learn to use it?"

Cy did.

The two wolves rented a studio in Burbank for two hours a night, and they practiced religiously. Mom thought it was therapy, but Cy hadn't gone in months. Jonah was paying an actor three hundred dollars per session to show up to the new psychiatrist and fake schizophrenia symptoms, all so they could have this alone time together. To train.

As for Jonah? Everyone thought he was on a lacrosse team.

* * *

On the drive home one night, Cy was rattling off answers to one of his brother's quizzes—this one was on exit node eavesdropping and basic safety precautions for staying anonymous on the deep web—when his phone buzzed in his pocket. *Bzzzz.*

He slipped it out and saw a text from his friend, Alistair: *Dude where the fuck have you been, I keep trying to . . .*

"Don't answer that," said Jonah, staring at the road.

Cy sighed. "I know." He silenced it, then put the phone back in his pocket. He was bleeding friends, but his brother didn't care; the lessons took priority. Always.

He aced the quiz questions.

At Kenter and Sunset, Jonah turned and took a brief detour to where Cy had parked his car—a silver Camry that Mom had given to him on his sixteenth birthday in February—so they could come inside separately.

* * *

At home, the two wolves kept their distance.

Jonah told their parents he was *"making an effort"* with his little brother, so it wouldn't be suspicious if they spent time together in the house, but most nights his door stayed locked. He had his own affairs to take care of. Secret things. His "art," he said.

Sometimes it was just a painting.

Sometimes, he'd sneak out and be gone overnight, and he'd refuse to say where he went or why.

Cy sat at the desk in his bedroom and stewed. He wasn't stupid; he was acutely aware of just how little he'd been told about what all this was leading up to.

So he was spying on his older brother.

He booted up his computer to check on Jonah's phone. For three nights now, he'd been running a nasty piece of software he found using Tor that exploited a flaw in the latest iOS update—*fix incoming. get it while it's hot!* its creator had warned on the private forum hosting it— to enable remote access to any iPhone's SIM data; all it needed was a phone number and a PIN. Jonah had muttered his when he was bleeding out in the Prius, and Cy remembered it: *8992.*

So far, Cy hadn't found shit. Nothing that helped explain all his brother's money or where he kept disappearing to at night. Jonah never sent any incriminating texts or emails to anyone. At least, not on his phone. Tonight was no exception, it seemed.

But then he noticed something in Jonah's contacts. A lot of them didn't contain any contact info. It looked like his brother had deleted the contacts from his phone, but the folders themselves were still archived on his SIM card. And the names didn't sound like people:

R&R Holdings
Romulus Industries
Romana Inc.

Pax Industries
R&R Mythica
Visigoth Workshops
Vandal Sciences

There were more, and they were all similar. Nineteen in total.

A list of companies?

Cy spent half an hour scouring the internet for details. He hit on four of the names. All four were corporations that had been registered in Wyoming for less than a year before going defunct. All created and dissolved within the last five years, never overlapping with one another.

And that was it; he couldn't find any other info. No websites. No mentions of what they had done or sold.

He sighed, frustrated.

The intercom beeped on the far wall, and Mom's voice blasted from a speaker. "Would my beautiful, beautiful children please grace us with their presence in the family room? Your father and I have an announcement to make!"

He rolled his eyes, tilted his head back until his neck felt like it might snap, and powered down his computer. Stared at the white ceiling and listened. No footsteps came from Jonah's room down the hall.

Nope. Cy wasn't going downstairs first.

Inevitably, the intercom beeped again. "It's good news!"

Silence.

A minute later, the intercom beeped once more. "Now. Get down here, both of you."

A creak down the hall. Footsteps, marching downstairs.

Cy exited his room and followed Jonah down the staircase. They met up at the bottom and marched grimly into the family room together. A misnomer, for the most part: the "family room" was just a formal living room, and it was the one Mom usually used to entertain guests.

"There you are!" said Diana, sitting on the arm of a big leather chair occupied by her husband.

Thad looked exhausted and bored. *Probably sober.*

"Sit, sit," she said.

The boys sat on opposite ends of the long couch and waited.

She tried to look coy. "Well?"

"What's up?" asked Cy, humoring her.

"You'll never guess," she said, giggling. "It has to do with a house."

Thad sighed. "Christ, baby, don't make it a game."

Diana's cheeks ran scarlet. "Fine. Sorry for being fun." She turned back to her sons and bit her lip. "I'll just say it: the house in Tennessee got finished early. Two years early!"

The brothers said it at the same time: "Yay . . ."

Diana jumped up off the arm of Thad's chair and danced in the middle of the room. Cy and Jonah shared a look. They'd both seen this particular take on the cabbage patch before. "Oh yeah!" She stopped. Looked around the room. "Guys? I don't get it. Why are you all so nonplussed about this?"

Thad snorted.

"I guess it's cool," said Cy, feeling bad, "but you're still not moving for two or three years, right?"

Mom and Thad had been building Wolf Hollow forever. The plan had always been to build their dream house, where they'd retire to after both sons left for college. *After. Both.* Jonah would be starting at NYU in the fall, but Cy was still finishing up his sophomore year at Harpers-Exeter. Then he still had two years of high school left.

"No, silly!" Diana sat on the couch between her sons and pulled them in close. "I made a decision with your father," she said, and this explained why he looked so haggard, "and we're moving in! We can be in the new house by the end of May if we put our minds to it and get down to packing. What do you guys say?"

Cy stared at her, dumbfounded. "But I have school."

Diana stared back at him. "So? There are schools in Nashville."

He opened and closed his mouth, on the verge of tears.

Jonah laughed. "Fuck you."

Diana was shocked. "Excuse me?"

Jonah stood up, pacing like a lion in a cage. "Fuck you, I said."

"Hey!" boomed Thad, still seated. "You do not talk to your mother that way."

Jonah turned on him. "Or what, old man? Are you gonna whip me with your belt?" He laughed coldly.

Diana sat stock-still on the couch, face white.

Thad leapt from his chair, squared up, and landed a right hook to Jonah's jaw.

His son fell. Diana screamed.

On the floor, Jonah laughed and blood ran from his mouth down his shirt.

Cy stood up and his hand went automatically to the hunting knife hidden in his belt, but Jonah glared at him. *Don't.*

"Don't get up," said Thad.

Jonah smiled. He stood up.

Thad threw a haymaker, but Jonah caught his wrist in one hand and twisted. The old man cried out in pain.

"*Stop!*" Diana wailed.

Jonah just held his father by the wrist, immobilized.

Thad grimaced, teeth locked, as he glanced meekly up at his son.

Jonah smiled, and his blue eyes burned. Then he let go. He left the family room and climbed the stairs without a word.

Diana wept.

Thad rubbed at his wrist, ego bruised but otherwise unhurt.

Neither parent seemed to notice when Cy left.

He flew up the stairs, two at a time, and got to the door before it had closed behind Jonah, so he shoved his way in.

"What?" Jonah retrieved a can of Coke from a mini-fridge, pressed it to his swollen jaw, and sat on the bed.

There was a new painting on an easel in the corner, almost finished. It was of a headless woman breastfeeding a limp child. Cy nodded at it. "I see you're branching out."

"Ha."

Cy got serious. "What the fuck was that?"

Jonah sighed. "I know. Sorry. I just hate how unfair this is to you."

Cy was taken aback by that. "You what?"

"She promised they'd leave after you were gone to school," said Jonah, voice cracking. "And now you're missing out on junior and senior year. It's not like skipping fourth grade. They're asking you to make all new friends, then leave again after two years."

Cy didn't buy it. There was an emotion in those oh-so-cold blue eyes he'd never seen before, hot and chaotic and noticeable. *Panic.* That would explain the thin excuse. A shiver tiptoed down his spine. He had never caught his older brother lying this badly. His phone still had that text from Alistair on it, unanswered. "Really?"

Jonah frowned. "Really."

Cy nodded. "Okay." He left.

He walked down the hall to his own room convinced of one thing. Jonah was mad about the move for some other reason.

He threw open his bedroom door, locked it, and sat at his desk. Booted up his computer.

*   *   *

Four hours later, he had gotten nowhere.

He was staring at an Excel spreadsheet containing all nineteen company names he had gotten off Jonah's SIM card, each of their registration dates and the dates they were dissolved, and not much else. He was out of ideas. It was pointless to keep searching for more info online.

He shut his eyes.

And then it was there, perched on his shoulder: *inspiration.*

He leapt out of his chair and ran downstairs, then out through the garage to the driveway.

Jonah was always harping on "practical hacks." The idea being that when people think of hacking, they think of a black screen with green letters and a guy typing five hundred words a minute, but that isn't reality. The most vulnerable part of any security system is the end user. Everyone is human. Even Jonah Wolf. And humans make mistakes. In his room, Cy had seen a mini fridge and a trash bin full of Coke cans next to it.

Nobody else in the family drank the red ones.

Cy turned on his phone's flashlight and unlatched the tall gate in the driveway that hid their garbage bins. Inside, he flipped open the lids of all three bins and searched.

Eureka. In the black bin were two big black trash bags and one small, clear bag full of red cans. Jonah's trash.

Cy lifted it out and it ripped, spilling cans everywhere. He cursed and froze in place, listening. It would be just like Thad to hear someone going through the trash and come stomping out with a shotgun. But no one came to investigate.

Cy sifted through the bag. At first, nothing but cans.

Then he noticed it—a piece of paper, crumpled up and torn. He smoothed it out and held the torn parts together, then shined his light on what looked like a shopping list, written in pencil: generator, lumber, nails, rivets, wiring, lights, zip ties, animal feed. All huge quantities.

Then there was a long list of addresses.

At the end of it, a scrawled note:

for M.T. —
1 from each. no english
min 4 total. needed 6 incl spoilage
did alone. watch back + check for blades
2–4 months

It gave him a bad feeling, but none of the words meant anything to him.

He googled the first address on the list: *2745 Teller Rd, Thousand Oaks, CA 91320.* It was a Home Depot, forty-five minutes away. He googled the next one, a Lowe's in Santa Clarita. The next one, a Home Depot. The next one, same, a different location. All of them far, far away from each other and from Brentwood.

Cy heard footsteps. He turned off his flashlight and hid behind the recycling bin.

A door shut softly—the side door that led into the kitchen. The steps walked past the tall gate, and he kneeled to get a look underneath at the shoes: black sneakers. Jonah.

Cy breathed in sharply, tensing.

But Jonah walked past the gate, oblivious to his presence.

Nearby, a car door unlocked with a quiet *beep.*

Cy checked the time: 3:21 AM. *Where the hell are you going?*

Heart pounding, he peeked over the gate and watched Jonah climb into his gray Prius. Once the engine came on, Cy could see his face lit up by the glowing dash display. Jonah looked unhappy, which was confirmed when he lashed out and punched the steering wheel.

Then his face reverted to a neutral mask, he put the car into reverse, and he drove.

Cy hesitated. *Fuck it.*

He ran back inside, grabbed his car keys, and ran out again. Jumped into his Camry and flipped a screeching U-turn back down Tigertail Road.

He caught up to the gray Prius at the light on Sunset. Two cars back.

Cy thought, not for the first time, about how he and his brother used to debate the utility of certain car colors. Gray and silver, they agreed, were the most anonymous. Cy's silver Camry probably had thirty thousand twins in Los Angeles. Same for the gray Prius.

But Jonah's car had a vanity plate, a whale's tail and a simple combination of letters: *TDJCW.* The first letter in each family member's name, plus a "W" for *Wolf.* It had been Mom's car, briefly, before she ditched it for a Tesla, then a Maserati, then a Jag.

Jonah turned right on Sunset, driving west toward the ocean.

Cy followed the whale's tail.

CHAPTER

31

Kerry

November 14, 2019. 7:51 PM

"THIS IS GETTING out of hand," says Kerry, eyes glued to his phone. "Like . . ."

Pink nods. Both hands rest on the bedspread at his sides, off his keyboard. "You possess a knack for understatement, my friend. This is worse than I ever could have . . ." He trails off and shakes his head at the laptop screen.

They sit in silence.

Neither of them has posted in hours. They don't need to.

The treasure hunt they started now has a life of its own. Hundreds of users are involved, and counting. Only one in fifty is helping, and twice as many anarchists are actively sabotaging their efforts, but each new helpful post brings some unique factoid or arcane observation to the table: the angle of the sun's rays hitting the cliff; a shadow under a protruding rock, no bigger than a few pixels; a curiously tilted layer of limestone jutting out of the dirt, left by an ancient earthquake. It's like watching piranhas devour a cow, darting out of the murk one after another until it's picked to the bone. And the cow's almost gone. In a single afternoon, the pseudo-hive mind has assembled a body of clues that no single person on Earth could've put together on their own. Not in a year.

It's dark out in Tennessee, but not in Malibu. Kerry and Pink know this because one of the trolls set up a livestream on Twitch where the whole world can now watch him driving a Jeep Wrangler out to the iron door—or, the set of bluffs where everyone on /pol/ thinks the iron door is. In an unholy turn of events, *4chan*'s infamous politics board was where the hoax had found most of its hardcore fans, which Pink blamed on the Krugerrands. "Your story was too good. Apartheid racism and buried gold are like catnip to frustrated white men."

Kerry glances down at the viewer count. *Holy shit.* "Pink, do you see how many?"

Pink nods gravely.

As the troll drives—his face is obscured by a black-and-white skull bandana, but he's pale, hairless, and his stomach is a tight fit under the steering wheel—he shouts out coordinates, using a satellite phone to keep track of his position. In return, viewers and /pol/ users plug in the coordinates and match still frames captured from the Twitch stream to the original photo, trying to triangulate the iron door's precise location.

Turn around, bitch! Turn! says one /pol/ user.

The skull-faced troll turns around. Heads back south on the Pacific Coast Highway.

Too far! Turn, bitch, turn!

The skull-faced troll flips another U-turn.

"That's the forty-sixth *different* popcorn-eating gif I've seen today," mutters Kerry, who's been keeping track to pass the time. "Why do people make so many? Do they convey different things, or . . .?"

Pink leans in closer, one hand covering his mouth.

"Like, is the Michael Jackson one for when you feel a little bad about eating the popcorn, but the Stephen Colbert one is like, schadenfreude?"

Pink shushes him.

Kerry shuts up.

THAT'S THE STREET! TUUUURRRRNNNN! says a chorus of Twitch users spamming the live chat.

The Jeep's tires screech—*skrrrrrt*—as the skull-faced troll veers right onto a small, steep side road. *"Winding Way,"* says the blue street sign. The road snakes uphill for a mile or so. At the end, it turns into dirt.

Memories of TPP intensifying, says one user, as the Twitch chat goes wild with minute directions, ninety percent of them conflicting.

"Guys, fuck off," says the skull-faced troll. "Where am I going? What's the consensus?"

RIGHT, MOTHERFUCKER, RIGHT! says a growing number of people in the chat, spamming it to drown out the anarchists, who are now just posting random Gameboy controller inputs.

"The road ends," says the skull-faced troll. "I'm parking. It's on foot from here, boys."

I'm not your boy . . .! This post includes the n-word at the end, only spelled with @ symbols instead of "G's." It gets a big laugh out of the skull-faced troll, who reads it aloud on his stream. The Twitch chat floods with vicious racial slurs, barely disguised to get past the site's language filters.

Kerry winces. "Ugh, these people are the fucking *worst*."

Pink nods.

"Oh, shit. The fuck . . ." says the skull-faced troll. "What do we have here?" He angles his camera down and shows off what he's found: a fake bush, old and fraying at the edges of its leaves but still realistic. He pulls on a branch, and it crumbles into a pile of rotted plastic, revealing a hidden path off the side of the dirt road.

WHAT THE FUUUUUUCCCCCKKKKKK!!!!!!! screams half the internet, it seems. The Twitch chat goes nuts. It's scrolling too fast for Kerry to read, there's so many people posting.

It's an internet legend in the making.

Kerry and Pink lean forward simultaneously.

The camera follows the path for a few minutes, pointed at the ground. The sun starts to set. The dirt path gets darker and darker. A black spider skitters past a pair of open-toed sandals. Pained, wheezing huffs punctuate each footstep as the noise from PCH and the beach dies off, absorbed by the undergrowth.

The feet stop. The camera rights itself. The skull-faced troll catches his breath, unable to speak.

There's a gray cliff face ahead, twenty yards away in a clearing.

There's a black door.

In the dark, it's tough to tell, but it looks like it's made of iron. Hanging half open on its hinges. Burnt.

"What do you think, boys?" says the skull-faced troll. "Should I go insi—"

The livestream goes white. Empty.

"*What!*" screams Kerry.

A message pops up from Twitch: *The community has closed this channel because of terms of service violations.*

"I don't get it. What did he do?"

Pink rolls his eyes. "Trespassing."

*　*　*

Two hours later, there's no update.

Kerry slaps himself on the cheek, struggling to stay awake. "What's the deal? What are people saying?"

Pink browses /pol/ and Twitch, ravenously hitting "Refresh" to see if there's any news from the cut-short livestream. "People are writing articles already . . . nothing yet we didn't know. Everyone's waiting."

"Articles?"

Pink sighs. "Thousands of people are going to read about this." He hangs his head in shame. "I'm sorry. I should've stopped you."

Kerry shakes his head, falls back onto his pillow and stares up at the ceiling. "Nah. Don't be sorry. It worked better than I could've *dreamed*, shit . . ." If he'd dreamed this, it'd be a nightmare. They couldn't have lost control of Cyrus Wolf's photo faster, or publicized it better, if they'd sent it to every major newspaper in the country. Which is exactly what Cy warned his mom not to do. *It only got more people hurt*, he said last time he went to the press.

Is that what they just did?

Pink yawns. "I guess we just wait and hope the morning brings good news."

"Yeah. Sounds good." The yawn was infectious, and it's not long before Kerry comes down with a bad case. "I can hope." He closes his eyes.

32

Cy

May 22, 2009. 3:48 AM

C Y FOLLOWED THE gray Prius at a distance, traveling just below the speed limit on PCH.

They were passing through Malibu when Jonah veered right up a tiny, near-vertical side street. *Winding Way.*

Cy veered right too. The street lived up to its name, curving back and forth like a snake and getting even more vertical and narrow as he drove, until finally it turned into dirt.

He saw the Prius, empty, sitting on the side of a fire road fifty yards ahead of him. No sign of Jonah.

Cy killed his engine and got out, then used his phone's flashlight to illuminate the ground as he walked to the other car. But there were no footprints in the dirt to indicate where his brother had gone.

Fuck.

Then he noticed a path on the side of the road across the street.

Someone had moved aside a fairly convincing plastic bush—it must have been concealing the path's entrance. The path was narrow, well-worn, and it led directly into the brush. Cy climbed onto the hood of the Prius to get a better vantage point. The brush stretched back into the palisades for miles, nothing but brown and gray bushes, weeds, and dried-up trees.

His stomach sank.

Uneasy, he got down. Picked his way down the concealed dirt path.

After ten minutes, he came to a small oval clearing, right up against a cliff face. The sea was close, maybe a mile away; Cy could smell the brine, dead fish, and seabird shit.

He also smelled gasoline.

He looked closer at a shadow on the cliff and saw where his brother must have gone.

There was an iron door cut into the cliff, wide open on massive hinges set into the stone with huge rivets.

Beyond its threshold, a dark tunnel.

Wood beams lined its walls and ceiling, and it looked like an old mineshaft, like a picture out of a textbook about the Gold Rush. There was something moving in the deep parts of the shadows inside.

Cy darted off the path to hide behind a tree.

Jonah backed out of the tunnel, holding an open can of gasoline in both hands. He swung it in sweeping arcs, making sure to soak the wood support beams.

When the gas ran out, he threw the plastic container into the tunnel and shut the iron door. Its hinges whined.

Jonah stepped back, dug a matchbook out of his jacket, and struck a flame on his jeans. Dropped the lit match at his feet.

A trail of fire raced under the iron door, and the gas beyond ignited with a *swoosh*. Flames licked the cliff as they tried to escape through the gaps at the door's edges, framing his brother's silhouette in a hellish rectangle of orange-red light.

Cy stepped out from behind the tree. Jonah heard him, turned around, and stared.

"What the fuck is this?" he shouted, breathless. "This is where you go at night, isn't it? Isn't it!"

Jonah said nothing.

Cy just stood there, blocking his path.

Jonah hung his head. Then he sat.

Cy wasn't sure what it meant or how to react. He walked closer.

Jonah looked up at his little brother. Silhouetted by the fire raging behind him, his face was tough to make out, but his cheeks looked wet. He sniffled. "This isn't how I wanted you to . . . I should've brought you here myself."

Cy gestured to the burning hellhole. "Did you build it?"

Jonah nodded. "And I thought I'd have another four months to use it. Then I was going to show you."

Cy understood. "This is why you blew up at Mom."

Jonah smiled weakly. "Sorry I lied."

"What the fuck is it?"

Jonah looked down at his chest, like he was ashamed. "I'm not a normal person, Cy."

"*No.* What's inside?"

"You won't understand if you see it now."

"Fuck you." Cy turned and walked back to the path. "I'm calling *911* before you start a wildfire."

He felt his brother's breath on his neck.

Cy whipped around, hand on his knife, but Jonah trapped his wrist against his side and pulled him into a viselike bearhug. "Don't."

"Or what?"

Jonah didn't answer, just held him in his grip like a python.

Cy grunted. "Let me go."

Jonah released him, staring.

Cy backed away. He breathed, filling his lungs with foul air. "Last time I'll ask. What's this *art* you keep talking about?"

"You know. Just say it."

"I don't." There was a new smell coming from inside the tunnel: *burnt hair.*

"Say it."

Cy shook his head, crying. "No."

"You know I kill people." Monotone and matter-of-fact.

Bzzzz. Cy's phone went off in his pocket. He didn't make any move to answer it. "Said you weren't a hitman."

"I'm not. No one tells me who to kill. It's mostly girls, and they never deserve it."

Bzzzz.

It was so blunt and so raw that Cy had trouble processing what he'd heard, and he stumbled over his reply. "But someone pays you for . . .?"

"The bodies. Parts. Or they get a ransom, I keep the girl. Other things."

Bzzzz.

"Why?"

"It's profitable. We use every part of the buffalo."

"No. I mean why are you killing girls?"

Jonah nodded, teeth slipping out of his lips into a smile. "Because it's going to make me famous."

33

Kerry

November 15, 2019. 7:28 AM

K ERRY WAKES UP first, squinting in a ray of morning sun that cuts right through his Ikea curtains. He yawns, wrapped up snugly in a burrito of sheets on his own big bed, and smiles. It's the best sleep he's had in a month.

In a rush, he remembers the livestream.

His hands shoot over to his side table to grab his phone. He navigates to */pol/*. Skims all the posts he missed since late last night when they passed out, waiting for news, then scrolls furiously down to the latest. He stops. Reads. *Oh no.*

"Pink," he says.

Pink is snoring on the floor, curled up like a rescued Labrador at the foot of his bed.

"Pink!"

Pink jolts awake and stumbles over to Kerry, who sits up and offers him the phone in a daze. He takes it, wordless. Then he does a double take. He looks at Kerry, horrified, then at the phone again. He hands it back like it's radioactive, sits at the desk where his computer is charging, flips it open, and types.

A minute passes while they read and absorb it. Both in shock.

"My god," says Pink.

"Fuck," Kerry agrees in a hoarse whisper.

The skull-faced troll did, in fact, enter the iron door. Everyone's talking about what he found inside. *The New York Times* gave the story top billing on its website: *"34 Bodies Found in Malibu 'Torture Chamber'; Bizarre Online Stunt Leads to Grim Discovery."*

There's a picture of the iron door with police swarming around it. A quote underneath it from the first officer on scene, whose eyes are staring far past the camera lens pressed in his face: *"They were shackled to the walls and kept alive while they waited to get cut into pieces. It's worse than anything I've ever seen."* The caption says the speaker is a twenty-eight-year veteran of the force.

Kerry's phone slips from his sweating hand and lands on his face, painfully.

He scrabbles for it, brings it back up to reading height. Rubs his eyebrow where it hit.

The article just keeps going. Luckily, the photos are minimal, but the language is graphic enough for his imagination to conjure a scene that'd give David Fincher nightmares. "Are you still reading it?" he asks, voice cracking. "These details?"

"No," says Pink. "I need to check something first."

Kerry feels a lump in his throat. "I think I'm gonna yack." Oh yeah. He's gonna.

He leans over and yacks all over his floor. It's gross.

Pink squeals. *"Kerry!"*

Kerry wipes his lip, smiles. "I'm okay."

"No. Not okay!" Pink waves him over, frantic, pointing at his screen.

Kerry jumps off the bed, goes to the desk, and leans over his shoulder. Reads. "Oh, come on!"

Pink flattens both palms on his face, peeking out from between his fingers. "Yes. This was not a smart idea."

"Yeah," says Kerry, monotone. "Fuck us, I guess."

They're both looking at /pol/, same board that Kerry searched. But he skipped this whole thread.

The trolls are back at work, even more feverishly than before. This time, there are no anarchists. They're all united in a single purpose: trying to dox Kerry and Pink.

Oh. Never mind. That post was old. No, they found his house in Nashville an hour ago, and they've already posted his address on twenty-plus sites. They know about all those fake identities he and Pink used too. They don't like that.

Samefagging cuck gets swatted? asks one user, in a post dated half an hour ago.

The others cheer.

Kerry wishes he didn't know what it means. Pink must know what's about to happen, too, by the way he's scared shitless.

They're gonna end up on the evening news.

"Okay," says Kerry. "Don't panic. We need to go."

"*Police!* Get away from the fucking door!" shouts a male voice magnified by a bullhorn. It's coming from the street.

Kerry runs to his bedroom window, but he doesn't make it in time to see what's out there.

Boom! He can hear splinters fly as his front door is smashed open.

Boots stomp up the stairs, shaking the walls.

Pink kneels on the floor and knits his hands behind his head, protecting his spine. "*Kerry.* You need to listen to me, now. They will separate us. Do not say a word to them, and they will let you go. I'll contact you again when it's safe."

Kerry, though, isn't listening, because he's already decided the smart thing to do is just open the bedroom door. As he reaches for the knob, he shouts: "We're in here, officers! Two of us, unarmed. Whatever call you got, it's fake. This is all a nasty prank some jerks online—"

Boom! The door explodes open and hits his head.

Kerry trips and falls on his back, and his ceiling fan spins faster than it ever did when it was on.

Thud. Something heavy rolls along the carpet.

A flash of light and noise: *KSSSSSHHH!* It's louder than anything he's ever heard.

Then silence—also, tinnitus.

Dazed on the floor, he goes to push himself up, but his hand slips in his own yack from earlier.

A knee slams into his neck, pinning his cheek to the slick floor. "Stop resisting!"

"*Not one word!*" he vaguely hears Pink screeching, like a banshee in heavy fog.

"*Fuck you, I'm tryi—*" screams Kerry, right as a fist swings into his face and the world ends.

PART IV

Philistines

When I was a boy and I would see scary things in the news, my mother would say to me, "Look for the helpers." You will always find people who are helping.

—Mister Rogers

CHAPTER

34

Jonah

June 29, 2001. 9:12 PM

A BIG CHARITY FUNDRAISER was being held at the house on Tigertail. Mom's idea.

People were starting to get drunk now that dinner was over, so
Jonah Wolf slipped away to be alone.

It should've been harder, not just since he was wearing a rented
tuxedo—*"Oh he's adorable, Dee!"*—but also because most parents
watched kids his age, ten, like hawks. Not his. It was easy. Most
nights, he could walk right out of the house and be gone for hours.
Mom never noticed.

No one did.

He ended up on the back patio, sharpening his pocket knife in a
secluded corner. As he ran it down a honing rod he'd stolen from the
kitchen, again and again, its blade caught one of the spotlights hidden
in the trees and he noticed a tiny brown spot: dried blood.

Jonah smiled at a memory, then rubbed at the brown spot with a
thumb, and it went away. He held his knife up to the light: *clean, sharp.*

"Going hunting?"

He turned and saw an adult standing in the shadows, halfway
between himself and the house. The man held a glass of shining brown
liquor in one hand. *Steady.* It was full.

"You're not drunk," said Jonah, eyeing it.

The man laughed. "Smart boy." He tossed the rest of his drink into a bush.

Jonah felt hairs standing up on his neck.

The man emerged from the shadows. In the light, he was just another rich guest in a tux: pale white skin, brown eyes and hair, in his early thirties. "You must be Jonah. I'm Frank." He didn't offer a hand to shake.

"So?"

Frank smiled. "I didn't come here for dinner. I saw a story on Fox 11 last month. Coyotes."

Jonah felt his hand unconsciously tighten around his knife. He said nothing.

"It's all right," said Frank. "You're causing quite a stir on your little street. But I think it's perfectly natural."

"What is?"

"Wanting to kill vermin. You enjoy it, or you wouldn't sign your work. Which is how I know you graduated to big game two weeks ago. Didn't you? And no one suspects a thing. No one but me."

Jonah stood up. Held the knife behind his back. "I don't know you. Go away."

Frank took a step closer. "Or what?"

Jonah thought about it. "I'll scream."

"Does that help when daddy gets drunk?" Frank's eyes got darker. He took another step.

"No." Jonah brandished the pocket knife, pointed it at the man's face. "But I will."

Frank shook his head. "No need." He took a handkerchief, reached inside his jacket and used it to pull out a piece of paper, folded in half like a birthday card. "I was told to give you this." He let it go and it fluttered to the patio floor.

Jonah didn't move. "What is it?"

"An invitation."

"To what?"

"A place where you can speak freely with others like you. *Us.* People who can help. Do you know how to use the internet?"

Jonah sneered. "I don't need your help."

Frank grinned. "Even the best hunters can use a little help, especially when we're so *young* and *stupid*. Mark my words. The next one who sees you for what you are won't understand like I do."

Jonah let his knife drop. A bead of sweat rolled down his nose. "What do you hunt?"

"Big game."

"Like what?"

"Buffalo."

"Liar. There's no wild buffalo no more." Not in Los Angeles. Just coyotes, rabbits, and stray cats and dogs.

Frank nodded, turned and walked away. "I wouldn't know."

"Wait."

Frank turned again, smiling. "Yes?"

"Who did you tell? Mom? Dad?"

"No one. Read it." He dropped the false smile and walked back inside, disappearing in seconds.

Jonah picked up the piece of paper. It shook in his hands.

When he unfolded it, two bills fluttered out. *Hundreds*. More money than he'd ever had of his own. He frowned and let the cash sit where it fell while he read the note.

35

Beau

November 15, 2019. 12:46 PM

B EAU PRUITT IS a big man. Six eight, pushing three hundred pounds and it's not fat: he does an Olympic lift program four times a week. Nothing superhuman, but he's a goddamn black Adonis compared to all the slob white boys he works with at the Federal Building in West-wood, a hulking brutalist skyscraper two blocks east of I-405. *If this were the Navy, these guys'd be shark food,* he still finds himself thinking on bad days.

But it's not the Navy. It's the FBI.

He gets depressed whenever he observes his coworkers too long. The analysts and upper-ranks guys at the L.A. field office are all pasty white, nearly to a man. Most of the other special agents are too, and the black and Hispanic ones he *has* met are just like them in every way but skin color. Frat boys. Schoolyard bullies who went pro. Meatheads and wife beaters who barely graduated from state and drink Budweiser heavies. Soft.

This isn't where he belongs. But he can't be a SEAL anymore. He tried. After Dolan drowned, he started getting panic attacks in the water. To this day, he has trouble near swimming pools. All those years diving in murky silt behind enemy lines, and now all it takes is the sound of a splashing kid to turn Beau into a blubbering mess.

They discharged him.

So . . . here he is, following in his dad's footsteps. Sort of.

It was his dad who got him set up at the bureau nine years ago, way back when Hank was just a section chief and not the first black FBI director in history. Those first five or six years, Beau had the best clearance rate on his floor. But in the last two, Special Agent Pruitt hasn't cleared a single file.

Not because he can't. He won't.

There are plenty of office rumors about why, but it wasn't any single thing that sparked his little personal rebellion. It was the time he overheard his new boss, Ryan Huckley, complaining on his phone about losing an agent who'd been caught coaching addicts to give false testimony in murder trials ("He's a good cop. We should take care of him . . ."); it was the day he walked in on two dozen of his coworkers glued to a TV in the break room, cheering on the riot police in Ferguson; it was when he realized his own father had been on the other end of Huckley's phone call, and the corrupt agent had been granted a pension. All his life, Beau listened to his dad talk about "changing the system from within." But now he thinks it only ever works in reverse: working within the system changes *you*.

One day, he just stopped trying.

He shows up, answers emails, passes any cases worth solving on to the appropriate inbox, and that's it. Call it civil disobedience. He'd have been fired months ago if not for his dad pulling strings.

Fourteen minutes shy of his lunch break, Beau rides an elevator down to the lobby, aiming to slip out and eat in his car. As always, he brown-bagged it: kale and sun-dried tomato salad, protein shake, and a canned coffee. While the elevator's display counts down to "*L*," he wonders idly: *Why coffee?* When he was deployed and his brothers needed him to stay awake on watch duty, caffeine was worth the jittery feeling. Nobody *needs* him now.

He decides to quit coffee.

On his way out of the lobby, he's looking for a trash bin to toss his can in when a squeaky voice stops him.

"Agent Pruitt!"

Beau sighs and turns around. It's Ryan Huckley's assistant, Karl. Cute little guy, roughly half his size.

Karl runs across the lobby. "Hey, Huckley needs to see you. It's urgent."

Beau frowns. "It's my break. What if I say, fuck you?"

Karl huffs and puffs. "I don't know. You'll get chewed out."

Beau nods. He doesn't feel like getting chewed out today. "I ain't gonna run."

Karl sighs. "Walk fast."

* * *

Huckley's office is messy and smells like moth balls.

Beau closes the door behind him and sits down. Ryan Huckley ignores him while he finishes up an email. *Power play.* This shit happens all the time at the bureau.

Beau glares at him.

Huckley fires off the email. Swivels in his chair. "There he is. Little Beau Peep."

Beau nods. "Huck." You just know he had a nickname like *the huckster* at some point. The man is everything there is to hate about cops crystallized into one being, like the opposite of that hot alien girl from *The Fifth Element*. He is a perfect piece of shit.

Huckley's mouth twitches. "You read the paper today?"

Beau shakes his head.

"Congrats. I'm putting you back in the field. Your new assignment is in *the New York Times*—should be first thing you see. Karl didn't have time to prep a case file, so read up when you get a chance. And no expenses. You only need to go to Malibu."

"Uh-huh." Beau looks up. "Wait, you're serious?"

Huckley grins like a demon. "What? Too busy?"

Beau pulls up the *Times* on his phone. Reads. "The torture chamber?"

Huckley nods. "Time to see if you can live up to your potential."

Beau feels his stomach churning as he reads details in the article. "But I'm a cold case guy." Even in his policing prime, he'd never take on something this scale alone. No one could. "You say no expenses, but I'm seeing at least two active crime scenes, thousands of miles apart. Thirty-four sets of bones, no one knows how old yet." *Jesus Christ.* The pictures aren't so bad, but the reporting is vivid.

"Tough titty."

"Don't you have a task force?"

"Serial crimes is busy. You're it."

Beau looks up at his boss's smug face, and he reads between the lines. "You know I won't clear this."

Huckley smiles menacingly. "The director's office sent me an email yesterday about you."

Beau says nothing.

Huckley leans back, hands on the back of his head. "It said I get to fire you if you pass on one more case. Hank thinks you'll snap out of it now that you know the stakes. Go prove him right. Or don't." He turns back to his computer screen. Adjusts his chair, pulls up close so it's a good spot for his back, and places his fingers on the keys like a maestro getting ready to compose a symphony.

Beau sits there, dumbfounded. "This case isn't cold."

"Don't give a shit. No expenses." Huckley types out the first lines of an email.

Beau stares out an office window at the I-405 below. Traffic's just starting to get bad at the on-ramp on Wilshire. He watches how cars in the 405's slow lane brake to let people merge, and how then all the cars behind them brake or switch lanes and cause someone in the next lane to brake, creating a ripple of inefficiency that goes back miles. One car, one pump on the brakes, and the whole system slows to a crawl.

Beau feels dizzy as he gets up and exits the office, still holding his coffee can.

"Psst!"

A little voice off to his left. Beau turns.

It's Karl, hiding in the nook where his computer lives. He waves Beau over and hands him a dark green folder bulging with papers and photographs.

Beau flips it open, wordless. It's a dossier on the torture chamber in Malibu. He looks up, brow furrowed.

Karl gives him a thumbs-up.

Beau nods. Mouths, "*Thank you.*"

Karl beams, spins in his chair to face his computer, and types loudly.

Beau tucks the dossier under one arm and walks down the long hallway in a daze.

When his senses return, he pulls out his phone, swipes into his contacts, and dials *"DAD."* The line rings. And rings. And rings some more. No message machine: Hank Pruitt likes to fuck with people. *Power play.* Beau hangs up. He takes the elevator to the lobby.

* * *

Sitting in his car ten minutes later, he picks at his salad. Sips his protein shake.

He flips open the dark green folder, the dossier. Reads.

As he turns the pages, he chugs his coffee. Starts his car. Pulls up directions to the airport on his phone.

* * *

When he lands in Nashville, Beau calls four numbers before he gets in touch with the cop in charge of the scene in Malibu. "This is Pruitt, FBI. I understand you requested an assist? I'm it."

The cop on the other end huffs. "Yeah. I know. Why the fuck are you in Nashville?"

Beau hails down his Uber. Gets in. "I'm headed to the station here to talk to the guy who put the photo online."

"Aren't you based in L.A.? You didn't feel like seeing it first?"

"Your scene? No. I'd normally send an agent, but it's just me. The bones aren't going anywhere. This mystery man is unless we charge him with something." Beau had talked to the Nashville station before he got on his flight. They had already let one of the suspects go home and were about to do the same with the other one until he begged them to stall.

"Just you. Christ."

Beau's face gets red hot. "Not up to me."

"Sorry. It's just . . . I was on a case where we got an assist before," says the cop, who sounds wary. "They had two people at the scene in a couple hours, and a whole team of analysts on it back at the field office. And that case didn't even make the local news. Now we got national news, and your boss, Huckley, all he sends us is you. One man. And no offense, but am I correct in understanding you got this number from the SMPD dispatch?"

Beau sighs. "Correct." He's rusty, but it's worse than that. He doesn't have the law enforcement connections he once did on speed dial. Those bridges are all burned.

The cop laughs. "Buddy, with all due respect, I think your boss fucked us."

Beau looks out his window. There's a homeless girl on the corner, begging for change. Young. "Yeah," he says, working out in his head what's bothering him. If Huckley just wanted an excuse to fire his worst agent, why torpedo *this* case? National news. "Where are you at on your end? What's the game plan?"

The cop sighs. Tells him.

He gathers a few more details, thanks the cop for his help, and hangs up.

Beau tries his dad one last time: eight rings. He hits *"End"* and puts his phone in his pocket.

His Uber pulls up in front of the Nashville Police Department HQ. He gets out and walks inside, frowning.

*   *   *

He sits down at the steel table and clears his throat. "My name's Beau. What's yours? No one seems to know what to call you."

No response.

Across the table, handcuffed to a ring in the center, is a thin man in his early thirties with hazel eyes and a jagged scar where an ear should be. His clothes don't fit.

Beau nods at his shirt. "Who loaned you the outfit? Your friend? You don't strike me as a Metallica dude."

The thin man says nothing.

Beau was ready for this. The local cops had told him what to expect. *Brick wall.* "Who are you?"

The thin man smiles.

Beau smiles back. "You know, they let your friend go. They almost let you go too. Why you think you're still here?"

A hint of concern appears on the man's face.

Beau presses his advantage. He pulls the ratty wallet out of his jacket pocket. Waves it.

The thin man shifts uncomfortably in his chair. "I want a lawyer," he mutters.

Beau teases open the secret slit, and all the fake IDs tumble out. "What do we have here?" He mimes counting on his fingers. "One . . . two . . . three . . . four counts of felony identity theft."

The thin man sighs. "Lawyer."

Beau nods. "Sit tight." He stands and makes his way to the door.

This has the intended effect. The thin man looks rattled, like he doesn't understand why the big bad cop is walking out so soon.

Beau smiles. "See you in a minute. Pink." He shuts the door behind him, satisfied at the look on the thin man's face. There are some skills that never fade: riding a bike, driving a car, mindfucking a suspect in the interrogation room. *Still got it.*

He turns and walks ten feet down the hall to the next room. Opens the heavy soundproof door.

Inside, Kerry Perkins looks up from biting his nails. "Oh thank God. You're here."

Beau sits down at the steel table, identical to the one in the previous room. Only this one's cuffs aren't being used. "I appreciate you coming all the way back here on such short notice, Mr. Perkins."

Kerry nods. "You found his fake IDs, right? That's why he's still here?"

Beau doesn't bother replying. They hadn't, until this bozo showed up and asked the receptionist the same question.

"They're mine. I made them for him as a gag."

"Uh-huh."

"Please," says Kerry, eyes pleading like it's the most important thing in the world. "Just let him go. This is my fault."

"I don't care about the fakes. Where'd you get that photo?"

Kerry wilts. "What do you know about it?"

Beau scratches an itch on his ear, casual. "I know it led to an underground tunnel with bones from at least thirty-four people inside. You wanna see?" He flips through the dossier until he gets to the part with pictures. Turns it around. "What do you think? Recognize either of these fellas? How about these six lovely ladies?"

Beau watches his reactions as he points out graphic details in each photo: the shackles lining the walls, some with bones still pinched in the middle; what remained of an operating table, kitted out with a light like they have in dentist's offices; a generator; an EKG machine. All burnt, only crumbling pieces left. Finally, he gets to a photo of a small design carved on the back wall of the deepest chamber, lines scored deep into stone.

Two wolves, maybe? From how close the crime scene photographer was when he took the shot, it's hard to tell.

The guy keeps it together for a second . . . then a light goes out in his eyes, and he faints. His head knocks on the table like an empty coconut and he lies there, facedown.

Beau sits in place, frozen. "Uh." *Shit.*

Right when he's about to go get help, Kerry's eyes open, and he sits up, groaning. Rubs his head.

"You knew it," Beau says softly. "That symbol."

Still groggy, the guy whispers: "I think it means it was her sons."

Beau pops a pen out of his shirt pocket. "Whose sons?"

Kerry sighs. He tells him.

Beau listens, taking notes.

*   *   *

In the hallway outside, he dials Huckley's office before he's even got the soundproof door closed behind him.

Karl picks up. "Ahoy, Agent Pruitt."

"Karl. I need a favor. And Huckley can't know about it."

The assistant's tone changes, matching the fear in his: "What is it?"

"Nothing bad," Beau says unconvincingly. He's been shaking ever since the bozo in there said a name he recognized, and his brain started putting pieces together. He overheard the name a week ago, walking by a closed office door. *I pushed it in a new direction. It'll stall out.* He didn't think much of it at the time, but now he has context.

Karl gulps. "Okay."

Beau steadies his breathing. "I want you to do a keyword search in Huckley's calendars and his email."

"Absolutely not. I'm not getting fired for you."

Beau can tell he's losing him, so he talks fast: "I just need to know who he was talking to last week about a man named Ellison!"

Silence on the other end.

"Big Rod Ellison?"

Beau's stomach sinks. "You know him?"

Karl pauses. "Serial Crimes Task Force is assisting on that case. It could've been a lot of people."

His task force really was busy. "Why are they on a missing person in Tennessee?"

"He's dead. And serial crimes is helping with the body because Ryan thinks it was the same guy they've been chasing all year."

He's pushed it in a new direction. Away from the Wolf family. A pump on the brakes here, a lane change there.

Beau lets the phone drop from his ear, staring at it in disbelief. He ends the call.

In his chest, he feels a familiar sensation. One he hasn't experienced in over a decade, and never in America, only in the shit: Afghanistan, the Congo, Kashmir, Sierra Leone. Most people would call it terror, but for him, it's a vital sign. He's *needed.* On his right hand, his trigger finger itches.

Beau walks back down the hallway. Calm.

He opens the door to the first soundproofed room, where the thin man is still sitting. Locks it behind him.

CHAPTER

36

Thad

November 15, 2019. 5:46 AM

THAD WOLF WAKES up at the crack of dawn. Throat itches. An automatic hand reaches over to his bedside table, fumbling at a bottle of George Dickel rye. Weight says empty.

Thad sits up. His eyes cross from the pain swirling in his head, where a nerve on the right side of his temple feels like someone has it in needle-nose pliers and keeps squeezing.

He finally gets his fingers around the bottle of rye, lifts it to his lips just in case there's a drop or two left.

But nope. Empty.

Thad sighs, stands up, and pulls yesterday's wrinkled slacks off the floor and onto his legs as he walks, hunched like a Cro-Magnon. He slips on his golf cleats, untied. Snatches a polo shirt off the rack in his closet and throws it over his head as he makes his way to his man cave, where he digs a fresh bottle of George Dickel out of the big oak barrel next to his chair, takes a swig—*heavenly,* first of the day is—then shuffles out of the house and to his red pickup truck.

* * *

At the country club, Thad tips his caddie with a fresh fifty-dollar bill. Members call the guy New York Mike and no one will say why if you ask, but it's because he's Jewish.

New York Mike nods his appreciation, then runs behind the club-house bar and grabs the bottle of scotch he keeps hidden specially for Thad Wolf's morning nine.

Thad tucks it under his shirt.

Gets in his cart, alone. Drinks.

Shanks his drive.

Drives the cart to it. Drinks.

Shanks his wedge shot. Gets mad and sails the club twenty yards into the bushes. Leaves it there. He can afford another.

* * *

Nine hours later, Thad drives home, despite the protestations of the new kid working valet.

Gonna talk to Haslem and get his ass fired, he thinks, careening down the highway. *Don't know who I am—shit, I been thirty-five years at that club.* No wait. That was Bel Air Country Club, back in Los Angeles. He's only been at the one in Tennessee for a little under a decade.

Shit. Still.

Thad gets home. Parks. Stumbles inside. Heads straight to his man cave, then slides the white double doors shut behind him. He flips on Fox News at full volume to hide the noise of him rummaging through his empties in the oak barrel, searching for the bottle of George Dickel he opened this morning. *There,* halfway to the bottom.

Three fulls left. Running low. He decides to bring one more in from the kitchen once the coast is clear, just so he has it.

He doesn't like to let Diana see him hoarding bottles. He told her he's down to one a day.

* * *

An hour after that, Thad picks at his guitar and watches golf on TV. Match play. Tiger's back, he notices, nodding approvingly. He never thought the guy got a fair shake. What'd he ever do anyway—just cheat on his wife? *Par for the course.*

Thad smiles at the pun he made in his head. He strums a celebratory D chord.

* * *

Two hours later, he eats dinner, with Diana sitting at the opposite head of their long dining table. Neither of them speak. Thad finishes his steak as quickly as possible, downs the glass of red wine she poured him, kisses his wife on the forehead, then retreats back into the man cave.

Lights his nightly cigar. Cohiba. The ones Fidel used to smoke.

When it's done, he lights a second.

*   *   *

Four hours later, Thad stumbles into the master bedroom with a full bottle of rye clutched in one hand. He sets it on his bedside table, unopened. Kicks off his golf pants, removes his shirt, and slides his legs under the covers—disturbing Diana, who grunts and does an alligator roll to escape his icy feet.

He takes a last swig of rye for a nightcap and then glances up at the fan with mahogany oars for blades, spinning above him. If the fan was actually on, he'd turn it off . . . but he knows better.

Five minutes pass, and he falls asleep.

He never dreams.

37

Diana

November 16, 2019. 2:11 AM

DIANA DREAMS OF her Mom.

In a twelve-year-old's body, she walks down the short hallway in their old apartment in East L.A. and pushes her mother's bedroom door ajar with a weak bony hand. "Momma?"

The door lurches open. It's dark inside.

On the bed, Bonnie Guthrie sits up like a rising corpse. Slow. She turns to face the doorway, and her daughter gasps.

The right half of her face—*only* the right half, like a clockface that counts only to six—is done up in full makeup: mascara, rouge, bright red lipstick. The works. The left half is untouched: a rat's nest of tangled hair covers her left eye and a popped pimple bleeds on her cheek.

Diana covers her mouth and backs away, crying silently.

Bonnie smiles, and her front teeth are red with errant slashes of lipstick. "Hey baby," she whispers hoarsely, "where're you going?" She hides her left hand, knuckles tight on something. "I want to talk to you. Come in here and sit with me."

Diana shakes her head. "No, Momma. Please."

Bonnie's smile cracks. "You don't think I'm *pretty*?" She stands. A long, thin boning knife hangs at her side, shining in a ray of light that cuts through the slatted window.

Diana spins, runs away as fast as she can.

Her mother's bare feet pound the carpet a few steps behind. *Gaining.*

Bonnie howls like a wildcat as she careens into one stucco wall, then the other, slashing.

Diana runs for her life, screaming. She feels a rush of air on her neck as the boning knife swishes through her ponytail and steals a few strands. She ducks and pushes off a wall as she turns a corner.

Bonnie trips and slams into the wall, screaming unintelligibly. "Fucker, I'll show you pretty! Fucker! Cunt!"

Diana scrambles for Luke and Kristen's bedroom door, opens it and skids inside, pulling it closed behind her. She locks it. *Bang!* The door shakes with the force of the impact and she falls on her ass. She crab-walks backward, watching it.

Bang! Its rusty hinges whine, but they hold. *Bang!*

Bonnie howls and screams in the hallway.

Luke and Kristen are both sitting up in their single, shared twin bed, crying, looking to their big sister to hold them, to protect them. Diana climbs into the bed and slips under the sheets. She pulls them both close, hands cupped over their ears as she gathers their tiny heads to her chest. "Shh," she whispers.

She peeks over the top of the sheets and watches the door.

Bang! It jumps again.

She hangs her head, closes her eyes, puts her flat hands together and prays: *O Lord . . . please let my Mommy die.*

Bang! Bang!

One last *bang* as the door splinters and flies open.

*   *   *

Diana wakes up in her bed at Wolf Hollow with a gasp, heart racing. She stares up at the white ceiling and the fan with mahogany oars for blades, a blooming flower of shadows in the dark.

As the night terror fades away, she breathes a long sigh of relief. Looks over at Thad's side of the bed.

She frowns. He's asleep with his mouth open, snoring quietly (for him), but that isn't what bothers her. There's a conspicuous half-full bottle of rye on his bedside table. Thad said he'd cut out the nightcaps. She makes a mental note to bring it up to him tomorrow morning, diplomatically, if he's around and in a good mood.

Diana lies on her back, eyes open. A few blank minutes pass before she closes them and tries to sleep again.

She doesn't. Time slips by in chunks.

At some point, she hears Thad sit up and reach for his bottle. He drinks deep from it and grunts. *If he's going to lie, does he need to make it so obvious?* She regrets the thought almost instantaneously. A neuron fires in her brain, a connection is made, and she's reminded briefly of Cy's email.

He said goodbye, says a sad little voice in her head.

No. It was a prank. It wasn't him. And if it was, he didn't mean it. He said it himself. He sent it when he was on drugs. Best thing to do is ignore it. Life is good. Cy is still alive, he's just too embarrassed to reach out again.

You blocked his number. Liar.

Diana shuts her eyes harder, and decides to invest in a set of ear plugs in the morning—but not the foam yellow ones. Fancy ones. Do they make artisanal ear plugs? She'll soon find out.

She sighs.

Thad freezes. He heard her. "Babe?"

She holds her breath, hiding in plain sight.

Eventually, he lies back down and starts to snore.

She keeps her eyes shut until morning, awake but thinking nightmarish thoughts.

CHAPTER

38

Kerry

November 15, 2019. 8:53 PM

"D ON'T BE MAD," he whispers to Pink when they're finally reunited in the lobby of the police station.

Pink ignores him. Just rubs at red circles on his wrists where the cuffs dug in, muttering curse words while a chubby cop behind a desk finishes up their paperwork.

The FBI agent coached them both on what to say to get out of the police station, but the cops still remembered the fake IDs, so . . . long story short, Kerry ended up eating a misdemeanor and a two-thousand-dollar fine.

"Pink," he whines as they emerge onto a yellow-lit street in downtown Nashville. "Come on. I'm sorry."

Pink shivers and blows into his fists, underdressed in the *Metallica* shirt and baggy jeans. The discomfort doesn't help his mood. *"Not one word,"* I said. "How was that unclear?"

Kerry hangs his head. The two men make their way south to an intersection, hands in their pockets. "I got let go, and you didn't, right? Bet it was because I wasn't a prick to them."

Pink throws his hands up. "They only kept me because you came back!"

Kerry pouts. They wait for the walk signal, huddled together in a cold wind. "I'm the one who's out two grand. Not sure what it is you're so pissy about." The signal changes. They walk.

Pink laughs. Shakes his head.

"What?"

Pink turns and yells at him in the middle of the intersection: "You told him every single thing! In detail!" A car honks, so they keep moving. "He is the FBI! He knows my nickname is Pink. He knows I help The Cuppa steal internet. He knows I stalked Diana Wolf and her family these past twelve years. And that means *they* know that now. Thank you so much."

"I said I'm sorry!"

Pink says nothing. Just walks.

Kerry scratches the back of his head, trying to come up with a way to explain himself. "I just felt like it's so insane, the only way he'd ever believe it is if I told him all of it. It worked, didn't it?"

Pink grumbles.

Kerry grins, knowing what it means. "Come on. It worked."

Pink half nods. "You got lucky. This agent Pruitt seems to be one of the good ones."

"What makes you so sure, all of a sudden?"

Pink shrugs. "I'm not. But he is appropriately terrified."

Kerry's smug grin dies. He shivers, teeth clacking as he scans the next block. "You see him yet?"

"No." Pink looks around for a street sign, finds one. "This should be it."

"I see him." Kerry points.

The gargantuan bald FBI agent is standing across the street in a long black coat, holding a loose pile of something white in his arms. Watching them, waiting.

Kerry and Pink trudge silently across the street to meet him, too cold to carry on a conversation.

Beau nods when they get there.

Kerry nods back, staring at him. Now that they're all standing, it's hard not to be in awe at the size of this man. He looks like an NFL linebacker, only taller and more muscular.

"You good?" asks Beau.

Kerry nods. "I'm not used to looking up at people."

"Where are we going?" says Pink.

"Someplace safe," says Beau. He tosses each of them oversized white sweatshirts with "I ✓ Nashville" plastered on the backs, bought from a novelty shop nearby. "Phones. I don't have time to argue." He makes the universal hand gesture for "cough 'em up."

They both reluctantly hand their phones over to him.

Beau puts them in his coat pocket, turns, and starts walking.

Pink follows, pulling the hoodie over his head.

Kerry tries to put on his while he walks, but gets his head stuck in an armhole and trips. He stops, gets it on, and then hurries to catch up. "Hold up. Are we walking?" The extra layer helps, but it's still miserable weather out.

Beau nods.

Pink nods too. "Rideshares and public transport are easy to track." They keep walking.

Kerry sulks. "How far is this place?"

Beau ignores him. So does Pink.

It's a long, quiet walk.

They go twenty-two blocks (he counted, to pass the time) before finally they reach an alley where Beau pulls out a ring of keys and stops at a metal door with a padlock on it. He flips through keys, reading labels, then fits one in the padlock and turns. The door swings inward to reveal a pitch-black staircase. Steep. It leads five stories straight up, no landings, to another padlocked door.

Beau waves them in after him, then shuts the door and locks it again.

They climb the stairs.

Kerry and Pink are both gassed by the time they conquer the last step, bent over and huffing. Beau comes last, swinging his keys and whistling quietly.

Kerry recognizes the tune. "Are you . . . *seriously* . . . whistling that right now?"

Beau smiles. Shrugs. "I forgot how good '*A Thousand Lies*' is, man. All this talk about Thad Wolf's kids got it stuck in my head."

"*Perfect* song," says Pink, gasping.

"Fuck that song," says Kerry. "Fuck The Pack. Fuck you both."

Beau unlocks and yanks open the door. Dust rains down.

Inside, it's like a luxury apartment.

Kerry's eyes immediately find the couch: a big L-shaped sectional made of beautiful, aged dark brown leather. He walks over to it and sits down reverently, afraid he's going to be told any second they're not allowed to touch it.

Pink isn't as quick to feel at home. He turns to Beau, who's grabbing a bottle of cream soda out of the refrigerator. "So, we're here. What is this place? What are we doing?"

"Fed safehouse. For VIPs only." Beau winks, as if to acknowledge their case is an exception.

"Cool?" says Kerry, nonplussed.

Beau glares at him. Grabs two more sodas. Closes the fridge and walks to the couch. "It takes a higher security clearance to know this place exists than it does to walk into Area 51, so unless this shit goes up to the cabinet, the three of us are invisible here. There's apartments like this in every major city in the country. Soundproof. Bulletproof"—he points at an aquarium-thick window on one wall—"and stocked so the three of us could last a month inside if we need to. Now, to answer your second question, what we are doing here is *waiting*. So get comfy." He hands them a brown bottle each, sits down, raises his own bottle in a silent cheer, then takes a long swig.

"For what?" says Pink.

"For a call. The cavalry. What we're up against, we can't fight alone. But we can't just trust anyone either."

Pink glares pointedly at his friend on the couch. "Hmm. You don't say."

"How long are we gonna be here?" asks Kerry, ignoring him.

Beau makes a face. *Don't ask me.*

"Fine," says Kerry. "Whatever." He stretches his legs on the long chaise, then uses the end of a candlestick on a side table to open his soda. *Chink.*

Pink sees him do it, and his brow furrows. "How did you do that without an opener?"

Kerry doesn't bother explaining. He stands up, walks over and opens Pink's bottle for him.

Pink sips at it, amazed.

Kerry sits again.

Pink coughs. He gets a dark look on his face and puts his soda down.

Kerry notices. "What's wrong?"

Pink whispers, pointlessly, "If only cabinet members know of this place, how does he have keys?"

They both turn to look at the FBI agent.

Beau heard, but he just looks . . . *embarrassed.* "I'm not supposed to. They're my dad's keys."

"Who is your dad?" asks Pink, pressing on. "Who are *you?*"

Beau flips open a badge. Tosses it to Kerry. "My full name is Beau Pruitt. My dad is—"

"Your dad is Hank Pruitt," says Pink, suddenly understanding.

Kerry looks at the photo. "You used to have hair?" He looks up, confused. "Who is Hank Pruitt?"

"FBI director," Pink and Beau say simultaneously.

"Okay," says Kerry. "That is a nice person for us to know. So that's who we're waiting on to call you back, right?"

"Right."

"Okay," says Kerry, starting to feel marginally better about their situation. "Well, while we're stuck here, let's put our heads together and make some sense of this. You said you think your boss is in on it?"

Beau nods. "I knew something was wrong a long time ago. I just didn't know what. Then you said that name, Ellison . . ." He explains where he heard it, and what Karl told him. "I think Huckley's been using his task force to throw off local murder investigations. He can't take over an investigation, but he can offer to help and then shove misinformation down their throats until they choke on it. And if the locals are really outmatched and asking for help, he can just send one fuckup like me and watch them drown."

Kerry breathes. *We really did get lucky.* "How much do you think it would cost to get someone like Huckley at the FBI to help cover up a murder?"

Beau shakes his head. Shrugs. "A million."

Kerry snorts. "That's it? To put a high-level fed in your pocket for a year?"

"Forever." Beau sighs. "Smart crooks only bribe you once. After that, they blackmail you."

"Still," says Kerry, "It can't just be Ellison and your boss."

"Right."

"So we're talking potentially tens of millions of dollars someone's spent on buying cops."

"Correct."

Kerry shakes his head, defeated. "So it can't just be Jonah."

"Um," Pink pipes up, "it can."

Beau and Kerry both look at him. "What?" they ask in unison.

Pink rubs the backs of his hands, nervous. "I used to think he was laundering money for someone. I found a slip of paper in his trash when he was just a teenager, a registration application for a shell company. I know he used it to buy a painting once, from Christie's. For $4.2 million. He wasn't quite eighteen years old."

Beau frowned. "Jesus."

Pink nods. "I never confirmed he bought more paintings, but I always had a feeling. I think it's why he works at the auction house."

"You're just mentioning this now?" says Kerry, annoyed.

"This is all happening so fast," says Pink, sighing. "His money was only something I paid attention to in . . . you know. When I was sick. During the bad times."

Beau blinks. "The *what*?"

Kerry brushes him off. "So he bought one painting, once. That doesn't mean he has enough cash to bribe cops on the scale we're talking about."

"You're missing the point," says Pink. "Art sales are anonymous. Once you own a painting, it's like having buried gold. No one will know if you never dig it up. I got lucky, this one sale I discovered. Of course I never found another. But knowing what we do now about Jonah Wolf and what he was capable of hiding . . . do you think it was the only one? You think a person who buys a $4.2 million painting ever has just 4.2 million dollars? And do you think a teenager with that much money is likely to have *less* money ten years later?"

Beau sucks air into his cheeks, then blows it out. "*Fuck*. Where'd he get it in the first place?"

Pink shrugs. "It wasn't from his parents."

They all sit in silence for a moment.

Beau breaks it. "The more money he has, the more dangerous he is. My dad used to say, one of the things that scares him about this country is how, for every law, there's a fine you can pay to get out of breaking it. Most just don't get written down."

Pink nods. "I think it's not unique to this country." He gets the dark look on his face again.

Kerry groans. "What now?"

Pink looks at the FBI agent again. "I think you are a good man, Beau. But waiting here is a stupid plan."

Beau pops his bottle cap off with an opener from the drawer, then takes an angry gulp. Waits.

Pink leans forward, elbows on his knees. "You said we're invisible, that only a cabinet member could access this place. But you have a key even though you aren't supposed to." He gestures with both hands, signing *do you see?* "Rules are bent by powerful people like your father when it's convenient. You think he was the only one?"

Beau's face says he gets it.

Pink sits back. "We're not invisible. This place isn't safe."

No one knows what to say to that. They stare at each other for a minute.

"So can we use our phones, then?" asks Kerry.

"No." Beau points at a bank of electronics charging in a wall socket. "The safe house has its own phones. Use those."

Kerry picks one off its charger, then walks back and sinks into the couch, dejected. *Android. Typical.*

Pink copies him and takes another phone off the wall. He sits back down, fiddling with it.

More silence.

All of a sudden, Kerry laughs. Pink and Beau look at him.

"I just checked my website," he says, smiling. "It's down. They DDOS'd it. And I've got fifty-six thousand emails."

Beau frowns. "Shit. I forgot. You two might be on the news." He reaches for the remote and turns on the flat-screen TV opposite the couch, then navigates to CNN.

The news isn't talking about them. Not directly.

"Oh fuck," says Kerry as all three of them lean in to listen.

A reporter is talking to a young woman on a Midwestern street, peppering her with questions: "When did you realize it could be connected to what was found in Malibu?"

There's a headline in bold letters across the lower half of the screen: *"BREAKING—Two More Torture Chambers Discovered in Nebraska and Idaho."*

"I was watching a highlight reel of the big thing from last night, the livestream," says the woman, whose face is as white as a ghost. "And when I saw that door in the cliff, I felt this chill. Because we go hiking in the state park a lot, and there's this weird *door* we found once way off this one trail. My husband and I, we just assumed it was some Parks and Rec thing. We never thought to report it. But it looked *just like* that door from the livestream. So we called the park ranger and . . ."

While the other two are glued to the screen, horrified, Kerry whips out his safehouse phone again and scours the internet for more info. He finds what he's looking for, but it doesn't make him feel any better.

Worse, actually. Way worse.

"Guys," says Kerry, but it comes out a hoarse whisper.

Neither of them hear him.

"Guys."

They turn to look, startled.

Kerry hands his phone to Pink. Closes his eyes.

Pink groans like he just learned a family member died. "Oh. Oh god."

Beau glances at them both impatiently. "What is it?"

Kerry opens his eyes, and they're glassy. "There are fucking nine so far. In nine different states. They only *opened* two."

Beau lets it sink in. "How many bodies?"

Kerry shakes his head. "No one's saying yet. It's a lot."

Pink reaches for the remote. He turns off the TV and looks at Beau angrily. "You still think we can wait?"

Kerry looks at him too.

Beau gulps. He stands. "I'm gonna try my dad again." He goes into a small bathroom near the kitchen and closes the door.

Pink gives the phone back to Kerry.

They sit in silence. No one touches the sodas.

39

Pink

November 16, 2019. 12:06 AM

AFTER AN EXCRUCIATINGLY long wait, Beau emerges from the bathroom. "Okay," he says, "he's still not picking up, so we're gonna be here all night. At least."

"If we last that long," Pink mutters.

Kerry deflates. "*Great.* Who else did you call?"

"Every old friend who ever owed me a favor," says Beau. "One of 'em even answered. Any family you two need to call?"

Kerry shakes his head. "All mine is dead or I don't know them."

They both look at Pink.

Pink nods. "Same." It's a lie, of course. "Sorry if this sounds rude, but your plan is still 'wait for Daddy to make it all better'? That's it?"

Beau sits on the couch and turns on the TV again.

"Be a man," says Pink.

Beau looks at him, and there's a fire in his eyes.

"*Dude.*" Kerry sits up, shocked. "Stop it."

"No," hisses Pink. "We are sitting ducks here, and we don't even know where Jonah Wolf *is.*"

Beau grins smugly. "Wrong. He is in downtown Manhattan, SoHo, sleeping next to some girl who isn't his fiancée. Tomorrow, he's got work at Christie's in midtown. I had that friend look him up just now. Guy is old-school surveillance ops. Took him fifteen minutes to track

Jonah's phone to this girl's apartment, and he's got eyes on him right now. I told you. We're good here for at least a day or two."

Pink sucks in air through his teeth, thinking, tapping his foot. "No. We are not *good*."

Kerry is the only one who looks concerned. "What is it?"

Pink grimaces. His hands make claws at his sides. "It's hard to say. I know his habits. Even before all this, he frightened me. This is a person who would've known what we did with that photo long before *the New York Times* did."

"Is he psychic?" asks Beau, facing the TV.

"*No.* Only very controlling, obsessed with details." Pink's heart is racing. His mind is racing. His foot taps faster, and he starts to sweat. The lights in the room get brighter, yellower, and more intense, until it hurts to keep his eyes open. *No. Not now.* He looks at Beau, and he sees a man in blue overalls standing over his shoulder. *"Look at me, Diego,"* says the man in blue. Pink averts his eyes. "I am telling you. If we stay here another day, he will find us."

"How?" says Kerry.

Beau stops pretending to watch TV. "He can't. Even if he does know these places exist, which is one in a million, he'd have to *guess* we're in one of them, then he still has to *guess* which safehouse I took you to. I told you. They're all over."

Pink counters: "Are any of them closer to the police station than this one?"

Beau glares at him, fuming. "Dad's never gone two days without checking his messages in his life. He'll call." He puts his feet up on the coffee table. "We *wait*."

Kerry shrugs. "I think it makes sense, Pink."

Pink says nothing.

The three of them nervously sip their sodas. There are four in the room, counting the man in blue overalls Pink sees behind Beau, but he doesn't drink soda. Or eat. Or blink.

He only whispers, *"Wait until they're asleep. Then do it."*

Pink does his best to ignore him, but that never works.

The lights keep getting brighter. Even when he closes his eyes, all he sees is burning yellows and blues.

* * *

An hour passes.

Beau cracks his fifth cream soda, channel-surfs away from the news, and lands on a *Judge Judy* rerun. Not much else is on in the early AM.

Kerry has had his face sunk into a soft leather pillow for forty minutes already, and he's snoring like a hog.

Pink sits in the same spot he has for hours, quietly and intently paying attention to the other two men.

When Beau's eyes flutter closed, he leans in and listens. Hears a snore.

Pink stands, tiptoes over to the big FBI agent and kneels. *Right leg.* He noticed the bulge earlier, when they were in the stairwell. He carefully rolls the pant leg up until a cyclopean ankle is exposed. Sure enough, there's a small Colt revolver strapped to it. It's loaded.

He uses two hands to undo the clasp, so it barely makes a *click* as it pops open, then pulls the gun out by its handle, slow. It slips free. Pink holds it solemnly, satisfied with the weight of it. He stands and sees the man in blue at the door they used to get in, holding it open for him with a rictus grin. *"Like you said. Be a man."*

He nods, tucks the gun into his waistband, and slips out.

40

Diana

July 9, 2000. 1:26 PM

D IANA SWERVED AND lead-footed the brakes. *Skrrt!* The Mercedes station wagon screeched to an abrupt stop, five feet from the curb outside the Bollenbachs' property.

Home was two blocks away, but she couldn't just go inside. What if Lupe was cleaning in the garage when she pulled in? She laughed at the mental image.

Her hands were shaking uncontrollably on the wheel, covered in dark brown smears. Blood. Not human. It was a coyote, she thought. But it had been so mangled when she found it, it could have been anything with claws and teeth. She just hoped it wasn't a dog. A pet would have been seen as a big escalation of Tigertail Road's unique . . . issue. Maybe enough to pique the interest of real police rather than just the ADT rent-a-cops.

Her heartbeat was going too fast. She felt light-headed, like she was about to pass out.

It was a big mystery in the neighborhood. Someone had been terrorizing Tigertail Road's hiking trails for the past year. And now she alone knew the culprit.

She glanced in her rearview mirror and flinched when she found his eyes waiting there.

In the booster seat in back, Jonah was staring at her in the mirror. He was soaked in blood from face to waist, his little shirt so saturated that it was stuck flat to his stomach. He sat quietly, waiting for her to make the next move.

Tears streamed down her cheeks. She opened her mouth, but no words came out. What is the right thing to say after you catch your nine-year-old elbow-deep in the chest cavity of a small mammal?

"I just wanted to try the butcher knife," he said simply.

Diana laughed. She put her forehead on the steering wheel and screamed.

When she sat back up and looked in the mirror again, Jonah was still in the same spot. Staring.

She turned around in her seat and looked at him directly.

He observed her, blinking. "Do you think I'm sick, Mom?"

She shook her head. "I don't know, baby."

He nodded. "I'm not."

She said nothing.

He smiled. "If you don't tell . . . I won't." Before he finished the sentence, his eyes moved onto something behind her. *The road.*

Diana spun, but there were no cars. It was quiet. Birds chirped.

Then she noticed Tina Bollenbach, their geriatric neighbor, walking two black standard poodles out of her front door and down the house's entry path. Fifteen feet away from their station wagon.

Tina was frowning, craning her neck.

Diana made eye contact and felt the blood drain from her face. She put her car in drive and gunned it, squealing the last fifty feet into her own driveway and parking in the garage.

As the garage door closed behind them, she shut her eyelids tight and prayed: *O Lord . . .*

A minute passed. In the backseat, Jonah coughed.

Diana opened her eyes again, her decision made. "Get out," she whispered. "Take off your clothes."

He complied. She turned the car off, then ran to the cabinets on the wall and opened the one with cleaning supplies. Took out rags, heavy-duty black trash bags, and a bucket, then filled the bucket with cold water at the utility sink and plopped it on the floor next to her son.

Jonah had stripped down to his undies. They weren't soaked like his shirt, but they were tainted.

"Off," she said, pointing.

He stripped naked, and dropped his undies on the reddish pile of seeping wet clothes.

Diana first gathered all the clothes into a trash bag. Then she triple-bagged it, so it wouldn't leak, and carefully walked the tainted clothes out to the little gated area where they kept trash bins, keeping a watchful eye out for Tina Bollenbach. No sightings. She tossed the bloody clothes into the black bin and closed it, then casually walked back into the garage.

Jonah was standing right where she left him, waiting patiently.

Diana took the rags and the bucket of water and she did a quick wipe down. When it was no longer so obvious that it was blood on him, and not just dirt, she stopped. She had made a split-second decision that it would be fastest to start cleaning in the garage now—the rags, the used bloody water, all the mess they made—and let Jonah finish cleaning his body off.

She shoved him. "Go. Straight to the shower in your room. *Now*." He started to walk, then she remembered and hissed: "No touching! I swear to god, Jonah, if I come in there and I find a single smear of red or brown on my white linen sofa, I will . . ."

Jonah looked over his shoulder as he climbed the three steps up to the kitchen door, smiling, and the look in his icy-blue eyes stopped his mother's train of thought dead. *Disdain*. Not hatred; it was colder and more dismissive than that. Arrogant. It was the same look she'd seen when she found him with the critter corpse.

Diana sputtered. "I . . . I'll . . ."

Jonah shook his head: *no*. "You would clean it." The naked little boy giggled like he had learned a fun new fact. Then he slipped into the kitchen and left her alone in the garage.

CHAPTER

41

Pink

November 16, 2019. 1:13 PM

TWO HOURS AFTER stepping off a red-eye at JFK, Pink sits on a
bench at the edge of a worn-out children's playground in Alphabet City. He expected children, but instead he's staring at an all-too-
familiar sight. Twenty yards away, two shadow-faced homeless men in
endless layers are nodding off under a plastic slide, too high to bother
concealing the spoon, lighter, and used needle on the ground between
them. They'd look like corpses if not for the steam billowing from their
open mouths.

Pink never touched heroin himself. But his father had. For the first
twelve years of his life, he was raised by addicts on the streets of downtown Los Angeles. Skid Row wasn't so different from the worst parts of
Manhattan. It was just a lot worse.

He can tell just by looking at these two that they'll be dead or in
prison within a year. If that. The light in their eyes is almost out.

But it's not pity he feels, staring at them. It's anger.

He knows no one is perfect, least of all him, so it makes him feel like
a hypocrite to judge. He still can't help but think this is what giving up
looks like. Kerry was right to remind him on that perfect afternoon they
spent as friends, before everything went to hell. *Trying* is everything.
No matter how unlucky you are in life, what excuse is there not to try?
Failure is a part of life. This is not failure. It is a denial of life.

His father had given up. For a long time, so had Pink, and to this day he needs to be reminded to try.

He wonders if that's what started all this. Thad Wolf gives up on being a father, so his son gives up on being a human being, so his brother gives up on the world, so their mother gives up on the truth. Or maybe it started a thousand years ago.

Beau and Kerry, now they want to give up.

Pink won't. Someone needs to break the cycle.

"Be a man," said the man in blue.

Which is how Pink suddenly found himself here in New York, alone, waiting for an afternoon appointment with Jonah Wolf at Christie's auction house in Midtown. With a gun. Against his ribs, he can feel the bulge of Beau's Colt revolver in one of his coat's inner pockets. Heavy, solid, and cold.

The gun was surprisingly easy to sneak through security at both airports. All Pink had to do was look up the body scanner being used at his departing terminal, do a keyword search on one of the big security forums, and in just a few minutes he came across a discussion detailing a known flaw in this particular scanner's software: an area just under the ribcage where it has a small blind spot . . . on most people.

Pink taped the revolver to his skin there, hid it under a lumpy sweater he stole from an unattended bag outside, and hoped he was *"most people."* Walked through security. Held his arms up. Got scanned.

Whirr.

Nothing on the scan.

No TSA agents stopped him. They just waved him through.

Pink thought about that on the flight. The TSA. Metal detectors. Sniffer dogs. Shoes off, laptops out. None of it is about security. It is about the *appearance of security.* An illusion. A trick of pageantry to make travelers forget how easy it is for a human being to hurt others if they want to—how easy it would be for *them* to shoot a rifle into a crowd, or to bash a sleeping family member's skull in with a rock, if they only wanted to. An uncomfortable truth is that modern society relies on a vast majority of people simply not wanting to hurt other people.

He checks the time: it's half past one.

Close, now. His appointment with Jonah Wolf—or Jonah's appointment with *"Hans Galloway,"* an art dealer who specializes in lesser-known Abstract Expressionist masters—is in an hour and a half, at 3:00 PM. It'll take half an hour at least to get uptown if he takes the train. Another twenty minutes to change clothes, get into character.

Truly, it's the *perfect* time to be having second thoughts.

Pink looks in all four directions and up. Coast is clear, other than the two living dead under the slide.

He reaches into his coat pocket, retrieves Beau's gun, and lays it flat in both palms. Looks at it. He can see his own reflection in the gray metal, if he looks close, but it's more like a shadow of his face than a mirror image.

He wants to throw it in a trash can. He wants to not be someone who wants to hurt people. But he is. He wants to hurt Jonah Wolf. Even now, long after the bad time has come and gone, he justifies it to himself. It's not just *her* in danger anymore. It can't be in his head this time.

And that scares him.

Pink sighs and slips the gun back into his coat.

He maneuvers into another pocket and finds the smartphone he stole from the safe house. He turns it on for the first time since the flight and is greeted by thirty-seven missed call notifications. All from the same number, one of its four lone contacts: *SH1*. No texts. No voicemails.

He can guess who it is.

He dials the number back. Waits two rings.

It picks up on the third: "Jesus Christ."

"No, just me. Greetings, Beau Pruitt."

"Where *the fuck* are you?" Beau sounds tired, like he woke up in the middle of the night and realized what happened. "Get back here. *Now*. If you fired a single round out that gun, I'll kill you, Pink. You hear me?"

Pink nods, even though the large angry man can't see him. "That is fair."

"Yeah. Fair." The voice trembles with rage. "You want to explain yourself, or—"

"No," says Pink, checking again to make sure no one's coming. "I do want to tell you my plans today. What I will do. Where I am. These things are important. Not why." The truth is, he can't fully explain *why* he flew to New York. To confront Jonah, to shoot and kill him in his office, sure—but *why*? No. Only the man in blue could say.

But if he had to guess, he would say he's here because he knows Jonah Wolf more intimately than his two friends do. The problem is not that they're too scared of him. Scared is appropriate. The problem is they think time is on their side.

Time is on the side that uses it. You don't wait out a monster like Jonah, same as you don't wait out a cougar with a taste for livestock.

You go hunting.

"Motherfucker," says Beau after a pause. "I can't believe neither of you idiots is in here right now, after I stuck my neck out."

Pink frowns. "Kerry's not there with you? Why?"

Beau laughs miserably. "He's out looking for you on the streets! I tried to stop him, but naw, he's convinced you're wandering around Nashville like a psycho bum, waving a gun at folks while you shout about dead girls and dirty cops." He restrains himself with a tactical sigh, calms down. "So was he far off? Where are you?"

"Manhattan."

Beau laughs again, harder. "You took my gun on a plane . . . to New York City?"

"Yes."

"Yup, no. Im'a fuckin' kill you, Pink."

"That would be fair," Pink agrees again, making a note not to mention how he stole Beau's credit card info and used it to buy his ticket, a few sets of clothes, and one or two other items he needed. There will be a better time for full truths. Plus, he'll need access to money again while he's in New York. The city is expensive.

"What are you *there* for?" asks Beau. Then he realizes, or seems to. "Oh. *Fuck.*"

"Yeah," says Pink. "I set a meeting for him with an art dealer, two hours from now."

Hans Galloway is an older identity of his, six years in the making, so Hans already had a substantial online footprint: LinkedIn, photos, an LLC in his name—even a fake article about a just-as-fake art sale eight months ago. With all that in place, it was easy to get an appointment with Jonah Wolf; as a fine arts specialist, he's obligated to meet with motivated sellers like Hans. "This art dealer is a fake person. He's me. You understand, right?"

"*How . . . ?* Never mind. Just don't do this." Beau's heart rate seems to have spiked, judging by his rapid breathing. "Come back. Fly back to Nashville, next flight. I'll buy you a ticket. Fuck it, I'll buy you *first class*. Hank's treat. Nothing has happened yet. Right?"

"Right." He checks his phone for the time again: an hour and twenty minutes.

"All good then! Nobody needs to know about stealing my gun, how you wanted to go kill the guy . . . look, I won't tell anyone. Okay? Pink?"

"Did Daddy ever return your calls?" he asks, knowing the answer. "Did he text you? Anything?"

There's a wait.

"No. Not yet."

"Then we need a new plan, don't we?"

No retort. Beau just breathes into the mic, furiously.

"I will speak to Jonah Wolf. Man to man."

"You will *not*. You can't go into an office building in Manhattan with my fucking gun! Listen. It is traceable to me. People might think I gave it to you or . . . this fucks me up, Pink. My job. My life. Maybe even my dad's job and his life. This is not just about you. *Please.*"

"I would say the same thing to you," says Pink, staring up at the looming skyline of Midtown in the distance. "You saw the news. This is bigger than all of us. He knows that we know. We cannot sit and cower while he plans his next move. What if he boards a plane, like me? What if he kills again?"

"I told you I know where he is!" Beau shouts. "He's at work. I got a guy watching him."

Pink sighs. "You were watching *me*."

"No! I wasn't. Didn't think I had to."

"I noticed. You and Kerry are very alike."

"Oh?"

Pink says it as nicely as he can. "You are uh . . . really good people."

"Oh. You got jokes."

Pink checks the time again. "I need to go."

"Did you seriously call just to let me know you're about to murder a man in broad daylight with my gun?"

"No. If that was my plan, I would never tell you, because you would do something stupid to stop me like call your friend or the police. I called to tell you he won't show. He will cancel at the last minute, because even if he is in that building, he is focused on *nothing but us*. It is like I told you last night: something is wrong."

"You don't say."

"*Think,*" Pink implores him. "If he saw the news, why go to work? Take low-value meetings?"

"I *think* you're an asshole. What if he does show?"

"He won't."

"Fuck you. If he *does*?"

Pink measures his response. "Great. I shoot his fucking face."

On the other end, Beau laughs and laughs. It's like he can't even form words, he's so angry.

"If he's there and comes to meet me," says Pink, nodding to himself, "we will end this. Together. Or I'm right, and I call to alert you to your mistake and hope it's not too late."

"So Kerry was right. You're sick in the head."

"I am." Pink hangs up.

He stands, buries his hands in his coat, and makes his way to the nearest F train.

* * *

The big clock in the Christie's lobby, hanging like a Sword of Damocles above the receptionist's head, says 3:01 PM.

Pink fidgets in a small pseudo-modern armchair, one of three along a wall adjacent to the street-facing windows. The chairs are blue, red, white, and yellow, and they got picked for style, not comfort, which is infuriating because they're still ugly as sin. He didn't have time to get his suit fitted properly, but now he wishes he'd gone in earlier and done it right. The modest navy suit he picked off the rack looks okay, but he can't stop noticing how the fabric bunches in awkward places: armpits, crotch, wrists.

"Mr. Galloway?" says a female voice.

Pink looks up. It's not the receptionist.

A woman in a sleek black top, white mini-skirt, and stiletto heels stands in a half-open doorway next to the reception desk, beckoning.

Pink stands and goes to her, hand outstretched to shake.

The sleek woman waits until he's through the door, then lets it shut and briefly grips his hand, just her fingertips. "I'm sorry about the wait. Jonah's just getting back from an in-home consultation. One of our usual sellers threatened to leave for Sotheby's unless we listed his grandfather's paintings in an auction coming up." The woman rolls her eyes, then turns and starts walking.

Pink laughs nervously. "Family."

The woman smiles a thin, polite smile. They get to an elevator. She hits a button and it arrives with a *ding*.

The elevator takes them up six floors.

The woman leads him down a long hallway to a glass-walled conference room. Pink takes a seat. "Would you care for a coffee? Bottle of water?" she asks. "Jonah will be in shortly."

Pink's mouth is drier than the Sahara. *He's coming.* "Water would be nice. Thank you."

"Voss, Fiji, or Smart Water?" she asks on her way out.

Pink looks at her, blank. "Tap, please."

She narrows her eyes at him, then leaves.

Through the glass wall, Pink watches her retrace her steps down the long hallway, heels clicking on white marble. At the end, she passes an impeccably dressed man coming the opposite direction: tall, wiry, short blond hair cropped short.

He watches the man approach the conference room—*his* room—and suddenly he realizes what's happening. *Security guard.* They know Hans Galloway is a fake. They made him. This man is coming to take him back to the lobby or a holding cell or a waiting NYPD van outside. Sweat breaks out on his forehead. It drips into his eyes.

"Hello, there," says a friendly male voice. "Mr. Galloway?"

Pink stands up, wiping his face.

His eyes open, and it's the blond man, the security guard, holding a big hand out to shake.

Pink takes it and shakes, confused. "Yes, call me Hans. Hello. Who are you?"

The blond man smiles as he discreetly wipes the sweat on his pants. "Your appointment. I hear you have a fine collection you're looking to bundle into our fall sale." He sits down at the head of the conference table. "I'm Jonah Wolf."

Pink's heart stops beating. "What?"

The man shifts in his chair. "My name. We emailed." He looks at Pink's suit with a critical eye. "You can take a seat, if you'd like."

"You're Thad Wolf's son?" All the sweat in his loose, bunched-up suit suddenly feels cold in the overworked air conditioning.

The man who claims to be Jonah rolls his eyes in a show of modesty. "Yeah. I try not to talk about Dad, to be honest. Especially at work. People tend to write you off when you've got a famous parent." He smiles winningly. Winks.

Pink pulls his wallet out of his pocket.

Fake-Jonah watches him flick through its contents in silence, tapping his fingers.

Finally, he removes a ragged old Polaroid. "You are not this Jonah Wolf." He slides it across the table.

The man takes a closer look: it's a Wolf family photo, dated November 13, 2005, in faded Sharpie. Diana and Thad are smiling and holding their two blond sons by the shoulders, standing on a grass lawn in front of a dual self-portrait the boys had made together. The brothers were twelve and fourteen. Pink dug the photo out of Diana's trash almost a decade ago, and he's kept it on his person ever since.

Even though the photo is of a teenager, seeing it right next to the man's face makes it easy to tell he isn't the same Jonah. Easy for Pink, at least. This man's eyes are blue; they're not *ice-blue* like the eyes of the boy in the photo. He hits every item on a superficial checklist of Jonah Wolf's features—blond, blue eyes, tall, thin and wiry build, good-looking—but the doppelgänger is warm in all the ways the real Jonah is cold. Soft in the places he's sharp.

The man's nervous smile disappears as he stares at the faded picture. "I am. That's me and my . . . younger brother. Cyrus. How did you get this?" He starts to stand.

Pink reaches into his coat and his hand emerges wrapped around the grip of the Colt revolver. Loaded. He flicks the safety off and levels it at the impostor's chest.

The man sits again, eyes like dinner plates, hands shaking on his chair's thin leather armrests.

Pink's hand is rock-steady. "Where is he?"

The man gulps. "I don't know."

Pink nods. "What you do know, then. Tell me and be fast. I'll give you four minutes."

* * *

Five minutes and six seconds later, Pink explodes into the lobby again. The receptionist screams as he makes a beeline for the revolving doors that lead to the street.

He digs his phone out. Dials the contact *SH1* and puts it to his ear.

It goes straight to voicemail. No rings.

A chill runs up his arm. Beau was waiting for a call; he would never turn it off.

He dials the next contact, *SH2*, hoping desperately it's the one Kerry took from the wall.

He gets lucky. It doesn't even take one ring. "Pink! Oh thank you. The *fuck,* man? Where are you?"

"Jonah Wolf is not in Manhattan!" Pink screams into his phone, out of breath. "He has more money than god! He bought more paintings and more police than we ever thought possible! He never worked in the auction house, has never worked any job or gone to school. All he has ever done is his life's work! If he is not already in Tennessee now, *he is coming!*" He stops and impatiently shoves his way through the revolving doors until, finally, they spit him out on the busy street.

Two blue-and-white police cars pull up to the curb and double park, lights flashing silently, "*NYPD*" written on the sides.

"*Dude,*" says Kerry, distressed, "what are you talking about?"

Pink turns and walks north up the sidewalk, steadily accelerating until he's running as fast as his suit will allow. He weaves in and out of the flow of pedestrians. *Maybe they were for someone else,* he hopes briefly, but then he hears two sets of sirens blare.

He glances down at his right hand. The Colt is still in it.

He drops it with a yelp, and it clatters behind him.

"Pink? What are . . . are those sirens? Are you still *you*?"

"*Yes!* Get far away from that safehouse!"

"Come back to us, Pink," Kerry whispers softly, ignoring him. "Please. Tell me where you are, and I'll come get you. It's okay. I told you. I'm gonna get you help."

"Fucking listen! You need to run!" Pink screams as he turns a corner and skids down an alley. A man on a smoke break looks up, offended. He shoves past him. "He is coming *now!*"

One of the cop cars pulls up and blocks the end of the alley. Dead end. Pink turns back. Another cop car screeches to a halt, blocking the way he entered. He's trapped.

"*Beau.* I need to warn him."

"You need *help*, man, ple—"

Pink hangs up and dials the last of the four contacts, *SH4*, as the cops on both ends of the alley raise black handguns.

One of the cops screams at him unintelligibly, but reading his lip reading, Pink knows he said, "*Show me your hands!*"

Pink raises one hand, holds the phone to his ear with the other.

One ring.

The cops start to jog. Pink meanders closer to the center of the alley, making them work for it.

Two rings.

All the breath leaves his lungs as he's tackled, hard, from behind. His suit rips at three different seams. The phone flips through the air and its screen shatters against a dumpster as he falls. His face slams into asphalt. "No, *please*, you don't understand!" he shouts through bloody teeth. The only response from the cops is to grunt, shove their knees in his spine, wrench both arms behind his back, and cuff his wrists together. Too tight.

Cheek pressed flat on the ground, Pink stares at his shattered phone lying a few inches away.

Listens.

It's faint, but he thinks he hears a voice: "... *person you are trying to reach has not set up a ...*"

A cop kicks the phone. It spins down the alley.

CHAPTER

42

Beau

November 16, 2019. 3:24 PM

B EAU MUST'VE FALLEN asleep while he was waiting for his dad to call, because the big leather couch is where he wakes up to two sensations:

One. The noise of a phone vibrating. *Bzzzzz.* His hand automatically digs in his breast pocket, but the one he's been using is gone. The sound is coming from the bank of chargers on the wall.

Two. A tiny *pain* in his neck, like a spider bite. Or a needle prick.

Beau's eyes open wide.

A rubber face stares down at him: peeling brown paint and white, dead eyes. Razor blades are sewn into its lips like teeth. The masked man wears all black. Two leather hands hover by his neck, pushing . . .

Beau knocks away the half-injected syringe with a fist, breaking its long needle off in his neck. *Ping.*

He kicks the man in the chest and scrambles to his feet, swinging. But the man in black just redirects the first punch and then slips out of his range.

The fog lifts in his brain and he gauges his attacker's size: tall and skeleton thin. Beau has four inches and close to a hundred pounds on him. But the man in black is wearing head-to-toe ballistic armor and other than the rubber mask, it's *real shit.* And there's an athletic ease to how he's moving that gives the big man pause. *He's not worried I woke up.*

Beau roars and rushes the man in black. He grabs an empty bottle off the coffee table and swings it.

The man ducks, and the bottle misses by an inch and smashes to bits on the nearby wall.

Beau slashes down with what's left, a razor-sharp knob of glass. But just as he thinks it's about to tear into shoulder meat, the man in black casually steps forward *into* the swing. A rising palm cuts the air like a snakebite and slams into his nose. Blood sprays into his eyes, blinding him, as his forearm lands on the man's shoulder and he drops the broken bottle.

The man swings onto Beau's back and gets an elbow wrapped tight around his neck, then tightens it. A calloused palm jams into the back of his bald head, forcing him into a triangle choke, and his eyes pop out of his skull. He gasps for air and swings his meat-hook arms, too musclebound to get at the man clinging to him with both legs.

The man in black whispers in his ear: "Hush now, Agent Pruitt. It's just a bad dream."

As he struggles to keep his neck tensed, fighting for breath, Beau notices a strange pain: toenails digging into his ribs.

Motherfucker's not wearing shoes.

He swallows one of the man's feet in his huge hands and squeezes, trying to crush it like a walnut.

The man grunts. Beau hears a bone crack, then a ligament pop as the arch collapses in his grip. The safehouse is fading to black when suddenly the pressure on his neck eases, his lungs fill with sweet air, and the man's foot twists out of his hands.

The man in black leaps off him, lands like a cat and circles, no sign of being injured.

As Beau spins to locate him, a bare fist slams into his broken nose. *Hard.*

The pain is unreal. He staggers back, one hand clamped on his nose, desperately holding the cartilage together. The back of his calf hits the glass coffee table, and he trips.

He falls, and his big ass smashes through the table.

Lying there in a pile of broken glass with his legs stuck above his head, it becomes clear he's not just out of shape. Not just old. The half dose of whatever was in that syringe is kicking in. His muscles feel like jelly, hands are numb, everything feels like he's underwater.

Beaten.

He holds his eyes shut and waits for the killing blow to come, hands shaking. But it doesn't.

He opens his eyes.

The man in black stands a few yards away, blocking the only entrance to the safehouse.

"You're him, right?" whispers Beau. He coughs, and blood sprays out his nose onto the rug. "Jonah?"

The man in black nods slowly before he lifts off the decrepit mask. Blond hair spills out. Ice-colored eyes pierce the half darkness. Just like he thought: Jonah Wolf is smiling. "Get up, Agent Pruitt," he says, not bothering to whisper. *Knows it's soundproofed.* "You're not dead yet."

Beau grunts and pushes himself to his feet, cutting his palm on broken glass. It hurts. He tries not to show it.

He stands tall and raises both fists, but his legs wobble under him. *Need to take this fight to the ground.*

Jonah licks his lips and places both hands behind his back.

Beau feints a haymaker, then he dives at his knees.

Jonah sidesteps at the last second, moving like a ghost.

Pain. White-hot. Beau doubles over, momentum still carrying him forward as warm liquid sprays out of his waist just above his belt. Too much. As his hand finds the wound, a bare foot slams into his ribs and sends him sprawling sideways.

He falls like a shot elephant. *How . . .?*

When he looks up from the floor, he understands. Still blocking the safe-house exit, Jonah now holds two long black combat knives, one in each hand. Cruel, ridged blades. The left-handed knife drips glistening rubies onto the wood floor.

Jonah waves at him with the bloody knife. Still smiling.

Beau stays down, gathers his breath. Puts a finger in the long gash in his gut, still weeping blood. He looks down and regrets it: a thin membrane of pale-yellow fat holds in a section of intestine, threatening to rip open any moment.

Going to die.

Jonah nods, as if he can read his thoughts.

Beau rises to his feet again, slowly, then bull-rushes straight at him, intending to brute-force his way to the door, but it's like running through molasses. His body won't do what he tells it.

Jonah trips him with a blade, cutting into the back of his knee and pulling through to the front.

Ligaments pop like kernels in a microwave, and he knows right away the leg is useless. He falls again.

A bare heel collides with his face, shoving him back to where he started: sprawled on his back on the couch, staring up at the big plate-glass window on the far wall. Bulletproof, aquarium thick. No hope of going out that way, even if he thought it'd be a good idea to fall fifty feet and go splat on the sidewalk. It's impossible.

Wait . . . is it?

Bleeding out on the floor, he's surprised to find a story his dad told him coming back in vivid detail. A Wall Street stockbroker used to brag to clients about how the plate-glass windows in his eightieth-floor office were shatterproof. He'd jump and slam his shoulder into one to prove his point, and it never broke—ever—but one day, the whole window popped out of its frame in one piece. The weak point wasn't the unbreakable glass; it was the little screws that held it in. The stockbroker fell to his death.

Beau stands up, holding his guts in.

Jonah stands by the door, waiting.

With a final sneer, Beau runs at the thick glass pane and jumps. *Slams* his shoulder as hard as he can into it.

The glass holds. Barely a wobble.

Beau bounces off and falls onto the floor again in a heap. He writhes in pain.

Jonah laughs, surprised and amused. "Do you know who makes that glass? It's designed to stop a fifty-cal. And we're five stories up."

Beau wills his body to stand. His knee gives out, and he almost falls again, but he rights himself and walks, builds up speed, *runs*, and leaves his feet once more. Slams into the window.

Bung.

A tiny screw pops loose and flies past his head. The plate glass vibrates as it escapes its metal frame, punched out by two hundred and sixty-odd pounds of muscle and bone. Fresh air rushes past and makes parachutes out of his lips and eyelids as he plummets from the sky, twisting wildly, suspended in free fall next to a massive square of glass with red stains smeared across it for what feels like an eternity—enough time to pray there's nobody on the sidewalk beneath him. He never got a chance to look first.

The giant glass pane smashes on the pavement. *Kssshh!*

So does Beau. *Thud.*

He's not dead. Not yet. Not even unconscious. Pain doesn't even register, just numbness and adrenaline. The world swims as he moves his eyes—the only part of him he *can* move.

A shadow rushes over to him, blocking out the sun. Face invisible, he's holding a coffee cup and wearing a flannel. He leans over and says something Beau can't hear. Words, maybe.

"Phone . . . paper . . ." Beau whispers, blood leaking from his mouth. "Pen . . ."

The shadow above him is dialing a number on a cell phone: three taps. Yelling into it.

Beau looks up at the empty window frame, fifty feet above him.

No one looks down.

The shadow above him gets off the phone. Leans down again.

Beau smiles when he realizes who it is: *Kerry fucking Perkins.* Back at last. "Pink was right . . . it was Jonah." The words are barely audible, even in his own head. "He might still be up there . . . but I . . . I doubt . . . tell Dad, it's not his fault if I . . ."

Kerry's eyes get distant, like *he's* going to faint now, so Beau doesn't say anything else. *Tired anyway.* He relaxes and lets his head rest on the hard, rough sidewalk, wet with his blood and warm in the midday sun.

Comfortable, almost.

More shadows gathering overhead now. A circle of no-faces, muttering.

Sirens in the distance. City noise.

The sun dies. Blue sky dims to gray, then black.

43

Diana

November 16, 2019. 8:21 PM

THE BATHROOM'S TILED floor is cold and slick on her bare shoulders. Wet hair is in her eyes. She can't feel anything below her waist.

Thad is screaming in her ear, but it takes her a second to discern the words: "... hear me? Baby wake up! I need you to wake up! Stay with me." He's trying to pull her up off the floor by her arms. It hurts.

Diana tries to tell him to stop, but it comes out a moan.

There's another male voice in the room, and this one sounds like it's coming from everywhere at once: "... *bizarre sequence culminated in a chase that was caught on video by bystanders. The NYPD has not released a name. They confirmed an arrest was made, but when we reached out ten minutes ago, all of a sudden they can't even tell us the man in the video is in custody.*"

A third man answers: "*I mean, this is clearly the same person. You can see the scar in both videos.*"

"*Like I said, the NYPD would not confirm that.*"

"*So he walks out of a police station in Nashville with a man who appears to be Beau Pruitt, the FBI director's son. No name. No charges. Then he shows up in New York, running out of a building with a gun. Same thing.*"

"Like I said. They are not answering any questions."

Thad yanks her up into a sitting position, until she's staring over his shoulder at the bathtub. It's full to the brim. The water doesn't look right: yellow and thick, and there's a crust at the top like pond scum. Gross. It looks like something you'd see on one of those YouTube channels with pool cleaners sharing professional horror stories. "What's wrong with my bath?" she asks, surprised to find her mouth working this time.

Thad looks at her like her hair is on fire.

It comes on fast: a wave of nausea from her chest up to her throat. Vomit spews from her mouth like a waterfall, down his shoulder and half into the tub, half onto the floor . . . and now she knows what the pond scum is. Case closed.

Thad heroically ignores the puke and the fact he's wearing his favorite golf shirt. He lifts her up, grimacing as he takes on her full dead weight. Lying flat against his chest, she tries to stand on her own, but her legs don't work as well as her mouth yet.

Thad holds her limp body upright, catching his breath.

"What did I do?" Last thing she remembers, she was in the kitchen making dinner, and there was only one bottle of Malbec open. Half full. And it doesn't feel late, not if the news is on.

". . . this is now fourteen potential locations in fourteen states . . ."

He shakes his head and lifts her up over his shoulder, like he's burping a little kid.

"Correct. But again, we're still waiting on word from the scene in . . ."

Thad turns and starts hobbling out of the bathroom, and she gets her first good look at the scene. There's vomit all over the floor and in the tub. A disturbing amount, most of it pure bile, like she ran out of meaningful chunks to expel. The outfit she wore today is strewn on the flower-print loveseat next to the door, but neatly, which means she wasn't drunk when she undressed.

She frowns.

She wasn't just making dinner. She was watching the news while she cooked, and that's why it's on all the house speakers.

". . . it begs the question: How do this many young women go missing, and no one notices?"

As if she knows where to look, her eyes suddenly find it: next to a leg of the tub, there's a fat pill bottle covered in yellow sick. It's empty, no cap in sight. It wasn't empty this morning. She can't read the text from so far, but she knows what it says:

"*Endocet 10/325*

#: 60"

Diana vomits again, and it hurts deep in her abdomen. "Thad," she whispers. "I need to tell you something."

He ignores her.

From the master bathroom, Thad waddles her all the way through their bedroom and her office into the living "room," then finally lets her go, and she collapses onto the couch.

Breathing heavily, Thad doesn't stop to rest. He gently lifts up her legs and maneuvers her body into a lying-down position, then tilts her onto her side and shoves little pillows under her back and neck to support her, so that if she vomits again she won't choke.

He takes a detour into the kitchen where she can't see him. Returns with a box of rags from the pantry and a glass of water.

He kneels and dabs the rags into the water, then uses them to clean her off. He starts on her feet and works his way up her thighs, but she can't feel it. Finally, he gets to her chest, and that feels just fine. His wrinkled and calloused hand hovers over her torso, from rib to opposing rib, just barely dragging the wet rag on her skin.

It sends a shiver down her back. A shiver that stops halfway down.

"Thad," she whispers.

He looks at her. "What?"

She opens her mouth, but the words won't come.

Thad sighs. "It's okay. An ambulance is coming. I'm gonna go get you some clothes, all right?" He takes her hand in his and squeezes once, softly.

She nods.

He jogs to their bedroom again.

If it were any other circumstance, she'd think all of this was beyond hot: feats of strength, heartfelt concern, playing doctor, intimate touching. Mm-mm-mm. Being completely at his mercy throughout all of it, like she is, would normally be the cherry on top of the world's sexiest Thad Wolf sundae. But it's not any other circumstance.

"Please, no, you don't understand!"

Diana frowns. She looks up at the big television set over the mantle.

The news is playing a shaky-cam clip of two NYPD officers subduing a man in a suit. The two cops are kneeling on the man's back as he pleads with them to listen. His cheek is pressed flat on the ground, so the side of his head with a large scar on it is prominently visible even from a distance.

"Diego?" she says, not believing what she's seeing.

It's him. She's never felt so sure of something in her life.

It's been a decade since she heard from him, but you don't tend to forget your first stalker.

He was stealing her mail and writing all the men back. Crazy letters. Raves and rants about how he'd hurt anyone who tried to hurt her, and about saving her from some vague threat only he could stop. Thad had to hire a private detective after the police were slow to move on it.

When he finally got arrested, all they told her is they had the right guy. The day she testified in court, Diana remembers how shocked she was to learn he was just a teenager. Here was the bogeyman she'd been so afraid of, for months: an orphan, like her, with a cluster B personality disorder and a horrible scar on one side of his head.

It looked fresher then. But it was the same one she's staring at on her TV screen.

They locked eyes exactly one time, when she first took the stand at his hearing. But that was it. After the courts granted a restraining order, the letters stopped. Diana never saw or heard about Diego Hillis again.

Until tonight.

She blinks, her mind running through all the implications of what she's seeing like a supercomputer playing a war game—but one of those 1960s computers, the ones that took up a whole room and were still useless. It's too much to take in. It feels like her head is shorting out.

Suddenly, she remembers what it was she saw on the news. It was a single crime scene photograph that drove her to run a hot bath and raid her medicine cabinet: two wolves. His signature. It was on the fourteenth door, the latest one, the one the cops think is just a hoax.

It's not.

Thad finally returns from her closet with a comfortable set of sweats and an old T-shirt of his for her to wear in the ambulance, plus a thoughtfully packed day bag with her toiletries, in case she needs to spend a night in the ER. "Hey, babe. You still with me?"

She nods.

He kisses her on the forehead, then gets on his knees and begins the arduous process of dressing her, socks first. It's sweet. It really is.

But she can't force a smile. She finds herself focusing less on how he's satisfying her damsel-in-distress fantasy to a fucking "*T*," not to mention saving her life, and more on an intrusive thought: he never tried to save his sons. He wanted them gone.

But now he's old, and you're all that's left, says a little voice, not her own. *Thad Wolf only cares about saving himself.*

Her mind wanders inevitably to what Cy wrote in his email. He never spoke the words, but in her head, she hears it loud and clear in his adult voice: *"He doesn't love you. He needs you, is all."*

It hits her: this isn't saving her. He's keeping her alive.

Thad sits on the couch. "Babe. Do you remember if you hit the tub when you fell? Your back is all fuckin' purple and yellow." He puts a trembling hand over his mouth. Starts to cry. "Why aren't you moving your legs, Dee?"

"I lied to that detective," she says, monotone.

Thad drops the hand and makes a face. "You what?"

A smile finally arrives, but so do tears. "It was his signature. I knew this whole time, I think." Diana nods at the TV.

He glances at it, and it dawns on him. He gets a dark look in his eyes, like he's begging her. *Don't.* Outside, a siren gets louder and closer until it's so loud, they must be in the main gate.

"Something's wrong with the boys," she whispers.

Blue lights flash in all the windows on one side of the house. She closes her eyes, and the darkness spins. Thad stands slowly and walks to the front door, leaving her alone on the sofa.

CHAPTER

44

Cy

November 24, 2012. 7:12 PM

THANKSGIVING AT WOLF Hollow was going well, as usual, which is how the boys were able to sneak away from all their drunk relatives and family friends assembled down at the firepit. Up here, at the top of the hill where the skeet range was set up, they could talk openly, and they had things to discuss. It was a big night.

Cy was nervous. "Pull."

Bang! Kssh. A clay pigeon broke into a hundred little pieces and clattered into the ravine.

"Nice shot," said Jonah, standing next to him with a pair of ear protectors on.

Cy smiled as he broke the skeet shotgun in half, ejecting a red-and-black shell. He clacked the gun back together and shouldered it. "What if I don't like it?"

Jonah rubbed his chin. "You probably won't. Not at first."

Cy handed the gun off to his brother, then set up behind the trap machine. "But it gets easier?"

Jonah rolled his eyes and brought the shotgun to his shoulder. "Yes. Pull."

Cy pressed a button. The clay pigeon rocketed out of the trap.

Bang! Kssh.

"No seriously," said Cy. "How much easier?"

Jonah smiled. "As easy as breathing."

Cy shook his head.

Jonah handed him the smoking gun. "You're gonna do great. Don't worry so much."

Cy broke the gun again to load a new shell, but he decided against it. He left it broken and laid it down on top of the trap machine. "Sun's down. Are we gonna do it tonight, or what?"

Jonah stopped smiling. "Did you roll that joint?"

Cy rummaged in his pocket, held it up between two fingers. "Yeah."

"Did Mom see you walk out with it?"

"Yeah. Made sure of it."

"Good," said Jonah. "Ditch it. Let's go. The truck's parked across the street, just off the road."

Cy ditched it in the tall grass. Ground it into the dirt with a boot heel.

As they walked off the property, ducking under the wooden fence half a mile from the front gate to avoid the security camera, Jonah chuckled.

"What's so funny?" asked Cy.

"You." Jonah didn't elaborate.

"Fuck you. What about me?"

"So nervous," said Jonah almost proudly, like he was talking to a kid about to graduate. "I told you already. I did all the heavy lifting for you. You get to do the easy part."

"Yeah. I guess."

"Remember what I said. The people who get caught are the ones who pick a victim, then wait for the perfect time and place. That's backward. Never pick a victim. You find the perfect time and place, first . . . then what?"

"Wait for a perfect victim." Cy has heard this before. Many times.

Jonah clapped a hand on his shoulder. "And I already scouted out a perfect time and place for you to pop your cherry, so that is *all* you have to do."

Cy sighed. "Okay. Where is it?"

Jonah shook his head. "It's a little spot off the highway. Black and quiet, all night. I've been visiting for a few weeks now."

"Jesus," said Cy. "I always forget how much free time you've got."

Jonah ignored the comment. "There's no cops. Ever. In the entire time I've been scouting it, I haven't seen a single black-and-white pass anywhere close enough to hear anything. It's this tiny path between two bus stations that leads into a tunnel under an overpass. In the AM, it gets dead silent. People only come by one at a time. And the bus that drops them off only comes every hour, so they're always spaced a long time apart. I saw two couples, but they were both johns with cheap hookers, so they're not gonna be nosy if they do wander past. It's *perfect.* You'll love it."

The Wolf brothers arrived at Thad's red pickup truck, parked behind some foliage just off the road.

Jonah got into the driver's seat. "Come on," he yelled out the passenger window.

Cy hesitated, hands in his pockets. But then he got in.

*   *   *

Four hours later, Cy vomited. Again.

Bile dripped down the cinderblock wall like snot in the dark.

"Cy. Look at me."

Cy's mouth stopped quivering. He tilted his chin sideways. Wiped his lips. Looked at his older brother squatting beside him.

"You can do this. I believe in you." Jonah hugged Cy's head to his chest, hard, with both arms, so hard it knocked the wind out of him. "I love you, big man."

"I love you too."

Jonah let go and stood back up. He put his hands in the back pockets of his black jeans and walked to the other side of the path, beneath the overpass and into the tunnel with no lights, where shadows swallowed him. A car drove past on the freeway forty feet above. The noise of the engine faded in the distance.

Silence again.

Jonah lit a cigarette, ten feet from where Cy had thought he was standing. The tip flickered orange in the dark like a stoked coal. Smoke drifted out from the tunnel in lazy, thin, twisting loops that dispersed halfway up the concrete pillars supporting the freeway.

Cy stood up, releasing his grip on the cinderblock wall, and lurched across the deserted road to the tunnel. As soon as he stepped inside, he was blind in the dark. It was impossible to see without a phone—Jonah had strictly forbade bringing them, said they could cause problems, and he was probably right—GPS and whatnot.

Cy found his brother's silhouette by watching for the cigarette. He was leaning against the side of the tunnel.

Cy joined him.

A number of uneventful minutes passed.

"Have you done it here before?" All these hours, and less than ten cars had passed above. No people. Not even a coyote or a lizard. It was the perfect time and the perfect place. *Is it really this easy?*

"No," said Jonah coldly. "Not here. Never the same place twice."

"Oh. Right. You said that."

"Take this. You know what it is." Jonah reached into a pocket, then handed a small object to him and closed his fingers around it solemnly.

Cy looked down. Unfolded his knuckles.

In the palm of his hand, he could make out the outline of a long syringe. Heavy. Full of clear liquid. He knew what it was: succinylcholine. *The sux.* They had sourced it from an NYU nursing grad student who needed money to pay off her loans. She had no idea who either of them were; they had used a proxy to buy it off her, and the proxy didn't know who they were either. They wore their masks when they dealt with him.

Blood pounded in Cy's ears. He clutched his stomach and tried to count his breaths. In. Out. In.

Out.

A branch snapped.

"There's a girl coming," Jonah whispered as he tossed his cigarette into the dirt and stamped it out, smiling so wide the moonlight caught his teeth. "Alone. This is good. Remember."

"I know."

"I'm here for you. I can catch you if you fall. But you won't."

"I know."

"Good." Jonah shuffled away, pressing his back against the opposite side of the tunnel and producing his mask. "Wait until she's in the dark. Let her come to you. Focus."

Cy heard it too now.

Footsteps. Light. It was a girl.

Tears rolled silently down his face as he watched her turn left and take the path down to the tunnel. He took his rubber mask out and slipped it over his head. A petite hiking boot fell just beyond the line where the overpass's shadow hid their presence from passersby and blocked the light and sound—nothing in, nothing out. She kept walking. The girl had no idea they were there, two feet away, on either side of the tunnel: tall, looming, breathing patches of black pressed against the walls.

One of the shadows lurched. A sneaker scuffed the dirt.

The girl turned her head. Sniffed.

Cy caught a glimpse of her face. She knew something was wrong, but not what.

The moonlit smile appeared over her shoulder. "Do it."

Cy lunged and stabbed the needle into her neck. He pressed down on the plunger before she even had a chance to scream.

When she did scream, Jonah already had his hand clamped on her mouth.

The effects hit her in seconds. It was a killer dose. As she started to go limp, Jonah let go and she fell to the ground hard, mumbling: "I was going to Asheville, Mom . . . Dad . . ." she said, flitting in and out of consciousness. "I was just going . . . to Asheville . . . on my way to see . . ." Then the words stopped. The girl's breaths became ragged, and she gasped like a fish on land.

Cy watched her dying. "Jonah. I don't like this."

Jonah didn't say anything.

Cy kneeled down and picked her up in his arms. She was dressed in traveling clothes, a loose hooded jacket with lots of pockets, boots, a big olive-green bag slung over one shoulder. Her eyes were hazel and unfocused, and her skin was pale white. There was dirt on her face and too much makeup, but underneath it all, he could see freckles. "I'm serious. I want to reverse it. Can we stop it?"

Jonah laughed. "No."

Cy stuck his fingers down her throat and made a claw, trying to get her to vomit. Then he realized it wouldn't do anything and felt stupid. He grabbed a bottle of water sticking out of her bag, opened it, poured it on her face. He was bawling loudly under his mask, he noticed all of a sudden. Acting irrational.

His mind left his body.

From somewhere in the air far above, he watched himself performing bad CPR. Pounding at her chest like an asshole, the way they do in TV shows for five minutes to drag out the tension before the character suddenly sucks in air and wakes up.

But she never woke up.

Jonah sneered at him, disgusted. "Come on. Get her up. Let's go."

Cy let her limp body fall to the ground. Dead.

*   *   *

The two wolves hauled her corpse into the back of Thad's pickup truck, got in, and removed their masks.

The whole drive, Cy couldn't stop crying. Jonah said nothing to him.

They stopped at a random exit—random to Cy, at least—and pulled over to the side of the road in a dark spot.

Jonah got out, then went into the backseat and retrieved the black trash bag full of his supplies.

Cy watched from the front seat as Jonah used pliers to pull all of the girl's teeth out, one at a time, putting each one into an individual plastic baggie. He watched as his brother took out a hacksaw and cut off her hands, then her feet, putting these into double-bagged black trash bags. It only took twenty minutes. When he was finished, Jonah gathered up all the plastic bags and dragged them into the woods, somewhere Cy couldn't see.

Half an hour passed in silence. Cy didn't move or think.

The girl's body, or what was left of it, was still in the bed of the truck. Right behind him. Inches away.

Jonah appeared and walked out of the woods. He mopped up the remaining blood in the truck bed with a big sponge, then covered it in a blue tarp and secured the tarp with bungee cords.

Then he walked over to the passenger side of the car. Opened the door. Motioned for Cy to get out.

Cy did.

Jonah tossed him the keys to the truck. "This is your night. I spared you the hard part, but that's over. You need to do the rest on your own. Drive."

Cy got out, moving like he was in a dream.

He drove to Leiper's Fork. To Wolf Hollow.

He pulled over a few miles from the driveway entrance and parked the truck.

He looked to Jonah for what to do next.

Jonah shrugged in the passenger seat. "Don't look at me. Get rid of her."

He got out, took off the tarp and slung her over his shoulder, then carried the girl's corpse into the woods alone. Deep.

He dug a shallow grave with a dead tree branch. It took hours, but he didn't notice.

He buried her.

* * *

When Cy got back to the truck, it was after three AM.

Jonah was waiting for him, smiling. "Where have you been? Did you use the treehouse?"

Cy shook his head.

Jonah groaned. "I built that basement for *you*, idiot. What did you do, bury her?"

Cy said nothing. Just cried.

Jonah softened. He got out, walked over, and hugged him tight. "I'm sorry. I get it. This was hard for you. It gets easier. Trust me."

Cy didn't hug back.

Jonah let him go. "Come on. You drive."

"No," he whispered.

"What?"

Cy stared at him, silent. There was nothing in his brother's eyes— no regret, no sadness, no happiness, nothing. Dead eyes, like hers. He crawled into the bed of Thad's red pickup truck and sat against the cab, tucked into a ball with his knees to his chest.

Jonah was furious. He stomped to the driver's door, got in, and started the engine.

As they drove home, one wolf stared up through the trees at the dark blue sky, watching the stars swirl and fade. The other used his turn signals and listened to pop on the radio. The backs of their heads were inches from each other across a metal and glass divide.

CHAPTER

45

Kerry

November 16, 2019. 9:32 PM

ALONE IN A sterile hospital room with his only son's lifeless body, Hank Pruitt cries.

*   *   *

Outside in the ICU hallway, Kerry Perkins watches the FBI director through a window. Hank may not be feeling so jovial given that Beau is in an artificially induced coma, but relief is flowing over Kerry's bones like warm water at a spa.

It's over. It's finally over.

Or it will be soon.

"Mr. Perkins?" says a voice.

Kerry turns to find a tall man in a navy suit, holding a hand out. He nods. Shakes the man's hand. It's cold.

"My name is Morrow. I work for the director," says the man, nodding at Hank in the room. "Do you have a moment?"

"Uh. Sure."

Morrow smiles politely. "We're diverting a sizable chunk of bureau resources into this manhunt, but first priority is our own backyard. I'm leading a task force looking into FBI personnel we suspect of taking bribes from Wolf and others like him."

"Others?"

Morrow nods. "That email you got the photo from. You only saw a partial—is that right?"

Kerry nods.

"We have the rest of it."

Kerry frowns. "How?"

Morrow's face is hard to read. His eyes are gray and still. "This stays here. Cyrus Wolf sent his evidence to more than one person. A lot more. We think a dead man's switch was triggered. My team moved on it last night: four arrests, all law enforcement. Ryan Huckley was one."

Arrests. Fuck yeah. "So the younger brother, Cy . . . he's dead?"

Morrow nods. "We think so."

"Is that good?"

"It is. And it isn't."

Kerry's stomach churns. "What do you mean?"

"The evidence raised more questions than it answered."

"What does it have to do with me?"

Morrow produces a notepad. Checks it. "Probably nothing. What can you tell me about your friend who flew to New York? The one you call Pink, with the scar."

"Not much." It's not a lie. "He used to stalk Diana Wolf, years ago. That's all I know."

Morrow writes. "What's his real name?"

"Never told me." Kerry raises an eyebrow. "Why don't you ask him?"

Morrow nods. "He's no longer in custody. We lost him."

Kerry's heartbeat speeds up. "What do you mean, *lost*?"

"He ran. NYPD let him out of their sight to use a bathroom, and he slipped out a second-story window. Cuffs on and all."

Goddammit. "Sounds like Pink." But at least he won't get far—not in Manhattan in winter.

"Hmm." Morrow looks just as annoyed as he is, if not more. "Will you let us know the second he reaches out to you, if he does? He's not in any big trouble. I have questions for him."

"Of course."

"Thank you." Morrow looks back at his notes. "Tell me: Do the initials 'B.H.' mean anything to you?"

"No."

Morrow looks up, staring. Then he nods. "When you first stumbled across Jonah Wolf's studio in the woods, you said you found a notebook with a set of coordinates inside."

"Yeah."

Morrow stares again. "Do you know what happened to it?"

"No." He'd always assumed Ellison had taken it home or burned it or something.

"Is there anything you forgot to tell Rod Ellison? Anything else you saw written inside? Anything at all?"

"I didn't look at every page. But no, not that I saw."

Morrow nods. "Do you remember those coordinates?"

Kerry answers without thinking about it. "Maybe." He cringes as soon it's out of his mouth.

Morrow raises an eyebrow. "Maybe?"

Kerry recites them perfectly. "I remembered when I got home," he mutters.

Morrow smiles. "Thought you might have." He doesn't jot the numbers down. Just reaches into a vest pocket, retrieves a card, and hands it to him. "I want you to contact me if there's anything else you remember about that day. Anything you saw in that studio, or heard, that you *forgot* to tell Ellison. Or any more pictures you took."

More. Kerry feels his face go white. "Okay. Will do."

Morrow lowers his forehead in a silent goodbye, then turns and walks down the hallway, disappearing in the crowd of busy hospital staff.

Kerry glances at the card:

M. Tani
Federal Bureau of Investigation, Cyber Division

There's a number to call.

He puts it in his wallet, then pulls out his iPhone and checks if it's set to automatically upload photos to the cloud. Yup. It is. Safe to assume the feds can see that stuff with a warrant, he guesses. *Oops.* Well, thank the gods he didn't lie this time.

Something tells him that whole weird interaction was a test, and he passed it. Barely. He shivers.

Fucking cops.

Kerry crosses his arms, closes his eyes, and breathes, whispering a list of thoughts—no, *facts*—in his head over and over like he's reciting a mantra:

Everything is going to be fine.
Beau's going to live, the doctors say. He's hurt, badly, but he'll live.
The system is working. The cavalry came.

It's out in the open. Every FBI agent in the country is searching for Jonah Wolf. No one can buy them all. They've already arrested four bad cops, and it's only been a day. Jonah's face—his *real face*—is plastered all over the television next to the nurses' station.

So is his. So is Pink's.

The nurses are all crowded around the TV, watching, sneaking looks at him like he's some daytime soap star. There are news crews shooting on the sidewalk outside the hospital.

It hits him. In a few hours, he and Pink are gonna be famous.

On a normal day, that'd worry him. For one, his career as a con man is over. No more selling Chinese maps for a hundred times what he paid, so unless he gets a book deal, he may finally need to get a real job. But not even that terrifying prospect can ruin his mood tonight.

Nope. Tonight, he gets to be glad.

He's safe. The bogeyman in his closet is out in the light, on the run, as vulnerable and powerless as any of his victims. It'll be days—or a couple weeks, maybe, or a month. But they'll catch him. Jonah Wolf will go to prison forever, and no one else gets hurt. It's over. *After all* . . . with all that evidence in hand, and all the budget and manpower the FBI has access to, how long could it possibly take to find one guy?

PART V

Legend

Life isn't fair.

—Every father, at some point

*Two years,
three months,
and four days pass . . .*

46

House of a Thousand Lies
by Adrien Halverstand

I AM STANDING ON the side of an empty road in the woods, staring at what locals have told me is the only entrance to the place they still refer to as *Wolf Hollow*, though there are no signs left proclaiming that name. I have seen photos of what this place used to be, when its owners were still proud and wanted others to know it was theirs. There was a tin mailbox on a post, dented; a carved sign hanging from it on chicken wire, proclaiming; a crude timber fence that ran parallel to the road, low and useless, with a matching gate; and a long driveway, paved, snaking down a hill in the distance. A call pad for the gate was hidden in a dead stump.

It was a place that lied badly, full of things that looked old and simple and lovingly made by calloused southern hands, but weren't.

Now, the raw honesty on display here is so repulsive, it forces one to wonder if truth is overrated. The new fence is nine feet high, made of chain links and endless coils of razor wire, and it hums if you listen closely enough. It is not useless. The only sign is a rectangular yellow plate that matter-of-factly warns trespassers just how many volts will pass through their bodies if they dare climb the fence. There is no obvious gate.

I was told the owner would meet me here, but our appointment was for an hour and thirty-three minutes ago. Perhaps Diana Wolf has had a change of heart about allowing *The New Yorker* to publish her profile, and is waiting for me to give up. It would not be the first time.

But then it happens: a motor comes to life, and a portion of fence splits in two. I jog through the opening. Immediately, it closes behind me, and I get the sense I am being watched. There are so many tall trees, the cameras might be anywhere.

Past the gate, I am surprised to find that the lies I was so nostalgic for just a moment ago are still here, preserved as if in amber. The driveway is still long, snaking, and paved. As I walk down the hill, a house comes into view: angular, large, built to look like it's been added to with renovations over the decades by four or five architects to reflect the evolving tastes of its occupants. But this is an illusion. The house is contemporary. It was built in a single burst of construction spanning three years in the late aughts.

At the bottom of the hill, the paved driveway gives way to a gravel parking circle around a fountain, where a small, clean John Deere four-wheeler is parked. Off to one side, there is a barn with ample room to park three more cars. A dusty green Jaguar coupe lives there; one of its tires is noticeably flat. A dirty burlap-sack scarecrow, dressed in jeans and flannel, sits in a wicker chair on the front porch of the main house. Dried-out straw spills from its wrists, ankles, and the holes in its chest, and a corncob pipe hangs from a slit in its mouth. A concrete ramp sloppily installed next to the porch steps clashes with the careful aesthetic.

Diana Wolf is not waiting for me in the gravel parking circle. Nor does she answer the front door when I ring it. Nor does she answer my second ring. Nor the third.

The fourth ring is the charm. Diana opens the door.

What strikes me first is that for someone living alone in the woods with a fairly severe T6 spinal cord injury, her self-care is impeccable. Her blond hair is washed and cut to shoulder length. Her clothes are clean. A scent of tasteful perfume floats around her, noticeable but never too overwhelming. A full glass of red wine sits in a special cup holder on the end of one of her powered chair's armrests. Despite everything that's happened, Diana Wolf remains an imposing presence and a beautiful woman. I find it hard to imagine how she does it. When she goes to shake my hand and struggles to lift her right arm, I start to wonder if the rumors of her isolation are untrue, and she keeps the help out of sight somewhere.

She invites me inside and offers me a glass of wine. I accept.

The interior of the main house is almost entirely a single large room. It's surprisingly cluttered with furniture for the home of someone with her practical needs: elegant armchairs, sofas, desks, and ottomans in all shapes, sizes, rustic woods, and rare fabrics, arranged to create four or five functionally and stylistically distinct spaces. It reminds me of a museum of miniatures I once visited. All of the little curated rooms are crowded, pristine, and unused. I get the feeling they were only ever meant to be seen.

I ask, "Did your boys enjoy living here?"

Diana snorts. She downs the remainder of her glass and directs me to a wine cooler. "They would have if they'd ever spent much time here. I built it for the family."

I feel certain neither statement is true, but do not say so. I pour the wine.

I ask her how she feels about the upcoming anniversary of her husband's death.

She snorts. "You don't waste time, do you?"

Perhaps not. But our interview was supposed to start almost two hours ago.

She sighs. "You'd be surprised. I'm okay. Honest to God. I think I was living without Thad for a long time before his accident, and then *especially* after I got hurt. He was here . . . but he wasn't. I got used to being mostly alone. It was good practice for the real thing."

The word *accident* sticks out to me.

"That's what it was," she insists simply. She drinks.

I press her on it, but it goes nowhere. She keeps using the word.

Thad Wolf died of a gunshot to the head from his own pistol. It was ruled a suicide, and the coroner's opinion wasn't seen as controversial. The man had strong motives that might explain him wanting to die.

She shrugs. "They ruled fucking wrong. I knew my husband, believe it or not. He wasn't suicidal. Period. Careless? Stupid? Yeah, those I can buy."

Stupid? I ask what she means.

She laughs bitterly. "He was walking home through the woods playing with a loaded gun, like he'd done a thousand times. I told him for years: you play with guns long enough, you get hurt. He probably took it out to shoot at a snake, tripped, and it went off. Simple as that."

Obviously difficult scenarios to imagine, let alone believe, but I decide it is best to let it go. If this is her way of coping with the loss, she is entitled to it. It seems a matter of semantics whether someone in the state Thad Wolf was in when he died (the neighbor who had last seen him alive claimed he had been so intoxicated as to be nearly incapable of speech, and forensic analysis of his blood backed up her story) is ever truly capable of committing suicide, or if anything he does must be thought of as an accident.

I was a fan of her husband's music. I hope I am not overstepping when I tell her I shared in her loss in some small way, as did his fans all over the world.

She smiles. "That's sweet of you. But most of his fans are as dead as he is."

Doubtful. "*A Thousand Lies*" still achieves regular play on classic rock stations.

"Radio's dead too, honey."

Touché. I ask her why she never leaves this place. Wolf Hollow. She chuckles. "Why do you think?"

Her son?

She nods. Finishes her glass. "My son."

Here in America, where serial killers of a certain stature are celebrated as cultural icons, it is common to hear or read Jonah Wolf's numbers rattled off like pitching statistics: seventeen iron doors and hatches in fifteen states; twenty-two thousand square feet of subterranean real estate; an estimated $8.6 million dollars' worth of lumber, heavy machinery, and various raw building materials; roughly $34.8 million dollars in known payoffs to law enforcement, both local and federal. They go on and on.

His calling card, and the number he is most famous for, is his kill count: a whopping *two hundred and forty-six*.

Officially, that is—and chillingly, so far. Two years have passed since the crimes were first brought to light, and his count still rises. Just three weeks ago, the seventeenth iron hatch with his now-familiar "two wolves" insignia etched onto it was found in Virginia, tucked into a dry riverbed just outside a Charlestown suburb. There were eleven desiccated corpses inside. A minor territory, for him.

The twelfth cavern found still dwarfs the rest: the so-called Wolf Hole in Illinois. A depression in the earth ten miles as the crow flies from Chicago's south side, geologists once thought it a natural sinkhole. It was while studying this "sinkhole" that a graduate student kicked through a dirt wall and found a collapsed tunnel, which he followed to its gruesome end in a vast subterranean cavern. Sixty-six unique sets of bone fragments were verified.

The vast majority of remains found go unidentified. Because it is theorized that he targeted undocumented immigrants, runaways, homeless, and other marginalized individuals unlikely to be missed (as far as the system is concerned), it is safe to say most will remain John and Jane Does forever. As was the case with Ted Bundy, it is unlikely we will ever know the true number of Wolf's victims, but the mass graves in his hatches serve as stark, grim reminders of an emerging fact:

Jonah Wolf is likely the most prolific serial killer in American history.

His omnipresence in recent American culture goes beyond numbers. It even goes beyond the myriad unsolved mysteries orbiting his case: the still-unidentified Scarred Man who conveniently escaped from NYPD custody hours after playing a shadowy role in the events that led to Jonah being identified as a primary suspect; the thirty-four minor masterpieces sold by Wolf's impostor at Christie's auction house that have never resurfaced, all of them priceless and now missing; the unknown source of his apparently vast fortune.

No, what truly sets his legend apart and makes it so wildly popular with murder buffs, conspiracy theorists, forum dwellers, and dozens of would-be Truman Capotes (three books were published last year alone, in four languages) is that Wolf has never paid for his crimes. He will soon top the FBI's Most Wanted list for a third consecutive year.

He is still *out there*. A young man in his prime.

Among law enforcement, there appears to be little hope of this changing.

The manhunt for Wolf has been unprecedented in scope. FBI director Hank Pruitt was once criticized in Washington for the staggering cost associated with the search—a congressman publicly accused him of prioritizing the case over more pressing national concerns to avenge his only son, a bureau agent infamously disfigured at Wolf's own hands. And yet, two years later, there has been no discernible progress.

This—all of it—is what Diana means when she says it is her son who forced her into this exile, living behind an electrified security fence surrounding nearly a thousand acres.

But from her tone, it is easy to infer that protection from the lurking monster himself is less of a priority for her than keeping people like me out, along with all the other things out there seeking to constantly remind her of her son. Inside this bubble, Diana Wolf retains control of her world. Comforting lies can still be told. It is difficult to escape the cult of Jonah Wolf as a mere bystander these days—imagine being the killer's mother. You might cut yourself off from reality too, if you had the means.

And then there is his art. I ask her how she feels about the prices his work has been fetching at auction.

Diana rolls her eyes. "Haley is a parasite, and you can tell her I said so."

This gets a laugh out of me. I was not expecting such a blunt response from the same woman who built and chooses to live in this house of lies, and who still insists her husband did not, simply *could not* commit suicide, so must have tripped on a root and shot himself in the face.

She means Haley Jackson, of course—her son's onetime fiancée and now the owner of hundreds of his artworks that he abandoned in the apartment they once shared.

Ms. Jackson, who was once a model for high-end fashion brands, used the paintings to reinvent herself as an unlikely power player in the art world. With a keen sense of social media, she has single-handedly kept herself and her ex-lover's art in the news almost nonstop for two years.

Promoting and selling Wolf's paintings has been lucrative for her. One of her most profitable sales to date was his *Ego 4*, a large canvas that sold for a low seven figures to an undisclosed buyer as part of a recent Christie's auction: *The Art of Evil*.

Shockingly to some, Jonah Wolf originals are now almost exclusively collected by legitimate institutions, who long ago priced out the fetishists slavering over Ms. Jackson's earliest offerings.

*   *   *

February 20, 2022. 12:31 PM

Haley Jackson stops reading and lays her copy of yesterday's *New Yorker* on the "don't care" part of her desk, where it blends in with the usual office clutter: half-written invoices, unopened mail, an invitation to speak on a panel at some sick true crime convention full of serial killer mega-fans.

She sighs. They didn't even have the courtesy to use a recent photo of her. It's the one from her *60 Minutes* interview, taken last year in her apartment. The one with Bear next to her leg, looking up at the camera like a little lion guarding her, and her staring out the window from her desk like she's pondering world domination.

Another hit piece. The article wasn't supposed to be about her, or even Jonah. It was supposed to be a profile of Diana, poor widow of Thad Wolf. That's it. That was the whole point. They even released it on the first anniversary of Thad's suicide. It should have been more obituary than tabloid column. At least that's what Ian told her when she pressed the editor for details over a dinner at *Bouchon* last month.

But Ian lied.

The writer mentions Thad's music what . . . once? Then it devolves into paragraph after paragraph of Jonah this, kill-count that, Ms. Jackson profited this much, hey Diana, how big of a parasite do you think Ms. Jackson is? What a *laugh*.

It gets tiring, reading about herself.

But so be it. Let the world not get it. Let the assholes call her a profiteer, or a merchant of sickness and rot, or a groupie bordering on accessory to murder. So fucking *be it*. It's not about him. It's about not letting a ghost haunt her.

Jonah haunted Haley for too long after he disappeared. His paintings too. When the news first broke, she shoved them all in the bedroom they'd shared and locked it.

There they slept, for months, in a room where she could never sleep again.

Today, she keeps a framed blue-and-yellow MTA card on the wall behind her desk. It's the exact card she used when she entered the subway two nights after Jonah's twelfth mass grave was discovered outside Chicago. The Wolf Hole is ten miles from the house she grew up in. Police told her he was probably scouting its location when she first met him, so she thought the least she could do was kill herself. She descended into the Houston Street station, intending to jump in front of a train or to lodge her bare foot under the third rail.

Instead, she just watched train after train pass. So broken, she didn't even have the guts to end it.

But then, through a blur of tears, she saw an advertisement on the other side of the station for his old employer—meaning, of his longtime body-double—Christie's.

They had a big art auction coming up. Haley can't remember whether the headliner was a Francis Bacon or *The Scream*, but it doesn't matter now.

It gave her an idea.

Instead of running from her past, she would wrap herself in it and wear it like spiked armor. Use it to subdue his ghost and bind it to her will. Use *him* to get what *she* wanted from life for once.

She called her agent and quit modeling. Then she unlocked her old bedroom.

Haley capitalized on the wedding ring he'd given her first. She booked herself as "Jonah Wolf's fiancée" on every morning show that would take her, and she told her sob story. The act took off. She brought it on a nationwide tour. Even cried on camera while Anderson Cooper patted her back. And she always managed to work in a teary-eyed anecdote about his paintings, and how she still believed they were great art, even after everything. There was shock value in saying that. The hosts usually asked to see one then, and she always had a new one to show.

It worked. Strangers started calling with offers—weirdos, at first. Anonymous buyers. But then it was art galleries. Then assistants working for big-name collectors.

Now it's museums.

He's never seen a cent of the money. He never will. It's not his. Not her parents'. It's hers. She earned it. All of it.

Haley sighs again as she realizes she's been staring at *The New Yorker* on her desk for five minutes, justifying her own actions. Five whole minutes. It shouldn't take so long if what she's doing is as empowering and noble as she acts like it is.

She wonders, not for the first time, *Am I really doing the right thing?*

He's not just famous anymore; he's respected. As an artist, by artists, not just the weirdos who idolize his *other* body of work. Is he watching? Is he happy with what she's done?

Yes, says a little voice.

A knock on her office door jolts Haley from the navel-gazing session, which has now stretched to eight minutes. "If that's you, Elsa, come in."

It is.

Elsa, her assistant, pushes the door open, takes a step inside and stands there, looking unsure of herself. "You have a call. It's Marc. I've been pinging you, but . . ."

Haley sighs. "No."

Elsa makes a face. "What?"

Haley stands, gathers up her purse and keys, and walks past the poor girl. She stops at the door. "I feel sick. I'm going home early. Tell him to fuck off. Politely."

Elsa nods.

Haley puts on her sunglasses and leaves.

*   *   *

It's a short ride on the 1 train back to her new place in Chelsea. She could afford a driver, but she likes it down here underground. It helps her remember where she came from.

*   *   *

Haley arrives at her townhouse and unlocks the front door. Walks in and slams it shut behind her.

Ba-bunk-bunk. The big crate where she keeps Bear while she's at work starts to rock in the far corner. He never did learn to stop scratching at the front door, so this was the best option.

"Hey, Black Bear," she says, smiling half-heartedly.

He wants out, clearly, but she decides she needs a few minutes to herself. She loves Bear, always has, but it's hard. He's a ninety-pound ball of muscles, teeth, and anxiety, way too big and scared of loud noises to live comfortably in Manhattan. But it's more that every time she looks at the dog, she wonders where Jonah really got him, and how. It wasn't at an airport.

She goes to her kitchen to pour herself a glass of wine.

The crate stops rocking.

Haley drinks, basking in the relative quiet.

Then the crate starts rocking again, harder than before. *Ba-bunk-bunk-buuunk.*

She frowns, peers around a corner into the living room, and screams.

A huge, bearded man wearing a black cap and steel-toed boots is standing just inside her front door, holding it closed. His eyes go wide, and as he starts to jog at her, he holds a finger up to his lips.

Haley runs.

But in a few strides, he catches her and throws his arms around her, bear-hugging her to his chest. "Stop," he grunts. "Not here to hurt you!"

She bites into his forearm and writhes, tearing at flesh. He cries out, but he hangs on. "Please. Stop. I just want my dog."

Haley opens her eyes and lets the pressure of her bite loosen. Tastes blood in her mouth. She spits and it runs red down the man's arm. "What the fuck did you just say?"

"I want to let you go. But I think you know I can't yet. You keep a gun upstairs, right?"

Bad fucking sign he knows that. She sniffs. Her senses must be going haywire, because the huge man *smells* familiar.

The man sighs. "Jonah stole him from me. It's my dog. I'm his little brother."

She screams again. The man clamps a calloused hand on her mouth, hard, and this time, she can't get loose enough to bite.

"Please. Please." He starts to cry, and tears drip on her exposed shoulder.

After a minute, she calms down.

Something is off: the man could've killed her ten times by now. "Cy?" she mutters into his palm.

The man says nothing, but his hand loosens a little.

Haley looks down at his arms, and realizes it's true. They're like his. Almost exactly like his, just thicker. "Thought you were dead."

"Me too." He takes a deep breath. "I'm sorry I came. Stupid. I thought you'd be gone, at work. I just read that article, and there was a photo of you in it, from in *here*, and I saw him sitting on the floor next to you, and . . . I'm sorry. So sorry."

"You can let me go." She's not sure if she means it.

He does, though. His arms relax, and she pulls free.

She spins and backs away from him, creating some distance. The man doesn't chase her. She looks him up and down, searching for any family resemblance, and there it is. His beard is blond and unruly, but the nose and blue eyes above it are unmistakable. "What did he do to you?"

Cy laughs sadly. "The same as he did to all of us." He looks at the floor, ashamed.

"No. I don't think so." She pauses. *Still broken.* If he really is Cy, how many more years must he have spent with Jonah than she did? Whatever hell he went through, it's nothing she could ever imagine. Pity swells in her chest. "Everyone thinks you helped him with the murders."

He shakes his head. "Only one."

The admission hangs in the air.

Haley shakes, unable to form a reply.

He breaks the silence. "It's the worst regret of my life. It's why I ran and tried to turn him in." He looks up from the floor at her. "But it never worked. So I just kept running. I still am."

Haley puts it together. "You're the one who gave them the photo. Those guys who put it on the internet."

He shrugs. "Yes and no. It's complicated."

She collapses until she's sitting cross-legged on her polished wood floor. "Fuck."

He stands there, waiting.

The crate in the corner rocks madly. *Ba-bunk-bunk-buuunk-bu -buuuunk!*

She speaks up: "What do you mean, *'it's your dog'*?"

His eyes find the crate as it dawns on him. They light up.

Haley stands, slowly, and makes her way over to it, watching him the whole way, just in case. He doesn't move. Just stares at the rocking crate. She flips the blanket off its door.

Inside, Bear wags his tail at warp speed, staring past her at the man and pushing his nose up against the bars.

She unlatches the door.

Bear rockets out, and at first she's sure he's about to go and try to murder the big scary intruder he heard attacking her a moment ago. But then he gets to him, and he just . . . stops. Stares up at the man's face like he can't believe it.

Cy smiles, eyes glistening. "Hey, Poot. I missed you, little guy."

The dog turns sideways and presses hard into his legs, head tucked and tail still.

Cy kneels down and hugs him.

Bear—no, *Poot*—licks his face over and over and presses into him harder.

Haley frowns. "He was yours." Not a question.

Cy nods.

She nods back. "Aren't you afraid I'll turn you in, as soon as you leave here?"

"Do what you want," he says, petting the dog, with a big wet grin on his face. "I deserve it. But you should know something first. If you do, you need to leave the city. Tonight."

She narrows her eyes. "Why?"

He sighs. "Because the people looking for my brother will come after you. Fast. And I'm leaving tomorrow, so I won't be around to protect you from them."

Protect?

She scrunches up her nose. "The FBI?"

Cy looks up, and the grin is gone. He shakes his head.

* * *

An hour later, Haley walks him and the dog she used to call Bear out the front door.

On the stoop, he turns and nods.

She nods.

He smiles.

She looks down at the dog, and they lock eyes. He wags his tail. She waves goodbye. "See you later, Mr. Black Bear. I love you." She holds her hand out to him.

The dog licks her, just once, then he pulls hard to the other end of the leash, trying to reach the pavement.

Cy grunts, holding him still. "Sorry. I think he sees my van."

"No. It's okay." She smiles.

Cy hesitates. "Thank you," he chokes out. He turns and starts walking, with Poot pulling him.

Haley watches them go, thinking about her next move.

Then she gets an idea, better than the last one . . . and her smile grows.

As she walks back inside and locks her door, she makes a mental note to stop and buy lighter fluid on her way to the storage unit tonight. Lots of it. There are more important things than money.

* * *

Across the street, a bodega security camera swivels to follow the man and his dog, blinking red.

It sits still and watches as he climbs into an old camper van.

Its lens shifts, just barely, to focus on the license plate.

CHAPTER

47

Sally

February 18, 2021. 6:21 PM

THE SUN WAS going down.

Sally Davis turned right out of the Puckett's parking lot onto an empty Main Street. It was ten minutes and three more turns before she was back home, pulling into her own driveway.

She pressed a button on her clicker. Her headlights passed over the slow-opening gate.

There was a man in black standing there, waiting.

She screamed. Then she recognized who it was, and stopped.

Thad Wolf stumbled over to her car, leaned against the driver's side window, and tapped with an index finger. Even through the tempered glass, she could smell him. He was stinking drunk. As usual.

Sally rolled down her window. "Thad. God. You gave me a heart attack." She'd thought it was his son.

No one knew anything had happened between her and Jonah except Diana. Sally knew she'd seen them in the cottage that one Thanksgiving, but then Dee never confronted her or told anyone else. It was the strangest, most fucked-up thing. She just acted like it never happened.

Sally had stopped messing around with the Wolfs after that. One of her best decisions ever, in hindsight.

Thad smiled. "I ain't supposed to be here."

She frowned. "Okay. *Why are you?*"

Thad looked confused by the question. He reached into her window with an outstretched hand, dirt under his fingernails, and tried to touch her cheek. Sally recoiled. Pushed his hand away.

Thad frowned. Tried again.

She reached into her purse on the passenger seat and came back up with a can of Mace, pointed at his eyes. His wrinkled hand came to a halt inches from her bare neck and hung in the air.

"I thought we could go on a date," said Thad, swaying. "You dun wanna? I ain't s'posed to be here. Uh . . . s'posed to be at the golf course still. Diana thinks that's where, uh . . ." He smiled again. "You look so goddamn sexy in red, girl. You still wear my color."

Sally rolled her eyes. Pushed his hand out of the window again, then rolled it up so there was only a crack to speak through.

She gave him the middle finger.

Thad barely registered it. He turned his head on its side, confused, like he couldn't imagine the idea that any woman would ever turn him down.

"It's fucking *over*, Thad," she hissed. "In a lot more ways than one, in your case. Okay?"

Thad nodded. "Sure. Fuckin' bitch." He stumbled away, muttering under his breath, back onto the street, then shambled through the red glow cast by her brake lights and disappeared into the night.

Sally rolled up her window the rest of the way, shaking her head.

48

Beau

February 20, 2022. 10:14 AM PST

Beau Pruitt is sitting at his desk in the big office Ryan Huckley used to occupy, answering emails, when his phone buzzes in his pocket. He yawns. Slips it out lazily. Looks down at the screen. Frowns.

There's a notification from Signal.

His eyes get big. He scrambles out of his chair and limps as fast as he can to his open office door.

Beau leans his head out into the hallway and looks once left, once right. Coast is clear. He closes the door and shoves his back up against it. Unlocks his phone, hands shaking.

From the far corner next to the window, Karl peeks around his desktop monitor. "What are you up to?"

Beau holds up a finger, silencing him. He opens the app. Logs in.

There's a single message waiting for him there. He thumbs it.

We need to meet. ASAP.

Beau types a reply: *More payments? names?*

He hits "*Send.*"

Another message comes in seconds: *Need to meet.*

Beau pulls at his tie, muttering curses as he types. *Can fly you in tn. Tell me where from.*

Karl pipes up. "Boss?"

Beau glances at him, then back at his phone. "I need permission for a civilian to join me at the scene in Carson tomorrow, no questions asked. You know how to get that?" In the two-plus years since the director helped him disappear, their special informant has never been too scared to share info over Signal before. Pink must be into something big.

Beau thought his dad had lost his damn mind when Hank first told him what he'd done, but the relationship has been productive so far. Without his help, they might still be wondering, like everyone else in the world, how the manhunt never found jack shit. Thanks to Pink, they know Ryan Huckley was just a sacrificial lamb. Eight dirty feds are in prison because of his tips, and two more are out on bail, but the press and the rest of the bureau can't know too many details. Not until they figure out where the money's coming from, and why.

Karl nods. "On it." He pops back behind his computer.

CHAPTER

49

Pink

February 21, 2022. 4:25 PM

*C*LICK. THERE'S A shutter sound effect.

Pink flips his phone and hardly recognizes the face in it. There are dark purple bags under his eyes, lips contorted in a deep frown, and soggy-looking wrinkles crisscross his forehead. The man in the photo doesn't look like a man at all—more like a corpse.

It's been two years, three months, and eight days since he first offered himself up as a tool to Hank Pruitt. Two years spent doing what he's best at: watching people, listening, sitting alone in the dark on a computer. Sneaking into private places in order to plant hardware when they're gone, or sifting through their trash for receipts and passwords. It all feels eerily similar to the years he spent off his meds, listening to the man in blue, stalking Thad Wolf and his family—only this time it's a lot more people than just the Wolfs he watches, and he never stays in one city for longer than a couple weeks. He takes lithium and speaks to psychiatrists on the phone semi-regularly, and he never, ever sees the man in blue. Beau tells him what to do now.

See? he tells himself. *Things are so much better.*

He sighs.

"Got you a coffee," says a deep voice.

Pink looks over a shoulder and finds Beau Pruitt hobbling up the ridge, holding two disposable cups, one in each hand. He offers the smaller one.

Pink nods, takes it and drinks deep. The too hot coffee burns his throat.

Beau walks to his side and takes in the scenery.

They're technically still in Los Angeles county, in a dirt field full of rusted oil pumps somewhere deep in Carson, but it doesn't feel like the L.A. he remembers. The air is cold and humid here, and not that salty wet cold you get in places like Santa Monica or Malibu where people shrug and say "marine layer" whenever it drops below sixty. It's a wet-blanket cold you'd only expect in the south. Say, Tennessee.

It stinks too, worse than Skid Row ever did—like burnt hair and plastic. Industrial waste pollutes every breath he takes. He doubts any-one lives or works near here by choice.

Beau notices him brooding. "You okay?"

An excavator rumbles in the distance, driving off a dusty access road toward a spot circled by black police SUVs fifty yards ahead. The place where Jonah Wolf's latest iron hatch was found two days ago.

"Yeah." It's the first one Pink has seen in person. "I just never expected to meet like *this*." When he first realized where they were going, he was worried one of the FBI agents might recognize him from the news way back when. But Beau waved it off and told him to stop being paranoid. The agents would be too focused on other things, he said.

The hatch is hidden in a five-by-fifteen-foot dirt trench, three feet deep, dug out with shovels and supported by a thin plywood frame. You'd never know it was there unless you stumbled into it, which is exactly what happened. Some luckless vagrant trekked out here think-ing it looked like a spot where the cops might leave a tent alone. No one has pumped any oil out of this field in decades; the original specu-lators sucked it dry before turning a profit, and when they abandoned the site, all the old pumps too rusted to be worth taking were left to rot. The current owner is an office supply company with a paper mill nearby, and the man who answered the phone when the feds called didn't even know it was part of their lot.

Beau shrugs. "Remembered how you said you wanted to see one before they stop popping up."

Pink nods. *If they stop.* "I appreciate it." He tries to keep the anguish out of his voice as he says, "Do you ever hear from Kerry?"

Beau nods, smiling. "Yup. He's still in Nashville. Working in construction, last time I checked in. Seems happy enough." The smile fades. "I get a sense he doesn't like it when I call, though. Think he wants to forget all this shit."

Pink smiles. "Good for him."

"You still on your new meds?"

"Yes." After he got the break-in notification from Haley's Ring doorbell cam, and it turned out to be Cyrus Wolf, he counted out the whole bottle of pills to be sure he'd been taking them on time.

Then when he took control of the CCTV camera across the street and watched them walk out, all buddy-buddy, an hour later, he checked his count again. He still can't make heads or tails of it.

"Can I ask you something?" says Beau.

Pink shrugs. "You can."

"What's with the nickname? You just choose a color at random?"

Pink slows his breathing, remembering painful times. Skid Row. The reason he finally left. "No."

"So what was it?"

"My father wore blue overalls most of his life, and he thought boys should like the color blue. And only girls like the color pink." He can't help but shake as he says it.

Beau looks worried. "Sorry."

Pink calms down. "I started going by this name online after he died." *Murderer.* He cringes at the half lie. "Then in real life too. Because I had no good examples growing up of what a man should be, but I had one of what a man should never be. So this is me, trying to be everything the man in blue was not. I'm not him. I'm what he hated. Pink."

Beau nods. "I hear you." He kicks idly at the dirt with a polished black shoe. "So, why all this urgency to meet? You get lonely?"

Pink sips his coffee. "Cyrus Wolf is still alive."

Beau spits. "Fuck off."

Pink shrugs. "It's true."

"How do you know?"

Pink explains it, being careful to skirt around most of the deeply unethical parts. "I don't understand how Haley fits into this yet. But we can track him now. See where he leads us."

Beau shakes his head, amazed and troubled at the same time. "So you were still watching his old fiancée that closely?"

Pink nods.

Beau raises an eyebrow at him. "And how about *her*? Same thing?" He means Diana Wolf.

Pink sighs, cringing. *"No."* Hank forbade it, as part of their deal—didn't want to encourage his new tool to fall back into any bad habits, said he'd rather him focus on identifying FBI agents with interesting spending patterns. Corrupt cops—that's Pink's primary focus as a so-called informant. Follow the money, score convictions, and move up the food chain.

But the deal doesn't matter. Results do. He tries to keep careful tabs on every single person who was ever close to Jonah Wolf, whether Hank and Beau like it or not.

He *would* watch Diana just as diligently as he does the rest, if only he could get past her fucking fence. She started building it in earnest a year ago, right after Thad shot himself, and over the next few months Pink lost access to her trash bins, both her webcams, and even the woods behind her house. It was no huge loss, though: she's confined to an expensive chair and too scared to leave Wolf Hollow these days. Ever. Even when he had access, there was nothing to keep tabs on that wasn't sad and useless to him.

He still keeps a trail cam in a tree across the street from her gate, so he'll know if that changes.

Beau frowns. "Uh-huh."

"I said no." Pink tugs his beanie down as a passing fed glances up the hill at them. He checks with a finger to see if his scar is still covered; it is.

Beau stares. "Don't lie to me, man." He gives him a sour look.

Pink growls. "I'm not."

Steam rises in curling wisps off of Beau's bald head. "Fine. Fuck you."

Pink sips his coffee.

A minute passes in silence.

"Where do you think he put the paintings?" says Pink. None of them have shown up, still.

"The ones his impostor sold to him?" Beau shrugs. "He probably already got rid of 'em, if he ever touched any in the first place. Sold 'em off to build all this shit a long time ago, and now they're all sitting on some rich asshole's wall until he dies and they end up in an estate sale."

"I doubt it."

Beau laughs. "You think he's on the run somewhere with thirty-four missing masterpieces? What's he hiding in, a U-Haul?"

Pink shakes his head. "I think he stashed them somewhere." Like buried gold. "Somewhere he could retrieve them, one at a time."

"You really think he could sell them still?"

Pink nods. "Easily." All he'd have to do is find a single unscrupulous art dealer to act as his proxy, and he could do it through Christie's. There are no requirements to report the identities of buyers or sellers in a fine art auction. "I wonder if Cy might know where he got the money originally. Who was paying him." Probably the same people still paying the feds he puts away.

Another silence.

Beau shakes his head and makes a *tsk*ing sound. "You hear they're using forensic sculptors to ID the victims, now?"

Pink hadn't, but he's not surprised. "Those poor families."

Beau nods. "One step up from psychics. That's where we're at." He sighs. "Doesn't feel like we made anything better, does it? I mean, maybe you did after, helping us put away those pieces of shit taking bribes, but we don't even know who or . . ." He trails off.

Pink looks at him. "No. It doesn't feel like it."

Beau smiles. "Guess we just gotta keep trying."

Pink nods.

Beau claps him on the back with a meaty hand, and he almost falls down the hill.

The excavator reaches its destination: the trench. Its arm rumbles down and catches on an edge of the iron hatch and starts prying it open. The heavy machine revs its engine. The hatch whines. Then, *clink*. A tiny chunk of metal breaks off and flies twenty feet in the air, and the manhole cover-sized hatch lifts up in a puff of brown dust.

The excavator flips into reverse, beeping. The tiny metal chunk hits the dirt behind it, harmlessly.

Blue-and-yellow-jacketed federal agents pour into the opening, flashlights waving. The first group climbs carefully down the ladder inside as they shout up descriptions and orders to those coming in behind them.

Pink takes a deep breath. Something's been bothering him. It's the real reason he wanted to talk in person, and he's waited months for a good excuse. "Do you ever think there are too many bodies now?"

Beau looks up. "Too many?"

"For one man to have killed." He pauses, letting his meaning sink in. "Think about it. How long would it have taken to scout and build each shaft? Even if he used slave labor and killed the workers after, he'd

need to supervise. It would take months. And this is the eighteenth."
Pink shakes his head. "I wonder: what if that was all he did? Dig or
design the caves for others to store bodies in, and then sign them."

Beau frowns. "Why would he do that?"

Pink shivers in the cold. "To take credit."

Beau pulls up his jacket, rubs his hands together. "You think he
wanted the title?"

Pink nods.

Beau blinks. "Fuck. That makes sense."

"Yes. And if I'm right, it means we've been chasing a ghost for
years, but the real killers never stopped."

"So you're saying he never murdered anyone?"

Pink bites his lip. "No. We know he did. But what if he was just
one of many? An employee. And above the many . . . something worse."

"Like what?"

Pink shrugs. "I don't know. But I keep thinking about this phrase
I used to find all over his old hard drives. *Buffalo Hunt.*" He shivers
again. "Have you heard it before or come across it anywhere else?" He
glances at his friend hopefully.

Beau shakes his head.

"Me neither." The crime scene hums with motion and sound,
assaulting Pink's senses:

Feds yelling.

SUV engines idling, lights flashing blue and red.

Factories churning on the horizon, pumping out black smoke and
stench.

Heavy footsteps running on dry dirt.

Windbreakers flapping in the cold, damp air.

After a minute, a man shouts *"Clear!"* from the top of the ladder
just inside the hatch, waving his arm. It's the go-ahead signal they've
been waiting for.

"You still wanna see inside?" Beau dumps the last of his coffee.

Pink nods.

The two men walk down the hill, and Beau shakes hands with
the feds at the top of the hatch. He and Pink flash their respective ID
badges, and just like Beau promised, no one takes a long look at the
face of his civilian tag-along. Too busy. Soon, every FBI jacket is stepping aside to let them pass like they parted the Red Sea.

They get to the ladder and start down it. It's rusty.

The air is even colder inside the hatch. It's dark at the bottom.

Pink puts one foot below the other. One rung at a time, he climbs down.

When they stop off the ladder, there's a cramped tunnel. Just like all the rest, it's supported by crude wood-and-nail beams, which makes it look like an old mineshaft. Portable spotlights are already being set up further down. With all the men in yellow-and-blue jackets shuffling around, the scene inside is not as frightening as it should be: empty iron shackles bolted to the wood supports, forty sets running the length of the tunnel; some that aren't empty.

A spotlight hits a deep alcove, and it's carpeted in bones.

Pink counts distinct victims as he passes. It looks like twenty or so new Jane Does when all is said and done.

The shackles run out, giving way to bare packed dirt. But the tunnel keeps going, too far to see an end.

"Shit," says Beau behind him. "Tell me it's not another Wolf Hole."

Pink keeps walking.

Suddenly, the tunnel widens out. Then the walls go from dirt to solid rock, and it widens out more—a lot more.

They come to the end, and find themselves standing at the entrance to a massive natural cavern of smooth, dry stone. A roughly circular space forty feet in diameter, with a domed ceiling half as tall. There still aren't enough lights to illuminate every inch, but there are enough pointing up at the ceiling for them to know there's a gargantuan mural painted on it.

All black-and-white. No colors.

More lights shine on it as Pink and Beau watch, mouths agape.

It's not just one mural on the ceiling: it's a grid of seventeen horrific scenes, arranged like panels in a comic book. Demons eating, fucking, killing, bathing in blood. All queasily realistic masterpieces, preserved for eternity.

Pink can guess what the narrative is without pausing on each scene to decipher it: a ghost story. A black and twisted Sistine Chapel devoted to the worship of its creator's myth. A future pilgrimage site.

And lording over all of it in the round central panel: a giant Cheshire cat smile. White teeth in the dark, laughing at them.

Pink breathes the cold air, exhaling mist. Staring. "How many years did Michelangelo spend painting one ceiling?"

Beau looks at him, blood drained from his face. "Four straight. I remember that from the Vatican tour."

They both knew it then: Jonah hadn't killed hundreds of people. How could he have, when he spent four years in this hole, painting his masterpiece? His altar. And Pink knew his suspicions had been right. The killing never stopped. There were other killers besides Jonah Wolf. Are *still* many others. And there's money involved. Someone worse is paying them all, and paying off cops to keep them from being caught. But why?

What is the Buffalo Hunt?

Pink nods. "Jonah played all of us." He's going to be sick.

He walks out of the cavern and makes his way back through the tunnel to the ladder, shoving feds aside as they look at him and mutter angrily. Climbs up as fast as he can and barely makes it up into daylight before he doubles over and vomits coffee onto the abandoned lot, the only contents of his stomach. The earth drinks it.

50

Thad

February 18, 2021. 6:58 PM

THAD WOLF WALKED down a winding road in the dark, feet heavy and unsure, one hand gliding over a gnarled wooden fence that marked the far edges of Wolf Hollow. Inches away from standing on his property, but miles from home. He smiled. It made him feel like a medieval lord, owning so much land that there were parts he'd never see. Rich and powerful and dangerous to his lessers—a great man.

If only his daddy could see him now.

Thad frowned. He spit.

There were no streetlights. A cold wind howled, blowing his thin hair back. The poplar trees on both sides of the road bent in a sudden rush of air, and their limbs whined and snapped. "Shaddup. Fuckin' trees."

The wind died.

Silence again. Not even an insect chirped.

Thad felt a twinge of something primal, instinctual: *eyes watching*. A finger moved to the pistol on his hip. He kept walking.

The feeling went away. He felt certain he'd scared off a potential mugger, and sneered.

To pass the time, he launched into a loud, warbling rendition of the first verse in *"A Thousand Lies"*:

How'd I ever wind up here in this smoky motel?
Neon blinkin' through the curtains and I'm hurtin' like hell.

I hear the streets, I smell the rain
But I don't feel a goddamn thing but pain . . .

A branch snapped. Off to his left, nearby.

Thad went quiet again. Stopped walking. The finger on his pistol grip became a clenched fist, trembling as he scanned the empty, silent poplar forest.

The noise had come from Wolf Hollow. Whatever made it was heavy. Either some neighbor's escaped animal or the biggest armadillo that ever lived had just strolled by. Or someone was trespassing on his property.

There.

He could hardly believe it when he saw it: there was a man standing in the woods, faceless in the dark.

"Who's there? Who is that!?" Thad unclasped the leather strap over his pistol and lifted it out of its holster, clicking off the safety.

He had always wondered what was stopping folks from walking into these poplar woods from off the street. *His* woods. He suspected it happened all the time, and he had just never been out here to catch any of the fuckers before. Too busy. "Don't you goddamn move. I got a weapon."

His heart fluttered with excitement as he pointed his gun at the trespasser, fifty yards away.

The man turned and ran off into the trees.

Thad lowered the gun and cursed under his breath. He stumbled off the road, ducking under the fence, and then jogged into the woods after the shadow man, pistol bobbing at his side.

A minute or three passed with no sign of him. Thad almost gave up and turned back.

But then he saw the silhouette again, standing less than a football field ahead, and he roared: "Where you think you're goin', huh?" He slowed, lining up a clear shot. "You someone's kid, boy? You got to a count of three to get on those knees and beg me not to tell your daddy."

The man said nothing.

Thad raised his gun. "One. Two."

The man ducked behind a tree.

Thad dropped the barrel to his waist.

Insects buzzed and bare branches shivered in the canopy above. It occurred to him that he must have covered some ground. The drone of distant cars on the highway was gone. Every labored breath he took sounded deafening in his head.

He ran from tree to tree, posing behind each one like James Bond. When he got close to where he had last seen the man, he stopped and caught his wind. Then he spun into the open with his gun up, ready to fire.

But there was no one.

Thad scratched his temple with the pistol's sights, confused. He wiped his face with a thin sleeve, and it came away damp. He shivered, suddenly aware of just how light his jacket was.

The man appeared again, closer this time. Maybe thirty yards off. He waved a black hand. *Leather gloves?*

Thad took off at a run.

He got within spitting distance, close enough to see the man was wearing some kind of mask. But before he could take aim, his quarry melted into the dark again.

Thad stopped in his tracks, suddenly unsure if he was chasing a man at all, or some sort of ghost. He threw his hands up, exhausted. His knees ached. Blood was pounding in his head.

He returned his gun to its holster with a disappointed huff. *Next time,* he told himself.

He turned in a circle, saw no recognizable landmarks, and realized with a pang of fear that he had no idea what direction would lead him back to the road. How long had he been chasing the man? It was hard to say. He closed his eyes and tried to retrace his last steps, but adrenaline and alcohol had fuzzed the time line.

There was a clearing a quarter mile off to his left. A moonlit gap in the trees. He made his way to it, slowly. The trees seemed thicker here than at the edges of the woods, and the forest floor was blanketed in brown leaves and twigs that crunched under his boots. It kept getting colder. His breath came out white now. By the time he got to the clearing, he was shivering bad.

Thad stepped out from the trees, squinting in disbelief. A smile crept onto his lips. He must've wandered onto someone else's property, at some point. *Thank the Lord.*

There was a small house in the clearing. The lights were on.

He stumbled through the grass, waving both arms and yelling so as not to surprise some hillbilly and get shot: "Ay! Neighbor! Just a neighbor! I need help out here! Not trespassing, just got lost, thass all!"

No one answered.

Thad came all the way to the front door. He knocked on it three times. "Anyone home?" As he waited, his teeth started to chatter.

Fuck it.

He tried the doorknob. To his surprise, it swung open.

Thad stood in the doorway, frowning. "Neighbor?"

No answer.

He took a step inside, leaving the door open.

It was dark in this part of the house. He passed a kitchenette on his left, with a big black-and-white stone countertop island in it. The entry hall hooked a sharp right up ahead, so he couldn't see what he assumed was the main room yet. But the light was coming from in there.

He kept shouting what he was doing: "I am coming in from the cold. Okay? I just—I need to warm up before I, uh . . . head on home. I'm inside now. Just a neighbor."

His shivering got worse as he walked. It felt just as cold in the house as it had been outside.

He noticed something odd and frowned. A wall up ahead was covered in paintings. Four neat rows of three frames—a *dozen* of them on one wall, taking up every inch of it from floor to ceiling.

All black and white.

Thad froze, teeth chattering.

There was a small noise behind him, like a rat skittering.

Thad whipped around, searching. "Who's there?" His eyes got big. The front door was closed.

He reached for his pistol and lifted it from the holster. Clicked the safety off and raised it.

He felt a tiny *pain* in his neck and slapped at it, dropping the gun. It clattered on the floor. He spun and tried to go after it.

A man in a crumbling rubber mask stood there, dressed all in black and wearing leather gloves.

Thad jumped halfway out of his skin and fell on his ass. He crab-walked backward, trying to put distance between himself and his son, but soon his arms felt like jelly and his head was too heavy for his neck. His left hand slipped. He fell sideways.

He tried to speak, to say his son's name, but the words came out garbled. "Oh-nah. Nuh. Nuh-uh-uh. Nuh. Nuh!"

Jonah squatted, staring into his father's eyes through slits in the mask. The razor blades in its mouth jangled together as he spoke: "Shh. It's just a bad dream."

Tears streamed down Thad's cheeks. This time when he tried to speak, nothing came out. His lips opened and closed like those of a caught fish gasping at air.

The world went dark.

*   *   *

Thad woke up bound in ropes. Hog-tied. No feeling in his hands or feet. A ball gag in his mouth.

The dead brown leaves and twigs blanketing the forest floor scraped his cheek raw and bloody as he was dragged.

Thad moaned in pain, twitching.

"Shh," said his son's voice.

The ground swam. His eyes closed again.

*   *   *

When Thad woke up the second time, he was sitting up in an old dining chair. Tied to it with rope and duct tape. Deep in the woods, in the dark. It was quieter than ever. The branches in the canopy were silent and still. Only insects made noise, but the sound filled his ears like it was a chainsaw.

Jonah was standing five feet away, arms crossed. Masked. "Awake?"

Thad tried to speak, but the ball gag was held taut in his mouth.

"You can nod."

Thad met his stare, breathing fast and heavy out his nose. After a while, he nodded. It felt like something heavy was tied to his head.

"And how are your fingers? Any feeling yet?"

Thad tried to move them. His left hand was bound at his side, but his right . . . it was bound too, but in a different place, up near his ear. And his fingers felt *cold*, like he was holding something metal. He wiggled them and a familiar knurled roughness met his touch: the grip of his pistol.

Jonah nodded.

Thad tried to scream. No use.

"Take your time." Jonah tilted his mask up at the black sky. There were no stars in it. "I have nowhere to be."

Thad calmed down. He stared daggers at his son, shaking.

No . . . not shaking. Shivering again. He looked down, as much as he was able to. He was naked. Worse, his hair and skin were still damp with sweat from running earlier. Violent tremors worked their way up his spine, like his body had only just realized how cold it was once he saw his clothes gone. He jerked and yanked at the ropes and tape.

Jonah shook his head, slow, like he was disgusted.

Thad moaned and shivered. His teeth wanted to chatter, but the gag held them in place. It hurt.

"Trigger is right there. Just pull it. And it's over." Jonah sighed. "Should I get comfortable? Nod. Or shake."

Thad was hyperventilating. He felt woozy enough to puke, but he fought it, terrified of choking on the sick if he did. He forced himself to breathe only at regular intervals.

He nodded, defiant.

"Stubborn. I figured as much." Jonah didn't sit.

*   *   *

Two hours passed. It felt like ten.

Thad's nerves had woken up, one by one, and they were on fire. Searing pain radiated from every inch of exposed skin, like he'd submerged himself in a bath of dried ice. He whimpered involuntarily.

He looked down at his feet, the only part of him that wasn't hurting. His right big toe was starting to turn blue. He thrashed at his bindings again, but all it did was bring more pain.

Jonah sighed. "If you're thinking rope marks will tell any half-decent medical examiner this was no suicide, you're right."

Thad thrashed harder.

"But I learned something from you and mom a long time ago: money buys *anything*. And one medical examiner is not expensive. Everyone else will only see what they want to see."

Thad stopped.

Jonah squatted, resting both hands on his knees. It made him look like a spider. "You know why I waited this long to come for you?"

Thad tried to scream again—he tried and tried.

"After this, I'm retired. I could have ended it sooner. I just wanted to wait until there was no question. Until you already knew it." Jonah took off his mask, and his lip quivered like he might cry. Then it was gone. "You were *wrong*. It did happen for me. Your son is more famous than you ever were, a hundred times over, and luck had nothing to do with it. It was will. I chose this." He sneered, baring his real teeth. "I consumed you, down to the last morsel. Your name. Your music. It's all just me now. You are a minor character in the legend of Jonah Wolf, America's most treasured ghost story."

Thad stared up at him, furious.

Jonah laughed in his face. "That is your only legacy. No one will remember you for anything else. And you know it."

Thad shook his head.

Jonah nodded. "But I have a secret." He made a big show of looking around to make sure the two of them were all alone. "A secret no
one can ever know except you. The truth is . . ." He leaned in close
and whispered in his father's ear: "You weren't a minor character, Dad.
Far from it. You were the most important person in my entire life. I
owe you everything. Your legacy is *me*." He stood, uncoiling to his full
height like a cobra. Put his mask back on. "Aren't you proud?"

Thad shook his head.

A dark cloud parted, and the razor blades sewn into the mask's
mouth twinkled in the moonlight. "Now pull it."

Thad thrashed. He moaned and cried.

Jonah stared with empty eyes and didn't move a muscle.

*   *   *

Eleven hours and sixteen minutes passed.

It was daylight in the woods—and had been for some time. Still
cold, but the sky was bright and blue, not a cloud in sight. Birds were
chirping.

Thad's breathing was ragged. He was in agony; he had been for a
long time. For years, if he was being honest. Not just hours.

Jonah had hardly budged. He squatted in the dirt like a gargoyle,
showing no signs of fatigue.

Ever since the sun had come up, terrible hallucinations had been
dancing at the edges of Thad's peripheral vision: his daddy standing
over him with a belt, speaking in tongues. A woman cowering in a
cave, bloodied and crying. The images blurred and ran together.

It was a circle.

Enough. He wanted out.

Thad closed his eyes. He put his index finger on the trigger and
pulled it.

CHAPTER

51

Diana

May 11, 1978. 7:22 AM

A N ALARM RANG.
Diana Guthrie was twelve years old, and she was exhausted. *Go back to sleep,* her body said. But her brain said it was a Monday, and the kids' summer break was still a few weeks off, so she shambled into the kitchen and cooked breakfast for her little brother and sister: leftover skirt steak and four eggs. The only food in the refrigerator. Pantry was locked, but there was probably nothing edible in it.

It'd been weeks since anyone bought groceries.

While the steak fried in a pan, she crept into Kristen and Luke's shared room down the hall.

She leaned over the twin bed. "Hey there, puppets."

Kristen's eyes opened first. Luke rubbed his and rolled over, grumbling.

Diana frowned at the sight of his ribs. *Too skinny.* Kristen was too, and so was she, but it wasn't as noticeable on them. Bonnie always said girls are supposed to be skinny. Diana didn't know if that was true, though. She didn't know if a lot of things Mom had said over the years were true. A lot of things Mom *saw* and *heard* weren't real.

She climbed onto their bed and started jumping, yelling, "Earthquake!"

The pillows and sheets popped up and down in the air. Kristen laughed. Luke was grumpy, but he woke up.

Diana hurried both of them into the bathroom and watched as they brushed their teeth. Luke faked it sometimes. *"Ariba, ariba.* School bus in thirty minutes. Where you gonna be?"

"Bus stop!" they both sang, mouths full of toothpaste.

"Correct. What are you gonna have?"

"All our school supplies!"

Diana laughed. "You better!"

Once she was satisfied their teeth truly were being brushed, she hurried back into the kitchen, where the steak was on fire. She took the pan off the heat, let it burn out, and opened a window. Fanned the smoke out with a paper plate from the trash.

When it was safe, she dumped the charred steak onto a plate and poured the beaten eggs into the pan, which was still hot enough to cook them.

Luke and Kristen wandered into the kitchen and sat at the folding card table in the corner, mostly dressed.

"Luke. Your shirt is on backwards."

"What about me, Dee?" asked Kristen.

Diana looked her up and down, keeping one eye on the eggs. "You're good."

Kristen smiled, delighted.

Luke grumbled something about liking his shirt that way, so when the eggs were done, she just walked over and fixed it for him against his will.

She split the eggs and steak evenly between two plates. Sat at the table and served both to her siblings. "I already ate," she said when they asked why. She hadn't.

As they ate, she took a deep breath and said a little prayer. *O Lord . . .*

Since they'd all be leaving in a few minutes, she walked down the long hallway to Mom's room to say goodbye.

The door creaked open. The bedroom was dark inside. Bonnie was nowhere to be seen.

In the back of the room, there was a door that led to a small master bathroom. Diana could hear water running. Under the door, she could see a strip of yellow light.

She crossed the room and opened it.

Inside the small bathroom, Bonnie sat in the bathtub, knees tucked up to her chest.

"Mom?" The bath was full, but the water was still on. It was running over the edge, spilling onto the floor.

Bonnie looked at her daughter, mascara running down both cheeks, and she smiled. She lifted a revolver to her own head. *Bang!*

Blood spattered the walls. It soaked Diana's face. It got in her eyes, but she kept them open.

The big, heavy revolver fell into the water. *Plunk.*

She stood in the doorway for a full minute, shaking. Stared at her mother's corpse as the bath water ran and ran, pooling across the tiled floor. It spread all the way to her shoes. It was dark red.

She took off her shoes, walked in and calmly turned off the spigot.

She closed her eyes, reached into the tub, drained it, and finally fished out the revolver from between the corpse's legs. She hid the gun on top of the medicine cabinet where Luke wouldn't be able to reach.

She cleaned the blood off the corpse's face with a fistful of toilet paper, as best she could.

A little scream: *"Mommy!"*

Diana turned her head and saw Luke standing in the doorway, bawling, barely tall enough to reach the knob gripped tight in his little hand. Screaming. Staring.

She rushed over, enveloped him in a hug. "Shh . . ."

Kristen ran in and then just stood in the doorway, not moving.

Diana slung Luke over her shoulder and whisked him back to the kitchen, where she sat him down at the table and told him to finish his steak and that Mommy was only resting.

He kept crying, but he ate.

She went to the landline on the wall, put it to her ear, and dialed 911. No tears in her eyes. A dispatcher picked up on the second ring.

52

Diana

March 3, 2022. 10:08 AM

DIANA WOLF WAKES up in pain. She's used to it—nerve damage or something from her fall into the bathtub that day. Nothing she can do but ignore it, so that's what she does.

It took almost a full year before she got comfortable swinging her numb legs out of bed and into her chair, but now she's a pro. The chair itself is a marvel. It's big, solid, and heavy as hell, painted the same dark green as her old Jag. It can climb up stairs like a Transformer, and its electric engine puts out twenty horsepower—more than she'll ever need puttering around the house, but if you can afford the top-of-the-line trim, why not go for it?

She powers on the chair and hums over to her closet, where she gathers a basic outfit: black pants, a white blouse from Christine, matching undies, socks, and black leather D&G flats. The time it takes her to get fully dressed every morning is embarrassing (socks are hell), but she bears it with a detached smile. And she looks fucking great in the mirror when she's finished.

She smiles at her reflection. She still *has it*.

That *New Yorker* article even commented on it—how "*beautiful*" and "*imposing*" she still is in spite of everything. Rest of it was pretentious and full of shit, but that part gave her a kick.

Diana rolls through the living "room" into the kitchen, where there's one less stool at the island than there used to be, to make room for her chair. She leans and cracks the wine cooler open, removing a bottle of Malbec and two custom glasses. She leaves one on the island and plants one in the beverage holder at the end of her left armrest, then gets a rabbit corkscrew out of a drawer and uses it to open the wine. Pours herself a generous glass.

A single *beep* emits from the bank of security monitors on the wall. She checks it and sees movement. Her groceries are here.

She stares at the small black-and-white screen as the delivery van's driver gets out and places two bags of food on the grass next to her gate. He looks nervous. Must be new.

She takes a long swig of wine and then presses a button next to the monitors, where there's a little microphone. "Good boy. Now get the fuck off my property, or I'll grind your bones to make my bread."

The driver jumps, looking up at the camera. He skitters back into his van and starts the engine.

Diana grins. It's the little things.

She leaves the house via the front door and takes the ramp down to her John Deere parked in the gravel circle outside. It takes more than twenty horsepower to get up a driveway as steep as hers, apparently, or maybe her chair's specs are just blatant false advertising. Oh well. The John Deere is gas powered. It chugs and belches a puff of black dust when she turns it on.

She unstraps herself from the chair and swings onto the bigger machine. Takes the wheel in one hand and uses a special stick shift to put it in gear and punch the accelerator. She blasts off up the hill.

The woods are full of birds chirping as she climbs the paved driveway. She enjoys her once-weekly trips up here, even if she's always on edge the whole time, worrying there might be something awful waiting at the gate: a journalist with a camera crew ready to film a "*gotcha*" segment; paparazzi hiding in the bushes; men in black and cops delivering more terrible news or yet another search warrant. All the reasons she built her fence in the first place.

Near the top, she passes by the old skeet-shooting ravine, still full of shattered orange discs. She slows to a stop, thinking of Cy.

She lowers her head and says a silent prayer:

O Lord, if he's still alive . . . keep him far away from here.

Diana revs the engine again and makes her way up to the front gate. As she approaches the fence and the deadly hum in the air grows louder, like a swarm of killer bees, she takes a second to check whether anyone's there. Nope. No one. The road is empty in both directions. She grabs a clicker off the John Deere's passenger seat, enters a code on its number pad, and presses a button. The hum dies, replaced by the rusty metal sound of her gate sliding open.

She takes a deep breath and holds it. Rolls out of the gate to where the two bags of groceries are sitting, and hoists them onboard. In just a few seconds, she's back inside the fence, pressing the button on the clicker again. A deadly hum fills the air. She lets the breath out.

This is the extent of her weekly interaction with the world.

Normally, at least.

But right as she's about to turn and start back down the hill, she hears a car coming and looks up.

A black SUV is approaching from the south. Slow, like its driver is lost.

Diana narrows her eyes—and waits. A bad feeling creeps up her neck, and the hairs there stand up.

Just like she thought it might, the SUV slows to a stop in front of her gate. Its passenger door opens, and a man steps out. She lowers her head instinctively, but then she recognizes his face.

Diana frowns. What the hell is Luke doing here?

He walks nervously up to the gate, looking just like the delivery driver did. Scared. Unsure what to expect. He bends down and tries to find a number pad or a button to press. There is none.

Diana hits the gas and starts down the hill. That's when he sees her.

"Dee?" he says behind her. "I can see you."

She stops, but she doesn't turn around.

Another car door opens, then slams shut. There's a sound like heels on pavement.

"Dee." It's a new voice, feminine, one she also recognizes. "Dee, please talk to us. We came all this way because we love you."

Tears fill Diana's eyes. She wipes them on the neck of her blouse. Then she turns her head, and sees both of her siblings standing just outside the fence and staring at her.

Luke has a scraggly beard she's never seen him wear, and Kristen has a string of gaudy pearls around her throat and too much makeup on. But it's them. They're here. *Why* are they here?

She drives up to the fence, still humming. Stares at them.

Luke waves. "Hi, Dee."

Diana doesn't wave back. "What are you doing here?"

Kristen gulps. "We read that article about you."

Diana sighs.

Luke looks at the ground. "We had no idea you were living alone."

Kristen's eyes get glassy. "Why didn't you answer our calls? Why won't you talk to us?"

Diana opens her mouth to answer, but no words come to mind. "What time is it?" She didn't bring a watch with her, and she never even charges her phone anymore.

Luke blinks. He slips a phone out of his pocket. "It's eleven." He puts it back, staring at her. "Can we come in? Or can we take you to brunch in town? Wherever you want."

"We just want to talk," says Kristen. "Please?"

Diana thinks about it. *Eleven.* That gives her two hours.

She grabs her clicker and enters the code.

*   *   *

Diana drops her groceries off next to the front door and then leads her brother and sister into the kitchen. She snatches up the glass she left on the island and dives into the cooler for one more, then splits the remains of the bottle she opened earlier evenly between the two.

Luke laughs as he sits at the island. "You still like Malbecs, huh?"

Diana nods. Pushes a glass his way.

He takes it.

Kristen sits next to him and eyes her own glass nervously. "I don't drink anymore."

"Why not?" It comes out defensive, and Diana wishes she'd said something else. Her social skills seem to have atrophied. That, or she's just nervous.

Kristen smiles politely. "Michael is in a program. Solidarity, you know? I want to help him."

Luke sniggers and takes a deep sip. "Kristen is helpful like that."

She frowns at him.

"I'm serious!" Luke rolls his eyes. "I am capable of sincerity, you know." He turns back to Diana. "Kristen helped me out when I was down on my luck a couple years back. Michael got me the job I'm at now, technically, but I know who really talked him into it."

Kristen smiles. "I may have mentioned his name once or twice."

"Uh-huh."

Kristen hits him softly on the shoulder.

Diana finishes her wine, hands shaking. She goes to the cooler and starts the process of opening another bottle.

Luke stands and walks to her. "Let me get that for you." He grabs the wine out of her hand, and after a brief struggle, she lets it go.

Diana blinks, watching him open the bottle with the casual, painless ease that every able-bodied person takes for granted. "Why are you here?"

Luke pours the wine for her. "To catch up. And to make you an offer, if you're okay with that."

Kristen nods. "We want to help. We love you. And we owe you."

Diana feels tears in her eyes again, and she looks away.

Luke kneels down and pulls her head up gently to look at him. "Why are you hiding in here? I know you've been through the wringer these last few years, but you can still live a good life. You deserve one. Especially now, after all the shit you've—" He stops. "I just don't get it."

Diana snorts. "I deserve everything I got."

Luke shakes his head and hugs her. He pulls away and looks her in the eye. "You can be an asshole, Dee. But you're the best person either of us knows. You saved our lives."

Kristen nods. "We miss you."

Diana shakes her head. "Can we talk about you guys, not me? Just for a while."

Luke gives her the glass of wine he poured, then he sits back down at the island. "Of course. What do you want to know?"

Diana smiles. "Tell me everything."

An hour and thirty-five minutes pass. The siblings talk. Three years' worth of gossip and small talk flows.

Diana laughs. "I can't believe you came all this way without even knowing if I'd answer."

Kristen's cheeks go red. "Neither could Michael. But I swung it."

Luke whispers: "She gets whatever she wants."

Kristen stares daggers at him.

Diana touches her brother's hand. "I missed you guys too. I'm glad you came."

Luke and Kristen look at each other meaningfully.

Diana frowns. "What?"

Luke takes a deep breath. "Well, I said we wanted to make you an offer, if you're okay with that."

"I'm not." Diana tries to say it politely but firmly, but it just comes out panicked. "Please. Don't."

Kristen frowns.

Luke turns his head sideways. "Okay, will you hear us out, first?"

Diana breathes, in and out. "I want to stay here. Alone."

"Why?" Kristen sighs. "*Why*, Dee? Look at this house. Look at you. Why would you stay here?"

Diana crosses her arms defiantly. "Because I built this house. It's mine."

"You paid architects and fifty other people to build it," says Luke. He frowns, regretting it. "Sorry."

Kristen glares at him, then turns to her sister. "That's not enough. I can't leave you here all by yourself like this. I won't."

Diana shakes her head, scoffing. "What should I do? Huh? Hire a nurse? Go live in a home? *This* is my home, and it always will be!"

"Live with us!" Kristen yells. She starts to cry.

Luke rubs her shoulder.

Diana looks back and forth between them, confused. "What?"

Luke looks up. "We want you to come live with us, at Kristen and Michael's place in Santa Barbara."

"He already said it's okay," whispers Kristen, sniffing. "And Luke offered to stay with you in the guest house and be your live-in nurse. You wouldn't have to hire anyone."

Luke nods seriously.

Diana feels tears streaming down her cheek. She looks at the clock, and her heart starts to race. "Get out."

Kristen stares at her. "What?"

Diana rolls to the front door and opens it. "I need you both to get out. Now. I'm sorry, and it was nice to talk to you both, but no. You need to leave."

Luke stands, confused. "Did we say something to offend you?"

Diana nods.

Kristen stands and goes to her. "Dee. No."

Diana laughs. "I said you need to fucking get out!"

Kristen recoils. She nods. Walks out the door, and then turns to look at her. "I wish you could see how much we both love you."

Diana nods. "I love you too. You don't know how much I do." She starts to say more, then stops.

Luke walks to the door, shaking his head. He looks at the two bags of groceries on the floor. "This is insane. It's stupid. How are you even going to put all this away? Let us help."

Diana points him outside. "Leave. Now. And don't come back unless I ask you to." She smiles at him sadly. "This is what I want, Luke. It's for the best. Trust me."

Luke opens his mouth, but he can't find anything good to say. He nods. "Okay." He walks out.

Diana shuts the door behind him, then she maneuvers her chair to a window and watches them from it. Luke looks for a long time at the house, and then Kristen pulls him away. They take each other by the shoulders and walk back to the black SUV she rented from the airport; then they both climb inside. The engine starts.

The car climbs the driveway, and her siblings fade from sight.

She heads back into the kitchen, where she follows their progress on the security monitors. When they get near the top, she enters the code on a pad, and her front gate opens. She watches the black SUV pause just inside the gate, then drive out and into the road.

She enters the code again. The gate closes.

Then Diana sits at the kitchen island and cries.

After ten minutes, she stops. Rubs her eyes. Turns her head and stares at the grocery bags sitting on the floor next to the front door, then at the clock on the wall: 1:03 PM.

She takes a long breath and closes her eyes. *You did the right thing,* she tells herself. *You protected your family, like you always have and always will. All of them.*

She rolls over to the back porch and looks out over her yard, and the gravel path that leads down to the woods. Follows it all the way to the cobblestone bridge spanning the ravine.

And there he is, right on time.

Jonah emerges from the woods and crosses the cobblestone bridge, carrying his backpack. He looks up and sees her, and he waves, smiling.

Diana smiles and waves back.

It's been nearly a year since her son returned home to take care of her. He's been living in the woods ever since, out at the treehouse he and Cy built back when they were kids, and he visits her daily to help out around the house. She wasn't lying when she told that journalist she built the fence for her son; it just wasn't meant to keep him *out.*

Only a few people on Earth know the truth of what he's been through. He told her all of it.

It wasn't him. Not one of those murders. He's just the scapegoat who took the fall for them. And now the real bad people who framed him are looking to kill him to keep him quiet, just like they probably did to his little brother. But they won't find Jonah here, now that she's protecting the only son she's got left. Her big, brave boy. Diana always knew he could never have done all those things they said; she and Thad hadn't raised their sons that way.

And like Jonah pointed out, there are too many bodies. It's ridiculous. He'd have to have been in ten places at once.

She goes to the kitchen and pours a new glass of Malbec for him.

Jonah enters through the back porch door and puts his bag down on the counter. "You're not gonna believe what I've got for you," he says, grinning. "Come look."

Diana rolls to him. "What is it?" She hands him his wine, and he sets it next to him.

Jonah opens the bag. "Voilà." Inside the bag, there's a DVD copy of *The Princess Bride* and a dusty old player to watch it on.

Diana swoons. "Oh, my god. Where did you get this?"

Jonah smirks. "I have my ways. And I know you unhooked the internet for the Apple TV, so . . ."

She frowns at him. "You left?" She hits him, hard. "Jonah. You can't."

He shrugs.

She hits him again. "I'm serious. *No.* You can't." Tears are in her eyes again. "I just got you back."

He frowns and bends down to her level, grabs her hand in his. "I know. I promise you, I'm not going anywhere. Not for a long time." He smiles and kisses her on the cheek.

Diana hugs his neck. "You better not." She laughs, shaking her head. "Can we watch it tonight?"

Jonah chuckles. "I was planning on it." He pulls away and stands. "Where'd you put the bags?"

"By the front door." She motions with her head.

He goes and picks them up, carries them into the kitchen, then starts putting away all the groceries in her cabinets.

Diana takes a long drink and wipes her eyes. "I had company earlier."

Jonah turns and gives her a look. "Who?"

She grins devilishly. "Guess."

He rolls his eyes. "Hmm. The delivery boy? You salty dog."

She drinks, laughing. "No! Guess again."

"Uh . . . Robyn Clarke."

"Haven't seen her in ages. Nope."

Jonah narrows his eyes at her. "Not Sally?"

"Jesus, Jonah. No."

"Huh. Was it friends or family?"

She tilts her glass at him. "Getting warmer. Family."

Jonah grunts. He shoves a bag of apples into the crisper drawer in the fridge. "Now you gave it away. How were Uncle Luke and Aunt Kristen?"

Diana sighs. "Good. They wanted me to come live with them, actually. In Santa Barbara." She scrunches up her nose.

"And? What'd you tell them?"

"Nothing. Just no." She smiles. "It was good talking to them, though, up until that."

Jonah finishes with the groceries. He throws the empty bags in a recycling bin under the counter. "That's nice." His tone changes. "Did they ask anything about me?"

"No."

Jonah grabs his glass of wine and joins her at the island. "Good." He clinks her glass and takes a drink.

*　　*　　*

Later that night, Jonah carries her to the couch and sets her down, and then he plugs in the DVD player. It takes a second to figure out all the hookups, since the tech is so outdated. But he finally gets it to work, and he puts in the movie and hits "*Play.*"

He sits next to her, and she leans into him. Rests her head on his arm and grabs his hand. He squeezes, and she squeezes back.

The Princess Bride starts, and they watch together. "Do you remember when I first showed you this?" she says while the little boy argues with his grandpa about whether it's a baby story. "You acted just like him."

Jonah snorts. "I admit it—you were right, and I was wrong. It's the best movie ever."

Diana gives him a suspicious look. "Now you're just buttering me up."

He shrugs. "As you wish."

She smiles and smacks him on the shoulder. "Dork."

The movie gets going. They watch in silence.

When the first sword fight starts, Diana tries to imitate Inigo Montoya and promptly spills her drink all over the rug. "Oh shit."

Jonah stands. "Let me clean that." He walks to the kitchen, rummages under the sink, and returns with a roll of paper towels and a bottle of white vinegar. Starts scrubbing.

Diana watches him, enamored.

You would clean it, whispers a little voice in her head, not her own. She frowns.

Jonah looks up at her from the floor, concerned. "What?"

"Nothing," she says, trying to forget.

He finishes with the stain and sits back down on the couch, and they keep watching. She rests her head on his arm again. Massages the back of his hand gently.

By the time it gets to the scene with Miracle Max, she's getting tired. She yawns. "There's a big difference between mostly dead and all dead," says Max onscreen. "Mostly dead is slightly alive."

Diana looks up at her son's face, smiling. She closes her eyes.

* * *

Jonah watches his mother drift off.

Once she's out cold, he gently removes his arm and shoulder from underneath her, propping her up on couch cushions so she won't fall. He stands and goes to the kitchen, where he slips a chef's knife out of the block next to the sink. Then he makes his way across the living "room," pads quietly into the hallway that connects it to the master bedroom, and opens a door that leads down to the basement.

He descends the dusty stairs in the dark. Pulls on a chain at the bottom to turn a light on.

A hundred black-and-white demons look up at him. He grins. *Old friends.* Some of them have been gathering dust down here for over a decade, ever since he was a teenager. But a third, he bought from Haley in the last two years.

When he disappeared, many things were left undone. The reveal of his legend hadn't gone as planned, after all.

In the haste of his escape, he had to leave behind many of his most prized paintings in the penthouse. For months, they remained in the uncertain care of his ex-fiancée. Jonah worried at first she might destroy them, or kill herself before he got a chance to reacquire them.

But in the end, it all worked out for the best.

When Haley started selling his paintings, he bought them up through proxies, one by one. At first, they barely cost him anything. But as he rebuilt his fortune, he started to bid against himself at auction, driving prices higher intentionally. The more he paid, the more the rest of his large collection of Jonah Wolf originals here at Wolf Hollow was worth, and the more commissions the auction house earned, and the more his fame and Haley's reputation as a dealer grew. Everyone profited. As the values ballooned, his art attracted the attention of real collectors. Real bidding wars.

Now museums display his work. And she thinks it was her idea.

No one but him knows the truth.

He bought back every piece he needed. They fight over scraps.

He walks up to a large dusty painting of his that he created when he was eighteen years old and purchased from Haley in the early stages of his reacquisitions: two demons drown in a black ocean, waves raging and swallowing them as they reach up for the clouds in agony.

Jonah takes his knife and slices into the edges of the canvas. He delicately peels away his own work and lets it fall to the ground, revealing another oil painting underneath:

Fishing Boats in a Stiff Breeze, by Joseph Mallord William Turner. One of his favorites.

He admires it, smiling. Still perfect after all this time, ready to be packed and shipped and sold. He pulls the chain again as he walks upstairs. The lights go out.

The demons under Wolf Hollow sleep.

53

Epilogue

March 7, 2022. 6:14 PM

Belle Morency eats dinner off a tray as she sits on her couch, watching TV.

It's a microwave meal. Mac 'n' cheese, two wrinkled sausages, a slop of mashed potatoes with some congealed gravy in the middle. *Cliché*, she knows. Her whole life is. She lives in a mobile home and cashes disability checks, struggling to raise a family. Four of them share one bed in the back: Mom, Dad, son, baby girl (she's eight, so not a *baby* anymore). It even used to be five people sharing it, before Alex ran away to go whoring after her boyfriend.

Belle can stomach the TV dinners and all the rest. She has to. Clichés are less expensive.

After the nightly news, *America: Unsolved!* comes on.

Belle leans in to watch her favorite show.

"Tonight," intones Tom Golden, the host, in a serious baritone, "we continue our series on the victims of Jonah Wolf, possibly the most infamous and prolific serial killer in American history. As our avid viewers will know . . ."

Belle feels a shiver. Tom is talking to her.

". . . almost all of Wolf's victims are known to us only by their charred remains. Investigators believe his preferred victims were migrant workers, homeless runaways, prostitutes, and addicts, and so police have been forced to rely on shows like ours as they search for the families—and names—of the forgotten dead. We are honored to help carry out the solemn duty of alerting families to the recovery of their lost loved ones' remains. These people, no matter who they are, deserve proper burials. They deserve to be remembered, celebrated, and mourned. They deserve names. Tonight, as usual, we focus on a single unnamed victim. A Jane Doe. As usual, we'll start by showing you, our viewers, a forensic sculptor's recreation of the victim's facial features. This is not an exact science. But hopefully, one of you good Samaritans out there will recognize this face and call us. Our number is at the bottom of the screen. All tips are welcome."

A realistic bust appears onscreen: a young girl.

Straight black hair. Button nose. Big blue eyes.

Nonvisual details run across a ticker at the bottom: she was five-foot-one inches tall and she weighed about a hundred pounds.

A chewed bite of sausage falls out of Belle Morency's mouth. "*Alex?* Mac! Mac! Come quick!"

Her husband sighs in the next room. "You're gonna wake up the goddamn kids."

"I don't give a goddamn, get in here! *It's Alex!*"

Mac stomps in, wiping a sip of beer off his mouth. "What?" he says, staring at his wife on the couch. "Jesus, Belle. Look what ya did, you spilled everywhere—" He stops when he sees the tears flowing from her eyes and the hand clasped tight over her mouth.

Belle points a shaking finger at the TV screen.

Mac looks.

His knees give out. He drops and sits, palms flat on the carpet. "It can't be her."

The bust rotates on a circular platform, spinning like a piece of costume jewelry on the shopping channel.

"Tonight's Jane Doe is unique among Wolf's victims in several key ways. She is, to date, the only victim whose body was not found in any subterranean tunnel or cavern. She was found, instead, buried in a shallow grave in the woods near Wolf Hollow, his mother's estate. We also have exclusive access to as-yet-unreleased correspondence written by Wolf's younger brother, Cyrus—yes, *the* email, for you true-crime fans—which seems to suggest that *he* killed this woman, not Jonah. He claims she was a hitchhiker walking along a highway somewhere near Leiper's Fork, Tennessee, nine years ago. In her last breaths, she told her killers that she was 'going to Asheville.'"

Belle stands up, knocking the rest of her TV dinner onto the floor. She screams into her hand. Mac stares at the screen, dumbstruck.

Their two young children wander into the room, rubbing their eyes.

The bust of Jane Doe rotates.

Tom Golden continues: "As with so many of the victims on our show, there is almost no physical evidence connected to tonight's Jane Doe. However, thanks to a young sheriff's deputy, Ignacio Rodriguez, who was present when Jane's skeleton was first exhumed, we have an exclusive lead to share with you. *America: Unsolved!* has learned there was a brass button found with Jane's body. A button with a distinctive slogan printed on it. An artist's recreation will appear onscreen momentarily . . . there it is. Now, for those of you who have trouble reading upside down, the edge of it reads: *'LOOK AT ME LOOK AT YOU!'* We were told it may have been from a pair of jeans, and so we have attempted to match the slogan to a manufacturer. But so far, no luck. That's where *you* come in."

Belle fires like a rocket off the couch and throws open the front door, then jumps down the three stairs outside and drops to her knees. She crawls into the tiny space under the house, searching. *There it is.* An old trash bag, holes in the side where critters have dug in over the years looking for food and been disappointed to find only clothes.

She drags the trash bag out from the crawlspace, oblivious to the cobwebs that now cling to her nightgown. She rips it open and dumps out all of Alex's old clothes . . . then picks up a pair of blue jeans, still creased from a neat fold after all this time. Nine years, it's been.

Belle examines a button in its fly: *"LOOK AT ME LOOK AT YOU!"* it says.

She collapses, rubbing the old denim on her face and weeping.

Mac stumbles out the door after her, still shell-shocked. "Belle, baby, was it . . .?"

Belle nods, sobbing. "She brought a bunch of these back from backpacking, from that market in Thailand. She wanted to sell 'em to make a quick buck, so she could help out around the . . ." She lets her face fall into the blue jeans again, damp now with tears.

Mac walks over to her and kneels. He holds her, stroking her hair with his fingers.

Belle sobs. "She was going to Asheville, Mac . . ."

Mac starts to cry. "I know. I heard. I can't—"

"Don't you realize what it means?"

Mac pulls away from his wife to look her in the eyes. He smiles through his tears, and nods.

Belle collapses into his chest again. *She was going to Asheville.* "Our girl was going to see Grandma, Macky. She was doing something good, something beautiful . . . so beautiful. She was going to surprise her Grandma in the hospital. I remember she said she wanted to be there to . . . to hold her hand when she died, but I just didn't think of it when she . . . she musta been hitchhiking. She was doing something beautiful, not ugly, and all these years we told everyone how she was so awful, but she wasn't . . ."

Mac strokes her hair. "I know."

Belle grips his shoulders so hard, her fingernails tear holes in his shirt. "I miss her so much, Macky."

"I know."

Belle whispers, over and over: "Thank you, God. Thank you. Thank you."

The two parents cry. They grieve.

An hour later, they call a hotline to claim their daughter's remains. Jane Doe no more.

Alex Morency was her name.

ACKNOWLEDGMENTS

MY WIFE, CASSIA, deserves more than half the credit for this book's existence. She is my co-author, my beta reader, my inspiration, my cheerleader, my rock. Writing a first novel is a long, arduous, risky process; I wanted to quit at least a dozen times, and at least a dozen times she convinced me not to. Here's to hoping this book sells a boatload of copies so I can finally spoil her rotten like she deserves. She's certainly spoiled me.

Thanks to my agent, Sam Farkas, who took a chance on me when my manuscript barely had a coherent ending. I owe her many big checks in the future.

To my editor, Sara J. Henry, who made me un-kill every single dead character but one because she loved them all too much (and was right to do so).

To my friends in The Chat, who bullied me into finishing my "book-length document" whenever my wife's Good Cop approach wasn't cutting it. I love you too, assholes.

And to everyone else who read my garbage early drafts and outlines: Noah (and your dad!), Jason, Arya, Kiran, Pat, Chantal, Kerry, Danial, Charles, Sarah, and my uncle Mark. You guys are awesome. I hope you'll keep reading my garbage.